I0658928

THREE ROADS OUT

The Sequel to

ALONG THE RED DIRT ROAD

Jane Yearout

Copyright © 2022 Jane Yearout

All rights reserved.

ISBN:978-1-7348280-2-3

The characters and events portrayed in this book are fictitious. Any similarity to real persons, living or dead, is coincidental and not intended by the author.

No part of this book may be reproduced or stored in a retrieval system, or transmitted in any form or by any means, electronic, mechanical, photocopying, recording or otherwise, without express written permission of the author.

Cover design: Ashfoard Associates

Cover Image: Ashfoard Associates

Illustrations: Jane Yearout

Printed in the United States of America

PREFACE

I never intended to write this sequel. Upon the release of *Along the Red Dirt Road,* my book club audiences and readers began pummeling me with questions. What happened after Annie left town so long ago? Did Hillview ever forgive what she had done? What followed that autumn afternoon by the old stone wall? What about Noah, Blink, Miss Mittie, KT, and the rest? Oh, my! Some answers were in my head, but another book was not my plan.

Three Roads Out was written over a thirty-month period during the first Covid outbreak and begins where *Along the Red Dirt Road* ends. Annie is gone, and now it's all on KT. Can she turn the page on Hillview and chart a new course as Annie had so long ago? So much has happened, but has anything really changed? The journey of Dr. KT Winslow is one of twists, turns, excruciating choices, duty, and friendship. Elements of the Civil War, Great Depression, the Holocaust, WW2 and post war years, the tumultuous sixties, civil rights, and current times are crucial to this tale. The story ends just before the pandemic strikes Hillview—or does it?

It takes a village!

Posthumously, I thank my mother and aunt who encouraged me, as well as elementary and high school teachers and my professors at the University of Oklahoma who told me to write. My husband served as a first reader and provided encouragement, editorial assistance, and marketing support. Judy M. and Leslie M. also served as first readers and gave me solid feedback on the plot and characters and convinced me this tale must be told. As with ***Along the Red Dirt Road,*** this book entailed a great deal of research, as I believe cultural, geographic, and historical accuracy is essential to good historical fiction.

Although the story is constructed around Dr. KT Winslow, the woodwork is teeming with other stories. I set out to craft a tale with serious societal value—something timely yet timeless, something entertaining and purposeful to a broad global audience. I hope you will be enriched by this multi-generational tale and will allow your imagination to go wherever it may wish to go.

Peace and love,
Jane Yearout

Table of Contents

SOIL, SEED, RAIN, FLOWERS

Mr. Anderson will be with you soon, Dr. Winslow. Please have a seat," said the receptionist. "Do you care for a drink?"

"No, thank you."

The receptionist exited the cavernous office and closed the door. Anna Ruth died three months earlier, and her affairs remained a mystery. Now, Dr. Kathryn Winslow awaited her first encounter with Anna Ruth's attorney, Roy Anderson.

She settled into a leather chair, drew a measured breath, and folded her hands on her lap. On one side of the massive mahogany desk before her, a laptop computer idled in discomforting silence as multi-colored lines danced across the screen. On the opposite side, a stack of file folders rested next to a somewhat dated telephone console. Legs crossed, Dr. Winslow tapped her left foot on the floor and glanced around the room. Behind the desk, an elegant, diamond-shaped window afforded a distinct view of the college clock tower several blocks to the north. Diplomas, awards, and framed photos dominated two walls, and floor-to-ceiling bookshelves with a puny ivy plant on top covered another

1

wall. For an inexplicable reason, the sight of this light-deprived plant bent toward the window elicited a nervous chuckle.

A side door opened, and a stocky, white-haired fellow in a rumpled gray suit swept into the room.

With a gracious smile, he said, "Hello, Dr. Winslow. Hope I didn't keep you waiting long." He reached to shake her hand with a firm, yet gentle grip.

"No, it hasn't been long. You're Mr. Anderson?"

"Yes ma'am! Anna Ruth spoke of you often. It distressed me to learn she passed away. I've served as your grandmother's attorney for going on forty years, and she was a gem. A rare and precious gem. I will miss Anna Ruth."

She acknowledged the lawyer's words with a faint, "I will, too. Please call me KT."

"You are kind. Thank you. Anna Ruth referred to you as KT, never Kathryn, so I shall do the same." The lawyer eased into the oversized chair behind his desk and extracted a folder from a pile of papers. "You mentioned on the phone you emptied her apartment here in town."

"I did. Nonnie, I called my grandmother Nonnie, lived in the Brookside Retirement Community. Management wants everything removed as soon as a vacancy occurs because they have a waiting list. Nonnie gave my name as the person responsible. I was unsure how to proceed, though. She possessed few furnishings or other belongings. I moved everything except her files to a storage facility here in town because I live two hours from here, and my condo doesn't have an abundance of room. Nonnie owned six filing cabinets. Six filing cabinets packed full, mind you! They are at my condo. Things must be disposed of if I have authorization."

"Well, my dear, you do. Your Nonnie, Anna Ruth, named me as her executor, but you are the person she desired to have her belongings. You can do whatever you please with any belongings, furnishings, personal items, contents of the filing cabinets, everything. After years of teaching at the college, those cabinets may contain a treasure trove of lectures and other interesting material. Have you seen a copy of her will?"

"No, and to be honest, I made little sense of my grandmother until her last day on earth. She never discussed her personal affairs with me. It's possible she did with Mother, but Mother died a few years ago. Cancer. Mother was Nonnie's only child. Nonnie explained I will inherit a piece of property near a town called Hillview back east in the Shenandoah Valley, and I spent the afternoon with her there the day she died. Nonnie never mentioned Hillview before we planned the trip, but she wanted me to see it. She needed to familiarize me with its story. Her story. She died as she sat in a chair where we enjoyed a picnic and spent the entire afternoon talking. Her heart gave out."

Anderson grimaced as KT's gaze fixed through the window at the clock tower. The attorney paused and cleared his throat.

"I have Anna Ruth's will here, KT. It may hold surprises for you. Before we review the will, I must offer explanations."

KT focused on the back cover of the document Anderson held in his hand, anticipating, dreading the disclosures yet to come as she fidgeted with her jacket buttons.

"Anna Ruth sold her house here in town when she moved to the retirement complex. Do you remember when the move occurred?"

"I do. Mother worried Nonnie made a mistake selling her home. Mother grew up in the house, and it held a lifetime of memories for her. It was the two of them. My grandfather died in World War II, and his remains were never recovered.

3

Nevertheless, Nonnie appeared content at Brookside after the move. She loved flowers, and her flowerpots overflowed with blooms every summer. She enjoyed her patio's privacy, listening to the brook running behind her apartment, and monitoring birds at her feeders. Nonnie ate dinner in the dining room with her Brookside friends, but she had this cute, tiny kitchen where she prepared her own breakfast and lunch. I visited as often as possible, but work keeps me busy. I should have visited more, and I'll always regret I didn't."

"Your grandmother liked Brookside. Anna Ruth made friends and played dominoes with her buddies, and she won most every time. She modeled the definition of an independent and adaptable woman, didn't she?"

"She loved dominoes and taught me how to play, but she always won. Independent and adaptable? Yes, Nonnie personified those traits."

Anderson cleared his throat again. "Anna Ruth received a hefty price for her home when it sold. Houses within walking distance of campus go for premium prices, especially ones in as extraordinary a shape as hers. Proceeds from the sale paid her rent at Brookside, but those expenses depleted the money."

KT shifted her weight in the chair, folded her hands in her lap again, and waited with apprehension for Anderson to continue.

"Anna Ruth left you the property near Hillview. It's a house on four acres, three miles from town. She inherited this property in 1970 from a woman named, let's see here." He leafed through his papers. "Susan McCormick Rutledge. Mrs. Rutledge must have held immense affection for your grandmother to leave her the house. I guess they were close, but not related to one another?"

"Did Nonnie describe Susie Rutledge as a friend?"

4

Anderson scratched his head. "Well, no. Um, she laughed when I mentioned the possibility to her. I always considered her reaction odd, but Anna Ruth sometimes appeared, uh, acted, uh, mysterious is the right word."

KT chuckled as she remembered her grandmother's words proclaiming Susie Rutledge left her the property out of pure spite.

KT explained, "When Nonnie and her parents lived in Hillview, they rented the house and grounds from Susie Rutledge's mother, a widow named Mittie McCormick. Susie Rutledge had no children, and for reasons known only to her, she willed it to my grandmother."

"You'll want to sell it, won't you? I mean, you have no reason to keep it and no connection to Hillview. I imagine it's a mess since it's been unoccupied lo, these many years. Anna Ruth listed it for sale but received only low ball offers. In recent years, a fella sent her contracts, which she tore to pieces. I don't recall his name at the moment, but she said his prices bordered on the absurd and he sounded like a weasel on the phone. If I questioned her on the Hillview property, she said, 'It's still there' and changed the conversation."

"You're right. No reason to hold on to it exists. My plan is to go to Hillview when spring comes. A private cemetery near Hillview is where I hope to bury Nonnie's ashes, and when I go, I'll find a realtor. I'm not familiar with the property or with Hillview itself. My single visit occurred when Nonnie and I went there together, and she died. We didn't enter the house, but she described its interior from when she lived there to me."

"It's a splendid idea to inspect it firsthand. I suggest you engage a realtor. He or she should be able to help with several decisions. The papers you'll receive today include the name of the realtor who listed it last. She liked him. I got the impression she cared nothing for Hillview, though. Are you sure you want to bury her ashes there?"

"Yes, Mr. Anderson. I believe in my heart it's what she would want."

With a puzzled shrug, the lawyer rose from his chair, ambled toward a beverage cart in the corner, where he grasped the handle of an empty coffee carafe. He buzzed the receptionist.

"Barbara, may we have coffee in here?"

KT stared out the window, noting ominous clouds forming on the northern horizon. A strange sadness overcame her petite frame, and she sank farther into the chair, appearing distant and lost in her thoughts.

Anderson cast a curious glance at her and strode to the door to the outer office, opened it, and asked, "Barbara, how's coffee coming?"

He returned to his desk and stood at the edge, toying with a pile of papers in between brief peeks at KT over the rims of his glasses. Motionless in the leather chair, KT's eyes lingered on the window.

"I need coffee!" boomed Anderson, breaking the stony silence. "You, too, KT?"

"No, thank you."

Anderson removed his glasses and sat in his chair. "Well, okay. We've covered Hillview. Did Anna Ruth mention her investments?"

KT's eyes pivoted from the window to the attorney. "Investments? No. She had investments?"

"She did."

"Oh, I never considered such. Her retirement from the college, I suppose?"

"Yes, retirement funds. But she inherited money from her parents, which she invested. In addition, she invested proceeds from selling the ranch in Oklahoma. She received stipends for her frequent Civil War lectures and invested those, too."

KT wrinkled her brow as she recalled the afternoon in Hillview when Anna Ruth expounded upon the time she and her parents lived near Hillview during the Great Depression. An oil company discovered oil on the Oklahoma ranch Anna Ruth's father inherited, and oil royalties gave the family a much-needed financial cushion. As for the ranch? KT never considered it, and she had no clue as to its location.

"You appear confused. Did she not touch on the ranch with you?"

"Nonnie mentioned the ranch when we were in Hillview, but she, well, there is much I learned and didn't learn in one afternoon, I guess."

A light knock on the door interrupted the conversation, and the receptionist tiptoed in, placed a coffee carafe on the beverage cart, and took her leave.

"Thank you, Barbara. KT, won't you have a cup?"

KT observed Anderson as he filled his king-sized mug and said, "I will, thank you. I take it black."

The lawyer set his giant vessel on the desk, filled a smaller mug painted with wildflowers, and passed it to KT.

"As a rule, I brew my own coffee, but I was in court until a few minutes before you arrived. Where were we? Oh, the ranch."

Without comment, KT took several pensive sips of the hot beverage and shifted her legs. Her right foot tapped the floor four times with a heavier whap than before, until she noticed Anderson's furrowed brow. She ceased tapping.

"Oil at the ranch played out in the 1940s. Your frugal great-grandparents saved much of the money they received from the oil company. Anna Ruth said when they lived in Hillview, those royalties served as a lifesaver, but after her folks returned to Oklahoma, most royalty money went into savings until the royalties stopped. The ranch comprised around seven hundred acres, and your great-grandfather held onto it. He leased pastures to neighboring ranchers for grazing, which provided enough income to pay taxes on the land, but not much more."

"I never met my great-grandparents. What happened to the ranch?"

"Anna Ruth inherited it when her folks died. Let me see." He put on his glasses and leafed through the folder before stopping on one page. His forefinger skimmed each line. "Your great-grandfather, Dr. Carter Young, died in 1972, and your great-grandmother, Ellen Young, died in 1975."

"Before my birth," KT acknowledged.

"Anna Ruth had an excellent business mind. She hung onto the ranch for years, but then she began selling bits and pieces. She sold the last seventy-five acres in 2001. It went to a developer for an upscale subdivision next to a golf course. Anna Ruth had sold a hundred and fifty acres for the golf course a few years prior, and the golf course buyer hounded her for the remaining land. He wanted to build expensive homes with views of the golf course and a lake. Your feisty grandmother held out until his price was as high as she thought practical!"

"Amazing," KT said in a soft voice. "I didn't appreciate her enough, and this saddens me. I perceived her as eccentric, and I never figured her for a businesswoman. Nonnie didn't speak of her past, other than to repeat to my brothers and me how she loved her parents. They were devoted to one another. I missed out on too much. My entire family did."

"Did you spend time with her when you and your brothers were kids?"

"Not much. My family moved a good bit. Dad coached college basketball at several schools. We visited Nonnie twice a year, maybe, but we never stayed in her tiny house. The six of us always stayed in a hotel. Her house had two bedrooms and one bathroom, and here we were with three rambunctious boys plus me! Mother spoke with her by phone each week, but I'm sorry to say we didn't see her as often as I wished. Dad took the boys on outings when we visited and always found a basketball court somewhere. Sometimes he dragged me along, too. May I have another cup of coffee?"

KT's mind wandered to those brief, infrequent childhood trips to visit Anna Ruth. Anna Ruth took an occasional summer trip to visit KT's family, but Coach Winslow's wealthy parents owned a massive dwelling which served as ground zero for holidays, with gatherings of cousins and other relatives. Anna Ruth attended Christmas there once, but the noise and ostentation overwhelmed her. She preferred holidays alone in her cottage near the college where she taught the Civil War period of American history. As a result, KT never spent significant time alone with her grandmother.

KT sat in silence, her mood darkening, as Anderson refilled her coffee mug.

"It works this way with families nowadays. Denuclearization, KT. We live in different places and don't see each other as often as we wish. My grandkids live in Boston and Texas. Dang it."

"Yes, it's too bad, isn't it?" KT took a sip from her cup before adding in a monotone voice, "Thank you for the coffee."

"You bet! Let's get back to the inheritance, shall we? Your grandmother was, as I mentioned, a savvy investor. She watched the stock market and traded in a smart way. Anna Ruth instructed me to sell her investments when she died and divide the proceeds among her four grandchildren. I have sold everything as instructed, settled the estate, and cut checks for each of you. Now, she didn't want the proceeds divided in equal amounts, which may surprise you, and may create, uh, angst among your brothers. I hope not, but her will spells out her wishes. She left the bulk of her estate to you."

"Oh? To me? Oh, my! Angst? Why might you expect problems?"

"Well, besides the Hillview property and her belongings, you inherit substantially more money than your brothers. She explains it in her will. You can read what she dictated, but she believed your brothers earn sizable incomes. Your grandmother believed you work in a not-too-lucrative field of medicine, and her money will be far more useful to you than your brothers. In addition, Anna Ruth confided she felt a special connection with you, much deeper than with your three brothers. She lamented she never spent as much time with her grandchildren as she wished. Anna Ruth said you reminded her of her own father, Dr. Young."

"Oh, I suppose she's correct in referring to a connection. I came to appreciate her after she died. It came too late, though." Tears filled KT's eyes as she fumbled in her purse for a tissue. "I wanted more time."

Anderson flipped through the papers inside the file on his desk, casting an uncomfortable glance at the freckle faced woman who dabbed her eyes before regaining her composure.

"Now, let's see if I have the correct information for your three brothers."

KT wiped her eyes again and sniffed. "Go ahead."

Roy Anderson recited the names and addresses of her brothers as KT affirmed their validity. One was assistant coach for a professional basketball team. Another was a district attorney in California, and the third was CEO of a software company in the Southwest. As a clinical physician serving indigent patients, KT earned much less than her brothers and most of her medical school colleagues. Although she matriculated from an Ivy League medical school, she found her calling in an arena her brothers disdained as, "Beneath your station and abilities, KT."

"All right, then. I'll send checks to them in tomorrow's mail. Here is a cashier's check payable to you for your share." He turned the check face down and pushed it across his desk.

KT turned over the check and studied it before her brown eyes fixed on Anderson. She gaped at the check again. Although determined to remain composed, her quivering hands confirmed her state of mind. Her eyes widened as her breath quickened.

"Are you serious? I'm, uh, I'm dumbfounded, speechless! She had this much money? Even more? This must be a mistake."

"I mentioned she was a savvy investor, didn't I? Do you expect your brothers may be unhappy because they don't receive as much as you?"

KT thought for a moment before giving a measured response. "No, I don't expect they will. My brothers pity me because I'm not the wealthy, renowned physician they assume I should be. They'll be fine. They weren't comfortable with Nonnie. Each thought her peculiar, out-of-step. The three of them related more to Dad's family. I'm the outsider, much as Nonnie was."

"I hope you're right. One never can predict how folks will react when someone dies and leaves money. Too often, old jealousies emerge, and someone figures they got the short end of the stick. You brothers will receive a copy of the will and a paid invoice for my services. I subtracted my fee and other costs from the total inheritance and detailed every expense, but if questions arise, call me. Once again, KT, Anna Ruth said your choice of medical practice and your nature made her think of her dad. She sure was proud of you. She expounded on what you were doing whenever we spoke. Now, you do whatever you wish with her belongings. I'd carry out a thorough inspection of those filing cabinets. You might find interesting tidbits in them or at least learn more Civil War history."

"I will. Thank you."

"Here's a folder with a copy of the will, the deed to the Hillview property, plus other documents showing how she gained it. You have everything you need."

"Thank you." KT accepted the folder and squeezed the attorney's hand. "I appreciate your diligent work and your friendship with Nonnie. If questions arise, I'll be in touch. Don't concern yourself with my brothers. They'll be fine."

With a paternal pat on the shoulder, Anderson ushered KT out the door and said, "This circumstance is difficult for you, KT. You lost your mother a few short years ago and now Anna Ruth. Your grandmother had a hard time when your mother died. The loss grieved her. Powerful grief. But her resilience amazed me. An absolute inspiration she was! The epitome of self-confidence and optimism. Best of luck in Hillview. I hope you can sell the old house and arrange a suitable resting place for Anna Ruth without undue trouble."

KT managed a meek smile. She bid Barbara the receptionist farewell, closed the outer door to the law office, and headed into the hall where an older gentleman in a dingy brown overcoat held the elevator for her arrival.

"Looks like rain, doesn't it? It's not cold enough for snow," said the old man as the car started its descent.

KT stared straight ahead. "Um, yes. Yes, you're right."

As the elevator approached its destination, KT faced the

man with a gentle smile and recited one of her grandmother's favorite adages, "Soil, seed, rain, flowers."

The elevator door opened, and Dr. Kathryn Winslow, clutching the zippered folder provided her by Roy Anderson, emerged and strode out a revolving door into the afternoon's blustery grayness.

LAY OF THE LAND

Three months after her meeting with Roy Anderson, the GPS on KT's Honda guided her through downtown Hillview toward the office of Wessler and Son Realtors. Main Street showcased a town bustling with eateries and specialty shops, flower-filled baskets hanging from lampposts, and colorful flowerpots adorning store entrances. The scene painted a far different picture from the day she and Anna Ruth traveled the same route on a quiet Sunday morning the preceding fall.

She turned west on Fourth Street, past more businesses lodged in Victorian styled buildings KT assumed once served as residences. A flower shop, a barber shop, and a music store occupied the north side of the street. A brew pub, an art gallery, and a restaurant called WhatYouWant consumed most of one block on the south side. KT chuckled at the restaurant's name but supposed the food and ambiance must satisfy since a line of patrons waited to get inside the door.

Two blocks and three left turns led her to the paved parking lot of another residence-turned-business. She parked, grabbed her backpack and clipboard, and eyeballed the overstuffed cardboard file box that occupied half of the back seat. Three-inch blue letters on the box's lid labeled the box "Hillview." She drew a deep breath and stepped into the office.

"Hello. Welcome to Wessler and Son. May I help you?" inquired a woman at the front desk.

"Hello, I'm KT Winslow, and I have an appointment with Graham Wessler."

"Yes, you do. I'll tell him you're here."

Within minutes, a tall, athletic-appearing man with thick, blondish hair appeared from a side office. With an amiable smile, he reached out to shake KT's hand.

"Dr. Winslow! I'm Graham Wessler. Pleased to meet you. Come into my office, and we'll discuss your property."

KT judged the realtor to be in his late forties or early fifties. He sported a casual chevron-style mustache, a white long-sleeve polo shirt, tan jeans, and a pair of lime green running shoes. KT seated herself in front of an L-shaped desk. The main section of the desk was vacant on top, except for a business card holder, a bottle of water, and a notepad with a mechanical pencil resting on top. A phone, computer screen and keyboard, plus a neat stack of file folders rested on the desk's side section. A hutch behind the realtor's swivel chair displayed books, award plaques, and photos of houses and landscapes, but no people. KT noted a tasteful, but sparse, office.

"When did you get into town, Dr. Winslow?"

"Just now. I left home before daybreak and drove straight through. Please call me KT."

"Pleased to do so, but you must call me Graham."

"You've got a deal! You're not as old as I expected. Are you Wessler or the son?"

He laughed, removed a business card from the holder on his desk, and handed it across to KT.

"I'm the son. My father was once the son, but after Granddad died, Dad became the Wessler, and I joined him to keep the name the same, I guess. May I ask if KT is your actual given name, or does it stand for something else?"

KT chuckled. "My name is Kathryn, but my mother called me Katie when I was a baby. I'm the youngest of four, with three older brothers, and the one nearest my age couldn't pronounce Katie. He put such strong emphasis on the second syllable it came out K . . . *Tee*. This sat well with my dad, who wanted another boy. I'm told Mother resisted, but she gave in and started calling me KT, too. As a result, the name stuck. Nobody calls me Kathryn or Katie."

Graham smiled as he retrieved a thick folder from the stack to his right and placed it in the center of his desk.

"I gather from our phone conversation you want to sell the property you've inherited. We have one heck of a file dating to before the street had a name. My grandfather held the listing on it for years. He referred to the property as McCormick House because a Dr. and Mrs. McCormick built it, and the name is what Dad and I have called it ever since." He plopped his right hand on the four-inch-thick folder. "This file holds a gazillion notes. We haven't entered them into the computer because your grandmother let the listing lapse years ago, but Dad left the sign in the yard in case somebody expressed interest. I drove out there last week, and the sign is in terrible shape, as is the entire property. We should inspect it before you decide how you wish to continue. You haven't been inside the house, correct? I have a key, and we can get in to assess its condition. Let's not discuss pricing or marketing until you see it. If you're not too tired, we can run out there now."

"Splendid! Now is fine. I've been there one time with my grandmother last fall, but we didn't go inside the house. Nonnie, I called her Nonnie, wanted to sit by a stone wall running the length of the rear boundary of the property. She died there. You may be aware of this."

"Yes, I am. I'm sorry."

KT shifted in her chair and asked, "Should we go in separate cars or in one? I don't recall the location, but my car will direct me."

"Oh, no. Let's hop in my car and go together. I'll return you here once we've inspected it. Shall we?"

They left the office and climbed into Graham Wessler's cherry-red Jeep Wrangler. The ride did not last long since the property rested a mere three miles outside Hillview city limits. Although the town had grown after Anna Ruth and her parents lived there during the Great Depression, acres of undeveloped land survived from the western edge of town to McCormick House. During her prior visit, an impatient KT paid no attention to the landscape on the drive to the property. On her drive back to town after dark, she saw only the backside of the vehicle carrying her grandmother's body to the funeral home. Hillview and McCormick House held no favored spot in KT's memory or her heart.

After a short drive, they turned left onto Apple Ridge Road, traveled a mile, then took another left onto a narrow asphalt lane with majestic red oak trees on each side. Graham's Jeep crept past three oversized homes on the right, each with a well-manicured lawn and generous setback from the road. Graham steered onto a neglected gravel driveway on the right after the lane curved to the left. The faded For Sale sign still hung by one rusty wire, and the lawn resembled a jungle of weeds and scrub. Although obscured by vines, trees, and overgrown shrubbery, KT saw the dilapidated condition of the house and clenched her teeth to hold back tears. Graham noticed her reaction and stopped the car short of the house.

"KT, I see you're troubled. Do you prefer tomorrow or another time?"

She shook her head with resolve. "No, I need to do this now. Now. Let's go."

They climbed from the Jeep and made their way through weeds and grass growing unchallenged through cracks in a once pristine flagstone sidewalk. Branches of an enormous boxwood encroached upon the steps leading from the sidewalk to the porch and upon much of the porch itself. Graham brushed aside the boxwood limbs, rendered KT a chivalrous assist onto the porch, pried open the screen door, and inserted a key into the lock.

"Let me go in first," he said. "Might be varmints in there."

She lingered on the porch, surveying the architecture and grounds, trying to imagine what used to be. Her mind pictured a tidy lawn with rock-lined flowerbeds and the dogwood her grandmother loved. She recalled Anna Ruth saying a rose bush Carter Young planted as a birthday gift for his wife Ellen once anchored a corner of the house. The sound of shoes squeaking on the hardwood floors upstairs broke the spell.

"It's fine, KT! Come in! I've been in houses where raccoons or squirrels have taken over and wrecked everything. The interior is a thousand times better than I expected!" His voice echoed throughout the empty dwelling.

KT entered and stopped. She yelled, "It's dark in here. I'm opening drapes to let in the light. We can see better."

"Good idea," came the response from upstairs. "I'll do the same here."

As she pulled back the drapes, she remembered Anna Ruth's description of Ellen Young's delight when she first arrived in 1933 and opened draperies, allowing sunlight to flood the rooms. KT surmised with overgrown shrubbery trimmed away or removed, such light could once again permeate the dark rooms. Even with its walnut-colored woodwork, the house offered hints of a bright and cheery setting.

Musty smelling wallpaper hung loose from a few walls, but KT detected no sour odor of mildew, which often accompanies leaky roofs or pipes. She saw no sign of water damage on the ceiling. When she entered the kitchen, KT encountered a dusty brown farm table with four chairs placed around it. The spacious window over the kitchen sink had no window covering, and she imagined her great-grandmother Ellen Young's African violets on the windowsill. When Graham came into the room, KT stood motionless before the window.

"KT, the stove and fridge are no longer in the room, but can you visualize it? It's a more-than-adequate size. The washing machine, one of those wringer types, occupied the space over yonder." He pointed to a space toward the exterior rear door. "I remember the appliances. I was a kid when my grandfather brought Dad and me here after your grandmother inherited McCormick House. An antiques dealer bought the fridge, stove, and washer. This table remains, and one old bed is upstairs."

She said, "It's a comfortable kitchen. I expected leaks, mold, and collapsing ceilings, but I don't see any."

"Your grandmother replaced the metal roof fifteen years ago. They can last forever. Several spots are on the plaster ceilings upstairs from when the old roof leaked."

KT walked to the windowed back door and stared through its filthy glass. The covered back porch, overgrown with vines, and a collapsed formation behind the house added to the dismal atmosphere.

"Let's go upstairs," she said.

Two bedrooms upstairs stood empty, and a clawfoot tub, pedestal sink, and vintage toilet inhabited the spacious bathroom. A third bedroom, the one at the end of the hall, contained an antique iron bed. A grungy, faded quilt gave it a forlorn presence, as did a feather pillow with its yellowed, dusty pillowcase.

"This must have been Nonnie's room. She described it to me. She said my great-grandfather guessed it was a sleeping porch at one time because it's long and narrow with windows on three sides."

"Yep, I'd bet the bathroom once served as a bedroom. Dr. and Mrs. McCormick may have converted this porch to a bedroom when they installed the bathroom. Homes didn't have indoor plumbing when the McCormicks built this house."

KT scoured the room. "I need to see the grounds. I realize we can't get through the underbrush to see everything, but I can get an idea."

They circled the house after exiting the front door. KT noticed many trees, several dead, around the house. Her eyes turned toward the dense woods her grandmother adored at the rear boundary, but she saw no signs of the boundary defining stone wall. Trees, weeds, vines, wild honeysuckle, and broken limbs hid the formation, but KT knew it was there. She had been there. She knew its history.

"Your thoughts?" Graham asked.

"What are *yours*? This place has been for sale forever. Some claim it's haunted, don't they? Will anyone buy it?"

"Dad says rumors and hearsay have been a problem. The former owner, Mrs. Rutledge, tried to sell it, but at too high a price. An absurd price. Your grandmother listed it for sale as soon as she inherited it. Yeah, people thought it haunted. I'm not aware of reasons."

KT said, "Susie Rutledge inherited it when her mother, Mittie McCormick, died. Nonnie spoke of them at length during our afternoon by the stone wall." KT made a conscious decision to stay silent regarding the rumors.

"Susie Rutledge was a family member?"

"Nope. Susie was the daughter of Nonnie's elderly friend, Miss Mittie McCormick."

"Dad said the nursery owner down the way took care of the grounds for a time, but . . ."

"The nursery? I didn't notice when we drove in here. Is it still there? Blink, uh, Tobias Hill? He was Nonnie's dear friend."

"Yeah, it's still there. A grandson owns it. Tobias Hill Nursery is the name of the business. We'll stop on the way out if you wish."

"Oh, please, let's do. Tobias was Blink's true name, but everyone called him Blink. I hope the grandson knows where the cemetery is. The one I must find. It's where I need to bury Nonnie's ashes, and I don't have a clue where it's located. Finding the cemetery for Nonnie is the other reason I'm here."

Graham brushed a fly from his face and asked, "Shall we go inside the house again, or are you ready to return to the office?"

"Let me check inside once more."

KT said nothing as she examined with painstaking thoroughness every space inside the house. She ran her hand across the woodwork and inspected each window. She stomped on the floors to see how much they creaked and if they appeared solid. KT lingered in one intimate room downstairs containing a wall of empty bookcases. This room served as her great-grandmother's sewing room, and KT imagined the whir of Ellen Young's sewing machine as it created fashions for Hillview ladies. Her fingers probed behind crumbling wallpaper and fondled the cheesecloth backing. She inspected boards behind the cheesecloth.

Upstairs, KT stared at the bedroom where Anna Ruth, known as Annie in her youth, spent hours peering through once bright yellow curtains sewn by her mother. A trail cleared years ago through the woods to the stone wall had provided Annie Young with her own pathway to history. Time after time, Annie stared through this window to the clearing and toward the stone wall, watching, waiting, and sometimes weeping. KT shuddered as her grandmother's story replayed in her brain.

A closer kitchen examination became the tour's last stop. Rusty brown stains on the porcelain sink hinted at many years of service and rendered a nostalgic glimpse back in time. KT faced Graham, who had followed her throughout the house, monitoring every moment of her inspection.

"My great-grandmother kept African violets in this kitchen window. The sill is wide enough to hold nice sized pots. See? Nonnie grew African violets in her kitchen window, too. I've never grown violets, and I don't have a kitchen window."

Graham studied the window's wide sill before observing KT as she reflected on her grandmother's youth in the house.

KT took one last scan, heaved an enormous sigh, and headed through the front door. As she made her way toward the red Wrangler, Graham locked the house and jogged the short distance to his car.

"We'll stop at the nursery on our way to the office," Graham said as he started the engine.

****

Located a short distance and on the opposite site of the lane from McCormick House, Tobias Hill Nursery sat at the intersection with Apple Ridge Road. Graham steered his car through the entrance, navigated a lengthy gravel drive, and parked in a paved lot lined with enormous wooden tubs brimming with colorful spring flowers. Straight ahead to the north stood a wood plank barn connected on the right to a stone office with a corral for handcarts in front. To the left of the barn, an elegant arched gate preceded a gravel path leading toward several greenhouses and fields with multiple rows of trees and shrubs. Posted a few yards west of the arched gate stood a hand-lettered wood sign reading "Hill Cabin, Established 1854." Built of logs, the simple and rustic cabin featured a covered front porch with a painted glider adorned with multi-colored pillows.

"My goodness, what an enterprise!" KT exclaimed.

"Yes," agreed Graham. "They have an immense inventory, the best you'll find in these parts."

A black man in khaki slacks, pale-yellow shirt, and a wide brimmed straw hat emerged from the barn. With keys in hand, he addressed the visitors with a wave and salutation.

"Hello, folks. Oh, hey, there, Graham Wessler! You've arrived at closing time, but I'll be glad to help you. What can I do for you?"

Before Graham spoke, KT hurried toward the man.

"Hello! My grandmother was a close friend of Mr. Hill, Tobias Hill. She and everyone else called him Blink. Are you related?"

"You bet I am. Blink? My grandpap. I'm Doan Hill. Did you know Grandpap Blink?" Doan's face beamed, and a wide grin stretched across his face.

"No, I didn't, but my grandmother mentioned him when she spoke of her time living here. He was her best friend. During her youth, my grandmother lived for a time in the old white house at the end of this lane. Her father was a doctor, and they rented the house from the widow who owned it, Mittie McCormick."

Doan Hill smiled, took a red bandana from his pocket, and wiped his forehead. "I didn't grow up here, so I'm not familiar with many of Grandpap Blink's friends. After he died, I moved here and took over the nursery. Grandpap left me a love of plants and digging in the dirt. I visited him and Granny Zell every summer when I was a boy, and, boy, he put me to work! Most kids hate such work, but I loved it. My wife and I live in the house Grandpap and Granny built. It's hidden from the street because of thick woods. It's across the lane from a ramshackle house . . ." He stopped and gave a start. "Oh."

KT gave a hearty laugh as she blurted, "Yes, I own the ramshackle house! I inherited it from my grandmother, and I'm here to get it ready to sell. Your grandfather used to care for it."

"He sure did. Grandpap said an old friend of his owned it. Your grandmother? Was her name Annie? When I visited each summer, Grandpap had me help him over there. It came across as welcoming and neat. We mowed and trimmed shrubs. He insisted on mowing a path to the rear of the property, where there's an old stone wall. A lot of the wall had fallen, and sometimes he tried to clear the space and put stones back on the wall, but it was an enormous job. He finally got crippled with arthritis, so he sent me to care for the grounds by myself. I'm sorry. I reckon I should have kept with it after he died, but I didn't. Continuing the business and getting settled took every bit of my time. Hope it sells fast."

As the sun slipped behind the mountain, KT pressed with one last question. "Mr. Hill, a small cemetery is somewhere nearby. Your grandfather tended it, too. It contained three

24

graves. Two of the graves held your relatives, Israel Hill and Ben Hill. Can you direct me to its location, please? I want to get permission to bury my grandmother's ashes there. Yes, her name was Annie. Her given name was Anna Ruth, but everybody called her Annie. Annie Young."

Doan pondered for a moment and shook his head.

"Relatives of mine? Sorry. I have no idea. They buried Grandpap Blink and Granny Zell over in Longtown, where Granny Zell's people hailed. She died first. My pap passed three years ago, and he's buried in Illinois where I grew up. Sorry I can't help you."

KT's winced and paused.

"Oh, it's okay, Mr. Hill. I'll find it. My name is KT Winslow, and I'm pleased to meet you." She clutched his hand once again.

"Glad to meet you, too. Don't call me Mr. Hill. My name is Doan. If I can help you with anything, I'd be glad to do it. Graham, it's good to see you."

"You bet," said Graham. "You've done a grand job here, Doan. People say your nursery is the county's best one."

Doan Hill beamed as he reached to shake Graham's hand.

"Thank you, thank you! I sure appreciate your kind words and the business you send me, too."

Graham suggested they return to town. KT nodded and waved back at Doan before climbing into Graham's Jeep. As they drove back to Hillview, KT expressed her pleasure at seeing the Hill property in such excellent hands.

"It is," Graham said. "Before he died, Tobias Hill put his property into a local program called Land Savers, which means owners must always use the land for agricultural purposes, such as a nursery. Doan moved here, kept the nursery, and has grown the business. The Land Savers program is one way we protect our rural landscape from excessive development. Most folks and several developers support Land Savers, but a few don't."

KT noticed the charm of the surroundings, with its lush and distinct views of the Blue Ridge Mountains to the east and the Alleghenies to the west. Anna Ruth had described how much Ellen Young appreciated the view, too. KT's unfamiliarity with her great-grandparents stung her heart.

"It's lovely here," she agreed.

"It is," Graham said. "Hey, it's almost six o'clock. Instead of going to the office right now, why don't we grab dinner and discuss McCormick House? I'll take you to your car after dinner."

"What a superb idea. I'm starved, to be honest."

"Hillview is blessed with a decent variety. What cuisine do you prefer?"

"I trust your judgment."

Graham mulled over the possibilities. "I suggest a popular local spot. We have chains, but I prefer to patronize local folks, if it's agreeable with you."

Graham steered his sporty ride into the parking lot behind WhatYouWant, the restaurant KT noticed when she arrived in town earlier in the day.

"What a hilarious name for a restaurant! I suppose they serve whatever you want, right?"

"They do."

After finding a booth in a rear corner, they settled in, placed their orders with a server, and Graham brought out his folder. He pulled a batch of printouts, descriptions, and prices of recently sold properties in the area and handed them to KT.

"KT, in my opinion, you have two ways to go. One, you sell it as-is. Two, you renovate the house, re-claim the yard, and sell it for more money. The second choice means putting in a significant chunk of change. A *lot* of money. The first choice provides the fastest and easiest result, but not as much money for you as the second choice."

KT took a drink of her iced tea and mumbled, "Hmm, I imagine you're correct."

Graham said, "The developer of the subdivision behind the stone wall at McCormick House built the three houses we passed before arriving at your driveway. He's been trying to buy your property for years. Your grandmother refused to sell to him because he aimed to demolish the house, divide the four acres into one-acre lots, and build four houses. The price he proposed bordered on the absurd, but his price didn't appear to be the reason she refused his offers. Dad says she thought the guy sounded slimy on the phone, comparing him to a snake or a weasel. She didn't take to the idea of demolition, either."

"Is he a snake, or is he a weasel?" joked KT.

"Well, I can repeat his reputation is not of a reputable, uh, honest businessperson. His houses, though large and impressive at first glance, contain shoddy workmanship, and he doesn't fix problems unless he's forced."

"What's his name?"

Graham swallowed his tea and surveyed the room before answering. He lowered his voice and leaned over the table, putting both elbows on the table before folding his hands.

"His name is Martin. He uses several names. Blane Martin. Thomas Blane Martin, Thomas Martin, T.B. Martin, Thomas B. Martin, Tom Martin. One never has a clue which name he will use."

KT's forehead wrinkled as she leaned in toward Graham.

His voice lowered again. "Nobody can figure out where he gets his money, but he somehow gets enough to buy property and build houses. He's an attorney, too, and does his own legal work. People have sued him with success several times, but he keeps building. He maintains a super-smooth demeanor. Comes across as too nice. Too considerate, if you get my drift. He tries to flatter the unsuspecting to grab an edge. Wears his religion on his sleeve and quotes Bible verses ad nauseam. The guy's a phony and a cheat, but by the time people make sense of him, it's too late. Maybe I shouldn't say what I've said, but even if a transaction made with him presents itself as easy, it may become problematic. I don't trust him one bit, and your grandmother read him right when they spoke on the phone. Dad says Martin hounded her to sell. He sent her contracts in the mail, which she tore into pieces and sent back to him. I'm surprised you haven't heard from him."

"No, I haven't. I'm surprised Nonnie didn't want the house destroyed. I won't go into details, but her life here had unpleasant, uh, well, let's say it wasn't always happy. Are you positive she didn't want it demolished?"

"Dad wrote it in his notes and reiterated it to me when I advised him you were coming. Dad received a leg wound in Vietnam and nowadays has trouble walking distances over rough ground. This is the reason he gave your file to me. He said you might want to walk the property, and he can't. He's semi-retired, anyhow."

KT nibbled her salad and tore a chunk of bread from the loaf in a basket on the table. As she spread butter on the piece, she watched Graham munch on his wedge of bread, peering from time to time through the window toward a patio packed with outdoor diners.

"Graham, with hearsay and innuendo enshrouding the property, will anybody buy it if I update the house and put it in livable condition? It's a lovely home on a quiet, dead-end lane, not grandiose, but adequate for a family. Four acres provides space, and the woods on both sides and at the rear afford ample privacy. Doan Hill's woods across the lane give him and McCormick House more privacy. It reminds me of an oasis, a serene oasis in a quality location."

"You're correct. Those ignorant rumors rise from the simple fact nobody's taken care of the property. Dad said years ago, talk of ghosts and a crazy girl who lived there circulated, but those stories are long forgotten. If you believe as your grandmother and don't want the house demolished, renovation before selling provides the best avenue to saving it. Anybody who intends to update it themselves will only buy at a low, low price. You may get rid of it in a flash, but such a buyer may decide to demolish it and build another house or subdivide the acreage, same as Martin. Once someone owns a property, they can do whatever they want with it. It will take real money to remodel and update the house, though. Lots of money. My records show Dr. and Mrs. McCormick erected it in the late 1870s. The home is one of many historic homes in this county. Are you unequivocally prepared to take on such a monumental and expensive task?"

KT suppressed a laugh and moved the salad around in its bowl with her fork. After she took a bite, she said, "The crazy girl of whom you speak was my grandmother, my Nonnie. Her maiden name was Anna Ruth Young, although people called her Annie in those days. I understand something about those rumors, Graham. Trust me, she was *not* crazy."

"Oh, I'm sorry. I wasn't aware your grandmother was the subject of the gossip."

"Don't be sorry. How much money are you estimating?"

"Gosh, more than a hundred thousand dollars at least, up to two hundred. Two fifty? The foundation needs examination. Electric wiring requires replacing, and the plumbing is old, old, old. The water well and septic are ancient. Drilling a modern well and installing a septic system cost serious money. Repair rotted wood. New

29

drywall. Update the kitchen and bathroom. Reclaim the outdoors. The list is endless. If you complete those chores and add updated landscaping, the property will command a premium price. The metal roof should be sound, thanks to your grandmother."

KT smiled a faint but optimistic smile. She sensed Anna Ruth's presence, her voice, her guidance. KT did not wish to destroy a witness to history and see its space turned into a grid of cookie-cutter homes. She understood why her grandmother never moved forward with what KT contemplated. Anna Ruth lived far from Hillview and harbored no inclination to return. Memories, many delightful, others grievous, stayed buried within Anna Ruth's heart, but the old woman never allowed a bulldozer to erase the delightful ones. The easiest course of action for the college professor was to let it be. Anna Ruth called the place an "albatross" when she spoke of it to KT, an honest description of McCormick House in Anna Ruth's mind. This inheritance was now KT's "albatross," and her personal circumstances dictated she find an expeditious and proper way to rid herself of this burden.

"Let me think it over tonight, Graham. I'll notify you tomorrow how I want to go forward. Nonnie used to advise, 'Don't make rash decisions, but never get caught in analysis paralysis.' It's funny. I wasn't around her too much, but she left me with several pearls of wisdom."

Graham smiled and said, "No hurry. You must decide what's best for you. I'm not going anywhere."

"I will. Once I decide, my search for the cemetery can begin. Let's enjoy our dinner."

THE PROPOSAL

K T retired to her hotel room and checked her cell phone for messages. Four popped on her screen. Two marked "urgent" came from the director of the clinic where she worked, imploring her to return his calls "at once." Her next-door neighbor in her condominium complex requested a return call. A medical school colleague's number showed as the fourth call, and his message urged her to reply "pronto."

She called her neighbor first, fearing a problem at home. No disaster. The neighbor caring for KT's two cats wanted permission to buy them a couple of toys. KT chuckled and replied the two always welcomed toys. After ending the call, she lamented her career absorbed virtually every minute of her time and denied her pets the attention they deserved.

"Lucky for them they have each other," she mused.

With a weary huff, she saved the message from her boss. His demands, his demeaning tone, and his definition of "urgent" no longer squared with KT.

"Nope, not tonight, Rightmore!" she spewed toward the phone. "I'm on my own time now, and I have important decisions to make. I'll deal with you in the morning."

Next, KT phoned her old med school buddy. Stub O'Connor and KT both completed their residencies in rural medicine, with special interests in prenatal care and public health. They had kept in touch—bouncing ideas off each other, discussing medical advances and the trajectory of their personal lives. Stub was the medical director for a clinic in Kansas before becoming a professor at a medical school, and now he served as Dean at another medical school in Maine. Stub and KT spoke not long after Anna Ruth's death but had not spoken since.

"Hi, Stub! It's great to hear from you. How's the family? Are you still loving it in Maine?"

"Hey, KT! Yeah, we're settled in. Kids are pleased with their school, and the school district notified Jeanie she'll be teaching fifth grade in the fall. I'm liking my job more every day. The people are fantastic, and Maine is gorgeous. Winter was snowy, but hey, skiing is superb. Are you at home? Can we talk?"

"I'm in Hillview to take care of the property I inherited from my grandmother. Arrived here this afternoon, and I've got important decisions to make. Either I sell the property as-is, accepting the fact the house won't bring much of a price and will presumably get torn down, or I spend a ton of money on renovations, try to recoup my investment, and save the house from demolition. The original owners built the house in the late 1800s, and its wooded four acres yield lots of privacy."

"When must you decide?"

"Tomorrow, maybe. Soon for sure. The sooner the better."

"Have you seen it?"

"Yes. The realtor and I inspected it this afternoon. It needs a *load* of work. A real *boatload*."

"I can't advise you. Big decision. Since you're in the midst of this dilemma, I'll explain in as few words as I can why I'm calling."

"Okay. Shoot."

"The last time we talked, you were unhappy with what's going on where you live in Bluff County. Has it improved or gotten worse?"

"Worse, much worse. As you know, our public health department reports directly to the county commission. The powers-that-be in our business community were unhappy they had just one of the three commissioners in their pockets, so they got a proposal on the ballot to increase the commission from three to five people. The issue received little publicity, turnout was light, and the proposal passed. Sad to say, the two new members hold zero interest in public health. One owns a gambling club, and the other owns a bunch of strip malls and rundown apartment complexes."

"Oh, I remember you mentioned the upcoming election. What's going on now?"

"It's bad. They cut our funding. Slashed it. The commission caters to businesses owned by friends—bars, tanning salons, gun shops, apartments, restaurants, tobacco shops, strip centers, and such. Those businesses are at odds with the public health department on many fronts, some with a history of health and legal violations."

"Not helpful. I remember a commissioner gave you grief for getting the no smoking ordinance passed."

"Yeah. After the election, they hired a Chief Medical Officer named Ron Rightmore, whose credentials are, uh, suspect. He's a local podiatrist who's hand-in-glove with three commissioners. Rightmore's in cahoots with them on a strip center and a humongous gentleman's club called The County Line."

"Wait. Aren't you the Chief Medical Officer?"

"I was. When Rightmore came on board two months ago, he demoted me to a staff physician position and cut the clinic and public health program's funds. He slashed the staff and now just one doctor remains. Me. Oh, we have Rightmore, who is too busy, he says, to see patients, and he's not qualified, anyhow, unless a patient has a foot problem. Two nurses administer immunizations and see patients, but now our services are minimal and pathetic. Rightmore says he plans to drop all medical treatment and only do immunizations. Last week he cut the health inspectors from two to one."

"This is awful! Where are your patients supposed to go for health care?"

"I don't know. He has no clue what he is doing, and I suspect the money we receive from the state is being misdirected to wherever Rightmore and his cronies wish."

"How can he do such a thing? Don't you have to maintain specific programs and standards to get funding?"

"We do, but I suspect he's falsifying documents. He asked me to co-sign a questionnaire from the state, validating we provide specific services. I refused because he discontinued the services mentioned on the paper. It's terrible because we've lost our prenatal education program and won't advertise our immunization program due to pressure from a state senator who is anti-vaccinations. I hate to envision what might happen if we have a veritable epidemic. We ran out of flu vaccines in February. It ran rampant in the county this year, and two people died."

"Gee, I didn't realize it was this awful. I'm sorry, KT."

"It's a real pisser. Bluff County is growing because people from the city are moving farther out for cheaper property and lower taxes. We now have no meaningful inspections of restaurants. There is no effort to curb substance abuse, and the program I created for healthy eating and exercise is gone. I keep hoping the voters will realize how dangerous these changes are and vote these characters out, but Bluff County has become a hotbed of apathy. I keep helping folks when they come in the door. They need me. I've considered reporting these problems to the state health department, but Rightmore is tight with the governor. If I get fired, nobody is there to help patients. Our two nurses are fed up and are searching for other jobs."

Silence.

"Stub, are you there?"

"Maybe it's providence I'm talking with you tonight, my friend. The medical school is expanding our rural health initiative and will need another professor next fall. You're the first person I thought of for the position. We have a brief window to fill the slot. It needs to be filled by July first. What do you think? I hate to toss this on you when you have other important decisions to make, but we received approval yesterday."

KT did not speak for a moment. This unexpected opportunity leaped through the phone and caught her off guard. It left her confused and shocked.

"I'm blown away. This is a tremendous surprise! Thank you for considering me. I must think on this, though. This is out of the blue. Gosh!"

"Of course. I didn't expect you to commit on the spot. Listen, let me send you a packet explaining the school and the position. You love working with patients, and opportunities exist for you to continue. Your expertise is what we need in every respect, KT, and you'd love it here. Maine is one gorgeous state. Mountains. The ocean. Moose!"

KT's hearty laugh rang through the phone. This offer tempted her. As much as she yearned to improve conditions in Bluff County, the thought of teaching others and imparting her love of public health brought a sense of excitement and adventure.

"Send it to me here at the Hillview Inn. I'm not sure when I'll get home. It's possible I can't study it for a while, but at least it will be in my hands. This sounds interesting. Mighty interesting. July first, you say? I'll decide before then. I must get home after I get McCormick House off my plate."

After an exchange of best wishes, the two friends ended their call. KT changed into pajamas and snuggled into the room's corner chair. She brought her knees to her chin and wrapped her arms around her legs as her mind raced from one topic to another. KT strove to sustain a solid effort for her patients, but she found the toxic scene at her clinic debilitating. The prospect of a medical school position brought hope for a brighter future. But her patients? What might happen to them?

"I must purge this from my mind. Oh, Stub, I wish you called me after I'm finished here. Right now, I've got to decide what to do with Annie's Albatross," she moaned aloud.

KT rested her head on her knees and rocked back and forth. She stretched and folded her arms over her chest. In the moment's stillness, she felt the embrace of Anna Ruth's gentle voice.

"Don't borrow trouble, dear girl."

ENVELOPE NUMBER ONE

KT tossed and shifted in bed the entire night. At morning's light, she awoke with determined resignation. Her heart implored her to do what Anna Ruth did not. She must save McCormick House. It required a fresh start with a new family.

"I can't allow it to continue as an albatross or be razed as if it never existed," she reasoned to her reflection in the bathroom mirror.

Graham received KT's telephone call with delight. "Hot dog! May we meet there at one o'clock? I will bring a list of contractors, and we'll go from there. KT, I can't wait to see the house in full bloom again, as vital as it was years ago. Oh, boy, this will be a challenge, but a fun one!"

As KT left the dining room after breakfast, the desk clerk approached and handed her a plain manila envelope. It showed no return address, just "Miss Kathryn Winslow" handwritten on the front.

KT sat in a chair in the lobby and opened it with care.

Dear Miss Winslow,

I am sorry to learn of your grandmother's death. Please allow me to introduce myself. I am Thomas B. Martin, Attorney at Law, developer of Briarhurst Estates, the exclusive subdivision adjacent to your property. My instincts apprise me you are desirous of selling. I am eager to welcome the addition of the property you inherited to my Briarhurst Estates and can assure you homes built on your land will be constructed to the highest standard, as is each Mansion by Martin home.

I have enclosed a contract for the sale of your property to me. The price I proffer here is a most generous one, considering the current real estate market and condition of your property. Without participation of realtors, the sale involves no commissions, making for a clean and easy transaction.

Please sign and return the contract to me at the address provided. I am out of town and will not return until next week, but I hope to meet you in person at a later date. I listed my cell phone number on the letterhead above if you have questions. Once you sign the contract, I will mail a cashier's check for the full amount of sale to your address on file.

Sincerely,

Thomas B. Martin, Esq.

"For we live by faith, not by sight." 2 Corinthians 5:7

KT marched to the front desk and addressed the clerk. "When did this arrive, please?"

The woman appeared taken aback and replied in a hesitant tone, "Fifteen minutes ago. I buzzed your room but got no answer. He left it with me and asked me to get it to you."

"Thank you."

KT shot straight to her car, jumped in, snapped her seat belt, and returned Dr. Rightmore's "urgent" call, which was not urgent. Focused on the task at hand, KT roared out of the parking lot and headed to her "albatross."

Upon making the turn onto the tree-lined lane, KT stopped the car. In the rear-view mirror, she caught sight of an imposing white house which fronted on Apple Ridge Road. It had to be the old Mueller home, she assumed, where Anna Ruth's kindred spirit, Mittie Mueller McCormick, lived as a child during the Civil War.

To her immediate left, brilliant flowers provided a friendly welcome to Tobias Hill Nursery. As she proceeded at a snail's pace, KT studied the three residences on the same side of the lane as McCormick House. She admired the dense woods concealing Doan's home across the lane from McCormick House and more woods at the end of the lane. She made a right turn into her own weed-infested gravel driveway and stopped the car. Thunderous crashing booms coming from what appeared to be the far back side of her property greeted her as the car door opened, but the impenetrable, overgrown thicket did not allow her to establish the precise source of the noise.

"I guess the neighbor is clearing brush or something," she said aloud, straining to see through the woods. "What a ruckus!"

Dressed in jeans and hiking boots, she grabbed her notebook and pen and began jotting notes on exterior improvements.

Another deafening crash startled her. KT spotted a deer path which appeared to lead through the woods toward the racket. Off she went, shoving limbs and vines aside as she forged her way toward the commotion.

Approaching the western edge of her property, KT spied her next-door neighbor's pristine lawn straight ahead through the trees. Another loud crash turned her ninety degrees to the south where, in the rear corner of her woods, a monster-sized bulldozer pushed and ripped at her trees. Was she confused as to the property line? No. The yellow Caterpillar had smashed onto her property, crushing everything in its path!

At a full sprint, KT hurtled toward the machine. She waved her fists and shrieked at the operator, "Stop! Stop right now!" He feigned not to hear, but KT accepted no part of his act.

"What are you doing?" she yelled at the man in the driver's seat.

"I'm clearing these woods," he snarled in a sarcastic tone. "What's it look like to you?"

"Why? You're on my property!"

"Huh? Nah, honey. Blane Martin owns it. I'm clearing a path for sewer and water lines before he builds houses here. It ain't yours."

KT's blood pressure rose. "This is *not* Blane Martin's land! It's mine! I am KT Winslow, and I own this land. You and your machine get off my property! Now!"

The driver shook his head. His dismissive countenance showed KT he planned not to obey her instructions. He put the bulldozer in motion and clanged forward as an oversized redbud tree cracked and crashed to the ground.

Infuriated, KT charged to the front of the dozer and planted herself in a stiff stance before the blade, blocking her face from the dust with her hands. She folded her arms and glowered at the driver square in the eye as the huge Cat growled to within a few inches of her body. Dr. Kathryn Winslow stood her ground.

He stopped, turned off the engine, climbed from the seat, and stalked toward her in a menacing manner.

"Don't you come near me!" she admonished as she took out her cell phone. "I'll call the police. You're on my land, and you need to go. Capiche? Blane Martin, or Thomas Martin, or whatever his name is today does *not* own this land, and he never will! If he claims he does, he's lying."

"Honey, he told me yesterday he'd bought it and to get started today. He's built these other houses around here." His hand swept across and behind his body. "Who are you, anyhow? A crazy old battleaxe owned this mess before he bought it. You ain't that old."

KT gripped the phone in her shaking hand and roared, "For one thing, buddy, my name is not Honey. I inherited this house and four acres from my grandmother, and she was *not* crazy. I have not and will not sell to your Martin friend. He's lying to you. Get your stinking bulldozer off my land this instant! Scram!"

The driver remounted the yellow machine, slouched into the driver's chair, and launched a disgusting wad of yellowish spit into the air. KT maintained her position as the intruder retrieved a cell phone from his shirt and placed a call. He spoke for several minutes before returning the phone to his shirt pocket. At the same moment, he launched the destructive beast, raised its ugly toothed blade from the ground, turned around, and rumbled off to a flatbed truck parked on the side of Apple Ridge Road.

KT shook. This confrontation rattled her. She glowered at the devastation the brute wrought to her woods. The day began with promise, but a bulldozer and a "weaselly snake" were fast turning KT's optimism into despair.

She cursed and stomped her way back to the dilapidated dwelling she now owned. "What type of person is this Martin character? Graham says he's bad news. Nonnie had him figured out without ever meeting him," she grumbled.

KT shuddered as she turned the key in the front door. Her episode with the "creep on the Caterpillar" rattled her. She stormed into the kitchen and slammed her notebook on the table, launching a voluminous cloud of dust into the air. Scouring the room, she visualized the image of it when her grandmother and great-grandparents lived there. Perhaps the kitchen could once more afford a welcoming and pleasant spot for a family to gather. She blew dust from one chair, opened her notebook, and sat, allowing her pounding heart to slow and her flushed cheeks to cool.

The cell phone in her rear pocket jingled. Graham's morning appointment did not last as long as expected, and his proposal to stop at a deli and bring lunch received an enthusiastic response. KT did not volunteer details of her confrontation, but she promised to fill him in when he arrived.

When Graham's red Wrangler arrived at the house, KT stood upstairs in the bathroom, jotting ideas in her notebook. She darted to the head of the stairs and waved as he entered the parlor.

"Come and get it, KT! I brought paper towels and a spray bottle of cleaning solution to wipe off the table."

She followed Graham to the kitchen and wiped the table and chairs as he set the food and drinks on top.

"Wow, check out this dirt," KT said as she crammed dirty towels into a large trash bag. She removed hand sanitizer from her backpack, slathered it on her hands and passed it to Graham. "Yuk!"

As they ate, KT detailed her encounter with the bulldozer driver and the contract Martin had left at the hotel. Graham did not appear surprised.

"This sounds like something he'd do," Graham said. "He assumes you'll sell to him, so he might as well get cranking. What are your plans for the contract he left for you?"

"Tear it to pieces. Where is his office? I want to take it there and dump it on his desk."

Graham snickered and said, "He doesn't have an office. The address on his letterhead is nothing more than a mail drop. It's a storefront where people rent mailboxes. Makes it appear as if he has an actual business location if you see it on a letterhead. Where he lives and works is a mystery. Martin's a phantom who disappears and reappears. It's unbelievable how he stays under the radar. He doesn't answer his telephone, and he changes the number from time to time. How much damage is back there?"

"I can't be sure. The fool cleared a hundred feet or more. He was next to what's left of the stone wall. The path is maybe twenty feet wide. I'm not sure. Where are the sewer and water lines he mentioned? Shouldn't I call the Sheriff? I'm furious!" Her mouth twisted, and a snarl blew forth from her nostrils.

"When Martin built the subdivision behind you, it included the three other houses on your street. He connected each house to the county's lines. I assume they run behind the houses on this street. Should you restore McCormick House to sell, you *can* hook into existing lines, but you'd need permission from Martin and the county. Because you are spurning his offer, I doubt he'll cooperate. Digging a new well and installing new septic may be your only recourse. It's legal in this county to have your own well and septic, even if county water and sewer lines are nearby, but it's expensive. Call the Sheriff? Hmm. Let me think on it."

Indignant, KT ripped a bite from her sandwich. She swallowed and said, "I want nothing to do with these creeps. What a presumptuous trespassing jerk he is! He's damaged my land back there, and he had no right."

Over lunch, KT calmed, and they discussed how to go forward with her renovation plan. Afterward, they toured the grounds around the house as she made more notes. Graham phoned a structural engineer who agreed to come assess the foundation at three o'clock.

"If he says the foundation is in poor condition, KT, you may need to reconsider your plans. It may not be worth it to renovate a house this old with foundation issues. The foundation seems solid to me, but he needs to see it. I called a guy who digs wells, too. Believe it or not, his name is Digger Wells, and he'll come in the morning at nine. The septic company will be here tomorrow at eleven. These three can deliver the best idea of whether you should continue with your plan."

"I'm beyond grateful, Graham. Thank you. This isn't your job, you realize."

"Oh, I figure if you go ahead, I'll make more money when it sells! Besides, you don't know a soul around here. I have contacts for honest craftspeople who do excellent work."

"You're right. I appreciate your help more than you can imagine, especially after my run-in this morning."

They meandered toward the back of the house for a cursory inspection of the collapsed shed. Graham shuffled a foot in the dirt near its entrance and said, "I've done something else, too. I'm not aware of the cemetery you're seeking, but I've made another appointment for you tomorrow with Emmaline Conrad, the head of the county Historical Society. She'll be able to find it, I believe. The appointment is at two o'clock."

KT threw her hands in the air and reached out to him. As she placed both hands on his arms, she broke into an immense smile.

"Thank you again, Graham. I can't wait!"

****

The structural engineer completed a thorough inspection of the home's foundation before speaking. "Whoever built this house did a bang-up job. Six joists need minor reinforcement, but it's stood for well over a hundred years, and it'll stand a hundred more. No termites, either. Don't let anybody flatten this house, Dr. Winslow. Years of life still exist in her, and our historical homes need protection." The fellow stomped his foot to confirm the soundness of the floor.

After the engineer drove away, KT clapped her hands and proclaimed to the sky, "Yippee! One down and two to go!" Her chestnut ringlets danced as her freckled face beamed.

Graham bellowed with laughter. "Not too fast!"

"I'm positive, Graham. It will be positive news. I can *taste* it. Rumors *won't* stop this property from thriving again. Somebody will fall in love with it, buy it, and turn it into a home filled with decency and love once more. Sounds corny, but it *must* be true."

As she latched the door and turned toward the porch steps, Graham glanced at his watch. "KT, it's five o'clock. An early dinner? We can discuss folks who can help you turn your dream into reality."

"Your invitation is kind, but isn't someone waiting for you at home?"

He paused. "My wife and my boy died in a car wreck years ago, and I've never remarried. I have a dog, but she goes in and out as she pleases through a doggy door."

"Oh, I'm terribly sorry. How tragic for you. I'm . . ."

Graham broke into her sentence. "Thanks. It was awful, but life often throws us a horrific curve ball. Losing my family was one helluva curve, but we must hoist ourselves from the depths and move forward on the road we are traveling, mustn't we? Now, follow me into town, and we'll try a different eatery. It's one of my favorites, and you can get another flavor of Hillview."

KT trailed Graham into town and parked in front of a cheerful establishment with an enormous blue and yellow striped awning in front. Two tables occupied spaces on the sidewalk, each decorated with a colorful tablecloth and a vase of bright flowers.

As they strode through the door, a diminutive ebony-skinned woman, perhaps in her sixties and wearing a blue and yellow checkered apron, greeted them with a cheery, "Hi, Graham! Nice to see you."

"Good afternoon, Birdie. I want you to meet KT Winslow. She's in town readying a property she inherited to go on the market."

The woman extended her hand to KT. "Welcome to Hillview and welcome to Birdie's Bistro. Pick any table, Graham. I'll be with you in a jiffy."

KT scoped the restaurant. Color splashed throughout. Each table sported a tablecloth of a different color, garnished with a vase of fresh tulips. White, gauzy valances dressed the front windows.

"How delightful!" KT put her hands on her hips. "If the food is as appealing as the décor, I can't wait to try it!"

They seated themselves by the front window at a table dressed in a purple cloth and topped with bright, yellow tulips.

"Birdie moved here over ten years ago from New York City after a messy divorce. Somehow, she discovered Hillview as a spot to start over. She owned a cafe in New York's East Village and brought her menus and know-how to us. This building had been vacant for years. Restaurants came and went. When Birdie bought the building, she uncovered lots of relics upstairs. She lives upstairs, and her apartment is a work of art. I guess others lived upstairs over the years, but I doubt any were as charming. If you check out the wall over yonder, you'll see photographs and old menus from Birdie's archives."

Birdie bustled toward their table and placed glasses of water at each setting. She handed each a menu and said,

"Maggie will take your order in a minute, folks." before scampering to the kitchen.

KT and Graham perused the menu and made their decisions before KT's attention turned toward the memorabilia on an opposite wall.

"I'd love to get a closer peek," she said, pointing to the wall. "Excuse me, please."

KT strolled past other diners and examined the framed menus and photographs. In a sudden gesture, she slapped one hand over her mouth when she saw a restaurant's name painted on the window in one photograph. Taken in the 1930s or 1940s, judging from the apparel worn by individuals standing by the door, the sign read "Olivia Watson's Diner."

"My grandmother mentioned this restaurant. It was Olivia Watson's Diner when Nonnie lived here!" KT gushed after returning to the table. "A different colored tablecloth covered every table as these do now."

"What a coincidence. I'll bet Birdie discovered the tradition and made it a point to decorate this way."

Birdie's Bistro differed from its years under Olivia Watson's ownership. KT observed diners of various ages and ethnicity, but when Annie Young and her parents lived near Hillview, Olivia Watson's Diner was a "Whites Only" establishment. Now, an accomplished black woman owned and operated the inviting eatery.

"Things have changed since the Youngs lived here. Changed for the better, Graham."

Graham acknowledged her remark with a smile and handed KT a list of names and telephone numbers.

"These are trustworthy folks. If you decide to press forward, they'll get your house in superb shape."

KT accepted the paper, folded it, and tucked it inside her backpack. She studied Graham as their meals arrived at the table and restated her unanswered question. "Shouldn't I call the Sheriff about Martin and his bulldozer?"

He drew a bite of his pasta dish, wiped his mouth with a napkin, and stared straight into her eyes.

"I'd not call the Sheriff, if I were you."

"But he trespassed and damaged my property."

"In technical terms, *he* didn't trespass. From what I gather from those who've had interactions with Martin, he'll deny he instructed the bulldozer driver to clear the space. He'll claim it was an operator error. As to damage, his dozer didn't get far inside the property. It's at the back where one can't see it from the house. When you return the contract, clarify the fact neither he nor any of his people may come on the property. I have No Trespassing signs at the office. I'll post them around the boundaries. You can use the law to go after trespassers only if you post signs."

She sighed, nodded, and concurred with his statement with a frustrated, "Okay. Thank you."

They ate dinner with no further mention of Thomas Blane Martin, or whatever his name was. KT spoke of her work and her childhood, but discussion of her grandmother's time in Hillview did not include details surrounding the furor a teen-aged Anna Ruth created.

Graham related details of his life's story. Reared in Hillview, he began a career with the United States government after college graduation. His work took him to foreign countries and locations within the United States. Frequent travel kept him away from his family, and he planned to retire from the government. One week before his last day at work, his wife and toddler son died in a car crash.

"When I lost my wife and boy, I almost canceled my retirement plans. I realized, though, my depression and frame of mind, uh, hindered my work and, uh, affected my colleagues. My wife and I both worked for the Feds. It's how we met. She quit her job when our boy was born. Granddad died not long after the accident, and Dad needed help in the business, which convinced me to walk away from my government career and come home. I needed a change and have been here ever since I came home."

"I, I'm at a loss for words, Graham. I'm sorry. How dreadful to lose your wife and your little boy. I'm sorry. Are you glad you came home?"

He gulped his iced tea. "Yes. Hillview is a right pleasant town. An influx of thinkers and visionaries can wake a sleepy village and make it vibrant. It happened here. Oh, we still have naysayers and the Old Guard who long for the old ways, but it's not what I imagine your grandmother and her parents experienced in the '30s. Dad's mother, my Gram, knew of your great-grandfather, Dr. Young. Gram said Dr. Young saved her father's life, my great-grandfather Graham, by performing an emergency appendectomy. Also, Dr. Young set Granddad Wessler's broken leg when Granddad was a boy. Granddad's stories of long-ago Hillview led me to believe it was not-too-friendly to outsiders."

"Nonnie might agree."

KT and Graham chatted, and Graham floated potential pricing and possibilities involving the restoration. KT declared her intentions to rebuild the stone wall at the property's rear, the wall which captivated a young Anna Ruth. It held the key that unlocked the clue to the secret its stones concealed.

"Maybe Blane Martin did me a favor by clearing a section next to the wall," she brooded.

Graham's nonchalance left KT with the idea he thought the stone wall renovation an unnecessary distraction from other improvements, but he agreed a restored wall added to the historical nature of the property.

KT detailed her progress with her grandmother's estate—how she donated most of Anna Ruth's belongings and began rifling through the six filing cabinets in her condo.

"I discovered one drawer labeled 'Hillview.' I hoped to discover a map leading to the cemetery, but I haven't. The contents of the Hillview drawer are in a cardboard file box I brought with me."

"I'll meet you at McCormick House at nine in the morning," said Graham as they strolled to their respective cars. "Digger will assess the well, and after the septic inspection at eleven, you'll have a clearer idea of the state of affairs. Don't forget, you have a date with the Historical Society tomorrow afternoon."

"I can't wait!" KT roared over the hood of her vehicle. "I'm going back to the hotel to write your Martin buddy a note on his contract and give him a piece of my mind before I drop it in the mailbox!"

Graham Wessler's hearty laugh rang out as he climbed into his trusty ride. He pulled out of his parking space and over to the spot where KT stood. Leaning out the window, he said, "I'm confident Blane Martin may have met his match with you, KT." before driving off with a toot of his horn.

KT frowned and slid into the driver's side of her car before heading to the hotel. At her hotel room desk, she penned a message to Martin before placing an enormous "X" and "VOID" on each page of the contract before tearing it into pieces and inserting it into the stamped, self-addressed envelope.

"Go away, Mr. Whatever-your-name is Martin! I don't want to hear from you again! My grandmother had your number, and I do, too. Goodbye and good riddance!"

She crammed the envelope into the hotel lobby's mailbox, waved at the desk clerk, and took the elevator to her room. After an online tour of the Maine medical school, she pushed everything into the recesses of her mind and fell into a sound sleep, ready to face the following day.

DIG A HOLE, DIG A HOLE

D igger Wells's lips drew into a narrow line as he stared over his glasses. "I reckon this well is shot, ma'am. Folks didn't case 'em in the old days like we do now, and they give out. This one's plain worn out. It's caving in. Ones nowadays last fifty to sixty years."

"I was afraid of this," KT conceded to Graham, who nodded his head in agreement.

Digger said, "Best fill this one in and drill another, but if you don't want the bother, hook into the county water line running behind those houses over yonder."

KT's dark ringlets bounced as she shook her head. "No, I won't mess with those water lines. We need a well. We'll drill a well. Where will you drill?"

Digger surveyed the vicinity and pointed to three possibilities. One spot appeared most promising. Its position near the house meant minimal cost for water lines and power for the pump. The location didn't endanger plants or trees. KT signed a contract, and Digger agreed to get the necessary permits. Once secured, he could begin work.

As Digger Wells drove away, KT sighed. "I figured this possibility, Graham, but I hoped for a better report."

"Old Digger's right. They dug wells differently; this one's been abandoned for years. You'd better prepare yourself for the same info on the septic."

The eleven o'clock appointment with Honey Wagon Services went the same way as the nine o'clock. KT found the company name amusing and snickered as she signed the contract. The Honey Wagon representative, same as the well driller, promised to gain permits and get started.

"I'm committed now," said KT. "I may be nuts, but I will make Annie's Albatross a fine home once again, Graham Wessler!"

"Annie's Albatross? I'm confident you will, and I'm glad. If you don't mind, may I tag along for your appointment at the Historical Society? Emmaline Conrad possesses a wealth of knowledge, and I'm interested in what she has to say."

"Oh, you bet! I'm concerned the cemetery can't be located. If I can find it, and this is an enormous question mark, then I need to learn how to gain permission to bury Nonnie's ashes there."

"Don't worry. Emmaline knows every inch of the county. I'm confident she can locate the cemetery, but I must get back to the office. Here's the location of the Historical Society. I'll meet you there at two o'clock. Okay?"

"Fine. See you at two."

KT lingered beneath an old oak shading one side of the house. The spring day was cloudless with a touch of wind, and birds chattered a symphony she found peaceful. Daffodils, wild onion, and a smattering of tulips peeked through tall weeds around and between two dead ash trees lying on the ground. KT expressed gratitude the enormous trees had not fallen on the house, and she added dead tree removal to the growing task list in her notebook.

"Hello, house," she addressed the decrepit dwelling, squinting as she spoke. "You're mine now, and you are safe. I will restore you and put you in the hands of a deserving family. I won't let snakes, weasels, or cruel rumors stand in the way, either. You'll be whole. There will be laughter. You'll enjoy love again."

The home's filthy, lifeless windows gaped at her. She gazed back for a long while, forming a mental image of how everything appeared when her grandmother and her grandmother's parents, Carter and Ellen Young, arrived in 1933. They had a dog, a terrier named Bitsy, who kept Annie company and entertained with an array of mischievous adventures. Dr. Carter Young had taken over the medical practice of the late Charles McCormick, M.D. His widow, Mittie McCormick, owned the house and rented it to the Youngs. Through this connection, Annie and Miss Mittie developed a cherished friendship. Over time, Miss Mittie admitted to a horrific event which poisoned Hillview, a tragedy long hidden from the light of day. The rest of the truth Annie exposed made it difficult for Annie and her family to continue living in Hillview; thus, when the family moved away, Annie abandoned the name of her youth, and those she met knew her by her given name, Anna Ruth. On Anna Ruth's last day of life, she and KT shared a picnic next to remnants of the old stone wall. There, KT learned in excruciating detail secrets confined to her grandmother's heart since she was a young teen. The reflection brought a cleansing flow of tears, followed by a warm smile of resolve.

"Okay, house!" KT hollered. "Get ready to shine! You'll be no one's albatross again!"

****

KT located the Historical Society. The wooden, Victorian style building sat on a side street, tucked among other businesses and residences, and she imagined these buildings had been grand homes in earlier times. This one stood out from the others because of its hue. Dark olive exterior walls, windows trimmed in beige, and a porch set off by ceramic pots filled with pansies provided an impressive welcome.

KT parked, strode the steps onto the porch, and entered Emmaline Conrad's office. Seated behind a desk, the woman who appeared to be in her late fifties held a phone to one ear with one hand while punching keys on a calculator with the other. She peered over rimless glasses at KT, brushed her shoulder-length light brown hair from her face, and motioned for KT to come to the desk. Oversized earrings swung backward and forth as she spoke.

"I have a customer. Check those amounts to see if you agree. I'll call you later," the woman said as she slammed the receiver in its cradle.

"Sit, sit! I'll bet you're Dr. Winslow, aren't you?"

"Yes, I am."

"I'm Emmaline Conrad. It's nice to meet you and welcome to Hillview!"

A sheer, flowered shawl draped from Emmaline's shoulders, and several long necklaces hung from her neck. A few faint liver spots covered her hands, and dark green polish adorned her nails. Each finger sported a ring. A thick copper bracelet girded her left wrist, and a cluster of thin bracelets on the other wrist emitted a welcome rattle when she shook KT's hand. Emmaline's warmth and colorful style connected with KT.

"Thank you. I'm glad to be here. I suppose Graham Wessler let you know why I'm in town. He believes you may help me find a cemetery."

"That he did. He notified me you inherited a piece of property you wish to sell. I'm familiar with the house, and I'm glad you'll restore it. Do you know it qualifies for listing in our county's Historic Register of Homes? Dr. and Mrs. McCormick built the home in the late 1870s. I expect it may qualify for the National Historic Register, too."

"What does qualification for these Historic Registers mean?"

"Our *county* designation means the home cannot be demolished, or its architecture altered. The *national* designation takes a while to receive and needs more documentation than our county one. The national designation is a possibility because the wife of the original owner, Mrs. Charles McCormick, Mittie was her name, was Dr. Henry Helton Mueller's daughter. Doc Mueller was a renowned physician here in the 1800s. We're aware he aided slaves in their escapes to freedom, and we've listed his house on both the national register and our county register. It's on Apple Ridge Road near your property, the white house with columns in front. We suspect his home was a stop on the Underground Railroad, but we can't be positive without further validation."

KT nodded. She set her backpack on the floor and smiled at Emmaline. "I'm aware of the house. My grandmother spoke of Doc Mueller's work. He was a decent and courageous man, wasn't he? My grandmother was a teenager when she and her family lived here, and she and Miss Mittie became 'kindred spirits,' Nonnie said. My grandmother and her parents rented the McCormick house while they lived here."

Emmaline started to speak, but a jingle at the front door stopped her. Graham strolled in and shut the door, causing the attached bell to emit a loud clang.

"Hi, ladies! Hope I'm not late. My calls took longer than expected." He proceeded to the chair next to KT and took a seat.

KT acknowledged Graham with a wave as Emmaline asked with a snicker, "Selling houses, are you, Graham?"

"I am. Do you expect you can help KT find her cemetery?"

Emmaline explained she had been speaking of historic designations. Next, she retrieved what appeared to KT to be a poster rolled into a tube from the side of her desk and opened it.

"We can discuss historic material later. Let's find your cemetery, shall we?" asked Emmaline.

"I don't know where the cemetery is," said KT, "but it's near the McCormick property somewhere. In searching through my grandmother's things, I hoped to find a map, but I've not found one. I only can repeat what Nonnie remembered. She said they drove on a rough dirt path barely wide enough for one car. The cemetery sat between three enormous sycamore trees next to a creek. The path may no longer exist, and the trees may no longer be there. This isn't helpful, is it?" KT wrinkled her forehead and searched Emmaline's face for any clue.

Emmaline pulled her hair back and adjusted her glasses. "This may be difficult. We have scores of cemeteries in this county. Many of them are old family cemeteries. Lots of creeks run through the county, too. But lucky for you, one of our projects has been to locate and map our cemeteries, and if one doesn't have a name, we give it one."

Emmaline unrolled the enormous sheet of paper and set it on top of the desk.

"This map shows the county cemeteries we've located," she said. "I'm trying to find your street. Son of a monkey, where the heck is it?"

Graham rose, walked around the desk, and stood beside Emmaline as he leaned over the map. KT observed them both, her nervousness becoming more visible, her heart beating hard enough she felt it in her ears. She feared time and neglect had erased every trace of the little graveyard.

"Here, Emmaline. Here's McCormick House. Right off Apple Ridge Road. Where is a creek?" Graham's finger moved toward the Mueller house on Apple Ridge Road. "Here's one on the Mueller property, near the original Mueller house, the big white house across from your lane. Is this it, KT?"

KT recalled another detail. "No!" she blurted. "In 1934, the cemetery sat on a strip of land owned by a man named Taylor. He gave it to James Hinshaw of Philadelphia. The strip once belonged to Morse Blanton, but Blanton sold it to Taylor's dad after the Civil War because . . ." She stopped.

"Taylor Farms?" Graham's finger moved on the page to a zone not far south of McCormick House and addressed KT. "Taylor Farms is a subdivision on what was once Charlie Taylor's farm. Charlie's son sold the property to another farmer in the 1950s, and he's the one who developed a subdivision in the 1970s."

"I'll bet it's this graveyard, Graham." Emmaline pointed her finger to a spot on the page. "Little Hanks Creek runs two miles south of KT's property, and we've a notation here saying three graves are off Creek Road right before Little Hanks Creek. Hey, Graham, see how Creek Road turns off Quail Run? Quail Run intersects Apple Ridge Road, which runs by the lane leading to your property, KT. We named the cemetery, uh, I don't see a name. We haven't researched it yet; it's a mystery whose remains rest there. KT, I bet you

Creek Road was the dirt path your grandmother remembered."

"That's it, that's it! Oh, Emmaline, it *must* be the right one!" KT scarcely contained her joy.

With a gleam of satisfaction, Emmaline leaned back in her chair as Graham returned to his seat. She and others had toiled to locate and map every tiny cemetery in the county, and this discovery and KT's reaction validated their work's value.

"We are pretty confident we've located every cemetery, and we're trying to document names on tombstones. Then, if someone is searching for a particular person's gravesite, we can find it. It's a tedious project. This cemetery isn't even in our file yet. We haven't researched the names of the folks buried there or who owns the plot. This may present a challenge for you, KT. One needs permission to bury a casket or ashes. In this state, a funeral home secures permission and handles the burial."

KT's confident reply startled both Emmaline and Graham. "The cemetery was owned in 1934 by James Hinshaw from Philadelphia. Whenever Mr. Hinshaw died, I'm willing to bet he left the cemetery to Ned Hill, Tobias Hill's father. Tobias Hill Nursery, you know. My grandmother said everyone called Tobias Hill 'Blink.' Nobody called him Tobias. The funeral home here has held her ashes since her death, so they'll arrange everything if I can find the cemetery's location."

Emmaline adjusted her glasses and responded with a sly smile. She peered at Graham and back at KT, who perched on her seat's edge. Graham tapped the map Emmaline had unfolded.

"Emmaline, since you don't have a record of the cemetery other than its location, wouldn't KT be wise to check at the courthouse?"

Emmaline responded with an affirmative nod as she reminded Graham residential subdivisions now blanketed much of the county. "Better drive there before you visit the courthouse. It's possible your cemetery is smack in the middle of someone's front yard." She slapped her hand on the desk.

KT conveyed her appreciation for Emmaline's help and rose from her chair. She reached across the desk to shake Emmaline's hand before turning to Graham.

"Do you care to go with me, or do you have appointments?"

"You bet! I'd love to see this mysterious graveyard myself and learn why it was important to your grandmother. My appointment isn't until six thirty tonight. Emmaline, will we get ticketed if we leave a car in front while we drive out there?"

"No, you won't," Emmaline said. "It's slow today, and the doctor next door isn't open on Friday afternoons. Please return and describe what you see because my curiosity is in overdrive now, too. I'll be working late tonight preparing for Hillview Days next week. KT, will you be here next weekend? I hope you will, because we'll put on a grand show and celebration next Saturday and Sunday."

"I haven't decided," said KT. "What are Hillview Days?"

Graham took her arm. "I'll explain later," he promised. "We should get moving. It may take a bit of searching to find this spot."

He waved to Emmaline as he and KT rushed through the door and climbed into the Jeep.

"I'm sorry I cut you off back there. Do you want me to clue you in on Hillview Days?" Graham asked as he drove.

"Of course, I do. Emmaline makes it sound fun and interesting."

61

"It's more than a festival or fundraiser. To fully appreciate Hillview Days, you need to grasp how our region has changed. Around twenty-five years ago, several of our oldest homes and buildings in town got leveled or *modernized* in the name of progress. Developers and builders were buying old family farms and orchards. Priceless historic artifacts got lost or thrown away, and it incited a bunch of folks to set off a preservation movement to protect our history, structures, land, and so forth. Participation in Land Savers increased, and before long, a group got together and formed the Historical Society. They held fundraisers and bought the building where Emmaline works for a super cheap price. People started bringing in memorabilia and writing stories. A museum is now on the top two floors of the Society's office. Right away, the Society launched a program to designate buildings as historical properties, and you'll see a bronze plaque on each one earning the designation. Hillview Days is one way we showcase, celebrate, and fund those efforts."

Graham's account delighted KT. In Anna Ruth's day, suspicion greeted each new resident. Jim Crow laws demeaned people of color, and secrecy enshrouded local history.

"This is marvelous! It's different from the town Nonnie experienced. Why, Nonnie thought it laughable the name of Hillview's founder remained a secret. He was a rascal, I gathered."

"He was, but his name is no secret today. The Thespian Troubadours put on a re-enactment of Hillview's founding during Hillview Days. They are a group of men, women, and students who do three plays a year besides Hillview Days. Emmaline is right. You should stay for the celebrations. It's fun and interesting, too. An arts and crafts fair runs the length of Main Street, bands play during the day and into the night, the library hosts local historians and authors, and three or four historic homes open for tours. Civil War re-enactors roam through, too. The money from admission fees goes to the Historical Society. People come from many places. We get charter buses loaded with lots of blue-haired ladies. Restaurants do a landslide business, and the B&B's and hotels are full. Because of this, if I were you, I'd extend your reservation through next weekend in case you stay."

"Sounds fun. I'll do it. I must hire contractors, and the process may take a while."

****

They drove south before turning left onto Quail Run. Graham maintained a slow speed, which enabled KT to take in their surroundings. They saw no quail, but modest, well-kept houses dotted the landscape on both sides of the road. In a few moments on the right, a street sign and brick wall with black letters announced the entrance to Creek Road and to Creek Road Meadows subdivision. Graham stopped the car.

"Are we ready for what lies in wait on this road less traveled?" Graham asked. "I'm familiar with this subdivision. Sorry to say, none other than Mr. Thomas Blane Martin developed it."

"Oh, brother. Just my luck." KT scowled as Graham turned onto Creek Road and headed south.

Impressive homes lined the way, each with a well-groomed front lawn and several varieties of trees. After the last house on the left and several yards before the bridge across Little Hanks Creek, Graham spied a gravel path. The narrow path intersected Creek Road at a right angle and ran for a short distance before disappearing into a stand of mature trees. Shifting the Wrangler into low gear, Graham drove on this path for a few yards and came to a halt. Through the passenger window, KT saw a wrecked picket fence forming a small enclosure. One enormous sycamore tree stood sentry outside the enclosure, while two stumps rotted nearby. Inside the enclosure, the tops of three tombstones peeked through a mass of overgrown vegetation.

"Here! Stop!" KT leaped from the vehicle and pushed through the weeds.

A dilapidated arbor laden with overgrown vines and branches of two long-ignored lilac bushes marked the entrance. KT fumbled with the mangled latch on the gate, but it did not open. The gate was further secured by a rusty chain woven into the fence and attached with a padlock. Even without the security measures, a tangle of wild rose vines prevented opening of the gate. As KT fussed with the chain, Graham found a section of picket fence where the upper rail and pickets had rotted and fallen away. This gap allowed both adults to squeeze through into the enclosure.

"KT, come here! We can get in over here."

She clasped his hand and navigated the rotten boards and vines with care, then headed toward three mossy, barely visible tombstones.

"Here is Israel's grave!" KT brushed away debris, revealing the faint, worn name of Israel Hill, year of death 1863, no month or day. "Ben and Noah's graves are the other two." With tears washing over her freckled cheeks, KT moved to the next marker and ripped back the vines. "Ben Hill, year of death 1863," she read aloud. She hastened to the third stone, pulled away vines, and brushed away a growth of moss. No surname graced this stone, merely the word "Noah" with 1863 as the year of death.

KT's reaction to the stones puzzled Graham. Who were these people? Why did three people who died in 1863 hold such meaning to KT Winslow over one hundred and fifty years later? Were they family? Should he go to comfort her or stand apart and allow her space? This was not the time for questions, he decided.

She wiped her nose on her sleeve and cried, "Nonnie, I found them. I found them! You can join them and rest beside Noah!"

As she blotted her eyes with her shirttail, KT turned to Graham and pointed to the three stones. One leaned backward forty-five degrees, one leaned forward, and the third twisted several degrees sideways. She struggled to catch her breath, but her face beamed.

Graham spoke. "They need straightening, don't they? Nobody has cared for this plot for ages. The fence is a total wreck. Brush and weeds are everywhere." Graham touched her arm and gave her his handkerchief. "Are you okay?"

KT gathered her wits. "Yes, I'm fine. I'm thrilled. Nonnie must rest here. It's a mess, isn't it?"

Graham glanced at his watch. "Because the courthouse closes at five o'clock, we'd best get going."

****

They arrived at the courthouse at four thirty, and a receptionist directed them to the proper office where ownership of the cemetery might be determined.

"May I help you?" asked the plump, purple-haired clerk glued to a glitzy romance novel.

"Hello, Mrs. Jennings," said Graham. "Can you help us?"

The woman raised her face and recognized Graham. With an embarrassed cough, she jammed a bookmark into the book and set it on her desk. "Oh, Mr. Wessler, yes. How are you today?"

"I'm fine. This is Dr. KT Winslow, Mrs. Jennings. She needs to learn who owns a tiny graveyard on Creek Road to the immediate north of Little Hanks Creek. It's old. Can you find the current owner?"

"I suppose, but it may take a while. Is this the only information you have?"

KT provided a precise location, divulged a man named James Hinshaw owned it in 1934 and may have willed it to Ned Hill, whose great-grandson Doan lived nearby. Mrs. Jennings took notes, nodding as she wrote. When KT stopped speaking, the woman stared at her notes for a moment.

"This may take time, Dr. Winslow. I must do research."

KT smiled and responded she appreciated the fact research took time. With knowledge of the cemetery's location, detective efforts to establish current ownership could advance. After giving Mrs. Jennings her cell phone number, a jubilant KT and a pensive Graham left the courthouse and climbed into the Jeep.

"I can't wait to find out who owns it now! Oh, I hope I can get approval to bury Nonnie's ashes there!"

"Me, too. I'll drop you off at Emmaline's so you can retrieve your car. Please clue her in on what we discovered. I must get to my office and prepare for my meeting, but I'll call you in the morning. We can discuss what needs to be done and who to call from the list I gave you."

As Graham sped off from the Historical Society, KT waved goodbye and entered the office. There she found Emmaline behind her desk, lifting hand weights and standing on one leg.

"Hi! How'd it go? Excuse my athletic flurry back here. I take breaks from sitting and do stretches, lift weights, and practice balancing exercises. Trying to keep the old body in shape."

"Don't stop for me, Emmaline!"

"No, I'm finished. Sit, sit. What did you learn?"

An exuberant KT described the cemetery and reported Mrs. Jennings at the courthouse promised to research ownership. Emmaline responded with a grin and two fists thrust into the air before suggesting they dine at a café a short walk from the office.

"I must return here afterward. I have work to complete before I go home, but I'm ravished because I skipped breakfast and lunch. What do you say, KT?"

KT agreed. A sign at the café entrance gate advertised organic and locally grown fare with seat-yourself dining outdoors or inside the quaint, Victorian style building.

"This is charming. I'm downright impressed with downtown Hillview," said KT.

The women entered the inviting brick courtyard and took seats at a patio table while KT surveyed the surroundings. No other diners had arrived, and the pleasing sound of a trickling water fountain among what KT estimated to be fifty potted plants added to the ambiance. The food was delicious, but secondary to their extended tête-à-tête. KT discussed her upbringing and career, and she learned Emmaline was a widow who moved to Hillview with her husband over twenty-five years prior. He had been with a beer distributor headquartered in Hillview. They had no children.

"Monty died a few years after we moved here," Emmaline said. "I stayed in Hillview because I loved it. A quiet and pleasant town, filled with history. This job became available after a while, and it suited me. I'm happy you filled me in on the Creek Road cemetery, and I'm thrilled beyond words to learn you plan to renovate McCormick House."

KT expressed her gratitude and took another bite of her quiche. When Emmaline asked why she wanted to bury her grandmother's ashes there, KT choked.

She gulped her iced tea and cleared her throat. She explained how a cold-blooded murder of two men led Anna Ruth Young to the graves. KT chose her words with care, hoping to avoid any discussion of spirits or a crazy girl which circulated when Anna Ruth was a teenager in Hillview.

"I called my grandmother Nonnie, but she was known as Anna Ruth as an adult and Annie when she and her parents lived here in the 1930s. She and Mrs. McCormick became devoted friends despite the considerable disparity in age. Nonnie's family rented McCormick House after Dr. McCormick died and Mrs. McCormick moved in with her daughter, Susie Rutledge. When Nonnie uncovered those murders, it created a major disturbance. Even though the murders happened years before, and everybody involved was dead, bringing the truth to light created a furor. The murderer buried his victims where I hope to bury my grandmother." KT omitted any mention of Noah.

"Oh, my, I've not heard any talk of murders. You must fill me in when you can! Gracious! I'll bet there's a juicy tale!"

They completed their meals and returned to Emmaline's office, where they bade each other goodbye.

"You must stay for Hillview Days next weekend. Please do!"

"I will!" KT shouted as she climbed into her vehicle and headed to the hotel, her heart filled with satisfaction and anticipation. Spent as she was, the Maine opportunity and Bluff County troubles swirled through her brain, making sleep an elusive endeavor.

THE DEED

Over breakfast, KT's thoughts drifted to her grandmother's teen years. Annie Young had embarked upon a quest for truth, one which exposed scandalous secrets concealed since Civil War times. A boy soldier from ages past aided Annie's quest, and the slightest hint of his presence deepened suspicion of the girl. Her friendship with Blink spawned an even deeper rift between Annie, her classmates, and the old guard. After all, Blink was black and Annie white. KT's grandmother confided her tale to no one until confessing it to KT on the day of her death in the woods behind McCormick House.

KT viewed her grandmother's story as a disturbing yet righteous one. Steeled by Annie's resolve, KT became the sole keeper of this sacred setting and saga. She must return the house to its former glory and hand it over to a new owner to begin his or her own story.

As she emerged from the hotel dining room, KT's cell phone vibrated in her jeans' hip pocket. Graham suggested they meet at the house in an hour. He planned to arrive earlier with several No Trespassing signs and post them on trees at the property boundaries, especially near the stone wall.

He said, "The property to the east of McCormick House is a thirty-acre nature park owned and maintained by the county. Besides wild habitats, the park features hiking and biking trails, an amphitheater, and a compact exhibit center. A twelve-foot chain-link fence goes around the entire park, which provides a secure barrier to your property on one side. No signs need to be posted there."

This information delighted KT. "This makes my real estate even more desirable, right Graham?"

"Yes, it does. Zero worries of a housing development or commercial enterprise next door!"

When she arrived at McCormick House, she saw the red Wrangler in the driveway, and KT assumed Graham to be installing the signs. She unlocked the front door and proceeded to the kitchen with cleaning supplies, paper towels, paper cups, and a box of granola bars purchased in town. In the absence of running water, KT lugged in a five-gallon water jug with a spigot for cleaning and drinking. She hummed as she wiped the kitchen with Lysol and wiped again with clean water, her mind racing with possibilities for the property. After stuffing dirty paper towels into a trash bag, KT strode into the dining room and turned to admire the results.

"What an improvement! It's a lick and a promise, but it's much better," she called to the empty room. "What a fine kitchen you will be!"

A loud thud on the front porch interrupted her musings. She raced to the foyer and opened the door. Graham, face and hands bloodied, lay sprawled on the porch, gasping for breath. His eyes darted around in search of KT.

"My God, Graham! What happened? You're bleeding! Your shirt! It's torn to pieces! Let me help!"

"Let me stay here a minute. Can you get me a drink of water?"

KT darted to the kitchen, filled a paper cup with water, and gave it to Graham. She attempted to clean the blood from his face, but he resisted.

"I'm okay. Please help me get on my feet, and I'll sit in the kitchen." Leaning on KT, Graham righted himself and limped into the kitchen, where he slid into a chair.

KT took his cup, refilled it with water, and returned it to him.

"What in the world happened?" she asked.

Graham rested his left arm on the table and took several deep breaths. "One of Martin's thugs." He gulped water from the cup. "I was tacking a No Trespassing sign on a tree by the stone wall when he came at me. He must have been hiding behind the wall, on the ground below the ledge. I guess he crawled onto your property without me seeing or hearing. I'd say he got the worst of it, though. Got a decent whack on him and threw him over the wall. Years of training in the, uh, let's say I can defend myself."

KT assessed Graham's wounds as he spoke. Damage was limited to several shallow, brier-inflicted lacerations, which KT cleansed with soap and water, then treated with a light application of Neosporin from her backpack. Graham sat straighter and rubbed his forehead with one of KT's damp paper towels. He started laughing as he recounted the intruder flying over the wall, where he landed face down in a pile of rocks.

"He was one of Martin's people? Why did he attack you? What was he doing back there?"

"Yeah, his shirt had Mansions by Martin on it. It's hard to figure why he was there. A utility easement goes along the rear boundary of Martin's subdivision. Maybe he was checking on utilities or maybe just snooping. He parked his golf cart on Martin's side, and he didn't take it well when I warned him to leave and never come back. Most of the torn shirt and blood come from briers and thorns. Glad it was my last sign to post. Now, you're covered in case a trespasser comes. Then you can call the Sheriff."

An infuriated KT stomped to the kitchen counter, where she filled her cup from the jug before returning to the table.

"Graham, I'm calling the Sheriff."

"No. Don't do it. I don't have a clue who the schmuck was, and he's gone. There's nothing the Sheriff can do other than call Martin, who won't answer his phone. He won't mess with me again. I may not look like much, but I work out in my home gym and run five miles each morning, which means I stay in decent shape."

KT sighed with resignation. She did not comprehend Graham's reticence on law enforcement and Blane Martin. She chose not to argue the point and plopped herself into an adjacent chair.

"Okay, but this is getting ridiculous. I want to meet Martin and toss him a piece of my mind! His hired goon may have seriously injured you!"

"I'm fine, KT. I posted the signs. If someone removes them, we notify Sheriff Cortez someone is messing around here. I should have detected his presence, but the hammering of the nail into the tree drowned out his approach, I guess. Not to worry."

"Oh, gee. Um, this makes me wonder if I should . . ."

"No! Don't you dare speak of quitting. No! You're doing the right thing, Dr. KT Winslow. Once Martin sees he isn't intimidating you, or us, he'll stop. Martin's not stupid. He's a bully until someone stands up to him, the same as all bullies."

KT shrugged her shoulders and exhaled with a noisy whoosh. Graham's breathing had returned to normal, and a slight smile had returned to his face, accentuating a deep dimple in each cheek. She reached over and patted the top of his hand.

"Hey, I am fine, KT. This shirt was ready for the rag pile anyhow. Listen, I've called a fellow to come look over what's needed. He's a fantastic carpenter and fix-it expert, and I swear he can do anything. The guy has been out of town and left me a message this morning saying he is home. He asked if I'm aware of any available jobs. He'll arrive here soon. I hope it's okay I called him."

"It's fine. I trust you. It's not every realtor who throws a thug over a stone wall for a client. What's his name?"

"His name is Larry Finler. Now, I need to prepare you for Larry before you meet him. He may not resemble many people you've met, I'll bet. He is the most talented craftsman, but he has issues."

KT's eyebrow arched. "Issues? Uh, oh, this sounds ominous. What issues?"

Graham took another sip of water, and his blue eyes crinkled. "Larry's from over the mountain," he said as he pointed to the west. "He's not school educated, but he's smart as a whip. He's had trouble with the law in the past, DUIs, public drunkenness, brawls and such, but he's stayed sober for a couple of years now. Larry quit smoking, too, and chews gum to stay off alcohol and cigarettes. His uses atrocious grammar, butchers the King's English, and he cusses a blue streak, but not in front of women. His habit is to anoint people with nicknames, so don't get insulted if he gives you one."

KT lowered her head before peering at Graham. "Um, all right. What work can he do? Do you have a nickname?"

"He calls me Cracker. Graham *cracker,* don't you know? Don't judge. The term is often an insult, but not coming from Larry. Larry's specialty is carpentry, drywall, electrical, painting, plumbing, and his work always passes code. His mind is a computer. He figures numbers and measurements in his head without paper, pencil, or a calculator. Every bit in his head! He got his driver's license back a year ago and bought an old Chevy truck with a blown engine. He painted it bright turquoise with a paintbrush. I can't fathom how he got it running, but as I explained, he can do anything."

"Is he dependable? Honest? I need this project completed as fast as possible in order to allow you to work your realtor magic."

"Larry is a hundred percent honest and dependable. Dad and I own six rental units, and Larry does the fix-it work on those places. He lives in the garage behind our office. When he drank, he lost his job with one contractor, followed by another and another. He lost his brand-new truck, every one of his tools, his belongings, and he was homeless for a time. A desperate plight, you can imagine, and we allowed him to move into the garage. The garage served as the real estate office when Granddad started the business, and before that, it was the housekeeper's quarters in Granddad's youth. It included a kitchenette and bathroom. Our current office is in the house where Granddad and Dad both grew up."

Graham leaned backward into the chair and mopped his forehead with a damp paper towel before continuing. "When Dad and I took Larry under our wing, Mom scoured yard sales and flea markets and found a couch, table and chairs, and a bed for Larry. He painted the garage inside and out, restored the kitchen, re-tiled the bathroom, and installed carpet. We bought basic things he needed, but he made it a cozy home for himself. I'm real proud of Larry. Far as I can tell, he stays away from the rowdy bunch of drunks and carousers he used to hang with, the ones who egged him into mischief. Larry's right much of a hermit these days, I suppose, but he reads tons of books. He checks them out from the library, and he took a computer class at the library."

KT rose from her chair and walked to the kitchen sink. She peered through the window and saw a vintage bright turquoise truck with shiny moon wheel caps creeping along the gravel driveway toward the house.

"Larry is here!" she announced. She and Graham walked into the foyer and stood at the torn screen door.

The truck came to a halt. A wiry hombre wearing a baseball cap emerged from the cab, giving KT and Graham a salute as he headed toward the porch. Wavy brown hair hung to his shoulders, and a tie-dyed t-shirt hung loose on his skinny-as-a-string-bean frame. Although his jeans and sneakers were long in the tooth, both were neat and clean. At five feet five and one hundred twenty pounds, Larry Finler reported for duty.

"Hey, Cracker! Good to see ya! Whoa, Nellie! What happened to you? You in a fight or somethin'?"

Ignoring his question, Graham winked at KT as if to say, "See? Nickname."

Graham shook his hand as KT absorbed the aura of Larry Finler. There he stood, chomping with loud smacks on a huge wad of chewing gum. His wide grin exposed the absence of several teeth as he eyeballed KT from top to bottom.

"Pleased to meet ya, Doc!" Larry drawled. "Graham Cracker allows you're gonna fix up this joint. Needs a bunch of work, don't it? Yup, I seen it from the road. Whoa, Nellie! Whatcha got in mind here?"

"I'm pleased to meet you, too, Larry. Graham and I made lists of the renovations. Please come inside and see if it's a job you'd want to tackle."

"Sure 'nuff. Look at them dead trees a lyin' over there. Too far gone fer firewood." He pointed to the two ash trees on the ground amid a once glorious field of daffodils. "Lucky they didn't fall on the house, ain't it? Them nasty ash borers got ever one of them ash trees around here."

KT acknowledged the comment and led Graham and Larry into the house, where they moved from room to room, discussing the range of projects awaiting the touch of a natural artisan. Larry expressed confidence in his ability to handle each job and suggested the need for a half bath on the main floor.

"This here space under the stairway? Perfect bathroom spot. It's next to the kitchen, which means plumbing won't be hard. I can do it easy. Yep!"

They headed upstairs, where Larry responded to each task with a nod and a chomp on his gum. Larry's self-confidence gnawed at KT. She wondered whether he possessed the ability to do this work or was blowing smoke. He asked no questions, took no measurements, and scrutinized nothing. He nodded his head and pulverized his enormous wad of gum while scanning each potential chore in what KT perceived as a haphazard manner.

"Yep, Doc, I can do it. Ever bit. Might need a tad of extry help with drywall and paintin' outside, and maybe electric, but I can do the job. Graham Cracker, what ya thinkin'?"

Graham addressed KT. "If Larry says he can do it, he can. I have experience with his work and am confident in his ability. If you hire Larry, you won't need to hire many other people."

KT hesitated for a few moments and said, "Okay, Larry. The job is yours! Please keep track of your hours. I'll pay you each week. Will you take care of obtaining any permits required?"

"You betcha, Doc! Now, Cracker called you KT. Is KT your actual Christian name? Only initials? No girlie name?"

KT let out a hearty laugh and repeated the story of how she got her nickname.

"Huh, your mama wanted to call you Katie, but your mean ole brother stuck you with them initials. Well, mind if I call you Katie Doc? It's more ladylike, dontcha guess? Slides off the tongue easy, too. Whaddya reckon, Cracker?" Larry drew a stick of Juicy Fruit from his hip pocket and crammed it into his mouth.

Graham chuckled as he navigated the stairs to the foyer. "It's not my decision, Larry; it's hers!"

Graham had been correct in describing Larry's uniqueness. KT stopped in the foyer, and as she opened the screen door, she addressed Larry, who was pushing his longish, wavy hair from his face. "Okay, Larry Locks, you can call me Katie Doc."

Larry laughed so hard he had to remove the huge wad of gum from his mouth to avoid choking. And where did the gum land? Back in his mouth, of course!

The trio completed a walk-around of the house and grounds before Larry Locks climbed into his turquoise 1965 Chevrolet pickup truck and opened the driver's side window.

"Katie Doc, I figure the old wall back yonder means somethin' to ya since you was real careful to point it out. Hard to see through them trees, but if you say it's in terrible shape, you've given me everything I need to stick in my brain. I got a cousin over the mountain, Clete, and he works with stone. He don't use no mortar and can get it lookin' same as it did. Ole Clete stacks them rocks same as they did in olden days. Okay if I get him to help with it? He can help me with everything else around here, too, especially drywall. He's strong as a dang ox and a real fast worker."

KT nodded. Neither Larry nor Graham understood why the stone wall held extreme importance to KT, but they did not question her. She held the secret of the stone wall in her heart, and she cared not to divulge its secret. Yet.

Larry promised to return the following day to take measurements and make a shopping list of necessary supplies. "Once we take care of everything at the house, we'll get right on fixin' the old wall out back fer ya."

Graham handed Larry a spare key to the house and written permission to use his account at the building supply store. Larry started his truck, spun around in the grass, and roared down the driveway hollering, "Larry Locks! Hot damn! Little ole Katie Doc is somethin' else, ain't she?"

Graham said, "I get why you may be nervous after meeting Larry. I'll reassure you his work is excellent, and he works fast. He's skinny and limber and gets into places another can't, and he knows what he's doing. Does he sound flakey? Yes, he does. He'll do a first-rate job for you, Katie Doc. Do you approve of your nickname? Didn't I warn you?"

She chuckled and brushed a curl from her freckled face before rushing inside to answer her cell phone.

"Hello, Dr. Winslow? This is Harriet Jennings at the courthouse. I have found the information you wanted, ownership of the graveyard on Creek Road."

KT's heart pounded faster as she took a seat at the kitchen table, motioning for Graham to come closer.

"Thanks, Mrs. Jennings. Let me get my notebook."

She fumbled with the notebook, trying to open it to a blank page, before dropping her pen under the table. Graham retrieved the pen and gave it to her.

"Okay, I'm ready," KT said into the phone.

"I'll confirm the history of the strip of land where the graveyard is. It's interesting. Back in the 1860s, it was part of Morse Blanton's farm. He sold the sliver of land to a farmer named Taylor. Taylor had the farm across the creek from the plat you're questioning. For your information, the

Taylor farm is now a subdivision called Taylor Farms. In 1934, Taylor's son Charlie deeded the graveyard to a James Hinshaw from Philadelphia. Mr. Hinshaw bequeathed it in his will to Ned Hill, who lived in a cabin on what is now Tobias Hill Nursery. When Ned Hill died, he willed the property to his son, Tobias Hill. Tobias Hill left the property to the county Historical Society in his will. The Historical Society owns it now."

This revelation shocked KT. Emmaline Conrad appeared to possess no knowledge of this information. KT heaped bounteous thanks on Harriet Jennings before sliding the cell phone into her hip pocket.

She faced Graham. "Mrs. Jennings at the courthouse says Blink Hill willed the cemetery to the Historical Society. The Society holds the deed. They own it! How is Emmaline not aware?"

Graham shook his head. He supplied no explanation or theory.

"When did they get it? When did Blink die?"

KT screwed her face into an exasperated snarl. "I didn't ask her."

"Why don't you call back and ask?"

KT clicked the most recent call received on her phone. "Mrs. Jennings, it's KT Winslow again. I'm sorry to bother you, but when did Tobias Hill pass away and transfer the cemetery to the Historical Society? Do you have the date?"

In a few brief minutes, Mrs. Jennings informed KT, "We settled Mr. Hill's estate in August 2001."

"Thank you," KT said as she ended the call.

"Graham, Blink died in 2001. When did Emmaline start at the Historical Society?"

Graham shook his head. He reached out, patted KT's hand, and in a calm voice assured her permission from the

Historical Society Board of Directors should not prove difficult.

"I cannot imagine the board objecting to you burying your grandmother's ashes there. It's obvious they aren't aware of the facts. Emmaline will help you; I'm convinced of it."

The two spent the remainder of the morning at McCormick House mulling renovation plans and a target date for completion. KT reckoned her one-month vacation from the clinic might not suffice for the task at hand. Graham concurred.

"I must assess how to pull this off," she said. "I didn't count on this one bit. My decision is correct, I'm convinced, but I want to stay here until the renovation is complete and I lay Nonnie to rest. An extended leave of absence won't go over well with my clinic's director. He's creating problems, and my absence makes it worse. Other pressing considerations need my attention, too." Stub O'Connor's proposition loomed.

Graham's blue eyes locked onto KT's brown ones. "You can count on me to supervise if you aren't here. This project means a lot to me, too. I don't understand why, but it's a magnet pulling me into its sphere. The history is intriguing, too. I get it. I'll help any way I can."

She smiled. She trusted Graham. Might she disclose the complete tale of Annie and McCormick House? Perhaps, but not now. Not yet. She shut her eyes a moment before whispering, "Thank you."

FRIENDSHIP IN BLACK AND WHITE

The next afternoon, KT drove to McCormick House where Larry's immaculate turquoise pickup sat in the grass. As KT rolled to a stop, Larry bounded from the house.

"Hey, there, Katie Doc! I've got my list together and will start first thing Monday mornin'. You okay out here alone?"

"I'm fine, Larry Locks. Thanks. I won't be here long."

The craftsman leaped into his truck, looped the yard several times, tooting the horn, before he drove away. A gentle breeze wafted through the trees, but dark clouds boiling over the western horizon caught her attention. KT scurried inside to inspect the bedroom where a youthful Annie Young had once dreamed. Creaky floorboards lent an eerie aura to the entire house, and her spine tingled. She returned to the main floor as a bolt of lightning lit the sky, followed by an immediate clap of thunder.

"Good grief!" KT exclaimed to no one. After locking the front door, she bolted to her car. Before she started the engine and snapped her seat belt, the gentle breeze gave way to roaring winds and gigantic raindrops splattering on the windshield. The downpour intensified but eased as she neared the hotel. Grateful to be spared a drenching, KT sprinted from the car to the hotel entrance.

Straight to her room she went and changed into pajamas. The cardboard file box on the desk commanded attention, so she removed its top with a resolute sigh. Rain pounded against the window, and thunder roared as she hovered over the box, leafing through a few of the file folders. One thick folder labeled "Blink" grabbed her attention. KT withdrew this cumbersome folder from the box, flicked on the nightstand light, and settled cross-legged on the bed with her back supported by three pillows. Packed with letters addressed to her grandmother from her faithful friend Tobias Hill, KT's heart twinged as she read the first one.

December 14, 1937

Dear Annie,

It was grand to get your letter. I miss our talks. Bravo! You are done with exams and have a break from school. It is convenient you can take the train to visit your parents for Christmas. I wish they still lived here. Please come visit sometime.

Mam got a letter from your mother last week. Miss Ellen said you were doing fine. I am sorry your grandfather is sick. Miss Ellen said your father is busy with patients because another doctor there moved away. Mam loves the sewing machine Miss Ellen gave her when your folks moved back to Oklahoma. Miss Ellen taught Mam how to sew on the machine. She used to sew everything by her hands, but this machine makes sewing easy and fast. Miss Ellen said she loves the machine she bought as soon as they arrived in Oklahoma.

I have been working hard at school. I want to graduate from high school and go to college like you are. Lots of schools don't want Negroes, but I am learning which ones do. Pap said I need to work to get money to help pay, so I got a job on Sundays after church helping Mr. Berger at his shoe store. Remember him? I sweep and dust and get the store ready to open on Monday morning. He is a nice man. He is Jewish. Mr. Berger says Jewish people are not welcome sometimes in places, and we are alike that way. It is the reason he wants to help me earn money for college. Mr. Berger said your father was his doctor, and he was the best doctor. He wanted me to ask you to give Doctor his best regards. Please do.

Pap and I put the graveyard in order yesterday. Weather was raw, and it snowed after we left. The graveyard is tidy and will be ready when spring comes. I wanted to visit Bitsy's grave and get it ready for winter, but Pap said I can't trespass on Mrs. Rutledge's property.

I am glad you enjoy it there in North Carolina. You said you want to find Noah's family and explain what happened to him. How can you? You never learned his last name. Why is your college town called Chapel Hill? Is there a church on a hill?

Pap planted pumpkins and took them to town in the truck. He sold every one of them in one day! He has not planted pumpkins before, but he will next year. People wanted them for Thanksgiving.

Merry Christmas.

Your friend,

Blink

October 28, 1939

Dear Annie,

I am sorry your grandfather died. I'm glad Doctor took care of him.

It is funny you lost my letters because you are organized. I keep your letters, too. Don't worry. You will never lose me as your friend. I bet you lost the letters when you changed rooms. How are your classes?

Everything is fine here. I still work for Mr. Berger at the shoe store on Sundays. It does not take me long to ready the store for Monday's opening. Pap taught me to drive the truck, and I drive myself to town. A lady called the police department last Sunday because she thought I had broken into the store. Mr. Berger gave me a key a long time ago because he trusts me. When the policeman came, he called Mr. Berger, who said I worked there and not to worry. It was Officer Collins. His wife buys vegetables from Mam and Pap, so when I gave him my name, he laughed and said he had to call Mr. Berger anyway. He advised me not to be scared. I was. My stutter got real bad because it scared me. Officer Collins patted me on the back when he left.

My teacher says I can graduate in spring, but I am not sure I will have enough money for college. I found a Negro school in a town called Normal, Alabama. It teaches agriculture. Isn't Normal a funny name for a town? Pap has taught me a bunch, but I want to learn everything relating to flowers and trees, too.

Mrs. Rutledge rented Mrs. McCormick's house to people who moved here from out of town. They did not stay long. Three months. They said the house is haunted. Can it be Noah? I thought he left. They moved into town and rented a house there. The man works for Mr. Rutledge at the mill.

Your friend,

Blink

February 13, 1940

Dear Annie,

Pap got a letter from a lawyer in Philadelphia yesterday. James Hinshaw died. This saddens me something awful. Mam and Pap feel the same way. Pap and James wrote to each other, as you and I do. James sent Pap a letter not long ago saying he felt poorly. I am heartbroken, Annie. I know you will be, too.

The lawyer wrote James had a will, leaving most everything he owned to us. He left money for me to go to college. It is not lots of money, but it will sure help. Isn't this a wonderful thing? He was generous and a good friend to us. I wish I could thank him. He left the graveyard to Pap. We take care of it. The lilacs bloomed and smelled sweet last summer. Sometimes we put flowers on the graves. The lawyer said James gave his house in Philadelphia to one of the Hinshaw people.

Guess what? Do you remember Mr. Edwards, who sings and plays in a band? He walks downtown on Sundays with his dog, and he stopped by the shoe store last Sunday as I locked the door. I get nervous when I talk to people I don't know. My stutter gets worse. Anyhow, he heard I can sing. Maybe someone from the church choir told him. You insisted I had a pleasing voice. Mr. Edwards said his band needs another singer, and he thinks singing helps with stuttering. He asked me to come to his house next Thursday night when they practice to see if I enjoy it. The problem is, he lives in town, and Negroes can't be in Hillview after sundown. You remember this. I reminded him it's true. Mr. Edwards was sorry. He said he forgot. When he asked if we had a telephone, I said we don't. He will drive to our house to let me know where they will practice outside the city limits. I am excited!

James Hinshaw's death grieves me. I yearn to thank him for the money and for his friendship. If it weren't for you and Noah, we would never have met James! Wasn't he an upstanding man?

Your friend,

Blink

June 8, 1940

Dear Annie,

I have been singing mountain music with Mr. Edwards and his band. We practice in the rear room at Mayfield's Market outside city limits. I can be there after dark. Pap lets me drive the truck because it isn't far from our house. I love it. We played for an audience on Saturday afternoon at Town Park, and I did not stutter. People clapped.

The school in Alabama accepted me. It's called the Agricultural and Mechanical Institute for Negroes. Alabama is a long way from here. Mam and Pap will drive me there and leave me. I am nervous. Mr. Edwards says he and the band boys will miss me, but he is glad I am going. His son Bobby joined the Navy in March, which means the band is short one singer and mandolin player. I'd never heard of a mandolin before I joined the band. It resembles a small guitar but sounds different.

Mr. Berger gifted me a briefcase to hold my papers for school. He is downright generous. I admire Mr. Berger. He is a friend, not just my employer.

Pap and I took our vegetables to the Farmers Market on Saturday. Mrs. Rutledge bought lettuce from us. She was sort of friendly. Mrs. Rutledge asked me if I ever heard from you, and I said you are doing fine and are in North Carolina at school. She told Pap nobody wants to buy the house you lived in, the McCormick place. She hired old Mr. Cobb to take care of it, but he does not do a thorough job. The graveyard is in excellent shape, though. Pap and I planted daffodils at the graves, and they bloomed this spring.

I hope you come visit sometime. You were my best friend. Harvey Woodard is a buddy now. Do you remember him? He and I go to the movies once a week. Have you seen the newsreels on Adolf Hitler? He invaded Holland. Mam listens to the radio and fears we will get into a war. She got a note from Miss Ellen, and war scares your mother, too. Mr. Berger is from Holland and has family there. He came to America when he was 18. Mr. Berger wants to get his sister, her husband, and two children over here in the United States because they are Jewish. Hitler hates Jews. Pap says the trouble is over there and won't affect us.

Good news! We got a telephone! Mam said she wants a telephone in case I get sick at school. Pap said we will get a telegram. She and Pap argued. It's the first time they yelled at each other. Mam said, "Ned, we need to come into the twentieth century," and Pap said, "Cora, we entered the twentieth century when I installed indoor plumbing." Mam reminded Pap telephone lines are already near our cabin since you had a telephone at Mrs. McCormick's house.

*The telephone people installed everything last week.
I miss you, too. Study hard.*

Your friend,

Blink

September 21, 1940

Dear Annie,

I am in Alabama. The school is agreeable. I have a roommate named Abraham Washington Tompkins. He is from Mississippi. He is a buddy. Teachers don't call me Blink. They call me Tobias. I almost don't answer when someone calls me Tobias because nobody ever called me Tobias except Pap when I did something wrong. It is okay. You wrote nobody at school calls you Annie, either. Anna Ruth sounds very adult. Anna Ruth is a pretty name, too.

It is hot here. Everybody at school is friendly. When Mam and Pap drove me here, we saw lots of colored folks working in cotton fields. They looked boiling hot. Abe and I do not go into town often, but I am deliberating buying a bicycle from another student.

I bet you are busy with school. Did you enjoy being with your parents this summer? Mam writes to me every day. She says she and Pap miss me. I'll bet Miss Ellen and Doctor miss you, too. I miss home. Do you ever miss Hillview?

My classes are interesting. I am glad I came here to learn agriculture. Pap says I can take over the farm and let him relax when I come home.

Mr. Berger wrote he is trying to get his sister and family out of Holland. He wrote to Washington, D.C. to find out how to get them here. It worries him because he's afraid the Nazis will hurt them. His sister wrote things aren't awful for Jews, and the only country available for escape is England. They cannot get passage on any ship to go to England anyhow because Nazis patrol the water and sink ships. Mr. Berger is frightened for them.

Mr. Edwards wrote to me and said the band is not playing much since I left. He has not found a replacement for his son in the Navy. His son Bobby is on an enormous ship. They name ships after the states. I want to see the ocean. Do you? Maybe someday we will.

Do you go to movies often? My buddy Harvey Woodard writes to me he is going to the movies with his brother since I am gone. Harvey has a limp from breaking his leg not long after you and your parents left town. Doc Morrison wanted to fix his leg, but Harvey's parents did not let him do it. They did not trust a white doctor, even though Pap promised them Doc Morrison is an honorable doctor. Harvey went to our place to help Pap plant broccoli and turnips before I left for school. Pap and I taught him about crops somewhat so he can help Pap while I am away.

Pap wrote a man from Maryland stopped at our cabin and asked if Mrs. McCormick's house is for sale. When Pap explained the real estate company's name was on the sign in the front yard, the man said no sign was there, so Pap got on our telephone and asked the operator to connect him to the real estate company. They admitted to Pap that Mrs. Rutledge got mad at them for not selling the house and removed their sign. Pap told the man how to contact Mrs. Rutledge. The man asked Pap if the Mueller property across Apple Ridge Road is for sale. Pap doesn't know who owns it. It has been empty a long time. Remember?

I need to study for a test. It is encouraging you have made friends there.

Your friend in Alabama,

Tobias Hill Ha! Ha!

November 28, 1940

Dear Annie,

Thank you for your letter. Hearing from you always makes me happy. I have been feeling blue because I miss home. Today is Thanksgiving, and I didn't go home. Taking a bus or train costs too much, and we had only today and tomorrow off from school. Did you have an enjoyable time with your friend Maxine and her family for dinner today? It is convenient they live near Chapel Hill, and you have friends there. I bet you are right when you say most students come from someplace else, which makes it easier to become friends.

Several students here, including Abe, did not go home. The school fixed us a turkey dinner with stuffing, corn, and green beans. Their rolls taste okay but not as tasty as Mam's. We had pumpkin pie for dessert. Tomorrow, Abe and I plan to go into town. I bought a bicycle from a student who quit school, and Abe has a bicycle, too. I am going to buy Christmas gifts for Mam and Pap.

Guess what? Mam and Pap went to town last week on errands and ran into Berta Simmons. She hugged Mam and Pap and asked them to her house for lunch. She fixed lunch for the three of them, and Mam said they stayed for two hours! Miss Berta is such a gracious lady. She still works for Mrs. Rutledge two days a week and works for another lady two other days. She asked how you are doing. Miss Berta corresponds with Miss Ellen. Miss Berta believes it is fine and dandy I am at college. Her brother-in-law, Frank Simmons, is doing well with his law practice. Miss Berta said Mr. Simmons asks about all of us whenever she sees him, and he told Miss Berta helping us and James Hinshaw was the best thing he has ever done as a lawyer.

When Mam and Pap left Miss Berta's house, they stopped at Mr. Berger's store to collect the work shoes he ordered for Pap. Mr. Berger was sorry I did not come home for Thanksgiving. His sister and her family are still in Holland. The Nazis made her husband register his business as a Jewish business, and this worries Mr. Berger. He's afraid Nazis will hurt Jews. A cousin invited the family to live with them and hide from the Germans. This cousin and his wife live in the country somewhere. Mr. Berger's sister wants to go, but her husband is not convinced. It's her husband's cousin who invited them. Mr. Berger says they should go stay with the cousin. No word ever came from Washington, D.C. in response to Mr. Berger's letters. Lots of Jewish people try to come to America, but I guess the ones in Holland can't get out. This is awful. Why does Hitler hate Jewish people? It somewhat resembles people who don't care for us Negroes here. It's kind of the same, isn't it, Annie? I don't understand it. It isn't right. At least that's what I think.

Will you be able to go see your parents at Christmas? I hold doubts I will go home. Traveling by myself on the bus makes Mam nervous, and she wants to come get me. I will write you what happens.

It is smart of you to get another degree after you graduate. You will be an outstanding teacher. Do you want *to teach there in Chapel Hill? You should be an adventurer and go somewhere different because you are brave.*

Your friend,

Blink

February 16, 1941

Dear Annie,

I haven't written in a while. Sorry. It has been busy here. Thank you for not giving up on me. You will always be my greatest friend.

I am sure it disappointed you not to visit your parents at Christmas. Mam and Pap drove here to take me home. I had two weeks for vacation. The drive is long. We spent nights in a hotel both ways because of poor weather. We colored folks have a hard time finding hotels to take us, but Pap found one in a book for Negroes who travel. It was a hotel just for Negroes. Pap's old truck keeps on running. Mam packed food, so we didn't have to stop to eat because most places won't let us eat in their restaurants. The hotel did, of course. They had yummy pancakes for breakfast.

It's nice your friend Velma invited you to spend Christmas with her family. I bet the holiday was different and fun for you. Thirteen people are lots of people! My holiday was Mam, Pap, and me. Pap gave Mam a puppy for Christmas. She named the puppy Ladybug. Ladybug is cute with brown fur and lots of white on her chest, and she has huge paws. Pap says she will be a big dog. Mam wanted to name her Bitsy after your Bitsy, but Pap said

Bitsy was not an acceptable name for a big dog. I reminded Mam there was only one Bitsy in the whole wide world, and it's not right to give another dog her name.

We had many tests at school, too, and I did okay. This term, I enjoy my classes. I find I am interested in flowers and trees more than crops. I hope I can talk Pap into planting flowers and trees. If we do, we will dig more rocks from a field. He has a giant rock pile now. He wishes you still lived in the McCormick house because the rocks are useful for re-building the stone wall.

Miss Mittie's house is for sale again. Mrs. Rutledge got a different real estate man. Remember the Maryland man who was interested in the Mueller property? He bought it from a bank, and it includes the land between the McCormick house and Apple Ridge Road. It is his country house. He must be rich! Pap says the fellow is doing many things to the house, and its appearance is much improved. He tidied up the Mueller cemetery on the property, too, even though he doesn't own it. His name is Mr. Foster, and he told Pap he can see the Mueller graveyard from a window. It should honor the folks buried there, he says. I don't see why Mrs. Rutledge doesn't take care of it because it's her family. Mrs. McCormick and her husband, Phoebe, Doc Mueller, and his wife are her family. Anyhow, it is terrific someone bought the property and is taking excellent care of it.

I feel bad for Mr. Berger. His sister and family went to the country. His sister's name is Elise. Isn't Elise a lovely name? They left at night riding their bicycles. Her husband abandoned his business in Amsterdam, and they left their house with every bit of furniture, too. Mr. Berger's last letter from Elise said the Nazis ordered Jews to register with the Nazi government by January. This made her husband decide they needed to run away before January.

They are staying with the cousin of Elise's husband on an isolated property surrounded by a forest. The cousin's name is Mr. Philips, and Mr. Philips works as a bookkeeper for a business in a nearby town, and he is aware of what is happening in Holland and in Amsterdam. Nazis took away radios from Jews in Amsterdam. Why did they do such a thing? The two families are enclosing a space in the barn as a hiding spot. It is a tiny room tucked in a corner, but it appears to be a feeding station for cows to eat hay. Hay sits on top and fills the space between the wall and open boards on the sides where cows can pull out hay. The room is inside. Isn't such a thing awful? I can't imagine. Mr. Philips is Jewish, but Mrs. Philips is not. Elise's husband's name is Mr. Schorr.

Mam says we will have a war. Pap still says we won't. How are your parents? Write to me soon.

Your friend,

Blink

April 16, 1941

Dear Annie,

    I count the days until this term ends because I have decided not to return to school next fall. Although I enjoy this school fine, I miss home. I will run short on money, too, even though I still have a quantity of James Hinshaw's money left. Pap saves as much money as he can, but it will be tough to save enough for a second year, even if I work at Mr. Berger's shoe store this summer. School is far from home, which makes it hard to go back and forth. I believe I learned enough to study agriculture books from the library and buy other books to teach me what I need to learn. Miss Berta asked Mam to call her whenever I want a library book, and she will get it using her library card. Mam and Miss Berta will speak in a code because they don't want the telephone operator to realize Miss Berta is getting a book for a Negro. Isn't it funny? It is the Berta and Cora Detective Agency! I don't understand why Negroes can't use the library.

    Will you live in the dormitory this summer while you stay at school? It is helpful to have a summer job at a store. You will get your master's degree quicker by staying there.

    Not much news. Mr. Berger's sister's family is still with Mr. and Mrs. Philips in the country. Nobody knows the Schorr family is there. The families finished the hiding place in the barn. I hope they don't need to use it.

    I wrote Mr. Edwards I will be back next month. He wrote back and said my spot in the band is waiting. He will teach me how to play his son's mandolin. His son Bobby plans to stay in the Navy. He will see the entire world.

My roommate Abe will not come back to school, either.

Your friend,

Blink

KT set the letters on the bed, clicked on the television, and frowned at the screen as a murder mystery cast a depressing glow into the room. She checked the clock and moved the letters to the desk before ordering a bowl of soup, a salad, and a light beer from room service.

KT addressed the stack of letters. "I need to take a rest, Blink. I'm uneasy about your next letters, but they must wait for another time. Thank God times have changed since you weren't allowed to eat in a restaurant or stay in a hotel. The library was off limits, too? No being in town after dark? Damn Jim Crow! What was wrong with people? Haters still lurk, though, and I can't fathom why. Blink, I wish I had known you! I yearn to have known my grandmother better. Too many things I wish, too many."

WHIPLASH

It rained through the night into morning, and KT still slept when Pastor P.G. Whitestone hit the airwaves. There he was, in living color, blaring his message of salvation by donation and the promise of eternal damnation for the non-compliant. KT had fallen asleep without turning off the television. Groping, she found the remote and aimed it straight at Pastor Whitestone.

"Poof! Goodbye, preacher man!"

She drew open the drapes, stumbled to the bathroom, and turned on the shower. Her mind drifted to her reading the night before as warm water caressed her body. The letters confirmed her grandmother's friendship with Blink flourished after she left Hillview. Anna Ruth and Blink remained loyal friends for life.

Saturday night's storm gave way to bright sun and an azure sky, but questions for Emmaline needed to wait until the next day, Monday.

"What a perfect morning to explore the countryside," KT said to the sky.

After breakfast, KT climbed into her car and pulled out a paper map of the county. Noting several places of interest, she set her GPS and rolled off to the west.

Stop one: the cemetery where she hoped to bury Anna Ruth's ashes. She stayed in her car, pausing long enough to soak in the scene. Its dismal presence troubled her, but her confidence in its restoration brought forth a smile. She proceeded south on Creek Road for a short distance, crossed the bridge over Little Hanks Creek, and entered Taylor Farms subdivision. These 1970s era homes, not as large as those in Blane Martin's development, were well kept. A man pushing a stroller waved as she passed, and she returned the wave before turning around and re-crossing the bridge. She passed the gravel path to the cemetery but slowed to study the Martin-built homes on Creek Road.

Her exploration led to a general store and tavern dating back to the early 1800s, still in service. Farther, a waterfall on Hanks Creek provided two families with the perfect spot for a picnic. The road climbed upon a ridge, where pink blossoms of peach trees glistened with droplets from the preceding night's storm. Then, the road narrowed to one lane and became steep as it wound its way up the mountain, where occasional breaks in the trees provided breathtaking glimpses of Hillview and the valley below. At the summit, the road widened and became less steep as it descended the other side into the next valley. From there, KT passed rolling fields with tidy barns and farmhouses and stopped at an ancient stone house to read a historical marker in front. On a hill behind the house, she spied a girl and boy riding horses. After a mile, a white wooden church of moderate size, replete with colorful stained-glass windows and a parking lot packed with trucks of every description, many covered in mud, caught her sight. As she passed, gospel music flowed through the open door. The road took a sharp turn to the right and stopped at a barricade. Ahead lay a smooth two-lane road back to town, but high water necessitated its closure. Back over the mountain she went, gripping the steering wheel, re-tracing each twist and turn, trying not to dwell on the monstrous drop-offs or lack of shoulders and guardrails.

Toward the end of KT's harrowing descent, an outline of Hillview emerged in the distance. Her parched throat craved moisture, and pangs of hunger knotted her stomach, so when she spotted Barney's Burgers at the base of the mountain, she parked and headed straight for the ladies' room. Empty towel dispensers and filthy sinks gave her the feeling better things were not to come. Nevertheless, two older men in the minuscule dining room appeared to enjoy their Barney Burgers. She ordered a burger with a bottle of water and took a seat in the booth next to the old codgers. Right away, conversation from the adjacent booth caught her attention.

"The joint won't sell. You heard what happened to Jimmy Gene Carlisle, didn't you?" rasped one man in a loud whisper. "A creature come out of the woods and tried to grab him!"

"I know ole Jimmy Gene," responded the other man. "I doubt his story. Jimmy Gene's a drunk, and he shouldn't oughta been there. He was trespassin', scroungin' for damn mushrooms in those woods. He was high on mushrooms and imagined the whole thing."

"Burger's ready, honey!" bellowed the woman behind the counter.

KT retrieved her order and returned to her booth. The men continued their back-and-forth conversation as she toyed with her burger.

"The property's been haunted ever since forever. Nobody's going to buy it. Spooky things go on out there.

Jimmy Gene weren't no drunk. Graham Wessler reckons he's going to get this gal who inherited it to sell it for a lot of dough. A sucker might buy it, but they'll be in for a surprise."

KT's ears burned. They were speaking of McCormick House!

"Folks swear it's haunted," retorted the other voice. "Nobody reliable has seen a gall dang thing. I bet it's been empty since before you and I were born. Common sense says folks might think it's haunted cause it's empty and overgrown. It's spooky, but spooky don't make it haunted."

"It ain't just Jimmy Gene," the first speaker said. "Junior Barker claimed a nasty little dog come out of nowhere and bit him. Drew blood, I say. Then the dog disappeared. It didn't run off. It plain disappeared into thin air after it bit Junior!"

The other man cackled. "Junior had no business there. How many years ago? He's been blabbing about disappearing dogs for at least twenty-five years. He was trying to steal a Christmas tree off Tobias Hill's nursery, and when Hill run him off, he sneaked over there to steal a tree from the abandoned place. I hope Wessler can sell it. Not to Martin the shyster, either. He should be in jail or dead."

"Well, your problem is you don't believe in nothing spiritual!" retorted the other. "Anybody who buys it will be sorry."

At this point, both men eased out of their booth. One headed straight for the restroom, and the other stopped to tip his cap toward KT before shuffling out the door.

This incident stunned KT. She understood rumors surrounded McCormick House, but these two gossiping in a greasy spoon out in the sticks dumbfounded her. One man referred to Blane Martin as a shyster, and his comment further sealed her decision not to sell to Martin. No way. No day.

100

Her cell phone jingled as she entered her car.

"How are you this magnificent Sunday?" quizzed Graham.

"I'm fine," she lied. "I was an explorer this morning on a trip around the countryside, and I finished lunch a minute ago. How are you?"

"Fantastic! I showed a house to a young couple earlier. It's near Town Park, and it's perfect for them. We presented a contract to the sellers, and I'm confident they'll accept it. Listen, my mom cooks dinner every Sunday. Might you enjoy a home-cooked meal tonight instead of restaurant or hotel food? She always makes pot roast. I can get you at six o'clock."

"Oh, how thoughtful of you! Are you positive it's okay with your mom to add another person?"

"You bet! Dad's eager to share recollections he learned of your great-grandfather."

"I'll see you at six. Thanks. I appreciate the invitation more than you realize."

****

Graham's parents welcomed KT to their home on Sunday evening. KT ate but a few bites of her lunch at Barney's, and the aroma of Mrs. Wessler's pot roast expunged the overheard conversation at Barney's from her consciousness. On a generous lot in town, the Wessler home featured a comfortable and uncluttered decor which put KT at ease. A spacious sunroom, enclosed on three sides by floor-to-ceiling windows, provided a cheerful setting for an oversized dining room table and eight chairs. Two easy chairs at one end of the sunroom hinted at the location where the Wesslers enjoyed their morning coffee and newspaper.

"As a general rule, I fix pot roast every Sunday, KT," announced Mrs. Wessler, an elderly woman with pewter colored hair and piercing brown eyes. "It has been a tradition in our family forever. It's a simple meal. I hope you're fond of salad and green beans. The roast cooks with potatoes, carrots, and onions. Rolls and pie for dessert come from Betty Lynn's Bakery downtown. I don't work hard in the kitchen anymore!" Her laugh exposed deep dimples in her cheeks, and KT saw where Graham's dimples originated. A thin woman, she appeared on the verge of frailty, but her pleasant facial expression and enthusiasm debunked the observation.

KT reassured Mrs. Wessler she loved every item on the menu.

"Mom, what pie did you get this week?" asked Graham.

"Custard pie. Betty Lynn doesn't make it often, so whenever she does, I get one. Do you enjoy custard pie, KT?"

KT cocked her head. "I don't believe I've ever eaten one. This will be a treat, though. Nonnie, uh, my grandmother, spoke of a family friend here in Hillview who made delicious custard pies. I'm looking forward to it!"

Laughter and conversation filled the sunroom. Mr. Wessler related his grandfather's gratitude to Dr. Carter Young for saving his life. "It was appendicitis, but nobody at the hospital diagnosed it. It stumped them, but Dr. Young diagnosed it without hesitation and performed emergency surgery. The old man came through like a champ. My grandfather died when I was fourteen, but I remember him saying he was alive only because of Dr. Carter Young."

"I'm touched by your story, Mr. Wessler," said KT. "Both of my great-grandparents died before I was born, but

Nonnie spoke of them with such love. I regret they weren't in my life."

Mr. Wessler resumed speaking. "Grandfather's last name was Graham. We named Graham here after him because we both thought it proper to carry the name forward."

Graham bellowed, "Yeah, Dad, thanks to you and Mom, I'm tagged with the nickname Graham Cracker. Thanks a lot!"

Graham's comment elicited a hearty laugh from everyone. Mr. Wessler listened with interest to KT's discussion of her work as a physician in Bluff County's public health clinic.

"A clinic similar to yours is here in Hillview, and it's a godsend to the public. The current director plans to retire soon, and the Board of Directors is searching for a replacement. Interested? I'm a board member and can put in a plug for you."

KT shook her head with a polite smile.

"Well, let me put in a plug for Hillview Community Clinic. We have the latest equipment and a fine staff. The county doesn't run the clinic; it's a well-funded non-profit, which allows us to sustain a high standard of care."

Mrs. Wessler intervened. "Al, everyone loves the clinic, but enough, dear!"

KT smiled again while shaking her head. "Thanks, Mr. Wessler. It happens I have an offer in Maine which will allow me to teach and treat patients, too. I haven't received the contract yet, and I haven't decided whether I want to leave where I am. My clinic back home has serious problems; with luck, it's possible I can help remedy them. When I get home, I must decide."

Mr. Wessler replied, "I suspect you will be a credit to your profession, wherever you may be. Maine is appealing. Best of luck with whichever choice you make."

Mrs. Wessler expressed delight with KT's plan to renovate the McCormick property and sell it as a charming residence.

Then, Mr. Wessler added, "I hope Graham is doing a proper job of helping with McCormick House. I turned your project over to him because I have trouble walking on uneven ground. Vietnam injury. I must tell you, whenever I spoke with your grandmother, she impressed me. What a delightful lady! Those who expressed interest in the property planned to demolish the house. Blane Martin kept after her like a darned rat snake, but she held no interest in selling to him. I don't blame her, either. The house and grounds need significant work, but if you follow through with your plans, you'll have a superb piece of real estate to sell. Such benefits the county, and you have my gratitude."

KT expressed her appreciation for his remarks, and after pie and coffee, Graham delivered KT to her hotel.

"Thanks, Graham! This was a delightful evening, and I appreciate the warm hospitality from your parents."

"They're great folks," he said. "My sis and her husband are out of town. They'll be sorry they missed you. Hope you can meet them another time. Listen, the job in Maine sounds exceptional!"

After bidding Graham farewell, KT entered the hotel. Before she made it through the lobby, the front desk clerk called to her and presented two large envelopes, one addressed to Miss Kathryn Winslow and one from Stub O'Connor.

"Oh, brother. I'll bet it's Blane Martin again," she sighed as she boarded the elevator to the third floor. KT placed Stub's envelope on the desk and opened the other one.

Martin began his letter with an apology for the bulldozer episode. The incident resulted from a "misunderstanding" as Graham predicted. Martin pressed KT to sell, and his new contract upped the price a measly five thousand dollars. His patronizing language and shameless Biblical footnote infuriated KT, and she slammed the packet on the dresser.

"Get out of my life, Blane Martin! You are *not* getting my property!" The blank television screen gaped at her in silence as she ripped off her clothes and plucked her pajamas from the dresser drawer. She stormed into the bathroom, but a calmer KT Winslow emerged in several minutes and crawled into the bed. Her gaze focused on the envelope from Stub and the file box containing Blink's letters, but she turned off the light and pulled the covers over her head.

****

"Good morning, Emmaline. Do you have a few minutes?"

Emmaline signaled KT to enter. She shuffled papers to the side, folded her hands, and leaned forward in her chair. "Sit! Tell me."

KT cleared her throat. "Courthouse records show Tobias Hill bequeathed the cemetery to the Historical Society in his will when he died in 2001. The Historical Society owns it, Emmaline."

"Huh? What? No, there must be a mistake. I have no record of owning any cemetery. We own only this building. Since 2001, you say? The date is before I started working here, but I've seen nothing related to any real estate besides this building. How can it be?"

"Mrs. Jennings has the paperwork."

Emmaline stood and faced the bank of black filing cabinets behind her desk. She opened several drawers and peered at the folders inside the drawers. Her earrings whipped back and forth as a frustrated Emmaline returned to her chair.

"KT, I know what's in these drawers. No deed or mention of a cemetery on or near Creek Road is in them. Where is such a document? I'm confused and embarrassed."

"I'll be happy to visit Mrs. Jennings and get copies of everything. Why don't I do it now? You're busy preparing for Hillview Days. If you write a note conveying it's your wish to get copies, I'm confident she'll copy the documents for me."

Emmaline jotted a brief note on the Society's letterhead and handed it to KT with the admonition, "Please bring it back today if you can. My board meets tonight, and we need to discuss this! This cemetery surprise means we must make decisions. One is to grant permission to inter your grandmother's ashes. If nobody has cared for it since 2001, it must be a God-awful mess! This mystery doesn't register with me. Not one bit. I'm stunned."

KT took the note and hiked three blocks to the courthouse, where she found Mrs. Jennings again engrossed in another steamy romance novel.

"Mrs. Jennings, how are you this morning? Remember me? KT Winslow? The little cemetery on Creek Road?"

Mrs. Jennings placed a marker in the book, closed it, and said, "I suppose you'll want copies of everything, won't you?"

"Oh, yes, please. Here is a note from Emmaline Conrad with the Historical Society requesting photocopies. She has no record of owning the plots. I'll pay for the copies."

Mrs. Jennings rose and shuffled through a door marked "Authorized Personnel." While KT waited, she noticed the other three women in the office appeared busy. Their fingers clicked away at computer keyboards; they searched, sorted, and stapled papers on their desks. Mrs. Jennings had no papers on her desk, and her computer sat idle with a kitten screensaver on display.

Mrs. Jennings returned in fifteen minutes with several pages in her hand and requested $10.00. KT removed the money from her wallet and released it to the woman. Mrs. Jennings pulled a receipt book from a side drawer of her desk, scrawled a receipt, and pushed the photocopies and receipt across the desk to KT.

"Here you go. Has this information solved a mystery for you and the *Hysterical* Society?"

"Yes, indeed. Thank you for your help. I appreciate it very much." KT flashed a smile. "I hope you have an enjoyable rest of the day."

Mrs. Jennings returned the smile and returned to her book.

When KT entered the Historical Society office, she found Emmaline in deep conversation on the telephone. Emmaline motioned to KT to sit while she concluded the call.

"Hi, KT! Let me see what you got!"

Both women examined the Last Will and Testament of one Tobias Hill, a map of the cemetery's location, and a deed showing the Historical Society as the current owner since 2001.

Emmaline leaned forward in her chair and addressed KT in a hushed voice. "I am flabbergasted, but here's proof. Tobias Hill put his nursery and his personal acreage into our county Land Savers program. A cemetery doesn't qualify for the program. I guess he thought we'd be perfect stewards of the cemetery, but we failed him, didn't we? For the love of Pete! I don't understand why we didn't have this in our files. I discovered a disorganized mess when I came on board, but the information should have been here somewhere. Maybe it got tossed in the trash by accident. Did the county fail to forward the material? It boggles my mind!"

"We can redeem the cemetery, Emmaline, as I'm going to do with McCormick House. Listen, if money is an issue, I can handle it. It can't cost much to fix the fence, right the markers, and clear the vines and limbs. It's a mere sliver of land. I want a pleasant resting site for Nonnie and the others, so will you please help me get permission to follow through on these plans?"

KT's persuasive determination impressed Emmaline, and she responded, "I'll ask, and I don't expect a problem. May I call you after our meeting tonight?"

"You bet!"

KT left the office, hurried to her car, set the GPS to the address on Blane Martin's letterhead, and hit the road. As Graham predicted, the "office" turned out to be a retail storefront with postal and packaging services, photocopying, and a wall of mailboxes. KT approached the young woman at the counter and asked permission to leave an envelope for Blane Martin.

"This is a mail drop for the postal service, ma'am. I can't let *you* put a letter in a box. The mail carrier does it."

"I see," said KT. "If I put these documents inside an envelope and mail it to this address, a mail carrier will put it in Mr. Martin's mailbox after it's gone through the postal system and arrived back here?"

The clerk's forehead wrinkled, and she replied with a sarcastic, "Yeah."

KT purchased a padded envelope, tore the documents into pieces, crumpled them, and took a notepad from her backpack. She wrote:

Mr. Martin, I will not sell my property to you now or ever. Quit sending me contracts. In addition, under no circumstances are you, any of your employees, or anyone you direct to set foot on my property. If such trespassing occurs, I will prosecute. Leave me alone. Dr. Kathryn Winslow

KT crammed the shredded documents into the envelope, placed her note on top of the pile, and taped it shut. She wrote Martin's name and address on the top and paid for the envelope and postage before tarrying long enough to view the clerk drop the envelope into the outgoing mail bin.

****

On to McCormick House she drove and discovered Larry inside, hard at work. He had torn out the space beneath the stairs for the half bathroom. It pleased her to affirm the space adequate for the improvement. The proprietor of Honey Wagon Services had been to the property earlier and spoken with Larry. The county should grant a septic permit within the week, and Honey Wagon planned to begin work as soon as the proprietor held it in his hand.

"Yes sirree, Katie Doc! Gonna get everything a flowin' and a flushin'! I do believe, though, I need help with electric. We must replace every single string of wiring. I can do the job, but it will take me a long, long time. If you want this done extry fast, better call Earl's Electric. Earl has a crew and does loads of work for Graham Cracker. They can knock this job out quick. Want me to call Earl?"

KT gave permission to hire the electrical contractor because the project required adequate electricity, and the sooner the better.

****

Emmaline Conrad phoned KT with positive news first thing Tuesday morning. In a unanimous vote, her Board of Directors approved KT's proposal. None held an inkling they owned the cemetery, nor did they have knowledge of its history. Upkeep of the slice of land raised concerns during the meeting, but KT assured Emmaline those responsibilities would not burden the Society.

The days of the week flew. The home's foundation received strong support beams. A crew of licensed electricians arrived and went to work rewiring the house. Larry bought a pedestal sink and toilet for the anticipated half bath. He peeled crumbling wallpaper from walls and piled everything in a dumpster. Lumber, nails, and other supplies arrived and were stacked on the front porch. Honey Wagon Services arrived later in the week to begin work. Larry darted from job to job, and KT marveled at the speed with which the renovation proceeded.

She engaged Doan Hill to clear the cemetery of brush and weeds, and although Doan asked for more information with respect to the graves, KT deferred.

"I'd prefer to explain the history of the cemetery to you and others at the same time. Members of your grandfather Blink's family are buried there, and this was the reason he cared for it. I want you to get the complete story, and I promise you will learn it soon."

Larry took a break from McCormick House to repair and replace fencing at the cemetery and apply a lustrous coat of white paint. KT hired a monument company to clean the three tombstones, refurbish the engravings, and reinstall them upright on solid footers. She ordered a marker for her grandmother, too. A visit to Jones and Little Funeral Home solidified her plan to bury Anna Ruth's ashes next to Noah within the fenced enclosure on Creek Road.

By the time Friday night arrived, an exhausted yet satisfied KT cast a brief glance at the file box. She did not touch it, and she did not open Stub's envelope detailing the job opportunity in Maine. She needed to be energetic the next morning for Hillview Days. KT Winslow slept well Friday night.

DON'T RAIN ON MY PARADE

D ressed in jeans and a light green windbreaker, KT clutched her baseball cap and mini-backpack as she climbed into Graham's spiffy Jeep Wrangler.

"Hi, Graham. Wow, you have the top off! Fun!"

"You ready to meet Hillview, Doc?"

"You bet. What's on the agenda?"

The day began with sunny skies, low humidity, and a refreshing sixty degrees. First stop: Downtown Hillview. Vendors under canopies lined both sides of Main Street, and bluegrass music greeted them at the north end. A garden club sold potted herbs and a picture book filled with photos of local gardens. A furniture maker displayed sample furnishings and handed out catalogs featuring his entire collection. Next to the furniture maker, three lines of squealing kids waited for free face painting. The smell of cinnamon rolls, barbecue, soaps, and candles added to the allure of art, crafts, jams, cakes, pies, and other merchandise. Men and women dressed in nineteenth century attire milled among the crowd.

"Hear ye, hear ye!" shrieked a man through a bullhorn. Dressed as a Revolutionary War officer, he sauntered along the midway. "The Thespian Troubadours will take to the stage in fifteen minutes! Discover the history of Hillview. Witness the diabolical demise of our founder's devious and disreputable life! Hillview's dangerous and duplicitous times during the American Civil War are depicted! Come to the Playhouse! Tickets are one greenback, one lowly clam, one measly buck, one thin dollar!"

"Come on, KT, you'll want to see this play." Graham took her elbow and escorted her through the crowd. Beyond a narrow side street, they came to what must have been a movie theater in earlier days. Its simple marquee, bordered by miniature white lights, read "Playhouse" in black letters. They entered and found seats two-thirds of the way toward the stage as throngs of people filed in behind them.

KT viewed neither an elaborate nor stark interior. The décor appeared freshened in recent times, and a faint odor of paint lingered in the air. Closed purple curtains hid the stage from view while several musicians stirred around the orchestra pit in front of the stage. KT twisted in her seat and spied the balcony behind her where a group of teens wearing shirts emblazoned with "Grover High School Band" giggled and chatted.

"A movie theater at one time, right, Graham?"

"Yeah. It may have been the sole one in town. A married couple bought it and invested an immense amount of time and money into renovations. Chairs aren't too comfortable because they're original, but folks don't come here to see first-run films. Most bring cushions for the seats."

"They show movies?"

"Twice a month. Old movies. Sometimes they feature a theme or particular actors or actresses. There's a lecture series in winter and a public talent show on St. Patrick's Day. The Thespian Troubadours perform here."

KT surveyed the surroundings again. Was this the theater where Annie Young spent occasional Saturday afternoons? Was its balcony the one where Blink and his family, indeed all persons of color, were required to sit?

The curtains opened, and the Hillview Jazz Band performed with perfection as the Thespian Troubadours depicted Hillview's origins. Their comical interpretation portrayed the town's founder in swashbuckling fashion, replete with a flowing black cape and oversized handlebar mustache. The first act concluded with Hillview's double-dealing founder meeting his demise at the hands of a cheated citizen.

KT whispered, "Is it true? Did someone kill him?"

"Nobody knows for sure, but it makes an excellent story, doesn't it?"

The second act presented Hillview as a peaceful farm village until cannon fire in the theater announced the arrival of America's Civil War. Thunderous noise and a blanket of smoke startled the audience and compelled a chorus of loud screams. Soldiers in blue and soldiers in gray engaged in ferocious battle on stage and wreaked havoc on the stage-crafted town. This part of Hillview's history was not comical because the region experienced hostile action. At the performance's end, the Troubadours bowed and thanked the audience. Everyone stood, clapped, and whistled approval, and as people filed out, the band played a spirited rendition of "When Johnny Comes Marching Home."

"What fun!" KT flung her backpack over her shoulder. "You say they put on a show three times during the year?"

"Yes. They'll perform this play again tonight and tomorrow afternoon. As to its historical accuracy, they may have embellished a bit. It makes for enjoyable theater, though. How does barbecue sound?"

Graham and KT found a table for two under a crimson umbrella at Poor Piggy's and enjoyed the ambiance and lunch.

"You mentioned a parade," said KT. "Where is it?"

"It should start around two o'clock. The route is on Third Street. It's an old-time parade with high school bands, fire trucks, old cars, and local yokels dressed in costumes. You'll see floats from different organizations. DAR ladies are always on a float in their Revolutionary War wigs and garb, and The Thespian Troubadours sell tickets to their next shows from the back of a flatbed truck. We have plenty of time to finish our drinks before finding an observation spot." Graham leaned back in his chair as a clown skipped past their table.

They made their way back to Main Street, stopping here and there to check out vendors' merchandise. KT bought a sun catcher for herself and a handcrafted leather wallet for a brother's birthday.

They arrived at Third Street and located a perfect viewing position on the porch of a hair salon closed for the day. A swing hung on each end of the porch, and they leaped into one, laughing and tugging the chain as they propelled the seat back and forth. Soon, the Hillview High School band approached their vantage point, baton twirlers leading the way. The parade was as Graham predicted. KT spotted the Grover High School Band, the one from the balcony. They played a rousing rendition of "This Land is Your Land" as they marched. Dance troupes, fire trucks, floats pulled by pickup trucks, and convertibles with politicians and beauty queens perched on back seats passed before a group called Cavorting Canines appeared to raucous applause and shouts of approval. When the act stopped before the two porch swingers, KT convulsed into laughter. Dogs dressed in people's clothes jumped through hoops, rolled over, and leaped over one another. Men and women dressed in dog costumes performed cartwheels as the act resumed its forward motion. A golf cart followed the troupe with one sign promoting the local humane society and another with a sketch of a donkey's rear captioned "The End."

KT reveled in a joy not experienced in recent times. Her career consumed her, and time to enjoy simple things such as a parade became rarer with each passing year.

Leaning back into the swing, she said, "This has been such fun, and I'm glad we came. Thank you for this delightful day!" She removed her baseball cap and shook her curls before pulling it back on her head.

"I haven't attended a Hillview Days parade in a few years. This was fun," Graham commented as he checked his watch. "It's four o'clock. We'll tour the historical homes tomorrow because they're closing now. We can take a short walk around the corner on East Thomas Street, though. Homes on Thomas Street are among the oldest in Hillview, and most have a historical sign out front stating who first built the house and detailing its history. None of the East Thomas Street houses are on the tour this year, but the markers give a glimpse of each one's past. If you enjoy dancing, the dance band starts at five o'clock. It's at the Town Square."

KT paused and acknowledged the homes enticed her. "I'm not much into dancing. Why don't we check out East Thomas Street and call it a day?"

Graham laughed. "I'm not much of a dancer myself. What a relief!"

They left the porch and strolled around the corner to East Thomas Street, where Hillview's earliest citizens of prominence once lived. KT and Graham perused the bronze plaques in front of each home before they arrived at 153. Its plaque read:

BROWN HOUSE
153 East Thomas Street
Established 1811 by Hiram Gideon Brown, Prominent
Hillview Merchant
This home remained in the Brown family until 1967
Brown descendants who occupied the home:
H.G. Brown, Jr.
William Walker Brown
Berta Brown Simmons

KT gasped.

"What is it, KT?"

She turned to Graham. "Are you familiar with these people? Nonnie told me about them!"

Graham peered at the sign and shook his head. "No. To be honest, I never paid much attention to our pioneers, I guess you call them. These names aren't familiar. What did your grandmother say?"

KT fidgeted with one strap on her backpack and stayed silent for a moment before exhaling a long breath. "William Walker Brown was an attorney and local historian. His daughter Berta worked as a housekeeper for Mittie McCormick's daughter, Susie Rutledge. Berta became a special friend to Nonnie and her parents, as well as to Tobias Hill's family." KT saw no need to elaborate further.

"Interesting," Graham said.

KT studied the house to ascertain which window might yield a view of William Walker Brown's study. This room contained a hidden compartment, the compartment Brown referred to as his "cubbyhole." The cubbyhole once guarded the missing pages of a manuscript whose pages validated a heart-rending truth to Annie Young in 1934. For several minutes, KT stood before the Brown House, lost in thought, scanning every detail of the home's exterior.

Graham stood in silence and waited.

KT took a few steps toward the next house but stopped and fixed her gaze back at the Brown House. She turned to Graham, her eyes twinkling. "I'm glad we came to Thomas Street! Thank you for suggesting it."

They meandered forward on the sidewalk while KT studied each plaque as if searching for a familiar name. When they reached the street's end, she stopped.

"Well, Dr. Winslow, do you wish to adjourn for the day?" asked Graham.

"Yes, thank you. I'm ready to get to the hotel. Are we still on for tomorrow?"

"You bet. I'll get you at ten o'clock again. We can visit the three homes on this year's tour. No doubt you'll find one of them of special interest. It's the Mueller house."

KT clapped her hands and threw her head back. "The Mueller house? On Apple Ridge Road? I can't wait!"

****

Graham deposited KT at the hotel, where she nibbled on assorted items from the salad bar and reflected upon her day. Hillview appeared to be a delightful town, an interesting blend of old and new. Upon entering her room, she stripped off her clothes and climbed into her pajamas. Seeing William Walker Brown's home drew her back to Blink's letters. Hadn't Blink mentioned Brown's daughter, Berta Simmons, in his letters? KT took the file, spread it on the bed, propped herself against the pillows, and read.

August 14, 1941

Dear Annie,

It is excellent you are having a fine time working at the ladies' store and enjoying your classes.

The band has been busy. Last Saturday night, we played at the Hillview Methodist Church for their anniversary celebration. Mr. Edwards arranged with Mayor Barbour for me to be in town after sundown since I am in the band. The other places we play are outside city limits, which means I don't have to fret on being someplace after dark. Grover is not a Sundown Town, and we play at their theater or town square any night they book us. I'm doing good learning how to play the mandolin.

Before I left Alabama, one of my teachers gave me a list of books to study and a list of bookstores where I can order them. They are expensive. Miss Berta asked Mrs. Albright at the library to order three of them for the library. She can check out the books and let me read them, but Mrs. Albright isn't aware they are for me. Miss Berta explained to Mrs. Albright that she wanted information on growing flowers and trees. Mrs. Albright will order two of the books now. Do you think she's caught on the books are for me? By the way, Miss Berta ordered me to quit calling her Miss Berta. She said to call her Berta. I will.

It is grand to be home. I help Pap and work for Mr. Berger. Sometimes Harvey Woodard helps Pap and me. Pap and I sell most of what we take to town on Saturdays.

Mr. Berger gives me a discount on shoes. I bought Mam a pair of fancy church shoes for her birthday. Mr. Berger's sister and her people are still with the Philips family in Holland because they don't believe it safe to go back to Amsterdam. The Germans rounded up a group of young men in Amsterdam and took them away in June. One of

119

them was Mr. Schorr's best friend. Mr. Schorr is Elise's husband, remember? Elise is Mr. Berger's sister. Mr. Schorr doesn't know where his friend is. Isn't it sad and awful? I wonder where the men are. Maybe the Nazis put them in their army like the Confederates did with Noah. I'll bet that's what happened. Don't you think so?

Mrs. Rutledge stopped by our table at the Farmers Market two weeks ago. She rented the McCormick house to the preacher at the Temple Baptist Church on Rock Howard Road. The house where the preacher used to live burned to the ground. I hope he will be a good-natured neighbor. The man who bought the Mueller place keeps it in fine shape. He is friendly whenever we see him. His wife is, too. She buys eggs from Mam when they are here.

I hope your parents are doing fine. Mam loves to get letters from Miss Ellen. Your mother was a precious friend to Mam. I can still hear them giggling in our kitchen!

Your friend,

Blink

October 30, 1941

Dear Annie,

I am glad your school is going well. You will finish in no time. Sometimes I'm sorry I did not stay in school. The remains of James Hinshaw's money are in a savings account earning interest.

I bought two more books on trees and flower raising. Berta checked out the books Mrs. Albright ordered for the library, and I wrote tons of notes. Berta can check them out again if I need to read them again.

The preacher at the Baptist church on Rock Howard Road moved into the McCormick house in August. He and his family moved out yesterday. Pap and I were planting red oak saplings on our side of the road when they left. The preacher claimed they could not live in the house because of demons! He talked gibberish, and I didn't make out what he was saying. Neither did Pap. The house is empty again after Mrs. Rutledge painted it on the outside and put the yard in order before the preacher's family moved into the house.

I am getting better at playing the mandolin. I practice when I have free time. Mr. Edwards says I will be as skilled as his son soon. We played at Grover on Saturday night.

Mr. Berger's sister and her family still live with Mr. and Mrs. Philips. Elise's last letter to Mr. Berger said Jewish children can't go to school anymore. Elise and her husband have two children, a boy and a girl. I don't know how old. Every letter Mr. Berger gets has Mrs. Philips's name on the return address because they don't want anyone to learn the Schorr family is there. Elise wrote that a strange man stopped at the house. He wanted to buy a pig from Mr. Philips, but Mr. Philips didn't have pigs. Elise said this scared both families. Was he at the wrong house, or was he a Nazi snooping? He didn't wear a uniform.

Mam tunes in to the radio each day. It scares her we will get into the war. Pap says we won't. He says England and the other countries over there will have to win their war themselves. My roommate Abe from school tried to enlist in the Army, but they didn't take him. I told him Bobby Edwards is in the Navy. Abe wrote the Navy only lets Negroes work in the kitchen, and Abe hates kitchens. I wrote him Mr. Edwards says his son Bobby loves it because *he gets to see faraway places, but Abe wrote he will keep working at his father's store. He says we will enter the war. I'm confused. What do you think?*

I have repeated every piece of the news here. Have you gone on another date with Robert? I haven't ever asked a girl for a date. My stutter might get worse. I will probably be a bachelor.

Your friend,

Blink

December 6, 1941

Dear Annie,

I am writing fast so Pap can take this letter to the post office. The band plays tonight at Longtown. Longtown is far, which means we will be late getting home. They are lighting their town Christmas tree, and we will play after they light the tree. Because lots of colored folks live in Longtown, I can be there after sundown. I don't think any white people live there. I hope they enjoy our music! We have practiced a few Christmas carols for tonight. I am getting better and better with the mandolin, and my stutter is improving. I don't stutter when I sing, and I don't stutter as much when I talk nowadays, either.

Mr. Edwards got a letter from his son Bobby. His ship is in Hawaii at the Pearl Harbor base and will stay there through Christmas. Bobby says Hawaii is magnificent. That is the word he used. He loves it and wants to return someday. Many ships are in port right now.

It is gracious for Robert's parents to invite you to spend Christmas with them. I will check a map and find Wilmington. You have never seen the ocean, and I'm excited for you. Please send me pictures because I want to see it through your eyes. You will miss seeing Doctor and Miss Ellen, but the distance is far, and you need to study. You must fancy Robert an awful lot. I am positive he is a first-rate fellow if you fancy him.

Nothing much to report here. Mam and Pap are hunky dory. Pap started repairing cars to earn extra money during winter. He sliced his hand on a car last week and called Doc Morrison. Doc Morrison came out and stitched him up fine. He will be good as new in no time.

Mam still sells her eggs to Mayfield's Market. Mr. Mayfield bought most of our vegetables this summer, and he will buy more next summer. Mam's dog Ladybug got sick from eating a deer carcass. She's okay now.

Mr. Berger gave me a raise starting January 1. He got another letter from Elise last week. Her family is okay. Mr. Philips works for a man who is not Jewish. Not long ago, the man asked Mr. Philips if he was Jewish, and Mr. Philips denied the truth. The man said he thought both Mr. and Mrs. Philips were Jews, but Mr. Philips lied to his boss they were not. The truth is, Mrs. Philips is not Jewish, but Mr. Philips is. Everyone was concerned by the question, so Mr. and Mrs. Philips hid their Jewish items. They dug a hole in the ground, shoved everything in a box, and buried the box in the hole.

The McCormick house is still empty. Mrs. Rutledge put a For Sale sign by the road. It has her telephone number on it instead of the real estate man. Berta continues to work for Mrs. Rutledge.

Doc Morrison said his wife Lou received a letter from Miss Ellen, and she said you were going to visit Robert's family for Christmas. Doc Morrison said we might hear wedding bells soon!

Have a grand time in Wilmington!

Your friend,

Blink

December 17, 1941

Dear Annie,

I do not understand. Why did the Japanese attack us? They killed over two thousand people and sank our ships. Do you understand why? We didn't do anything to Japan. Now the Germans are against us, too. The bombing and war declaration upset everybody here. Mam has been crying and crying.

Mr. Edwards has no word from his son Bobby. Bombs hit Bobby's ship. Mr. Edwards is afraid his son is dead, and I believe he is right. Don't you imagine he should have gotten word if his son were alive? This is awful. I am sad. Everyone is sad and frightened.

Pap and I drove to the recruiting station last week to join up. The recruiter man rejected Pap, but when he found out Pap farmed, he wrote Pap's name and address on a form. I got nervous, and my eyes started blinking fast, and my stutter got worse. I wanted to join the Navy, but I wasn't allowed to join any branch of service. The recruiter man said I was unfit for duty. He told Pap I am feeble minded. I tried to tell the man I went to college, but he ordered me to leave. Pap and I came home. I will do whatever I can to help here.

Harvey Woodard tried to enlist, but nobody accepted him either. Harvey limps. Remember? Two of the band boys will join the Army, but they haven't yet. When they do, it will leave Mr. Edwards, Yancy Barnes, and me in the band. Yancy Barnes and Mr. Edwards are too old to enlist.

Mr. Berger worries about his sister Elise and her family. He says he won't get mail from them anymore because Nazis control Holland. Mr. Berger says they will not let letters go to the United States or letters from the United States go into the country. I hope the Philips and Schorr families will keep safe.

I am afraid and worried. What will happen? Praise be we have President Roosevelt.

Your friend,

Blink

December 31, 1941

Dear Annie,

This war is a terrible thing. When I got your letter, I laughed because you said you wanted to come to Hillview and slug the recruiter man for calling me feeble minded. He is a whole lot bigger than you are! It's okay. People have called me that and worse. It does not bother me.

I am happy you enjoyed being with Robert and his family at Christmas. Thanks for the pictures. I long to see the ocean someday. You found lots of seashells at the beach!

I bet Robert and his father are correct when they say the new shipbuilding company in Wilmington will be important to the war effort. Has Robert decided what he will do? Will he return to school? Will he work for the shipbuilding company or enlist? Is Wilmington near Noah's hometown?

Mr. Edwards got a telegram confirming his son Bobby died at Pearl Harbor. It is horrible. Mayor Barbour held a service on the town square Sunday afternoon to honor Bobby Edwards. He is the first person from Hillview to die. I hope nobody else from here dies. Mam, Pap, and I went to the service and stood with the other band boys. I feel powerful sorry for Mr. Edwards and his wife. Bobby was his only son.

Mayor Barbour started a civilian defense group. He says if the Germans come, we must be able to alert everybody. He is organizing time slots for people to watch from the Methodist church steeple because it offers the tallest spot in town. If watchers see something, they will ring the church bell. Mam volunteered to be a watcher, but Mayor Barbour said she had to bring her own binoculars. We don't have binoculars. Berta says they keep binoculars on a shelf in the steeple for each watcher to use. I guess Mayor Barbour doesn't want colored folks using the same binoculars the white folks use.

Berta fixed the basement in her house as an air raid shelter. She put chairs in a circle and bought canned foods. She filled jugs with water. We are welcome if need be. Pap says the house might collapse on top of us if a bomb falls. We will stay here and take our chances.

Mr. Berger has gotten no word from his sister Elise. He hopes she is okay, and I do, too. Harvey Woodard and I went to the movies and watched the newsreel. It showed Pearl Harbor and the ships on fire. Have you seen those newsreels? One showed the Nazis fighting in Russia. I hoped they might show pictures of Holland, but they didn't. I guess nobody is in Holland to get pictures to the United States. The entire country is under German control.

Study hard. You will finish soon. Maybe the war will end quick.

Your friend,

Blink

February 6, 1942

Dear Annie,

Congratulations on your exams! You will soon finish your master's degree. Your progress is one promising thing during this terrible time.

I bet it pleases you Robert will complete his work at school. I bet he is correct the government will draft him, but it will be convenient if he can finish his degree first. It is admirable you both want to be college teachers. Mam and Pap are glad you fancy him as much as you do.

There is plenty of news. Because the band is the three of us now, we are changing our music since the guitar player and harmonica player joined the Army. Now the band is Mr. Edwards with his fiddle, Yancy Barnes with his banjo, and me with the mandolin. Mr. Edwards and I do most of the singing. We played at a rally to buy war bonds at Town Park in Hillview Saturday afternoon. When I finished singing, everybody clapped!

Mrs. Rutledge rented Mrs. McCormick's house again. It's a man from New Jersey who works at Mr. Rutledge's mill. The mill plans to manufacture material for the war. I am not aware of what. The mill hired more people because many of their employees joined the fight. When we were at the rally last Saturday, I saw Mrs. Rutledge buy a war bond. She wore a mink coat. Mam says they are expensive.

The owner of the Mueller place, Roy Foster, called Pap long distance on the telephone. Mr. Foster works in Washington, D.C. He can't come here now because of the war, so he hired Pap and me to take care of his property. He will mail Pap a key to the house and the barn. He will pay us an acceptable sum of money. Isn't this splendid? The man who worked for him here joined the Marines. We will take care of the Mueller cemetery with Miss Mittie's grave as nice as we do for the one where Noah and my kinfolk lie. Mr. Foster wants us to plant trees along his side of our road, the same as we planted on our side. The property between the McCormick property and Apple Ridge Road is his, remember? We will plant the trees in spring. Green trees will line both sides of the street in spring and summer once these saplings grow big.

Mam said people in town are saying Mr. Blanton has trouble at his bank, but I'm not sure what trouble. He still owns the orchard behind the McCormick house.

Mr. Berger has received no word from his sister. I am sorry for Mr. Berger. His wife died years ago, and he doesn't have children.

Please stop fretting because you can't find Noah's family. There is no way you can locate them, Annie. You never learned Noah's last name. You know his people's first names, but lots of people have those names. They are long dead. It is admirable that you want to pass on details of what happened to his family, but you can't. Please don't get *sad. You said the town near his home no longer exists, anyhow. Noah would understand. He would, Annie!*

Mam got a letter from Miss Ellen last week. Mam misses your mother. Miss Ellen wrote Mam she misses her, too. Miss Ellen wrote she doesn't have any friend back in Oklahoma as true-blue as Mam.

Your friend,

Blink

KT sighed, gathered the letters scattered on the bed, and placed them on the dresser. She crawled under the covers and stared at the ceiling, reflecting on Blink's unsettling revelations. World War II came to Hillview, claiming one of its sons at Pearl Harbor. No branch of the armed forces accepted Blink or his father Ned, in all probability because of their race, and the recruiter's cruel treatment of Blink brought angry tears. Mayor Barbour didn't even allow Cora Hill to volunteer in the civilian defense group, although the thought of Hillview as a Nazi target elicited a slight chuckle of dismay from KT. As for Mr. Berger's family, their plight in Holland brought a deep sense of dread. Then, there was Robert. Who was he? Was this her grandfather, the father KT's mother never knew? Guilt washed over KT as these questions hammered her brain.

"I don't even know my grandfather's first name. I'm ashamed. It's inexcusable."

KT tossed and turned the entire night as sleep failed to embrace her. Around four o'clock in the morning, she fell into a shallow sleep before awaking groggy and exhausted.

WEASEL ROAST AND CHOCOLATE PIE

G ood morning and welcome to the Mueller House. Please come in and allow me to introduce you to this historic home," said the docent, a short, square-built woman attired in clothes of the late 1800s. She greeted visitors and ushered them inside the home's foyer.

KT and Graham entered through the glass paned front door and waited with six other guests. KT scoured the foyer and peered into other rooms. From Apple Ridge Road, the house appeared larger than its actual size.

"Mueller House was the home of Dr. Henry Helton Mueller, a physician and farmer locals referred to as Doc Mueller," the docent began. "Construction of the home started in 1774 by a British loyalist who fled to England when Revolutionary War hostilities broke out. After the Revolution's end, Doc Mueller's father, Wallace Mueller, purchased the estate and finished construction. This house is a log home covered by plaster on the exterior. At one time, the property encompassed two hundred thirty acres. Research leads us to believe Doc Mueller aided slaves in their flights to freedom. He treated both Union and

Confederate soldiers during the Civil War, either in the kitchen or in the former stable under the dwelling. Doc Mueller's children sold the property after his widow's death, but the purchaser lost it in foreclosure during the Great Depression. It stood vacant for several years before Roy Foster of Washington, D.C. bought it from the bank as a vacation property and did extensive renovations to the house. Following more owners and the sale of most of the land, the current owners bought the home on five acres in 1990 and completed more renovations. Please continue to the dining room and kitchen."

Another costumed guide took over the tour. KT imagined her grandmother's beloved Miss Mittie as a child playing in the spacious kitchen where an antique pot hung inside an enormous stone fireplace. One window provided a westward view of the mountain and allowed afternoon sun to illuminate the home's original pegged oak floors.

"This fireplace mantle and corner bathtub are both original to the home," the docent droned. "None of the antique cooking implements are original. Our current owner discovered the bathtub in the basement and placed it where they believe it sat when Doc Mueller and his family lived here. Crafted of tin, the tub is lightweight and easy to move from one location to another. During winter, the Muellers most likely bathed in this space before the fireplace. During summer, they often bathed outdoors."

While others in the group stared at the bathtub, KT moved toward it and ran her hand over its smooth, rounded top. She fingered the handles on each end and assumed it was the tub in which Miss Mittie's sister Phoebe bathed when her mother and Blink's great-grandmother Thea soothed bruises and washed grime from her body. When KT turned to Graham, her eyes brimmed with tears.

"What is it?" he asked. "What's wrong?"

"Nothing. Nothing is wrong. I'm remembering what Nonnie related to me. Miss Mittie's sister Phoebe witnessed a dreadful crime. I'm positive she bathed in this tub afterwards. Tragic." KT paused for a moment. "I'm okay. We need to find our tour group."

KT and Graham rushed upstairs to re-join their group. They discovered more-than-adequate closets and updated bathrooms rendered the home modern and accommodating. Exquisite decorating created a pleasant air of history, comfort, and convenience.

The original bones of the house came into view when the group descended into the basement. Old stone walls and rough chestnut beams greeted the tourists, but polished concrete now covered the original dirt floor. The house sat on a hillside where barn doors on the lower level once opened to the outdoors. Now, instead of barn doors, wide French doors opened to a patio, allowing sunlight to flood the interior space. Three portable dehumidifiers hummed as the docent explained a horse stable once occupied most of the basement. These horses, she explained, were Doc Mueller's personal mounts. A nearby barn demolished long ago provided shelter for other riding horses, carriage horses, draft horses, mules, oxen, and such. Through the windows, KT and Graham viewed remains of a smokehouse and spring house in the distance. Tucked into one corner of the basement, a tiny room compelled attention. This room, the docent theorized, served as a hiding space for runaway slaves. She explained boards surrounding the exterior of the room allowed for hay to be stuffed between the boards and the room's walls. This camouflage caused any unknowing observer to see the space as a livestock feeding station, not a room where runaway slaves might hide.

"Please examine the carvings and sketches on the posts and interior walls," she urged. "You'll see a few names, but most slaves could neither read nor write, so most are depictions of faces, animals, trees. Doc Mueller was of the Quaker faith. He despised slavery. Rumors circulated he helped those in need of escape, and these carvings and the tiny room confirm those rumors, in our opinion."

KT and Graham still scrutinized the chamber when the docent announced the tour's end and suggested visitors leave through the French doors. Once outside, the guide pointed toward a flagstone pathway and recommended a visit to the Mueller cemetery. She further suggested the cabin across the road at Tobias Hill Nursery may be worth a visit. KT made no mention to Graham of the similarity between the Mueller hiding place and the one in Holland described in Blink's letters, but the similarity stunned her. She paused and shuddered before returning her attention to the docent.

"As to the cabin," continued the docent, "A freed former slave named Russell Hill built it on twenty acres in 1854. Doc Mueller gave Russell the land as a gift. The Hill cabin is not part of our tour, but the nursery owner, a descendant of Russell and his wife Thea, opens it for visitors each year during Hillview Days. You can find lovely flowers at the nursery, too," the docent concluded with a wink. "Thank you for coming."

"Shall we visit the cemetery?" Graham asked.

"Please," KT answered.

Dwarf boxwoods lined the flagstone path leading to the Mueller cemetery where a wrought-iron gate marked the entrance. Once inside, they both noted the current owners maintained the graveyard with meticulous care.

"Here is Wallace Mueller's grave and his wife's," said Graham. Next to those, two more stones noted the resting places of two infants, a girl and a boy. KT soon spotted Doc Mueller's grave memorialized by a simple stone:

Here Lies Henry Helton (Doc) Mueller, Physician
Freedom is the Greatest Gift
December 30, 1813–February 2, 1899

Doc Mueller's wife, Hannah, Miss Mittie's mother, rested beside her husband.

Graham noticed KT's reverence for these historical figures and scrutinized her as she removed her cell phone and photographed the two tombstones with care and solemnity.

"This man was a hero. Someday I will tell you more. Nonnie passed stories to me she learned from Miss Mittie and from Blink's family. Doc Mueller was the best of the best."

Graham nodded without speaking. He followed KT as she moved to a lone stone, not plain as the others, but engraved with flowers, angels, and hearts encircling the name.

"This is Phoebe's grave." KT's hand caressed the stone before she photographed it.

"Phoebe? Oh, yes, you mentioned the name. Who was she now?"

"Miss Mittie's sister. She saw the murders."

"What murders?"

"Oh, the story is too complicated to explain now. Townspeople tormented Phoebe, according to Miss Mittie. My grandmother explained everything to me right before she died in the woods behind McCormick House. I can recap Phoebe's life in one word, and the word is tragic."

"I'm sorry," Graham muttered as he stroked his mustache.

After a few moments, KT moved to the next grave, one belonging to Dr. Charles McCormick. Her focus next locked onto his wife's stone belonging to Mittie Mueller McCormick.

"Here is Miss Mittie! She may have been, besides my great-grandparents, the most influential person in my grandmother's life. Nonnie adored her." KT's cell phone camera clicked again. She stood in reverence, not moving, staring in silence.

The chatter of women at the gate startled them, and a mockingbird perched in a nearby apple tree scolded the intruders before taking to the sky. A group of five, cackling and slurping from paper cups, barged into the cemetery and commenced to mill around the graves. KT faced the women with a stony stare. She considered a graveyard a venue for quiet, for reflection, and for respect.

The group tromped around, walking over one burial site after another before becoming bored.

"Oh, come on, Carol. These are dead people. Who cares? Let's get to town before the twelve o'clock rush!" one woman called.

Incensed, KT stepped in front of the women and pointed to Doc Mueller's grave as she admonished, "This isn't a playground, ladies! It's a family cemetery, a sacred plot! You should leave and reflect on your behavior!"

She pushed past the women and pounded the flagstone pathway back to the house. Graham excused himself, leaving the dumbfounded women silent, and hurried to where KT stood.

"Whoa, KT! Hang on! Wait for me!"

She stopped. He took her arm and saw tears streaming over her cheeks. She fumbled for a tissue.

"Those sorts of people infuriate me! I'm sorry my temper got the best of me, but I can't *stand* disrespect. The Muellers, of all people, deserve utmost respect." She wiped her eyes, fumbled for another tissue, and blew her nose.

Graham put his arm around her and patted her shoulder. "Hey, I feel the same way. You don't need to apologize. The Mueller graves mean a lot to you, and the Muellers were important to your grandmother. Let's ignore those insensitive hags and forge ahead. Do you still wish to visit the Hill cabin across the way?"

She agreed. They strolled across the lawn and crossed Apple Ridge Road. At the entrance to Tobias Hill Nursery, a sign announced the historical Hill cabin was open to the public during Hillview Days. KT and Graham hastened through the entrance and along the shaded gravel driveway to the nursery.

The full parking lot and the sight of customers loading vehicles with plants hinted that Hillview Days brought significant business to the nursery.

"Blink would be proud of his grandson's work," KT surmised in a near whisper.

"Are you ready to see the cabin?" Graham asked.

KT's perky spirit rebounded. "You bet! Nonnie spent plenty of time here when her family lived at McCormick House. Her mother Ellen and Blink's mother Cora became the best of friends. Ellen Young often sat at the kitchen table in this cabin or at McCormick House drinking coffee with Cora Hill."

The two approached the front porch. There, a cherry-red front door and a matching antique glider with multi-colored pillows created a welcoming scene, but a hand painted sign informed any potential seat-takers to stay off the fragile glider. KT and Graham traversed the wooden steps, and a statuesque black woman greeted them.

"Hello, friends!" greeted the hostess whose rich sepia complexion and yellow period costume KT found stunning. "Thank you for stopping by the Hill cabin. Russell Hill built this cabin in 1854. Russell and his wife Thea, freed slaves employed by Doc Mueller in the white house across the way, were devoted to the Mueller family, and the Muellers returned their devotion. Doc Mueller gifted Russell twenty acres during a time when no people of color owned property here. I will be happy to show you the interior where a few original furnishings and items survive. Nobody has lived in this cabin since 1967, but the cabin remains in the Hill family. It, the nursery, and a nearby residence on the property are now owned by Russell Hill's great-great-great-grandson and his wife. Please join me."

KT and Graham followed the slender woman. As the modest crinoline of her yellow skirt swished along the floor, she pointed out rooms added to the original construction and spoke of its inhabitants. She discussed the property's evolution from farm to nursery after Blink, whom she referred to as Tobias Hill, inherited the tract from his father Ned. The tour lasted less than fifteen minutes before the woman escorted KT and Graham out the front door.

KT addressed their guide. "Thank you so much! My grandmother once lived in the McCormick house and was grand friends with Blink, uh, Tobias Hill. Her mother and Blink's mother Cora became fast friends, too. The cabin is as my grandmother described, complete with its red front door and porch glider."

The woman's countenance switched from dutiful docent to family friend. "Oh, my gracious! You're Dr. Winslow, aren't you?" She reached out and grabbed KT's hand. "It's wonderful to meet you! I'm Doan's wife, Amy. Amy Hill."

The moment Amy introduced herself, three other visitors arrived and entered the cabin. "Please excuse me, Dr. Winslow, I must help these visitors. I hope we'll visit soon. Doan and I are thrilled you're here reclaiming the McCormick property!" Amy pivoted a brisk one eighty and trotted inside to resume her duties as tour guide.

"Well, I guess you're glad we came over here, aren't you?" Graham asked.

"Oh, you bet. This is marvelous! What other surprises will this weekend bring? Thank you! Since we're near McCormick House, may we check on it? Larry is there today."

The two meandered back to Graham's Jeep, climbed in, and drove the short distance down the lane to McCormick House. Larry's truck sat in the driveway, and behind it a full-sized black Mercedes Benz sedan dominated the narrow entrance. Graham parked on the street.

As they approached the house, a six-foot tall smarmy-looking man emerged through the front door, planted his feet commando-style on the flagstone sidewalk, and stared in their direction. His ill-fitting suit and shirt emphasized his bay window and pudgy, out-of-shape frame. Thinning, oily, blondish/brown hair, sweaty forehead, and a pallid complexion presented a man who appeared more suited to darkness than normal daylight.

"Miss Winslow, I presume?" he asked, as he held out a puffy, pale hand.

KT accepted his gesture, unable to ignore his hand's smoothness and buffed fingernails as she accepted the extended appendage. There was no grip as his limp, damp, baby-soft palm slid into and from her hand in the manner of a lazy, fat eel.

"Let me introduce myself, Miss Winslow. I am Thomas Blane Martin, and I am pleased to meet you."

"It's Dr. Winslow," she corrected.

"Oh, I didn't realize. I'm sorry," Martin muttered before acknowledging Graham with a nod and a curt, "Wessler."

Graham responded, "Martin."

After an awkward pause, the uninvited visitor turned to KT once again. "I dropped by to see if you received my latest document."

"Yes, I got it," KT said. "And I tore it into pieces and mailed it back to the mail drop you present as your office. If you check there, you will find it."

Martin shifted his feet as more beads of sweat formed on his face. He stared at the ground before his squint returned to her and what resembled a growl erupted from his throat.

"Why did you do such a thing? I'm willing to pay a premium price for the property. You don't want this old dump, do you?"

KT straightened her frame into a stiff stance and eyeballed Blane Martin from the top of his sweaty brow to the bottom of his wide, spit-shined shoes. She squinted.

"It's none of your business, Mr. Martin. In my note to you, the one mailed to your box at the mail drop store, I instructed you to never set foot on this property. Not you, not any of your employees, not anyone acquainted with you. Now, leave me alone and leave. Get it?"

Martin glared at Graham, who stared back at him without blinking.

"Now, Miss, uh, Dr. Winslow. Your grandmother agreed to sell me this property before her death. Such a genial woman she was! Don't you want to honor her wishes? I'm confident you'll find our contract among her belongings."

This lie infuriated KT. She moved closer to Blane Martin, pointing her finger upward toward his ashen face. She remembered Anna Ruth's description of Phoebe Mueller accosting Morse Blanton after the murders of Ben and Israel Hill in 1863. KT felt Phoebe's rage invade her body as she laid it out in plain English.

"Don't you dare spout your vile, lying garbage to me, Mr. Martin! My grandmother never agreed to sell you this property. She tore up your contracts. If there's one thing neither my Nonnie nor I can stand, it's a liar, a conman, a bully, and you're all three rolled into one. You don't even use the same name. Are you Blane Martin? Thomas Martin? Thomas B. Martin? Tom? Who are you? You with your hypocritical *Christian* quotes on your stationery! You. Are. Repulsive! Leave this property and never come back. Understood?" KT's finger still waved at the target of her fury.

KT's rage took Martin aback. A petite, freckle-faced female in a baseball cap castigated him in the company of another man. Nobody, especially a female, did such a thing to Blane Martin! He peered around KT, seeking relief from the realtor. Graham raised his eyebrows, drew his lips into a thin line, and pointed to the black Mercedes, indicating Martin should leave.

"I'm sorry you've come to such an erroneous conclusion, Miss Winslow," Martin muttered.

"It's D-o-c-t-o-r Winslow," KT spelled out. "Now, go!"

Martin sneered, "Yes. Goodbye." With a huff, he stalked past KT and Graham toward his car, leaving a faint but disgusting whiff of hair oil and cheap cologne.

KT and Graham observed Martin enter his car and back out of the driveway, being careful not to throw gravel. Once on the asphalt lane, he gunned the engine. With tires squealing, he accelerated toward Apple Ridge Road and disappeared.

"Boy, howdy! You let him have it, Katie Doc!" Larry yelled from the front porch. He had followed the entire interaction. "Come inside and have a sit. Graham Cracker, bring her in here. I bet she needs a drink of cold water!"

Larry escorted KT and Graham into the house. They headed to the kitchen, and each sat at the table. Larry grabbed a paper cup, filled it from the jug on the counter, and handed it to KT. She nodded her thanks and took several gulps.

"Martin's one slick son-of-a-biscuit eater, ain't he, Cracker? I told him Katie Doc wasn't sellin' to him when he sashayed in here without knockin'. He peered around to see what I was doin' like he owned the place. He seen the well dude's equipment out front. Don't believe he seen the septic work out back, though."

"He shouldn't come back, Larry," said KT. "If he does, call the Sheriff. He has no business here. I see why Nonnie called him a snake."

Graham walked to the kitchen window and gazed through it to the front yard. He stood there for several moments before turning to KT and Larry, his face showing concern.

"Larry, how much longer before the well is ready? The septic?"

Larry reported electrical work, septic, and plumbing should be completed within two weeks, along with the well.

Graham said, "Promising news."

"Yup," said Larry. "Katie Doc, if you pick out a stove, fridge, dishwasher, and such, I can get the kitchen goin' right soon. Do you plan to use these old cabinets, or do you want modern ones? I gotta tear out the ones by the sink anyhow to install a dishwasher."

KT, her brain still on overload, appeared overwhelmed. The experience with Blane Martin drained her. She had not experienced anger of such intensity, perhaps ever. Her head swayed, signaling an uneasy state of mind.

"Oh, Larry, I'm clueless! I've never selected appliances. Cabinets? Lord, what have I gotten myself into here?"

Larry kneeled before her and took her left hand into his dry, calloused one. His other arm, sporting a naked lady tattoo, rested on the table next to where KT sat.

"Now, looky here, Katie Doc, don't worry one whit. It ain't as hard as it sounds. Martin is a blowhard bully. A conman. You take a breath, relax a minute, and go. Graham Cracker, since Katie Doc here is leery of pickin' out things, won't Miz Wessler help her out? She picks out what to get for your rent houses. She's got a talent."

Graham smiled. "She can, and she'd be happy to help. KT, let's let Larry finish what he's working on right now. I'll ask Mom to help you with the cabinet and appliance chore. It can overwhelm anyone."

KT hung her head. "I feel genuinely stupid because I let Martin light my fuse. I'm sorry to have made a scene. Oh, Graham, if your mother will help me, I'd appreciate it more than you or she will ever know. I've never considered this sort of stuff before today."

****

"Come in, come in!" Al Wessler welcomed KT and Graham to the Wessler home. At over six feet tall, his shock of white hair, bright blue eyes, and kelly green vest made Al Wessler a dazzling and imposing figure. "You'll get wet in this rain. The weather guy didn't call for rain, did he?"

"No, Dad. We were on the Hillview Days' home tour when Mom called and invited us to Sunday dinner. Rain cut our tour short."

KT and Graham set their umbrellas on the porch and entered the house.

"Graham?" came a query from the kitchen. Mrs. Wessler entered and chuckled at the two souls standing in her foyer.

"Thanks for the invitation, Mom!" Graham said. "We were heading into the second house when you called. The rain started when we left it. I'm glad KT noticed the clouds and grabbed our umbrellas before we went inside. Because of the rain, we didn't go to the third house. We came straight here."

Mrs. Wessler said, "I'm sorry you couldn't finish your tour. I imagine downtown is clearing out earlier than expected due to rain."

"It's fine," KT replied. "We saw the Mueller house and the Hill cabin, which interested me the most. Thank you for welcoming me to dinner again. I appreciate the invitation."

Graham said, "My sister and her husband can't come today. Mom adores company on Sundays, and she's pleased as punch you came, aren't you, Mom?"

"You bet I am, honey. Al is, too. Everyone take a seat because dinner is ready." Mrs. Wessler escorted KT and Graham to the table and pointed to where they should sit.

Mr. Wessler retrieved the pot roast from the kitchen, set it on the table, and returned to the kitchen to bring out other dishes. He then took his seat and passed each plate around the table while chatting with KT and Graham. Periodically, he paused to chew and focus their way.

"Now, listen here, KT," Al Wessler said. "Quit calling us Mr. and Mrs. Wessler. My name is Al, and her name is Gabi. This Mr. and Mrs. nonsense is too formal."

"Gabi?" KT asked.

Gabi Wessler laughed. "Yes. Al says my parents knew I'd be a talker!"

Animated conversation flourished throughout the meal. KT discussed the Mueller property and the Hill cabin. She divulged no details of her grandmother's stories, but she mentioned she was aware of both places because of those stories. Her mood darkened as she recounted the experience with Blane Martin. Al muttered something incoherent under his breath. Silence followed.

Gabi stood and announced dessert and coffee. Soon, a piece of chocolate pie from Betty Lynn's Bakery and cups of coffee sat at each place. Over an hour of conversation followed, during which KT and Gabi scheduled shopping the next day to select kitchen appliances. By the time they finished dessert and coffee, the rain had stopped.

"I guess I'd better get KT back to her hotel now," said Graham as he moved toward the front door. "KT, can you get Mom around nine in the morning? She doesn't drive anymore. Better drop by McCormick House first so Mom can check out the kitchen."

"You bet," KT said.

Gabi gave Graham a peck on his cheek and planted a kiss on KT's forehead. "KT, I'll see you in the morning!"

When Graham dropped off KT at the hotel, she again expressed her appreciation for his help and for the hospitality shown by his parents.

"I'm glad to help, as are they!" he hollered as he drove away.

Inside her hotel room, the file box sat on the floor, waiting, longing for attention. The folder containing Blink's letters rested on the desk, enticing her, but KT read no letters. The unopened envelope from Stub O'Connor waited on the nightstand, but she stole a side-wise glance at it and wrinkled her nose. She checked her phone for messages and clicked on the television to a nature documentary, which took her mind off the nasty incident with Blane Martin. Her lack of sleep the preceding night prevented her from seeing the entire show. Within thirty minutes, she fell into a deep and sound slumber.

SUE WHO?

KT and Gabi Wessler took off on their excursion Monday morning. After a brief stop at McCormick House, the women agreed the existing cabinets and built-in hutch needed nothing but paint. They next trekked to the home improvement store and ordered kitchen appliances. With their mission accomplished, KT took Gabi to lunch at the café near the Historical Society, and they lingered until after two o'clock.

Before returning to McCormick House, KT dropped Gabi at her home, stopped by the hotel, and changed into a sweatshirt and jeans. The front yard bustled with equipment and machines, ear-splitting racket, and scurrying workers. Larry toiled inside the house while his favorite music blared forth through the open front door, eliciting a smile and chuckle from KT. The aroma of freshly cut lumber greeted her as she walked through the front door and maneuvered through piles of debris to the stairs.

"Hey there, Katie Doc!" Larry bent over the stair railing and waved to KT, who waved back from the first step. "How ya doing?"

"I'm fine, Larry. Mrs. Wessler and I ordered kitchen appliances. The store will call you to schedule a convenient delivery time. We decided to paint the cabinets instead of replacing them."

"You betcha! Easy peasy! Them boys outside is gettin' the job done. I'm takin' a gander at the bathroom. The drawing you gave me is easy to figure out. I'll order a flusher, vanity, and sink. You wanna keep this here bathtub, don't ya?"

KT joined him upstairs in the bathroom, where KT scanned the room. She assessed the clawfoot bathtub, which appeared to be in excellent shape, should appear brand-new after refinishing.

"Yes, Larry. It's lovely. Uh, oh, people often prefer showers. I didn't consider a shower!"

"Yup, they do. It's a fact. See this corner over here? I can install a shower in it easy. Make it roomy. This is a ginormous bathroom, Katie Doc. It's got plenty of room for a decent sized shower."

"A shower is a necessary addition. I guess you'll want to install tile. Oh, gosh. More decisions for me."

Larry let out an enormous snort. "Get Miz Wessler to help. She loves to pick out decorating stuff."

KT exhaled a soft whistling noise, fluttering her lips. "I will. I can't express to you how much I appreciate your enormous help. You, Graham, the Wesslers, Emmaline at the Historical Society, everyone I've met. Except Blane Martin." Her mood darkened.

"Don't you worry about ole slime-ball, Katie Doc! I'll take care of him if he shows his pasty face around here! I may look scrawny, but I'm mighty!" He flexed a wiry arm muscle, forcing a cackle from KT.

KT descended the stairs. "No violence, Larry. I need you!"

Her spirits lifted, and she began collecting debris and tossing it into the dumpster by the front porch. Her cell phone vibrated.

"Hello, KT." Graham's voice echoed on the other end, "Mom said you two picked out great kitchen appliances."

"Yes, we did. I'm beyond grateful for her help. I'll need her help with bathroom tile, too!"

"She'll love it. Listen, I must leave town for a few days. I do consulting jobs for my former employer, and I need to take a sudden trip. If you need any help, call Dad. Things are progressing, and you'll be fine."

"Yes, I will. Have a safe trip. Where are you going?"

Silence on the other end. In a moment, Graham said, "Oh, off into the wild blue yonder! See you soon."

KT shrugged.

"Strange," she muttered before she resumed straightening the living room. After completing this chore, she returned upstairs and removed the dingy, dusty pillow and quilt from the bed in Anna Ruth's former bedroom. After depositing them in the dumpster, she called for Larry to help her drag the floppy mattress out of the house. They maneuvered it down the stairs and plopped it into the dumpster.

"Larry, let's leave the iron bed frame in the room. It's an antique, and Nonnie slept in it. I want to take the bed frame home with me. The kitchen table and chairs, too. I may have to rent a trailer, but I'll handle it later."

"Okie Dokie. Will do."

"I'm returning to the hotel. I'm reading a collection of my grandmother's papers and learning tons of stuff pertaining to Hillview from them."

"Okie Dokie! Hey, Katie Doc. Listen, there's a funny pint-sized dog hangin' around sometimes. This mornin', it come upstairs and stared at me while I measured in the bathroom.

After a few minutes, the dang dog disappeared. I didn't catch sight of it comin' or goin'. Don't know how it got inside the house, but it don't act as if it wants to bite. If you see it, don't let it scare you."

KT stopped. Her face turned white. Her eyes widened.

"Describe the dog, will you, Larry?"

"Cute little pup. It's white with black and tan on it. Ears stick up and flop over. Has a beard. Wiry fur."

"Oh. Uh, I'll watch for it. It, uh, it may live in a house beyond the stone wall. Thanks for alerting me."

Her legs trembled as she pushed open the screen door. Still shaky, she stumbled to her car and gripped the steering wheel. "Bitsy," she mumbled.

****

In the comfort of her hotel room, KT retrieved the file containing Blink's letters and eased into the corner chair. She propped her legs onto an ottoman and began reading. The next batch of letters, dated 1942, provided insight into the worlds of Blink and Anna Ruth Young during the early days of World War II. Blink and the band still performed and marched during Hillview's Fourth of July parade. He attached a miniature American flag to his hat and delighted in the crowd's cheers as the boys played a song by The Carter Family entitled "When the World's on Fire." KT learned Mr. Rutledge's mill operated twenty-four hours a day, seven days a week manufacturing parachutes. Blink and his father Ned each worked two shifts per week. Harvey Woodard, Blink's friend, worked at the mill six days a week. Mr. Berger continued to employ Blink at his shoe store on Sunday afternoons, and Ned sold much of his produce to Mayfield's

Market. When the government introduced gas rationing in May, Ned bought a bicycle and built a compact trailer, which he attached to the bike. He used the bike and trailer for transporting produce to Mayfield's. He built a trailer for Blink's bike, too. No word involving Mr. Berger's sister and family in Holland arrived.

KT snickered when she learned the renter of McCormick House moved out because of peculiar happenings at the residence. "Yes!" she squealed when Anna Ruth received her master's degree. Upon reading Anna Ruth and Robert visited Carter and Ellen Young in June 1942, KT muttered, "Robert must be my grandfather!" as she set the letters on the floor, stood, stretched, and checked her watch. KT ordered room service, turned on the television news, and monitored the program while eating. Following this respite, she set the empty tray outside her door, made a cup of decaf, and settled into the chair once again to resume reading Blink's letters.

1943 brought changes to Hillview. Monthly scrap metal drives collected every type of metal for the war effort. Minnie Mouse and Pluto endorsed efforts by the American Fat Salvage Committee, and local women responded by saving cooking fat. Mayfield's Market paid four cents per pound for leftover grease, which was used for manufacturing munitions. KT had no clue kitchen fat helped make bombs. She learned another Hillview soldier died, this time in North Africa, bringing Hillview's war dead total to two. The band's performances dwindled due to gas rationing. Mr. Berger fretted for his sister's family in Holland, and Ned, Cora, and Blink toiled on their farm. Cora again tried to volunteer as a watcher in the Methodist church steeple, but the mayor declined her request. McCormick House remained empty while Ned and Blink cared for the Mueller property and the graveyard off Creek

Road. More letters contained Blink's admonition for Annie to stop searching for Noah's relations in North Carolina.

A letter written toward the end of 1943 congratulated Annie on her engagement to Robert and expressed concern Robert had enlisted in the Marine Corps. Learning these details of Anna Ruth Young's life pained KT. Her ignorance of her grandmother's life shamed and saddened her, and she delved into more letters with furious abandon.

A January 1944 letter addressed Robert's furlough from the newly dedicated Camp Lejeune. This furlough allowed Anna Ruth and Robert to marry in a private ceremony at the Forest Hills home of Robert's parents in Wilmington. A honeymoon included a visit to Carter and Ellen Young via train, followed by Annie's return to Chapel Hill to resume work on her PhD. Robert returned to Camp Lejeune.

A paragraph in one of Blink's letters reassured KT her grandmother's choice of husband pleased Dr. and Mrs. Young.

Mam and Pap and I are thrilled for you and Robert! Miss Ellen wrote Mam she and Doctor have not stopped smiling since you and Robert returned to North Carolina. I hope to meet Robert someday. I showed Mam and Pap the picture of Robert and you, and Mam says he is a dreamboat. Promise me you will bring him to visit, Annie. It is grand you are happy.

To read Cora Hill's description of KT's grandfather as a "dreamboat" produced a snicker, followed by a moan of sadness as she set the letter on her lap. The island of Okinawa claimed him as a war casualty in 1945, not long before World War II ended and soon after Anna Ruth gave birth to their daughter.

Her cell phone's buzz broke KT's thoughts, and she answered the device to find Larry on the other end.

"Katie Doc, electric's working! I put bulbs in the fixtures, and what a change! Oughta have water and septic right soon, too. These fellas work fast."

"Marvelous, Larry! I can't believe the progress we're making. This is glorious!"

"Everything should go fast. You can rest easy. I'll get it done before you blink an eye. Graham Cracker can put a sign out front and sell it, and you won't worry with it anymore."

"Thank you. I *will* rest easy, Larry. You take care!"

She set the folder with Blink's letters on the desk. A nagging mystery forced her to open the lid of the file box labeled "Hillview." She thumbed through folders until she found one labeled "Noah." Blink's letters often mentioned Annie's search for relatives of the young soldier who inspired the girl's crusade for truth.

A stack of papers, penciled in a young girl's handwriting, detailed Noah's escape from a Union prison and his futile attempt to return home to North Carolina. KT scanned the pages for family names and jotted them on a notepad: sisters Ibby and Mamie, brothers George, Jacob, and Theodore. No other first names and no surnames did she discover, but one notation mentioned a town near Noah's family farm. As a historian, Anna Ruth was no stranger to research, yet the internet did not exist, and family Bibles provided the primary means of documenting ancestry. Could modern technology provide the key to clues that remained out of reach to KT's grandmother?

****

"Hello, Emmaline," KT chirped the next day when she strode through the Historical Society door. "I'm trying to uncover current relatives of a Confederate soldier, but I don't have the person's rank or last name. How can I achieve this, or is it even possible?"

Emmaline responded with information involving online genealogy research networks, explaining a knowledge of first names, places, and dates might produce answers, and she gave KT the name of her preferred site.

"Thanks! I'm on a scavenger hunt, I believe. I enjoyed Hillview Days immensely. You and Graham have my appreciation for insisting I stay for it."

"Glad you enjoyed it. Sunday's rain ended outdoor activities early, but we consider it a successful event. Please stop by for lunch soon!"

When KT entered her hotel room, she set her laptop on the desk and joined the popular genealogy website Emmaline suggested. She began typing and first checked the 1860 census records for North Carolina's Rockingham County, entering only the first names of Noah and his siblings. She estimated Noah's birth year based upon Anna Ruth's notes and did the same for his young sister, Mamie. In what struck KT as a nanosecond, each sibling leaped on the screen in one household, the household of Hezekiah and Abigail Poole.

"Oh, my word!" KT shrieked at the computer. "There they are! Each one of them! I don't believe this. Nonnie, you spent ages and ages trying to find these people, and here they are on my computer screen!"

Her fingers flew on the keyboard as she clicked on each sibling's name. She took furious notes as to birth dates, death dates, marriages, children, and places of residence. After she discovered a treasure trove of information, her stomach rumblings proclaimed the lunch hour had come and gone.

"I'd better eat something," she chuckled as she headed for the door, but a call from Larry interrupted her as she started toward the elevator.

"Katie Doc, a fella come to the door and asked for you. When I relayed you wasn't here, he took off. He had an envelope in his hand, and he looked mean, I tell ya."

"Oh, don't worry, Larry. I'm sure it's Martin sending another sales contract. I'm grabbing a late lunch and will see you tomorrow."

She more or less skipped into the dining room before settling into a chair near the door. After the server took her order, a squatty man in a rumpled brown suit stopped at her table and addressed her in a hoarse, squeaky voice.

"Are you Miss Winslow?" he asked. "Miss Kathryn Winslow?"

"I am Kathryn Winslow."

"Here," he squawked. "You've been served." He tossed an envelope on the table before turning and waddling through the lobby and out the hotel's front entrance.

KT opened the envelope to discover it contained a summons, a "Service of Process." Thomas Blane Martin was suing her for breach of contract. The summons proclaimed KT's grandmother signed a contract before her death to sell McCormick House to Martin, and Martin intended to enforce the contract.

KT's heart raced, and her face turned the color of Graham's Jeep. Her hands shook as she put the glass of water to her quivering lips.

"Honey, are you okay?" asked the waitress as she set KT's lunch on the table.

"I'm, I'm okay, thank you. I'm okay."

Okay, she was not. She took two bites of chicken salad and shoved the plate away. What course of action should she pursue? Anna Ruth signed no agreement to sell the property to Martin. How brazen for Martin to claim she had! His assertion was a lie, but here lay proof he cared nothing for the truth, and his willingness to take her to court over his lie infuriated her. KT realized she required an attorney, but she knew none in Hillview. Could Martin win? Could she lose McCormick House after all her work and see the house demolished? Concerns and emotions flooded her brain, and when she put her head in her hands and rested her elbows on the table, her elation at finding Noah's family members faded into despair.

"Honey, you aren't okay," insisted the returning server, putting her hand on KT's shoulder. "Can I help you?"

"No, thank you. Please put this on my bill. Room 372. Thank you."

KT hurried from the hotel to Wessler and Son Realtors. Graham was out of town, but she hoped to find Al. The receptionist advised he did not aim to return from visiting a friend in Lexington until the following day. A frantic KT drove to the Historical Society to ask Emmaline Conrad for help. A locked door and a sign showing Emmaline's return at four o'clock deepened her desperation. KT peered at her watch. It read three-thirty. She recalled her grandmother's attorney, Roy Anderson, saying Anna Ruth refused to sell and destroyed contracts sent to her. Fumbling with her phone, she found Anderson's telephone number and called. He had left his office. Might Gabi Wessler have the name of a reliable attorney? KT discarded the idea of asking the eighty something-year-old woman for advice. She phoned Graham.

"You have reached the voicemail of Graham Wessler. I cannot speak to you now, but please leave your name and number. I will return your call as soon as possible."

Exasperated, KT left the following message: "Graham, it's KT Winslow. It's urgent I speak with you. Blane Martin has sent me a summons. He's suing me for the property. He claims Nonnie signed a contract to sell to him. What should I do?"

She stared at her phone and asked herself if something in the file box might prove Martin to be wrong, or worse, correct. "Annie's Albatross," she mumbled under her breath, before starting the car and driving to the hotel, placing the file box on her bed, and thumbing through the folders. Folders containing Blink's letters and the folder labeled "Noah" stayed on the desk. None of the remaining folders in the box produced anything resembling a sales contract. There were invoices, pages torn from tablets written in Annie's youthful penmanship, and routine correspondence to and from the Wessler Real Estate firm, but nothing connected to Martin.

"I must not panic," KT hissed. "I must not panic."

Her cell phone jolted her. Graham's reassuring voice calmed her. He advised she should not worry; meritless lawsuits comprised another of Martin's bullying tactics.

"It's unfortunate, but you must hire an attorney," Graham lamented. "My business concluded sooner than expected, which means I'll be home tomorrow afternoon. Here are names of two excellent attorneys."

KT wrote the names, thanked Graham, and ended the call. She telephoned the first name given, and the man was in court. She phoned the second attorney, a woman named Lyntha Bishop. KT reached attorney Bishop as she prepared to leave her office for the day. Lyntha Bishop's professional manner and the fact she was aware of Blane Martin's reputation eased KT's mind. After arranging an appointment for nine o'clock the next morning, KT settled back into the corner chair and grabbed the television remote control, hoping for a diversion from her dilemma. Stub's unopened envelope lay buried under papers, and displayed on her laptop, the Poole family tree awaited her next click.

"I can't do this now," KT sputtered to the computer. "Not now."

LADY WITH A BLUE DRESS ON

yntha Bishop, Attorney at Law, greeted KT with a firm handshake and a warm, "Good Morning, Dr. Winslow. I'm sorry you're having difficulties with Blane Martin, or whatever name he's using today. What's in the folder you're carrying?"

KT handed the lawyer a folder containing Anna Ruth's will and deed to McCormick House, then detailed her encounters with Martin. While Lyntha perused the documents, KT scanned the room. Unlike Graham's office, photos of smiling children filled the shelves. A framed diploma, nestled among photos and law books, bore witness to graduation from a prestigious law school. KT estimated Lyntha Bishop to be a woman in her mid-fifties. Her smooth, dark amber complexion, pixie cut hairstyle, tailored navy-blue suit, and simple sterling jewelry created an image of refinement and professionalism, yet this black woman attorney's presence struck Anna Ruth Young's granddaughter as ironic. When the Youngs lived in Hillview, Jim Crow laws prevailed, so KT doubted a black man or black woman of the time could have held the title Attorney-at-Law.

"Dr. Winslow, why are you confident your grandmother didn't sign a contract with Martin? Did she exhibit any signs of dementia or confusion which might have contributed to her not mentioning she had? She *was* in her 90s."

KT bristled. "Absolutely not. I have medical knowledge in those matters, and she possessed a crystal-clear mind. Both her attorney, Roy Anderson, and Al Wessler said she ripped to pieces the contracts Martin sent her. She never met Martin, but she described him as a 'snake' from her phone conversations with him. She rejected selling to him because he planned to bulldoze the house. Mr. Anderson would be familiar with a contract if she ever signed one. Please call me KT."

Lyntha smirked as she said, "I believe your grandmother was a perceptive lady, KT. Martin has a reputation. I've never dealt with him myself, though, but he's an attorney. At least, he holds a law license. And please call me Lyntha."

Lyntha requested Roy Anderson's contact information. She planned to confirm KT's assertions with him and do the same with Al Wessler.

The attorney said, "I'll answer the summons. He has scheduled a court date of June 13. He's trying to scare you into folding. I'll ask for a dismissal, but dismissal is a long shot. You must decide how to proceed with the house. Do you wish to continue with renovations, or do you want to stop until we settle this? One never predicts how a lawsuit will turn out. While you believe, while you *know* you are right, it can turn out wrong. The judge may believe him. Face it, you aren't from around here. Your grandmother was old, quite old. To an objective observer, your grandmother selling the property to Martin makes total sense. Maybe she didn't inform her attorney, or she forgot! As grand as it sounds to say you'll win because truth is on your side, you may not. The search for truth is fraught with adversity, and your adversary will try to thwart the search any way possible. Truth doesn't always prevail in our courthouse. Sometimes truth gets buried. It's happened many times, I am sorry to say. I've been successful in my career, but success is never assured. I'll do my best for you, and I believe you."

"Well, I guess I must decide whether to go ahead with renovations, don't I? Thank you," KT said with a nervous sigh. As she trudged to her car, she remembered words written on a piece of paper handed to her by Anna Ruth on the fateful day by the stone wall: *The pursuit of truth is a restless endeavor, yet with it comes understanding.* Miss Mittie spoke these words to a fourteen-year-old Annie Young in 1934, and KT carried the paper containing them in her wallet.

KT started the car engine and blurted to the car's dashboard, "Nonnie, this pursuit makes me plenty restless. The only thing I *understand* right now is Blane Martin is a treacherous, dishonest, sorry swine who doesn't abide by truth!"

****

Larry crawled from beneath the pedestal sink in the half bathroom on the main level. His wide toothless grin and sudden military salute brought a meek smile from KT.

"Hey, General Katie Doc! Looky here! Water's a comin' out of the faucet real fast. Ain't it great? We got water everywhere. And check this out." He flushed the toilet. "Voila! That's French, ain't it?"

KT laughed aloud this time. "This is great, Larry. I must tell you something, though."

Larry leaned against the stair railing and recoiled. "Uh, oh. This don't sound good, Katie Doc."

KT explained the case with Blane Martin's lawsuit and expressed her uncertainty whether to continue the renovation.

"I'm confused and torn, Larry. The heating and air conditioning company is coming day after tomorrow to begin their installation. Maybe I should postpone it. I don't want you to keep working if I'm going to lose the property. If demolition is its future, there's no use in continuing."

Her sorrowful eyes spanned the home's interior—its walnut-stained woodwork, the high ceilings, the living room with its handsome stone fireplace and polished walnut mantle. The thought of demolition brought her to near tears.

Larry shifted from one foot to the other. He studied the floor. He gazed at the ceiling. His lips pursed when he addressed KT.

"Now, you listen here, Katie Doc! The ole son-of-a-motherless-goat ain't gonna take this away from you. No sir! He won't do it. No sirree! You got truth on your side, gal!"

"I hope it is, Larry. Boy, I hope it is. Truth doesn't always win, though."

Larry pulled more Juicy Fruit from his pocket and stuffed it into his mouth. He insisted he harbored no intention of stopping as he chomped the huge wad.

"If you postpone the heat and air dudes, I'll keep workin'. There's plenty to do here. Don't you worry, it'll be okay."

KT scrutinized Larry's hardened face as it softened into his more familiar grin. He wagged a finger and mouthed the silent words, "It'll be okay" before heading upstairs to test the bathroom fixtures.

She wandered into the kitchen. From the sink, KT gazed out the window into the front yard, imagining again the view when Ellen Young stood at the same sink, African violets blooming on the sill, long ago.

"Katie Doc, you still here?"

Flustered, she called, "Oh, I'm daydreaming, Larry. I'll leave you now. I won't delay the HVAC work. Do you realize your confidence is contagious? Call me if you need me."

KT strode through the door toward her car. When she collapsed into the driver's seat, she cupped her hands around the steering wheel, rested her head on them, and closed her eyes. Her petite body decompressed and slumped against the wheel as if comforting arms embraced her, and within a moment, she felt a force. Peace? Love? Trust? A spirit? She delayed for an indeterminable period of time, silent, taking soft breaths, before she sat upright, started the engine, and drove away.

****

The little bell clanged as KT closed the door at the Historical Society office.

"Hello again, Emmaline. Got a minute?"

"I do. How are you?" Emmaline pushed a couple of papers to the side and rested her elbows on the desk, her umpteen bracelets clanking as she did. "What's going on, lady?"

"I've received a message from the monument company advising me they have cleaned and straightened the three tombstones at Creek Road Cemetery. They installed a tombstone for my grandmother. My plan is to drop by their office and pay this afternoon. The funeral home can bury Nonnie's ashes whenever I say. Does the Historical Society need to schedule the time, or may I do it?"

"You may bury the ashes whenever you wish. Are you planning a service?"

"Um, I doubt it. Nobody who knew Nonnie lives here. It will be me alone, I guess." A frown crossed her face.

Emmaline read the sadness and confusion on KT's face.

"I'll be happy to go with you. You shouldn't be alone. Please tell me when you plan to bury your grandmother's ashes, and I will go with you or meet you there. Please."

KT clutched Emmaline's hand in both of her own before expressing her appreciation. Her mood darkened as she related the news of Blane Martin's lawsuit, challenging her ownership of McCormick House. The scowl on Emmaline's face morphed into anger.

"I'm glad Graham suggested you call Lyntha Bishop. She's an excellent attorney, and if anyone can beat him. . . the . . ."

"Snake?" KT interjected.

"Snake is a kind word for him! How dare he try to cheat you out of your property! I wish I could help you, but I don't know how! If anybody can whip this skunk, I'd put my money on Lyntha Bishop."

"I hope so. We have accomplished a ton. It's not only the money, either. The thought of everything being torn apart makes me sick. My grandmother didn't want it to happen. I'm going to the hotel now, Emmaline. Unfinished business waits for me on my computer."

Before KT left, Emmaline called to her, "Did you locate the people you were searching for in North Carolina?"

KT's smile returned. "I did! I found the family through the site you steered me to. Now, my mission is to locate any living descendants and speak with them. Thank you for your help. You're a marvelous friend!"

Emmaline rose from her desk and escorted KT to the door, giving her a long hug.

"Oh, Emmaline, one more thing. Have you ever seen a manuscript written by William Walker Brown entitled 'A History of Hillview and its Surrounds?' Nonnie told me about it. He wrote it in longhand on loose pages, and when Nonnie lived here, the public library kept it in a box in their storage room."

"No."

"Where is the library?"

"It's at the corner of Main Street and Market. It's not the same building your grandmother patronized. They expanded back in the 1960s by removing three houses next to the original building."

****

KT parked at the front of the rambling building. True to the 1960s, the library now assaulted the eye with a fading, multi-colored metal facade. "This is one ugly library," she muttered under her breath as she opened the double glass doors.

KT waited at the counter. Soon, a middle-aged woman appeared from a room behind the counter. The librarian's muddy brown hair and brownish dress presented a dreary air, but her inviting smile erased KT's initial impression.

"Howdy doo! May I help you?" the woman chirped.

"Yes, you may. I am trying to find a manuscript, a handwritten manuscript. This library held it back in the 1930s. They didn't display it on a shelf because it wasn't a bound publication, but the librarian kept it in your storage area. I'm wondering if it might still be here. I've written the title and author on this paper. If it's here, I'd love to see it."

The librarian examined the paper. She clicked on a computer keyboard, searching for William Walker Brown's manuscript. Perplexed, she shook her head and opened a drawer from under the counter. Thumbing through cards filed in the drawer, she hummed a tune with an occasional, "Nope" emitting from her lips.

"We're computerized nowadays," she said. "These files in the drawer contain titles of obsolete or damaged books not listed on the computer. I don't see it here, and it's not on our computer. Why do you think it was here?"

"Mr. Brown wrote it in the late 1800s, and it was fragile. Folks considered Mr. Brown a historian, and his children gave the manuscript to the library when he died in the 1920s."

"Let me get our head librarian. Won't you step over here, please? I'll be right back."

KT stepped aside. She noted a bank of occupied computers against one of the library's walls. Another librarian assisted a young man at the counter while several patrons browsed shelves. KT's hopes of getting her hands on Brown's manuscript faded. She feared it thrown away when construction turned a small-town library into a larger one.

Soon, the librarian emerged with an older lady attired in a cobalt blue dress. The blue dress lady requested KT follow her to a back office, where she closed the door and sat behind a desk, pointing to an adjacent chair in which KT should sit.

"My name is Lacy Albright. I'm the head librarian, but I'm retiring next month. You're searching for Mr. Brown's history?"

"Yes. Are you familiar with it?"

"I am."

"Do you know where it is?"

Lacy Albright scrutinized KT with suspicion. Lacy came across as being in her mid-70s with gray-streaked umber hair. More stylishly dressed than the woman who earlier assisted KT, she peered at KT through circular blue spectacles which matched her dress.

"How did you learn of this manuscript, may I ask?" she asked KT.

"From my grandmother. She lived here for a time when she was a young girl and was a friend of Mr. Brown's daughter, Berta Simmons. I am KT Winslow, and I've inherited the old McCormick property west of town where my grandmother and her parents lived. I'd love to read it if possible."

Lacy's cocked eyebrow made it apparent she knew the identity of KT's grandmother. Her hushed voice asked, "Was Annie Young your grandmother?"

"Yes! Annie Young. Anna Ruth Young. Did you know her?"

Lacy laughed at KT's comment and snorted, "Oh, no! I may appear ancient, but that was way before my time! My grandmother was Georgia Albright, and she was the librarian here. She was acquainted with your grandmother and briefed me on the story of Mr. Brown's manuscript. Annie's discovery of it and the manuscript's secret created a disturbance in Hillview. Did your grandmother relate details to you?"

"Yes."

"Well, after Annie left for college and her parents moved away, Grandmother moved the manuscript from the library to her house because she caught the other librarian trying to toss it into the garbage. Grandmother took the train into Washington, D.C. and had the loose pages bound into a proper book. The bookbinder did a first-rate job. Those handwritten pages were fragile beyond belief. Grandmother waited until the other librarian died before she brought the book back to the library and placed it on a reference section shelf. It was around 1955. Anyhow, she confessed the story to me when I was a child, and when she retired, she asked me to keep an eye on the book to make sure nothing happened to it. Well, when the city took on library construction in the 1960s, the library staff started packing books in boxes to get ready. I was a teenager. Grandmother instructed me to get the book. Because my grandmother was Georgia Albright, the librarians let me mill around and snoop. I found Brown's manuscript while they were busy packing, so I sneaked out with it. We had no library for close to two years while they built the addition and remodeled the old section, and Grandmother died during the time of renovation. Years later, when I became the librarian, I believed such a fragile book could deteriorate sitting on a shelf manhandled by people, so I kept it home where it sits today. I plan to donate it to the Historical Society, but it either slips my mind, or I don't get around to it. I believe Emmaline Conrad will take proper care of it, and I must deliver it to her."

KT had difficulty believing her ears. How encouraging to learn someone besides Annie and Berta Simmons, a person still alive, valued the manuscript! KT doubled down.

"Did Berta Simmons ever . . ."

"Replace the missing pages?"

"Yes! Did she?"

Lacy chuckled and clapped her hands together. "You bet she did! But with those pages replaced, old, oh, what was her name? The other librarian? Ah, yes, Florence Bigler. Miss Bigler wanted to get rid of Brown's manuscript. Those missing pages exposed the secret of one of Hillview's finest families, don't you see?"

"I have been working with Emmaline on the cemetery where those murder victims are buried, Mrs. Albright. I am planning to inter my grandmother's ashes there. The Historical Society owns the cemetery because Tobias Hill left it to them in his will. The Society wasn't aware they owned it until my recent discovery."

Lacy Albright slapped a hand on her desk and hooted a muffled, "Whoopee!" before grabbing a notepad from her desk.

"What splendid news. Please write your telephone number here, and I will call you tomorrow after I come to work. I will bring Mr. Brown's book for you. Please get it to Emmaline and explain the story behind it. Oh, I'm not a Mrs. I'm a Miss and proud of it. I never married, which makes me an old-fashioned old maid librarian, and I love it! Please call me Lacy."

KT smiled and wrote her name and telephone number on the pad. Following a few minutes of chit-chat, KT exited the library and all but floated to her vehicle. A day beginning with worry and fear moved toward a satisfying end. Her computer waited at the hotel, primed to yield the information KT's grandmother longed to discover. She knew the location of William Walker Brown's manuscript and would soon hold it in her hands. Creek Road Cemetery was ready to receive Anna Ruth's ashes, and optimism began to replace much of the darkness in KT's heart.

Before KT could start the car, her cell phone alerted her to a call. Graham had returned to Hillview. He suggested dining in quiet and discussing recent developments. KT agreed to rendezvous at Birdie's Bistro, where she found Graham at a corner table for two near the window.

"Hi, KT. Have a seat. Are you okay? How are you doing?"

"I'm fine. Believe me, I am. I met with Lyntha Bishop this morning. She will take my case and answer the summons. I feel somewhat better after meeting her. Do you believe Martin can win this?"

Graham hesitated. He drew a deep breath and said, "I wish I had an answer. My gut says he cannot. But he's sneaky and conniving. He wants your property, and he will do whatever he can to get it. The word honest doesn't apply to Martin, but Lyntha is a talented lawyer. I'm sorry you're having to face this. Everything has proceeded as smoothly as possible before this. How are things at McCormick House?"

"Fine, fine, fine. Water, septic, and electricity are operational, and the heating and air conditioning guys arrive tomorrow. I considered postponing installation, but I'm going ahead with it. Larry is busier than . . ."

"Ants at a picnic?"

"Yep! A perfect way to put it."

Graham said, "Let's eat and forget Blane Martin for a while."

KT brought Graham up to date on the Creek Road Cemetery clean-up and her plans to speak with the funeral home on the topic of Anna Ruth's ashes. She even leaked a sliver of information regarding William Walker Brown's history of Hillview.

"I want to tell you more, but I wish to do it when Doan Hill is present, too. I must arrange a proper time."

They bade each other goodbye, and KT went back to her hotel, climbed into pajamas, and eased into the desk chair. Despite the day's tiring events, her curiosity involving North Carolina's Poole family restored her energy, and she clicked at computer keys well into the night.

SISTERS, BROTHERS, AND UNSUNG HEROES

T hanks to material Euladora Monroe posted on the genealogy website, solid information on Noah Poole's family appeared within reach. KT gasped when an essay written by Noah's older sister Ibby flashed upon her computer screen.

My Family Story
By Ibby (Isabel) Poole Kirk
August 14, 1924

My children solicit reliable recollections of my early life, so said recollections will not be lost when I leave this earth. I shall divide this document according to time periods.

KT skimmed through Ibby's remembrance until she arrived at the section of most interest to her, which she read with rapt attention.

Pa cared not for talk of war. He refused to engage in such discussions with neighbors. Brothers George, Jacob, and Theodore spoke mightily of it as they worked the fields, but my younger brother Noah appeared unconcerned. When war arrived, our house erupted into conflict. Pa refused to consider secession, but North Carolina seceded. The state's action caused Pa acute distress. What further distressed him was the fact my brothers' beliefs split our family into two factions. George and Jacob agreed with Pa to stand by the Union. Our grandfather fought in the Revolution, and Pa did not abide breaking the Union. Despite Pa's stance, soon after secession, my brother Theodore joined the Confederacy. George and Jacob fled to east Tennessee to join Union forces there. My beau at the time accompanied George and Jacob. He perished at Shiloh.

Hard times haunted us after the brothers left. Pa's health deteriorated. Noah, Ma, and I kept the farm going with as much help from young sister Mamie as possible. Pa died one afternoon in the field. As a result, our lives took a powerful downward turn. We let fields go and experienced difficulty finding food.

The worst befell us in March 1863. Rebel soldiers arrived at our house and kidnapped my sixteen-year-old brother, Noah. Ma attempted to stop the marauders, as did I, but they rode away with him. Those foul, uncouth men forced Noah to take one of our horses. A cloud of red dust as they rode off burns my mind as a last memory of my younger brother. We never saw nor did we receive word from Noah again. I believe this loss scarred Ma worse than losing Pa. Noah, a mere boy, stolen from us! Ma attempted to learn his fate without success. She badgered people who kept military records to no avail. It was as if my brother never existed. She prayed to receive a letter from him, but none arrived, nor did word of his fate. I often caught her staring at the front gate, hoping to see him ride toward her, a jubilant smile radiating across his sweet, youthful face. We assume he joined the thousands slaughtered in their dreadful battles. Where his body rests is known to the Almighty alone.

Ma, Mamie, and I suffered more food shortages and barren fields after Rebels abducted Noah. The Home Guard stole our pigs and most of our chickens. They returned the following day to steal our cow. Their constant threats of violence toward us made for an unease I never hope to experience again. We were fortunate nothing came of their threats, and we suffered no more damage from the Home Guard or other roving savages.

An encounter with a group of Union soldiers occurred at one point. These men apprehended three hens, but Ma pleaded with them, explaining two sons served in the Union Army and we had no food. An officer questioned Ma as to my brothers' regiments, but she did not possess those details. She showed the officer Jacob's most recent letter, which the officer read with intent interest. After instructing the other soldiers to set the hens on the ground, he and each soldier tipped his cap to Ma and me as they rode away.

A neighbor's kindness provided us meager sustenance from time to time, such as boiled field greens and, once, a delicious wild turkey. We boiled pine needles for tea because of coffee's scarcity. Although distasteful at first, we accustomed ourselves to its pleasant aroma and found its taste satisfying. Our neighbor's circumstances grew as dire as ours toward war's end.

Townsfolk shunned us because George and Jacob fought for the Union. When Ma first applied for county assistance, Old Man Gimble denied her application, but when she reminded him two of her sons were Confederates, he relented and tossed her a bag of flour. He knew Theodore, and he claimed to have heard rumors of Noah's conscription. Ma suspected Gimble himself sent the Rebels to take Noah. She thought him an unsavory man, as had Pa. Her pride never allowed her to seek relief again. I roamed the farm, searching for any critter I might shoot using Pa's gun, and I found rabbits plentiful for a time. With no salt to cure meat and no flour to make bread, our diet became one of catch as catch can. Thank the heavens our remaining chickens produced eggs, and because the Home Guard did not steal our rooster, our tiny flock multiplied.

Theodore suffered an acute injury at Chickamauga, severing his left leg below the knee. After lengthy hospital stays and infections causing further amputation, he returned to us before war's end, but his inability to be of use in the fields contributed to his turn to the drink. He received the position of postmaster in town, but his troubled mind and physical disabilities, coupled with overindulgence in spirits, led to his dismissal. Bitterness toward his situation in life contributed to his death in late 1866 after Jacob and George returned home following Lee's surrender. In a stupor, Theodore fell from his bedroom window. Jacob and George placed Theodore in the wagon and delivered him to the doctor in town, where, despite the doctor's efforts to save him, Theodore met his demise.

George, though injured in a skirmish, suffered neither Theodore's trauma nor his fate. George's injury comprised a crushed leg suffered when his horse fell upon him. The leg healed, but its twisted and stiff circumstance with frequent pain prevented return to battle. His superiors assigned George to a unit called the Invalid Corps, and he served as a guard at the Union prison camp in Point Lookout, Maryland. At war's end, George returned to us. George employed the loveliest hand carved cane to assist him in walking. He explained the doctor who treated his injured leg presented the cane to him. This man, not a military doctor but a civilian member of the Quaker faith, lived outside a township in the northern Shenandoah Valley. George spoke of a delightful colored man named Russell, who worked for the doctor and carved the cane. A tall basket containing canes for those needing such accommodation sat on the doctor's back porch. George's grandson has the cane now. I always admired it.

Jacob experienced no injuries during the conflict, and I remain astounded at his ability to come through unscathed. He achieved the rank of Major. When he returned to us following Lee's surrender, he slept for one entire day and through the next afternoon. Jacob appeared his former self, but he often retreated to a swing in the front yard where melancholy overtook his countenance.

Ma's health deteriorated toward war's end, and afterwards her age, heavy toil, stress, and grief took its toll. She fell ill on a Wednesday, and despite a visit from the town doctor, she succumbed on Saturday, March 16, 1867. George, Jacob, Mamie, and I buried her next to Pa and Theodore.

Hard times during and after the war left the farm in wretched condition. Before Theodore's death, relations between Theodore and my other brothers grew more troubled because Theodore refused to accept Confederate defeat due to his belief in The Lost Cause. The other brothers considered him a traitor. George and Jacob did their best to plant and return the farm to production, but *this task proved daunting. George's gimp leg prevented participation in heavy work, and after Theodore's death, Confederate sympathizers in town turned against us again. Because of this, purchasing available supplies grew more contentious, so with enormous reluctance, George and Jacob sold the farm to Old Man Gimble. His low price offended us, but we required the pittance we received to move elsewhere. George and Jacob's pensions aided our finances. With much trepidation, the four of us, George, Jacob, Mamie, and myself, bade farewell to our home place. We headed to Raleigh, which was spared the devastation endured by other southern cities.*

Leaving our farm proved to be the wisest of decisions. Not long after our arrival in Raleigh, George secured a position with the old "Sentinel" newspaper while Jacob and I found employment with the Briggs Hardware Company. Later, George helped young Mamie get a position in the editor's office at the newspaper, and within two years, she married Arthur Robbins, a delightful journalist. Mamie and Arthur later settled in Illinois. George became successful in the newspaper business and ended his career with what is now "The Raleigh Times." Although Jacob struggled for a time, his leadership experience during the hostilities led him into a successful legal and political career after leaving North Carolina for Maryland. Both brothers ultimately married, and I, of course, met the acquaintance of my dear Mr. Kirk, the finest of gentlemen, and we married two years after my arrival in Raleigh. I returned to our home place once when Mr. Kirk and I traveled west to his cousin's wedding in Asheville. We discovered our former farm overtaken by fields of cotton. Sharecroppers lived in our house, and we solicited permission to place flowers on my family's graves. The most accommodating woman who lived there joined us.

She informed me she cared for the graves herself. I thanked her for this mighty generous gesture, and after placement of the flowers, Mr. Kirk and I continued on our way. Sadness and memories accompanied the rest of our journey until celebratory wedding festivities relieved my mind of such emotions.

KT's throat tightened as she read Ibby's traumatic recollections. The sad and often miraculous story of Noah's family and thousands of others traversing mine fields of starvation, scavengers, grief, and illness amazed her. She now understood how Noah's abduction affected his family, and she understood she must honor Anna Ruth's unrealized mission. At that moment, KT accepted the obligation to enlighten Noah's family regarding the boy soldier whose only goal after abduction was to return to his family.

One revelation in Ibby's remembrance left KT thunderstruck. Had treatment for George's crushed leg been at the hands of one Doc Mueller? Everything made sense—the location, a Quaker doctor, the cane carved by a black man named Russell. Russell Hill, Blink's great-grandfather, carved canes for Doc Mueller's patients, and Mueller paid him handsomely for his work. KT learned this truth from Anna Ruth.

"Oh, please! What if George was at Doc Mueller's when his little brother Noah came upon Union troops in Blantons' field behind the stone wall?" KT said to her blinking laptop screen. "Where was *George* injured? It had to be near the Mueller property. Is it conceivable the Union patrol was George's? Was *George* in Blanton's field the same time as Noah? Could *George* have shot his own *brother*? Oh, my God in Heaven, I don't believe this!" She covered her face with two trembling hands.

****

Sleep did not come. KT tossed in bed for hours, her mind racing from Noah to Stub O'Connor's offer, to Bluff County's problems, and back to McCormick House and Blane Martin in a never-ending circle. As a result, when the sun rose, she lay awake still, dwelling on the previous day's happenings, annoyed at herself for not yet examining Stub's proposal and berating herself for getting no sleep.

Sunlight peeked into her room beneath the curtains. "It's no use," she sighed as she rose to start the day.

When she reached McCormick House, it bustled with action. Installation of heating and air conditioning was well underway. Larry, a saw in hand, emerged from beneath the overgrown boxwood in the front yard. A pile of cuttings consumed a corner of the yard.

"Good mornin', Katie Doc! You strike me as plumb tuckered out. Want coffee? I brought my coffeemaker and plugged her in next to the kitchen sink. Them dudes is workin' everywhere inside, so I figured I'll make myself busy out here. This here boxwood will be a baby tree after I get done. Doan Hill can plant somethin' small under it. Don't worry. I won't kill it. It's lived a long time and deserves to stay."

"Thanks. I believe I will have a cup. You're one thoughtful guy."

"Nope. Not thoughtful. Coffee keeps me a goin'. It's pure selfishness!"

They entered the house, and KT spoke to the HVAC supervisor, who assured a complete installation within three days. She and Larry poured themselves a cup of the hot brew and returned outside to sit on the front porch steps.

"Katie Doc, if it's okay with you, I want to sleep here at night."

Larry's statement startled KT, as she observed solemnity overcome his usual perky self.

"Well, uh, it's fine, Larry, but why?"

He took a long sip of coffee, and his eyes narrowed. "I worked late last night. With electric, I can work at night now. When I started to leave, I seen a light way out back in the woods near the stone wall. It was movin' toward the house. I went to my truck and got my super-duper light-up-the-skies flashlight and shined it back there. When I did, the light disappeared. Didn't see nothin', but I believe with the trouble you're having, it's best for me to stay out here. I'm a real light sleeper. Everything I need is here now."

KT hung her head in resignation. She longed to believe the light belonged to teenagers living in homes beyond the stone wall and not to persons of ill intent, but her gut calculated otherwise.

"Where will you sleep? The bed upstairs is a frame with no mattress. You can't sleep on it. I don't want to put you in danger or to make you uncomfortable. Your suggestion is most thoughtful, but I can't ask you to forego the comfort of your own home."

He snorted and stomped his foot on the bottom step. "Katie Doc! I got me a sleepin' bag as puffy and comfy as can be. I camp and fish and hunt with it. Don't you worry. I'll be fine. The idea of that son-of-a-biscuit-eater beatin' you out of this don't sit well with me. It don't sit well with me one whit! I'll be fine and dandy. It's settled, now, ain't it? Ain't it?"

KT paused as a slight whooshing sound left her lips. "I'm not crazy about the idea, but I guess it's settled. Please call the Sheriff if you suspect mischief."

Larry rose from the steps and, with a sweeping salute, roared, "Will do, General Katie Doc. I will do!" He stomped over to the front flowerbed and resumed his shrubbery trimming project.

KT returned the coffee cups to the kitchen, waved goodbye to the men working inside the house, and strolled toward the woods at the property's rear. She worked her way through nearly impenetrable underbrush, tree limbs, and vines before stumbling upon the deer path she and her grandmother had traversed the previous fall. When she reached the stone wall's remnants and the clearing where Anna Ruth unveiled her secrets, KT surveyed her surroundings. Signs of spring peeked through the covered ground, and it did not appear as dismal as when she last trod the land, but the scene depressed her. Three cigarette butts and two empty beer cans littered the ground under one of Graham's No Trespassing signs. Homes on the other side of the wall and rock ledge, the ones Anna Ruth referred to as "monstrosities," were faintly visible, but emerging foliage would soon obscure them from view. KT plunged her hands into her jacket pockets and ambled back to the house.

"Larry, I'm returning to town. Call if you need me."

Hidden among limbs of the overgrown boxwood, Larry's voice boomed forth. "Bye, Katie Doc! Don't you fret on nothin'!"

As she hurried past Larry's turquoise truck, she stopped to peer into the bed of the truck, where a sleeping bag, a camping stove, and a box of assorted canned goods sat. Next to a suitcase rested a cooler, filled, KT assumed, with Larry's favorite brand of sweet tea, but the sight of a shotgun in a rack across the truck's rear window elicited a gasp from her lips. She debated with herself whether she should confront him, but she realized the reason for the gun and Larry's wish to stay overnight at the work site might be legitimate. Downcast, she returned to Hillview.

****

KT arrived at Jones and Little Funeral Home the next morning. The receptionist greeted her and buzzed Mr. Jones, who invited KT into his office. The two agreed upon a date for burial of Anna Ruth's ashes, one week from Friday at three o'clock in the afternoon. KT drove to the library and met with Lacy Albright.

"It's a grand morning!" Lacy grinned. "I have William Walker Brown's volume here for you. I read it again last night. My, oh my, he delves into secrets! I can only imagine how disturbing it was when your teen-aged grandmother exposed the biggest one."

KT accepted the leather-bound manuscript. With a tender touch, she thumbed through the thin parchment pages for a moment before addressing Lacy.

"Thank you. I wish to read it myself. With your permission, I'll take it back to the hotel, read it tonight, and deliver it to Emmaline tomorrow. I'm grateful beyond words your grandmother took such care with it, and you have, too."

Lacy acknowledged KT's gratitude and asked, "When do you plan the service to bury Annie's ashes?"

"Funny you ask," KT replied. "I this minute came from the funeral home, and we scheduled the burial a week from Friday at three o'clock."

Lacy stammered, "This, uh, this may be presumptuous of me, but do you mind if I attend? I feel, I feel as if I, I know her. Grandmother thought her a delight, a brave girl who followed her heart."

"Why, I'll be honored for you to come. It will not be a traditional service, but I am inviting a few others. Please join us. You learned Annie Young's story first-hand from your grandmother. You *must* be there! Please come."

Lacy took KT's left hand into her wrinkled one and brought it to her lips. "This library was my grandmother's life besides my father. My grandfather died young, leaving Grandmother and my dad, nine years old, alone. She passed her love of books to me, and she related stories of Hillview's people. Grandmother shared the tale of this manuscript, of Annie and old Mrs. McCormick, as well as her uppity daughter, Susie Rutledge, with me several times. Grandmother adored Mrs. McCormick, and she admired your spunky grandmother. Georgia Albright hated when Dr. and Mrs. Young and Annie left Hillview."

"Thank you. I needed to hear these words today, Lacy."

After a quick hug to Lacy, KT hurried to her car, phoned Emmaline, and scheduled an appointment for the next morning. KT promised Emmaline an exciting surprise and asked her to put the burial service on her calendar. A phone call to Graham went to voicemail, so she left a message about the service. She drove to Tobias Hill Nursery to apprise Doan Hill.

After KT went over the arrangements, Doan retrieved his cell phone, logged the date and time of the burial on his calendar, and asked, "Will you explain every piece of this mystery to me, please?" His puzzled smile begged an answer.

"I will, but at the cemetery. Others must learn the story, too, and it's best to explain at one time. I promise you, it's important. Please bring Amy if you can."

Still puzzled, Doan shrugged and replied he planned to attend. "Amy and I will be there, you bet. I always welcome any Grandpap Blink stories. I loved him a lot, and I couldn't be here doing what I love if it weren't for him. Amy and I enjoy mysteries, too! Thanks, KT."

****

A hasty check at McCormick House affirmed the boxwood resembled a small-scale tree, but HVAC work blocked the front door, prohibiting entrance into the house, so KT returned to the hotel. With William Walker Brown's manuscript clutched in her arms, she entered the elevator and punched the third-floor button. As she headed toward her room, she spotted a scrawny older chap standing in front of her door, shoving something under it.

Her spine tingled. KT whipped around and raced to the stairway, where she flung open the door and galloped down the steps to the lobby. When the man exited the elevator, she pointed toward the fellow and in a breathless whisper asked the desk clerk, "Is he a hotel employee?"

"No," the young woman said.

KT hastened out the hotel door and observed him entering a rusty SUV caked with mud before driving out of the parking lot. She scribbled the license plate number on a page inside the notebook she carried and returned to the lobby.

"Who is that man?" she asked the clerk.

"No clue."

"Is he a guest?"

"Maybe."

Exasperated, KT rushed to the elevator, reached the third floor, zoomed toward her room, and flung open the door. A yellow page torn from a legal pad lay on the floor, its message scrawled in red marker.

Get out of town. Now. You can't win. Let him have it. He will hurt you.

Her phone's vibration caused her to drop the device.

THE SHADOWS KNOW

Graham's voice reverberated through the phone. "Hi there, Dr. Winslow. How's it going? I got your message. Next week at the cemetery is fine, and you can bet I'll be there."

KT did not respond. The man at her door and the message he left unsettled her. Words did not come, and she stood mute in the room's doorway.

"KT? KT? Are you there?"

A meek, "I'm here" response alarmed Graham.

"What's wrong? Where are you? I'll be there in a minute! Is everything okay at the house? Are you hurt?"

"No, I'm not hurt. I'm scared. I'm at the hotel. Can you come, please? I'll wait in the lobby."

Graham appeared in the lobby and found KT slumped in a chair holding the yellow paper. He rushed to her and settled in the chair beside her.

"When I got out of the elevator, I saw a man shove this under my door. I've never seen him before. What does this mean?" She gave to note to Graham.

Graham read the note, set it on the table between the two chairs, and took his cell phone from his shirt pocket. He punched numbers and said, "Glenda, Graham Wessler here. Is Sheriff Cortez available? Great. Thanks."

Graham provided Sheriff Cortez a brief recap of the circumstance surrounding KT's property before advising he and KT would meet him at the Sheriff's office in ten minutes.

****

Sheriff Cortez, a burly fellow with a handlebar mustache and round belly, welcomed KT and Graham. After KT gave him the mysterious man's license plate number, Cortez, muttering incomprehensible noises, plunked away on his computer.

"The car is registered to a Stanley Clinkenbeard. You heard of him, Graham?" Cortez asked.

"Name isn't familiar."

KT inserted, "The desk clerk said the man wasn't an employee. How did he have my room number? Desk clerks are careful not to divulge such information, aren't they?"

"I'll call the hotel manager," responded Cortez.

Sheriff Cortez learned from the hotel manager no one named Stanley Clinkenbeard worked there, but a woman named Betty Clinkenbeard worked in the hotel restaurant as a hostess. She was on duty. The hotel manager summoned her to his office and handed her the telephone.

Sheriff Cortez took notes as he spoke with Betty Clinkenbeard and inserted several "Um, hmms" as he listened to her answers to his questions. When he completed his questioning, he asked to speak again with the manager.

"Cal," Cortez addressed the manager, "Don't be hard on her. She was trying to be helpful. Sounds as if she's upset and afraid she'll get fired. Thanks for helping me."

Cortez leaned far back in his chair, and KT thought he might fall over backwards. He twirled his mustache and put on a pair of bifocals before glancing at his notes.

"This Stanley Clinkenbeard does odd jobs for Martin, and he overheard Martin talking to somebody on the phone describing this lawsuit he's got going against you, Dr. Winslow. Whatever Martin said alarmed Stanley, and he asked his daughter, one Betty Clinkenbeard the restaurant hostess, if you were staying at the hotel. She found your room number on one of your restaurant receipts and gave it to her dad. Of course, she shouldn't have done it, but she believed she was doing the decent thing. Betty confessed her dad fears Martin might harm you. I don't wish to cause her trouble, and I don't want to put the old codger in a predicament with Martin. He needs the work, even though he can't stand his boss."

Graham asked, "What should KT do? Someone has been prowling around after dark. If you try to reach Martin, I can guarantee you he won't answer your call. He's a phantom. This crafty hombre doesn't have an office; where he lives is a mystery, and he evades internet searches to the point it suggests he doesn't even exist."

"I'll order a patrol car drive-by day and night. I can't do much else because Martin hasn't made direct threats. Is this old gent making a mountain out of a molehill? It's conceivable. Dr. Winslow, be aware of your surroundings. Alert your lawyer to this development. I instructed Betty to have her father contact me if he has knowledge of any plans or actions harmful to you or your property, and I reiterated I will keep his information confidential. We'll keep tabs on the house to make certain everything is okay."

KT and Graham left the office and drove to McCormick House, where they found Larry upstairs framing the bathroom shower, trying to steer clear of the HVAC workers.

"This place is on the move!" Graham's cheerful declaration, an attempt to raise his client's spirits, elicited a meager half-smile from KT.

"Hey, Graham Cracker! Hey, Katie Doc! Ain't this joint lookin' spiffy? Them dudes is working fast, and I'll be ready to tile the shower lickety split."

"It's a remarkable improvement," Graham said. "I understand you intend to stay out here at night. Still the plan?"

"You betcha!"

"It's a solid idea, and here's why." Graham explained the latest development while KT wandered into the kitchen and studied the two men on ladders.

Larry assured Graham he would pay attention for possible mischief and agreed to call Sheriff Cortez if anything was amiss. The two men spoke in whispered undertones before Graham gave Larry a thumbs-up sign and strolled into the kitchen where KT stood, staring out the window over the sink. He put his arm under her elbow and escorted her to the front door. She said nothing.

"Bye, Larry. See you tomorrow!" Graham yelled to the second floor as he and KT left the house.

"I'm frightened and deflated," KT confessed as Graham backed his Jeep out of the driveway and headed toward Apple Ridge Road. "I've been optimistic. Bringing the house into the twenty-first century and turning it into a pleasant home for someone gave me a sense of purpose. The cemetery is in fine shape and ready to receive Nonnie. My research on Noah is panning out, too. I've discovered his last name and family story thanks to Emmaline, and I expect to locate Noah's relatives and deliver the story of what happened to him. I'm eager to solve this family mystery for them. Now this mess happens because of a slimy, dishonest sleazebag. Nonnie called Martin a snake. He *is* one!

Graham, I feel as if someone punched me in the gut and kicked me to the curb."

"I can empathize. Who is Noah?"

KT shook her head and said, "It's a long story, and it's one you won't believe."

"I'll bet I will. Why don't you try me? Listen, I've got dinner in the slow cooker at home. I'm uneasy about taking you back to the hotel right now. You're disheartened, and you don't need to be there alone. Come have dinner at my house and introduce me to this Noah person. I'm a decent cook, if I say so myself."

She reflected for mere seconds. "Thank you. I appreciate your thoughtfulness. To be honest, I dreaded dinner at the hotel, especially if Miss Clinkenbeard is on duty."

****

Graham's home, a stone and brick two story dwelling near Hillview's Town Park, featured a well-kept lawn and inviting front porch. It reminded KT of English cottages seen in travel magazines.

"Don't be afraid of my killer guard dog. Jingle will try to lick you to death, but she won't bite," Graham advised as they walked through the front door. Sure enough, the minute they entered the house, Jingle greeted Graham with wags and licks and ran around him three or four times before fixing on KT.

"Should I pet her?"

"Of course."

KT held out her hand, and the timid Sheltie retreated, yet within seconds her tail wagged again, and she accepted KT's attention, then zipped back to Graham for another lap around him.

"She's sweet, Graham. How long have you had her?"

"Four years. A friend had the mother, and he thought I needed a companion. He gave her to me when she was a puppy, and I must admit, she's my best buddy. She runs with me every morning and hogs the bed at night. Ready for dinner?"

KT found the eclectic décor of Graham's home appealing. The aroma from the slow cooker drew her to the kitchen where she concocted a salad. In less than twenty minutes, they sat at the dining room table enjoying a simple meal, with Jingle concentrating on every move, hoping for any spilled morsel.

"You were going to come clean on who Noah is," Graham reminded her as they completed their meal. "Let's go to the living room. It's more comfortable. I'll handle the dishes later."

Thus began the tale Anna Ruth related on a crisp fall day. Ensconced in a comfortable easy chair, KT divulged the entire story to Graham: Miss Mittie, Blink, the murders, and finally, Noah's story. The revelation took a while, and Graham absorbed everything without expressing emotion, surprise, or disbelief. His acceptance of the narrative surprised KT.

"Whew, you've told me one helluva story!" He rubbed his hand over his mouth and stroked his mustache. "I appreciate why you want to bury your grandmother's ashes in Creek Road Cemetery and why you're determined to restore McCormick House. Your grandmother was something, wasn't she?"

"Yes, she was. You're not weirded out? I spilled the beans on a strange, an extraordinary tale."

"No. If it's what your grandmother conveyed, it's what she experienced. I'm glad you trust me enough to confide in me. Everything is obvious now. I wish I'd met her. Dad enjoyed and respected her tremendously, although he never met her in person. They spoke on the phone and corresponded through email. He thought her a delight. I'm guessing you are telling me this story in confidence."

"I am, for the time being. Thank you."

A relieved and grateful KT returned to the kitchen and began clearing the table. Graham followed, and they put the kitchen in order. When KT confessed to being tired, they started toward the door where she spotted a framed photo on a table near the entrance and took it in her hands. She faced Graham.

"My wife and boy," he said. "I took the picture a month before the accident. He was a spunky little guy. I keep this photo on the table so I can talk to them when I pass by. Your story of Noah? I hope someday *they* will visit me."

They left for the hotel, and Graham walked KT to her room instead of saying goodbye in the lobby.

"Thank you for being such an exceptional friend, Graham. I'm optimistic. I'm not afraid of bully Blane Martin, and I'm confident I'll win my case. Don't worry, if something is amiss, I'll brief Sheriff Cortez and you." She began an almost uncontrollable giggle. "If you can throw Martin's buddy over a stone wall, I can see you launching Martin himself into the air!"

Graham flexed his arm muscles, and they both laughed before he departed. The hour was late, but William Walker Brown's yellowed manuscript lured her to its fragile contents. She settled into her pajamas, snuggled into bed, and began reading. Within minutes, KT fell asleep and did not awaken until morning.

Lyntha Bishop's call awoke KT, whose groggy, raspy voice answered.

"I'm sorry to call at such an early hour, KT, but I wanted to alert you the judge will not dismiss the case. Didn't figure she'd agree, but we needed to try. I've received an affidavit from Roy Anderson, your grandmother's attorney, and Al Wessler sent me one yesterday. Both help confirm our position asserting your grandmother didn't agree to sell to Martin. I requested an earlier court date, and the judge granted my motion. She scheduled the hearing a week from next Thursday because a slot opened. Ten o'clock."

KT thanked Lyntha and provided details on the note shoved under the door.

"We don't want to cause Mr. Clinkenbeard trouble, Lyntha, but can you present this threat without betraying his identity?"

"It's possible. Please drop off his note at my office. I'll be in court this afternoon, so leave it with my administrator. Oh, KT, do you have any papers with your grandmother's signature? We may need it."

"I'll go through the files." KT dressed and took William Walker Brown's manuscript with her to breakfast.

She mulled over the manuscript as she ate when her cell phone intruded.

"Katie Doc, ole Larry here! Somebody come drivin' up without no lights on around midnight. I jumped out of my sleeping bag when I heard the pup I done talked about barkin' and makin' a ruckus. Well, I grabbed my shotgun and ran to the first floor and peeked out the front window. A dude got out of a truck and started a walkin' to the front porch, but I flipped on the porch light. Then I opened the door. When I asked him what he wanted, he saw me with my gun and started a runnin' back to his truck. Man, he peeled outta here like crazy!"

"Oh, gosh, did you call Sheriff Cortez? Did you recognize him?"

"Too dark to see. I called. A deputy come, but the dude was long gone. I thought the barkin' pup was gonna take off his leg. Then, poof, no dog! It always disappears; it's magic. Guess what I got?"

KT, shaking, asked, "What?"

"The license plate number! Ain't it somethin'? And guess what else?"

"I can't imagine."

"Dumb fool was drivin' a truck with Martin's name on it. Ain't it the most stupid thing? I reckon he thought nobody was out here. I can't figure what he was goin' to do, but he didn't do it!"

"Did you pass on the license number to the deputy? And describe the logo on the truck?"

"You betcha!"

"Oh, Larry, thank you for being alert! They have moved my court date to a week from Thursday, so we should settle this mess then. I appreciate you more than you'll ever know!"

"It's okay. I'm gonna get to work now. Don't you worry. Everything's gonna be hunky dory. I already left a message for Graham Cracker. You don't need to call him."

KT finished her coffee while pondering the possibilities of Bitsy standing guard and the likelihood of more trouble. She retreated to her room and devoured the rest of Brown's manuscript. The section disclosing the murders intrigued her the most, and she grieved for Albert Blanton and his best friend William Walker Brown, as well as for Brown's father,

H.G. Their innocent involvement altered their lives, and fifteen-year-old Phoebe Mueller never recovered from what she viewed in the field beyond the stone wall. The tragedy of an 1863 early summer's day remained a secret until Annie Young verified it through Brown's manuscript and exposed the secret.

KT closed the manuscript and, tucking it under her arm, left the hotel for the Historical Society, where Emmaline greeted her with a loud, "Yo, KT!" Emmaline's bracelets clanked as she waved at KT.

KT explained William Walker Brown's manuscript to Emmaline and presented it to her with a flourish.

"Lacy Albright at the library wants you to have this. Her grandmother, Georgia Albright, took pains to protect it. She even had it bound into this book. You'll find it illuminating."

Emmaline embraced the book with care and swished back and forth as her flowing skirt created a slight breeze. Her joy at receiving the treasure radiated throughout the sunny room. With reverence, she placed the manuscript on her desk, patted it with a tender touch, and told KT she planned to take it home with her after closing time to "learn more of this intriguing town's history."

After a few minutes of conversation, KT returned to the hotel. It pleased her the monument company agreed to add Noah's surname to his gravestone in time for her to take a photo to share with his Poole descendants. Yet, thoughts of Blane Martin and his attempt to steal her property consumed her, which postponed the search for Noah Poole's living relatives. Now, she must sift through every scrap of paper in the cardboard file box for something bearing Anna Ruth's signature.

KT thumbed through the box until a folder at the back caught her attention. Labeled "For Sale" on the tab, the folder held notes to and from Graham's grandfather, Harry

Wessler, and from Al, dating back to the 1970s. KT discovered no contracts from Blane Martin, but copies of letters between Anna Ruth and Al Wessler contained her signature. These were not originals, but copies, and KT found no correspondence referring to Martin. However, a contract with a roofing company for the tin roof installed fifteen years prior displayed her original signature across the bottom.

"Will we need more samples? Oh, I wish I had those six filing cabinets here," she hissed. "Those must hold her signature on lots of things. I have letters from her in my condo, too! I bet Al has the originals of these letters in his fat binder Graham showed me. We'll have to trust what we have."

Following her declaration, KT began her search for living branches of Noah's family tree. Her fingers flew on the laptop's keyboard. Research confirmed Ibby Poole Kirk's descendant, Euladora Monroe, served as the Poole family genealogist. Further finger tapping and exploration led KT to record Euladora's telephone number and address before turning off the computer.

KT pulled the folder containing Anna Ruth's account of Noah. The notes refreshed KT's memory of the tortuous journey leading Noah to the field behind the stone wall and the events which followed his arrival there. She heaved a heavy sigh and closed the folder before returning it to the cardboard file box.

She spoke to her image in the mirror over the desk. "Okay, Kathryn, if I contact this Euladora Monroe, how on earth do I explain this whole bizarre thing to her? I can't mention *Noah* told my grandmother this tale. She won't believe!"

The mirror returned a blank stare, which KT countered by sticking out her tongue and making a clownish face. She slammed her laptop shut and placed the papers with Anna Ruth's signatures and the warning note from Stanley Clinkenbeard into an envelope. Then, KT drove the short distance to Lyntha Bishop's office, where Lyntha's assistant accepted the papers and promised to give them to the attorney.

KT arrived at McCormick House and found the HVAC crew cleaning debris. Larry thundered greetings from the upstairs shower where his tile installation was underway.

"Hey, Larry, it's getting near dinnertime. I'll be back in a flash with eats!"

She drove to town and purchased two takeout orders of hamburgers and onion rings. When she returned, she and Larry ate at the kitchen table, enjoying a conversation which allowed her worries to retreat for a time. Larry planned to start work in the kitchen soon, painting the newly installed drywall and cabinets and installing a new floor before appliances arrived. His exuberance for the entire project reinvigorated KT. Larry's optimism comforted her, and she thanked him for "keeping me sane" several times.

"It's gonna be okay, Katie Doc. Don't you bother about no tomfoolery around here, neither. Between me and the dog, nothin' bad gonna happen. My cousin Clete comes tomorrow. You wait and see. Everything will be tickety-boo. Go on, now and don't worry none!"

TRUTH AND CONSEQUENCES

C lete arrived to assist with drywall, other chores, and to rebuild the stone wall. He brought his sleeping bag. Sounds of hammers, loud music, and laughter split the silence for hours upon end, and within several days, Larry finished painting kitchen cabinets and installed kitchen flooring. Appliances arrived to complete the bright and engaging kitchen space, and the built-in hutch begged for dishes to grace its cream-colored shelves.

"Whaddya think, Katie Doc?" bellowed a voice from the study where Ellen Young once spent hours at her sewing machine. Larry peeked around the corner. "Clete's a whiz at drywall, and we'll finish dang soon. I'm gettin' excited!"

The progress pleased KT, but Blane Martin worries nagged as the court date loomed. More calls from Rightmore frustrated her, and a perusal of the contents in Stub O'Connor's envelope elicited consternation over her inability to reach a decision on her future. As a result, she busied herself with preparations for Creek Road Cemetery's intimate burial the day after the hearing. Survey stakes now marked the boundary around the sliver of land Charlie Taylor gifted to James Hinshaw years ago, and KT's visits to the cemetery delighted her with its pristine, straightened tombstones. Noah's full name now graced his stone. A spanking-new stone stood next to Noah's, this one etched with Anna Ruth's name, birth, and death dates, and Larry's repaired and painted fence glistened in dazzling sunlight. Thanks to Doan Hill, the pruned and restored lilac bushes Ned and Blink planted in 1934 rendered the spot one of peaceful reverence. The sign company would install a sign declaring the graveyard Creek Road Cemetery in coming weeks.

KT postponed contacting Euladora Monroe, keeper of the Poole family tree, until after the hearing and burial of Anna Ruth's ashes.

****

Thursday morning of the hearing arrived, and KT met Lyntha Bishop at her office. They discussed strategy and proceeded to the courthouse, where Graham and Al waited. The men's presence provided moral support, and Al came prepared to testify to the fact Anna Ruth refused Martin's offers. KT squeezed both of their hands before she and Lyntha took seats at a table facing the judge's bench. Graham and Al selected two seats behind them.

Soon, Blane Martin sauntered into the courtroom. He held a thick folder in his hands, and his shoes clunked on the floor before he slouched into a chair at a table across the aisle from KT and Lyntha. No acknowledgment of either the two women or the Wessler men came from him, but the powerful aroma of men's cologne lingered in the air as he passed, causing KT to scrunch her nose.

"All rise," instructed the bailiff standing by a door.

The judge entered the courtroom. Her meticulous makeup, her stern face, and the brisk click of stiletto heels hinted at a no-nonsense tribunal. She took her seat behind the elaborate judicial bench featuring an intricate carving of Lady Justice and cleared her throat. Lyntha had prepared KT with the information local attorneys referred to this judge as "Fashionista Fran." She was, in Lyntha's opinion, fair.

"Good Morning," the judge intoned as everyone took a seat.

"Good Morning, Your Honor," replied Lyntha as KT smiled at the judge and repeated the greeting.

Martin said nothing. He glared at the robed woman behind the bench, an intimidating glare, and he did not acknowledge her greeting with word or gesture.

KT wondered if Martin may have responded in his same bullying manner if the judge were a man. Here he sat in front of a female judge, with a female attorney seated across the aisle who planned to rebut his claims. Based upon Martin's reputation as a blowhard and bully, KT decided his reaction to a male judge or attorney might have been the same.

Fashionista Fran shuffled through papers on her desk and addressed both parties. Her demeanor implied annoyance, but KT could not discern the object of the judge's displeasure. Martin, the plaintiff, spoke first, prefacing his remarks with a biblical quote.

"Judge, to quote Romans 7:15, 'For what I am doing, I do not understand; for I am not practicing what I would like to do, but I am doing the very thing I hate.' Judge, I despair I must resort to pursuing this legal action against Miss Winslow. Completing my mission of developing the ignored and neglected property her grandmother sold to me and turning it into a masterpiece of significant value, providing four elegant homes for Hillview residents, is my fervent desire. I do not wish to be present in this courtroom today. In all sincerity, I do not. However, I am forced to press on with this judicial proceeding because Miss Winslow refuses to concede to my ownership of the real estate once owned by her grandmother. She continues to defy my legal contract with her grandmother and makes reckless improvements to an uninhabitable dwelling. I am standing before you in this hall of justice to enforce what is righteous. Righteous!" Martin's voice grew bolder and more forceful as he spoke, while glaring at the judge with each word he spit forth.

The judge nodded and directed her stone face toward Lyntha, who rose to speak. In a calm voice, Lyntha explained the facts. She emphasized Anna Ruth willed the referenced property to *Doctor* Winslow. She insisted no signed contract between Anna Ruth and Martin existed because Anna Ruth rejected Martin's attempts to buy her property. Martin made no payments to Anna Ruth, and he attempted to buy the property from Dr. Winslow by sending *her* contracts which she returned.

"Why, Your Honor, did Mr. Martin present my client with contracts to purchase the property if he already possessed a signed contract from Dr. Winslow's grandmother? This makes no sense."

"Mr. Martin, did you present Dr. Winslow with contracts to buy the property in question?" the judge asked.

"No, Judge, I did not," Martin deadpanned. "Why on earth would I send contracts when I am the rightful owner? *That*, Your Honor, makes no sense."

KT gasped and grabbed Lyntha's sleeve. Lyntha did not flinch, nor did she exhibit emotion at the lie flowing from Martin's pursed lips. KT, furious with herself because she did not make copies of the contracts Martin sent her, felt her heart race and fiery blood permeate her freckled face, turning it the color of Lyntha's crimson scarf.

Back and forth between Lyntha and Martin kept going as the judge questioned both. No, KT did not keep the contracts he sent her; she tore them into pieces and returned them to him. Martin persisted in denying such contracts existed. He presented the judge with a contract between Anna Ruth and himself, unsigned by Anna Ruth. When the judge pointed out the absence of the woman's signature on the contract, Martin passed the judge a copy of a letter from him to Anna Ruth. Dated two weeks before she died, the letter thanked her for agreeing to sell to him at an insultingly low price.

I enjoyed speaking with you this morning when you agreed to sell me your house and four acres near Hillview.

The contract containing my signature is enclosed, as is a stamped and addressed envelope. Please sign the contract, keep one copy, and return the other copy to me. As soon as I receive the contract, I will mail you a certified check for the proceeds. It is my pleasure to conduct business with a delightful and generous woman such as yourself. Rest assured, homes built on the property will be of the highest quality, as is each Martin home.

Yours truly,
Thomas B. Martin, Esq

"You will be enriched in every way so that you can be generous on every occasion, and through us your generosity will result in thanksgiving to God."

2 Corinthians 9:11

The judge examined the contract and the letter and glared at Martin before admonishing him with a sarcastic sneer. "Mr. Martin, Dr. Winslow's grandmother did not sign this contract. What are you intending here?"

Blane Martin, aka Thomas B. Martin, aka Thomas Blane Martin, aka whatever name he used for the day, retorted, "Judge, Rule 847B dated September 27, 1968 states when a verbal agreement exists to a contract, one party's signature validates the contract. This constitutes precedent. My letter to Miss, er, *Doctor* Winslow's grandmother proves she agreed to sell me her property. Under the precedent of Rule 847B of the state statutes, the contract is valid."

KT's heart felt as if it might burst through her chest. The term "Annie's Albatross" stabbed her brain again, raising her ire and making her wish she had never heard of Hillview or McCormick House. She sat as still as possible as Lyntha rose to rebut Martin's assertion. Lyntha presented a copy of Anna Ruth's will, an affidavit signed by Anna Ruth's attorney Roy Anderson, and the affidavit signed by Al Wessler, each stating Anna Ruth refused to sell to Martin. An affidavit KT signed attested to the fact Anna Ruth advised KT of her inheritance of the property in question. Lyntha specified Rule 847B, issued during the Vietnam conflict, followed a precedent set in 1944 when a state resident serving in the armed forces during World War II could not sign a contract in person to sell his home because he was fighting Nazis in France.

"Your Honor, Dr. Winslow's grandmother harbored no intention of selling to Mr. Martin. As the affidavits I've presented state, she ripped up every contract he sent her. Mr. Al Wessler will testify to that effect under oath. She intended her granddaughter to inherit the place. The woman was lucid, and she wasn't fighting in France or Vietnam. Mr. Martin claims he did not send Dr. Winslow any contracts. This is false. False! Dr. Winslow handled those contracts as her grandmother had and returned them to Mr. Martin in pieces. Dr. Winslow will testify to this truth under oath. Under oath, Mr. Graham Wessler will testify Dr. Winslow advised him of the contracts, plus he was present when Mr. Martin trespassed on the property in question and discussed the contracts he sent to Dr. Winslow. The letter Mr. Martin purports to have sent Dr. Winslow's grandmother is dated two weeks before she died, but I suspect Mr. Martin wrote it a few days ago as a ploy to prove his false point. Dr. Winslow is renovating *her* property for resale. *Her* property, Your Honor."

"Mr. Martin, nowadays, legal documents are often signed electronically. Why didn't you send the contract to Dr. Winslow's grandmother in that manner?" asked the judge.

"Your Honor, the woman was incredibly old. Why, I did not consider she could navigate online documents. Her mind was, well, let's leave it at the fact she was old."

Lyntha rose from her chair. "Your Honor, Mr. Martin's assertion is false. Dr. Winslow communicated with her grandmother by email each week, and Mr. Wessler's affidavit contains email correspondence from the woman. She possessed a rational mind and navigated online documents without difficulty."

Judge Fashionista Fran said nothing for several painstaking moments. She thumbed through and re-examined the papers presented to her before leaning back into her chair and rocking for a few interminable seconds. The judge placed her elbows on the bench and entwined her fingers with each hand, sizing up Martin. Her gaze pivoted to KT, who perched as still as she could, considering the fierce fluttering of her insides made her fear she resembled a shivering dog in a frigid rainstorm. The judge examined pages again before turning to Martin. His face bore the earmarks of every schoolyard bully as he attempted to intimidate her. He did not blink; he stared, his eyes shooting invisible daggers at the woman. The judge sighed and curled her lip. She shuffled more papers before her focus again rested on Blane Martin.

"There is no need for witness testimony. I find for the defendant. Mr. Martin, considering the lack of credible evidence to support your claims, those claims appear to be fabrications. You waste my time, Dr. Winslow's time, Attorney Bishop's time, and the time of the Wessler men who appeared here to testify. In addition, I find you responsible for attorney fees Dr. Winslow has incurred and for all court costs. Dr. Winslow, continue your renovations with the knowledge you are the rightful owner of the property in question. Best of luck to you. Good day. Court dismissed."

"All rise," bellowed the bailiff.

The judge shot a disapproving scowl at Martin, scooted her chair behind her, and swished out of the courtroom, her heels clicking on the hardwood floor before the others could stand. The bailiff closed the door behind her with a bang and motioned toward the courtroom's exterior door as a signal for the others to leave. KT squeezed Lyntha and stumbled over her seat to hug Al and Graham. Her face exuded joy as tears flowed. When Graham provided his handkerchief, she dabbed her eyes and leaned into him, nearly collapsing into his arms.

Martin turned to leave but paused to face KT with a menacing sneer across his pale, anemic face.

"You won't sell the place to anybody else. I'll see to it."

Graham held KT closer, and Lyntha rushed to plant herself between KT and Martin.

"Are you threatening Dr. Winslow, Mr. Martin? Are you? If you are, I'll have you in court again. You lost. Get over it. Your cheating scheme didn't work. You lost. I'll get a restraining order against you if you don't leave right now!"

With beads of sweat forming on his face, Martin stormed the aisle and exited the courtroom, slamming the door behind which left a disagreeable scent in his wake.

"Come on, gang!" exclaimed Graham. "Let's get a celebratory lunch before the stench of Martin and his cheap cologne asphyxiates us. What say you?"

"Yes, let's go!" cried Lyntha. "Birdie's Bistro, here we come!"

* *

The foursome met at the restaurant and selected a yellow clothed table in a corner. Their laughter caught Birdie's attention, and she asked what they found humorous when she brought water to the table.

Graham said, "Guess what, Birdie? Truth and justice prevailed at the courthouse today! It's a fine day in Hillview!"

Birdie's smooth dark skin radiated as she joined in the laughter. The diners made their selections and kept up the jovial banter as they ate. KT's obvious relief at Judge Fashionista Fran's decision extended to the other three.

Al admitted Martin concerned him. "He may be the sneakiest businessman I have encountered or heard of in my entire real estate career. I can't fathom how he stays in business. Where does he get his money? What type of lawyer is he? He changes his address so often, nobody can find him. Truth prevailed today, thank heavens."

"Thanks, Al," said KT. "I must admit, it scared the wits out of me to think he might win."

Graham addressed Lyntha. "You asked KT for examples of her grandmother's signature. Were you concerned he might present a forged signature on his contract?"

"Yes." Lyntha scanned the room, assessing other diners, before speaking to her companions. The attorney whispered, "The forgery possibility worried me. I learned day before yesterday Blane Martin is facing disbarment in the three states where he holds a law license. The contention is Martin withheld settlement funds owed to a client from an automobile accident in which she sustained severe injuries. The client alleges he forged her signature on a document increasing his share of the settlement; she never signed such a document. He transferred the funds in question to his personal bank account. This is serious. He may be disbarred and prosecuted. It concerned me he might try this forgery tactic on KT. This was the reason I wanted samples of your grandmother's signature, KT. He's in boiling hot water over this other allegation; it's possible he was afraid to try forgery today. I can make you aware of his problem because the case is in the public domain."

"I didn't realize Martin has legal clients besides his development business. Wonder how he gets these clients?" Graham asked.

Lyntha shook her head.

"He's a phantom, flitting from one state to the other, always pretending he's a devout Christian. What a phony. What a crooked phony!" Graham growled.

"Yes," agreed Lyntha. "Shakespeare wrote a line in *The Merchant of Venice* which applies to Martin. 'The devil can cite Scripture for his purpose. An evil soul producing holy witness is like a villain with a smiling cheek.' The quote has been on my mind ever since I took your case, KT."

Al said, "A perfect description. Old Will Shakespeare was an observant soul of the human condition, wasn't he?"

Everyone agreed with wry chuckles.

KT cleared her throat and addressed the others. "Thanks to each one of you for your help! I can't imagine how I could have gone on without your support and your friendship. My gratitude and love for you overwhelms my heart right now. My grandmother compared life to travel along a red dirt road, and this stop on my red dirt road of life has strengthened me, I believe. It's solidified my faith I am doing the right thing in resurrecting McCormick House. As Lyntha warned, the truth doesn't always prevail, but today it did. Thank heavens it did! After lunch, I'll drive to the house and tell Larry. Thank you! I cherish each of you."

The group departed and promised to reconvene the following afternoon at Creek Road Cemetery. Before exiting the restaurant, KT stopped to remind Birdie of Anna Ruth's recollections of Olivia Watson's Diner.

"I'm going to rustle through my box of pictures and memorabilia. Maybe I'll find a photo of your precious grandmother if I'm lucky!" Birdie declared.

****

Larry whooped and hollered when KT revealed the judge's decision. He danced around the living room, grabbed KT's arm, and swung her around the room before a sudden halt.

"I shouldn't have grabbed you," a sheepish Larry mumbled. "I'm sorry if I offended you."

"Quite the contrary, Larry Locks! I felt like dancing myself!"

"I done told you not to worry, now, didn't I? Don't you worry no more! Clete and me will get the indoors finished as soon as we can. We'll beautify the outside, re-build the stone wall, and it'll be ready for the new owner. Another coupla weeks should do it, I do believe. I thank you for invitin' me to the service tomorrow, but I stay away from them spooky places. Don't never go to no graveyard. Thank you kindly."

KT reached out and touched Larry's tattooed arm. "I understand," she said before turning to leave. "Call me if you need anything. I'm headed to the hotel now."

"Oh, Katie Doc! I almost forgot! Looky here what Clete and me found behind the bookcase in the little room yonder. We unscrewed the big ole bookcase from the wall so we could install drywall and paint. A bunch of papers lay crumpled on the floor behind it like they fell between the

shelves and the wall. I put 'em in a bag for you. Here ya go."
He grabbed a plastic bag from next to the front door.

A curious KT removed the contents from the bag as Larry returned to his chores. She saw invoices, newspaper clippings, a few architectural drawings, and pages from medical journals. Two tissue-like papers, carbon copies of letters typed on the letterhead of Dr. Charles McCormick, Miss Mittie's husband and Susie Rutledge's father, piqued her interest. Each was addressed to Sister Margaret at the Magdalene Home in Richmond. The first one, a 1911 inquiry from Dr. McCormick, discussed his daughter Susie's tragic loss of two infants within a period of one year.

My daughter's infantile uterus abnormality allowed the first child to gestate a full nine months, but the child weighed a mere three pounds at birth and died within two weeks. Despite my medical advice to refrain from pregnancy, Mrs. Rutledge became pregnant again and suffered early pregnancy loss. Severe bleeding and internal organ damage nearly caused her death. She is desirous of adopting a child and asked me to facilitate. I understand your establishment contains many wee ones ready for a permanent home. Please advise the procedures Mr. and Mrs. Rutledge must follow to adopt a child.

Anna Ruth indicated Susie and her husband had no children, so the letter puzzled KT. Dr. McCormick's second letter offered a gut-wrenching explanation as to why the Magdalene Home never received a completed application.

While Mrs. Rutledge still aspires to adopt, Mr. Rutledge will not accept a child other than one of his flesh and blood. My daughter is depressed and bitter toward her husband, and I fear further mention of the subject may cause the collapse of their marriage. Thank you for your assistance and for your righteous work assisting the unfortunate young women in your care and finding homes for their wee ones. I am enclosing a check for $100. Please use it as you see fit.

KT's heart grew heavy. Susie, the haughty woman whose demeanor raised eyebrows and forced others to ponder her behavior, experienced tragic loss accompanied by her husband's indifference and insensitivity. In that moment, KT reached a fuller understanding of Susie Rutledge and reasoned the bitterness Susie held toward Mr. Rutledge triggered her behavior. Susie spent Rutledge's money with a vengeful flair and played her role of society matron with a distinct aura of superiority. Did she leave McCormick House to KT's grandmother out of spite for resurrecting a secret as Anna Ruth believed, or did Susie envision Annie Young as the daughter she never had? Newfound sympathy for Susie McCormick Rutledge gripped KT as she trudged from McCormick House to her car with the bag of papers tucked under her arm.

WAR AND PEACE

K T set the bag aside, retrieved a ginger ale from the mini-fridge, and poured half the can into a glass half-filled with ice. After moving her laptop to one side of the desk, she took a sip of the fizzy beverage and settled into the desk chair before exhaling a deep sigh and opening the folder containing Blink's letters to Anna Ruth. She had not touched this material for days, but an urge to read as much as she could before Anna Ruth's service the next day consumed her.

A letter written soon after D-Day in 1944 expressed great optimism peace might be at hand. Besides describing mundane happenings, Blink announced a shocking scandal and a startling clue.

June 8, 1944

Dear Annie,

I'm sure you have been listening to the radio describing the invasion in France. I feel in my bones this war will end soon. Mam and Pap danced around the cabin when we caught the word, and Ladybug jumped and barked as they cavorted. Mam grabbed me, and we danced, too, before Pap grabbed us both. We celebrated while Ladybug joined in the fun. Such grand news! Our brave soldiers will take care of business.

Do you imagine Robert will come home soon? Have you gotten letters from him lately? I know how hard it must be to have no guess of his whereabouts, but I bet our boys will win before too long and come home. Everybody can get on with our lives. I hope the end comes soon.

Nothing much is going on here. We started our crops, and the early ones are coming in now. Pap will take them to Mayfield's Market. We don't go to town on Saturdays much because Mr. Mayfield buys most of what we bring in, and gas rationing limits gas. Pap and I still work at Mr. Rutledge's mill, but with crops coming in and taking care of the Mueller property, we plan to quit. Our decision is right. Other folks need the work.

Mayor Barbour asked the band to play at Town Park on Saturday at noon for a celebration of the invasion. There will be speeches and a war bond drive. According to Mayor Barbour, Hillview will have a parade when we win the war.

Berta told Mam Mr. and Mrs. Blanton left town! It's a mystery where they went. Everybody is gossiping about it. An auditor from the federal government came to Blanton's bank and found something wrong. I haven't learned what was wrong, but it was awful, I guess. A bank person from Richmond is running the bank now. We don't keep money there, of course. It's a strange thing, isn't it? I wonder what will happen to their house and the orchard and the rent houses he owns.

*When I went to the shoe store to clean on Sunday, Mr.
Berger was there repairing shoes. He began doing repairs
not long after the war started, and with leather rationing,
people aren't buying shoes. Mr. Berger is busy with repairs
and needed to work on Sunday to keep up with his
customers' demands. He holds hope his sister and her
family can come to Hillview after the war, but he worries
every minute. I hope they are okay. He showed me a picture
of his sister Elise and her children. They are cute. The boy's
name is David, and the baby girl is Gabi. It's an old picture
before the family fled to the country. The children are older
now, of course.*

Write when you can. Peace will come, Annie.

Your friend,

Blink

KT gulped her drink and studied the letter again. Gabi?
Her brain reverberated with confusion and astonishment.
Graham's mother's name was Gabi. Could Graham's mother

be Mr. Berger's niece? If true, Elise's family must have survived the war, or was it a simple coincidence? This duality of names stunned KT, and she vowed to ask Graham as soon as feasible.

Another paragraph elicited a raised brow from KT. "Hmmm, old Clay Blanton left town, huh? Wonder what caused the Feds to take over the bank? I'll bet it was theft." She swirled ice at the bottom of her glass, poured in more ginger ale, and took a sip.

KT read the next two letters, which contained more details of wartime life in Hillview. The government designated one young man missing in action in France, gas rationing limited the band's performances, and lack of rain presented concern for the Hills' crops. No more mentions of Clay Blanton and his wife made it to the pages of Blink's newsy correspondence until the third letter, which astonished KT when she read it.

September 28, 1944

Dear Annie,

A baby! I am excited for you! This is wonderful! Mam and Pap are tickled pink, too. Mam called Berta. Berta called Mam this morning to say she went to the library yesterday and spread the word to the librarian, Mrs. Albright. Mrs. Albright always asks how you are doing when Berta goes there. Everyone is glad for you and for Robert. How long before he gets your letter with the news? Do you know where he is? Won't he be proud? It is wise to go to Doctor and Miss Ellen's and wait for the baby's birth. I hope you get this letter before you leave on the train.

I do not have much to tell. Pap and I are busy with crops. We turned the section Pap gave me permission to use for planting flowers back into crop land so we can help feed folks here. We took the truck to town on Saturday because we had gas, and we sold everything. Mrs. Rutledge came to our truck and bought beans and tomatoes. Annie, she was friendly! She mentioned you, and Pap told her a baby was on the way. She smiled. I have never seen her smile an actual smile before Saturday.

Nobody has found out where Mr. and Mrs. Blanton are. Their house is empty, and nobody has worked in the orchard this summer. The people who live in the Blantons' rent houses aren't paying rent because their envelopes with rent checks came back in the mail. It is the strangest thing. He withdrew every bit of his money and stole other people's money from the bank before he disappeared, but I'm not clued in on details. I'm repeating what Mr. Berger said.

Take care of yourself. Write to me. Robert will be a happy soldier!

Your friend,

Blink

"Oh, my, Annie's baby was my mother, my precious mother," KT said to the page in her hand. "It will thrill Lacy Albright to learn what Blink said about her grandmother Georgia in his letter."

KT felt extreme gratitude to recognize Anna Ruth still had friends in Hillview after her kindred spirit, Miss Mittie McCormick, died. Of course, Blink proved devoted, but others cared for Anna Ruth, too, including Susie Rutledge.

KT bit her lip as she read a letter written in late March 1945.

March 26, 1945

Dear Annie,

We got Miss Ellen's telegram yesterday. We are thrilled to learn the baby has arrived. A girl named Joellen! You are thoughtful to name her after Robert's mother Josephine and your mother Miss Ellen. I am glad Doctor delivered your baby. How satisfied he must have been to deliver his own granddaughter. I hope Robert hears the news soon. He will be over the moon. The reports we get on the radio hint the war may end soon. Robert can come home to you and the baby when it ends.

I bet Joellen is a beautiful baby. Mam says for you to stay in bed until you are in fine shape. With Doctor and Miss Ellen there, you have excellent help. This is wonderful!

Things keep moving forward here. Nobody has found Clay Blanton. He stole a ton of money, and the theft is a federal crime, which means he is in lots of trouble. The bank people closed his bank, and its customers go to the bank across the street or the one on South Pike. His orchard is in terrible shape because nobody has paid attention to it since he and his wife skipped town. Did I write you that people went to his orchard and picked apples last fall? The apples fed a whole bunch of folks. Mr. Mayfield went and said the fields resembled a gigantic party. There were loads of ladders and people from everywhere picking. Pap accepted apples from Mr. Mayfield, but he didn't pick any himself.

I need to go help Pap prepare our fields. Your happiness makes us happy, Annie. You will always be my best friend.

I want to meet Joellen and Robert someday when this war ends.

Your friend,

Blink

KT's tears flowed as she recalled Anna Ruth's husband Robert died during the fierce battle for Okinawa in early May 1945, a few days before VE Day. Did he ever learn he had a precious baby daughter named Joellen? It was advantageous for Anna Ruth to return to her parents' home to have her only child, and Anna Ruth and baby Joellen lived with Carter and Ellen Young for one year. However, when a professorship opening led Anna Ruth and her daughter to a Midwestern college town farther northeast, the town became Anna Ruth's home for the rest of her days. Ellen Young accompanied the two to their new residence and stayed to care for Joellen until Anna Ruth hired a babysitter. Ellen then returned to Oklahoma.

"Nonnie, you were so brave," KT murmured as she scanned the room, as if expecting to see her grandmother appear. "You deserved much more than you received from us. Oh, I wish things had been different. Please trust how I love and respect you. I doubt I could have been as brave as you. You are my hero."

KT paused before smoothing Blink's letter and re-reading it before tackling more letters in the stack.

August 16, 1945

Dear Annie,

Thank goodness this horrible war is over, but this does not bring you happiness. The Marines took a long time to send word Robert died at Okinawa. My heart hurts for you, Annie. You must stay strong. You always are. Joellen needs you to raise her as you and Robert both wanted. Annie, you are the bravest person I know. I am glad you are with Doctor and Miss Ellen and not alone.

What else can I say except I am sorry? Mam and Pap send their love. Berta is writing you a letter, and Mam is writing Miss Ellen a letter now. Please take care of yourself and Joellen. I am sorry, Annie.

I will always be your most devoted friend,

Blink

Blink's next letters described Hillview's return to normality. The town held a massive parade to celebrate victory, and Blink's band of three marched the entire route through downtown. Hillview lost three men to the war, but one survived a POW camp in Germany, another survived the Bataan Death March, and two boys came home with injuries. The end of gas rationing brought the band more jobs. The mill run by Susie Rutledge's husband ceased its wartime production of parachutes and laid off employees as it prepared to return to its prewar business of manufacturing medical uniforms. Three doctors' return meant the hospital, shuttered for the duration, re-opened. Clay Blanton and his wife remained missing despite a national search by law enforcement agencies, and Blink enclosed a newspaper article detailing Blanton's crime. The article reported Albert Blanton's son committed mortgage fraud and fled after draining the bank of all cash assets.

Because of the war, a shortage of bank examiners existed; therefore, Blanton's fraudulent activities went unnoticed for a longer period than usual.

One letter announced Mr. Berger's sister Elise Schorr and her two children were coming to Hillview to live. They and Mrs. Philips survived the war hiding at the Philips farm and in its surrounding forest. Regrettably, Nazis captured Mr. Philips and Mr. Schorr and transported them to Amersfoort concentration camp in the Netherlands before shipping them to Buchenwald in Germany, where they both perished. The businessman for whom Mr. Philips worked aided the women and children's survival after the men's abduction. He and his wife sneaked food, clothing, and blankets to them. The hiding space in the Philips's barn proved well worth the effort constructing it, and although soldiers ransacked the house and stole livestock, they never learned of the barn's hidden room. The businessman believed the local postmaster alerted the Gestapo to the men's presence at the farm based upon letters mailed to Mr. Berger prior to the entry of the United States into the war. It saddened KT to learn the Holocaust claimed the two men, yet knowledge of Elise's and her children's survival and their subsequent travel to Hillview brought a sense of profound relief.

"Gabi? Gabi! Graham's mother must be little Gabi. Her age sounds right. Oh, what a marvelous turn of events if this is the truth!"

KT continued reading. She gleaned insight into the tranquil first year of Joellen's life Anna Ruth and Joellen experienced in Carter and Ellen Young's loving home. The courage it took for Anna Ruth to leave her parents and travel with her tiny daughter to a faraway college town where she knew not one soul awed KT. Although Anna Ruth's dream job awaited, life as a single mother awaited, too. A group of war widows embraced Anna Ruth and became her constant friends as they shared their grief and daily challenges. KT determined from Blink's letters Anna Ruth and Joellen found happiness and contentment in their surroundings.

Darkness overtook the hotel room. KT switched on a lamp, headed downstairs for a light dinner, and returned to prepare for the next day. An agenda of sorts, written earlier, awaited edits, and KT completed the tribute to her grandmother she planned to read at the cemetery. She cared not to rely on her physician's handwriting in the company of her newfound Hillview friends and typed her tribute on her laptop before printing it at the hotel business center. Upon returning to her room, she jotted a handwritten note of thanks to Lyntha Bishop for representing her in such a professional manner and set the envelope next to her backpack. A hurried check of messages on her cell phone displayed another frantic one from Dr. Rightmore seeking her dates to return to work. The clinic needed her. He needed her.

"I have too much to do here," KT sighed as she typed a reply advising she needed more time than the vacation days already scheduled. She vowed to study Stub O'Connor's contract again after the cemetery service. The prospect of starting an unexpected and alternative life's chapter intrigued her more than she thought possible.

"Hmmm," she brooded aloud. "Wonder if I'll still have a job when I go home? Maine sounds better and better every day." She brushed aside the thought and gathered more of Blink's unread letters. She smiled as she read his newsy correspondence, but a 1947 letter brought forth a huge grin.

September 29, 1947

Dear Annie,

I love the picture of you and darling Joellen. She is cute. Thank you for sending it. What was your class's reaction when you took her to class when her babysitter was sick? I wish you had taken a picture of her sitting at a desk drawing pictures. She is a sweet girl, isn't she?

I have news for you. You will not believe it! I have a girlfriend. We met when the band played at Longtown three months ago. I have not mentioned it because I have never had a girlfriend or dates with anybody, and I didn't want to get you excited thinking I had a girlfriend. But she is great, Annie. It's amazing, but I can talk to her without blinking too much and without stuttering. She is real pretty, too. Her name is Ozella, but people call her Zell for short. Pap has let me take the truck to see her a few times, and the band has played there twice since I met her. I really like her. We get on well and see things the same way.

I've enclosed a newspaper clipping dealing with Clay Blanton. The bank building, his rent houses, his house, and the orchard and farm will sell at public auction because nobody has paid taxes since he skipped town.

Take care of yourself and Joellen. Everyone is fine here. I am doing more of the farm work because Pap's back and knees bother him. I planted one small plot in tree saplings I harvested in our woods, and we built a greenhouse behind the barn for flowers. We are selling them. Pap even took out a newspaper advertisement!

Your friend,

Blink

PS. Mrs. Rutledge rented Miss Mittie's house to a family who is moving here from Georgia. Mrs. Rutledge cleaned and painted the outside, and it looks real presentable. I wonder if they will stay? Ha! Ha!

KT unfolded the yellowed clipping which announced Hillview received word of Clay Blanton's death in Florida. His wife Esther pre-deceased him by two years. They lived in Florida under assumed names, so their whereabouts remained a mystery to everyone except possibly their three children, who claimed no knowledge of their parents' location. Law enforcement never found the couple, leaving Blanton's misdeeds unpunished.

"Well, well," KT mused. "Two scions of Hillview society ended up on the lam and died in Florida. I'll bet their kids knew where their parents were! This isn't much of an obituary. I wonder how his true name came to light. This article doesn't say what their assumed names were. Odd." She shrugged and set the letters aside before preparing for bed. KT desired the next day to be one of celebration and revelation, so she needed to be rested and prepared.

"Goodnight, Nonnie," she breathed as she settled under the covers and turned off the light. "Tomorrow you will be with Noah." She chuckled, winked, and added, "But you already are, aren't you?"

PARALLEL UNIVERSES

Friday morning dawned cloudy and gray, with sparse, oversized raindrops hitting the parking lot as KT opened her car door. A sudden wind gust jerked the door from her hand, almost slamming it into the adjacent car.

"Good grief," she declared to the sky, climbing into the vehicle as claps of thunder grew closer. "Oh, come on, Mother Nature! You can't rain today. You can't mess with Nonnie and me! Nope, don't do this!"

KT gripped the steering wheel and planted herself in the driver's seat as scattered drops became torrents, pummeling the car with a deafening roar. Wind whipped across the parking lot, driving waves of water against her car, causing it to sway. She clenched her teeth, glaring at the raging storm, cursing it in silence. Flustered, she waited, attempting deep breathing exercises to control her frustration. Within fifteen minutes, the wind stopped, the rain lessened, and quiet once more prevailed.

"Okay, okay, I guess one of my choice words convinced you!" KT laughed. Staring at the clearing sky, she again addressed Mother Nature with a quiet, "Thank you."

KT's first stop was Creek Road Cemetery. She needed to verify its readiness for the afternoon's ceremony. After replacing her tennis shoes with rain boots from the car's trunk, she strolled along the gravel path next to the fenced space and entered the gate. Doan Hill had pruned the two lilacs Ned and Blink Hill planted in 1934, and leaf buds sprouted. Doan cautioned KT the bushes might not bloom because of his extreme pruning, but tiny flower buds formed microscopic bulges on the greening stems. The repaired arbor with its bright white paint welcomed visitors, and feathery grass seed Doan sowed would soon be ready to mow. Daffodils had bloomed, yet their graceful and erect blades persisted. Before Anna Ruth's tombstone, a newly dug space awaited the box containing her ashes. KT stood motionless, trying to absorb the setting's tranquility and simple grace.

"This scene is as I imagine it was when Nonnie and the rest of her truth tellers stood to honor those buried here," she addressed the lone remaining sycamore tree. "You saw a horrible incident in 1863, didn't you? Yet you still stand, as grand as can be. You, Mr. Platanus Occidentalis, are the towering sentry for this little graveyard. You're over two hundred years old, and I hope you stand another two hundred. Thank you."

"You talking to the tree, lady?" barked a voice from behind her.

Startled, KT turned. "I was. It's a grand tree, isn't it?"

The speaker ignored her question. "I live next door. I've seen this reclamation and wondered what's going on. These your kin?"

"No, uh, these are friends, I suppose you might say. I'll return this afternoon with a few others to bury my grandmother's ashes here, though. The Historical Society owns the graveyard and plans to erect a sign at the front of it. Have you lived next door long?"

"Three years. To be honest, my wife and I plan to sell the house. We're trying to do repairs and put lipstick on this pig to sell it quick. When the graveyard stayed overgrown and hidden, it wasn't too objectionable, but now it's cleared, and it spooks us. Sorry, but it's true. Our house has a jillion problems, too, with cheap materials, shoddy workmanship, shortcuts everywhere. The builder did a poor job. Windows leak, bathroom tile cracks because the floor isn't level, nothing works right. I could go on, but I won't. It's one of those Martin houses. Never buy one of those."

KT frowned. "Oh, I'm sorry. I should imagine a cemetery is a peaceful neighbor, though. Did you buy your house from the builder?"

"Nah. We bought it cheap from the original owner. He said it needed a heap of work, and we took it because I'm handy. It needs more than I can do, and this graveyard isn't quiet. Sometimes at night, the sounds resemble men arguing. And digging. My wife says it's the wind in the trees, but I don't care for it one bit. We hope we can sell the house to somebody who doesn't mind being next to a graveyard. Good day to you. Sorry your grandmother died."

He shuffled across the gravel path and through his front yard before entering the house and slamming the door.

KT frowned. Graham said most of Martin's homes, fraught with problems, created massive headaches for their owners as they dealt with remediation. She sighed and tossed one last glance at the cemetery before returning to her car.

As she drove off, she remarked aloud, "Men arguing and digging, huh? Trees in the wind? Interesting!"

****

The day passed in a flash, and three-o'clock arrived with a bright sun shining upon the glistening white fence and four sparkling tombstones. Nary a cloud tarnished the sapphire sky. Did KT's admonitions to Mother Nature work their magic? Mr. Jones from Jones and Little Funeral Home stood at the gate when KT arrived. They engaged in conversation until more attendees approached. Graham, Al, and Gabi arrived together, followed in quick succession by Emmaline, Lyntha, Doan and Amy, and Lacy. KT greeted each person with a hug and a "thank you for coming" before everyone stood together at Anna Ruth's monument.

Mr. Jones performed the burial as required by county law and within ten minutes bade everyone farewell. At the same moment he exited the gate, KT placed bouquets of spring flowers on three graves, reserving a single red rose for Anna Ruth. She moved to face her friends.

"None of you knew my grandmother," KT began. "Al, you spoke with her on the telephone and corresponded, and Lacy, you knew *of* her from your grandmother, but none of you met her in person. May I introduce her so you can wrap your heads around why this graveyard is her proper resting place? Her story is one you may find unbelievable, but it's true."

KT related the story of the Young family's Great Depression journey which brought them to Hillview, where Dr. Carter Young took over the medical practice of a deceased physician. She elaborated on Annie's friendship with the physician's widow, Mittie McCormick, and of the terror Miss Mittie's fifteen-year-old sister Phoebe experienced on a spring afternoon in 1863. KT spoke of Annie's friendship with Tobias Hill, and when she addressed Doan and Amy, their tears flowed as she described Blink's letters. KT divulged the existence of Noah Poole and how his assistance uncovered the truth of what Phoebe witnessed. This revelation brought shock, perhaps disbelief, but she kept talking. The name James Hinshaw was, of course, unfamiliar, yet through KT's illuminations, each gained a profound respect for the man and the other principled people KT mentioned.

"When my grandmother and I arrived in Hillview on the day she died, she told me this story, never divulged to anyone. When she left Hillview, nobody except her husband and parents called her Annie. Well, Blink did in his letters. She went by Anna Ruth, her full name, because as she explained to me, she left Annie here. I found this truth sad, but it's the reason I had her tombstone engraved with the nickname Annie instead of her full name. My grandmother spoke to me of her search for truth and of how important truth is. Life, she believed, is a bumpy and dusty red dirt road filled with potholes and obstacles, and the destination is never clear. She came to Hillview on such a red dirt road. Her parents returned to Oklahoma on that same road, and Noah Poole left his North Carolina home in a cloud of red dust. I believe her view through the dust and dirt is honest and true. No matter what color the dirt, or the sky, or the skin, we each travel an uncertain road throughout our lives, and I am deeply grateful to have met each of you on this part of *my* journey. Thank you for your friendship and your willingness to hear my grandmother's remarkable story. Thank you for coming today!"

Lacy Albright addressed the group. "KT is correct. My grandmother, Georgia Albright, recounted Annie's story to me. I was unaware of each detail I learned this afternoon, but I'm far richer for learning. This spot is sacred. I am grateful Georgia Albright befriended and defended Annie in those days. Doan, Emmaline has the William Walker Brown manuscript. You must read it to learn more of your wonderful family."

"Don't worry, I will," Doan replied, wiping a tear from one cheek. "Grandpap Blink may have mentioned bits and pieces of this, but I was the same as lots of kids and thought family stories boring. I wish I had listened to him. KT, thank you for opening my view to more of my history. I'm proud to descend from Russell, Thea, Billy, Ned, and Cora Hill. I'm proud of Grandpap Blink. Gosh, I'm proud, plain proud!" He beamed as he thumped his hand over his heart. "They lived during a time I cannot fathom, and they paved a better road for me to travel. My road isn't one of red dirt, but it's the one they gave me, and I owe them everything. I hold a stronger appreciation for old Doc Mueller in those hard Civil War times. I've heard the story he helped slaves get to freedom, but it never hit home with me. If not for Doc Mueller, I wouldn't be living on Russell's land and following my dream. And James Hinshaw! His gift let Grandpap Blink further his education. Your grandmother's persistence made it happen, KT. I'm grateful, but grateful isn't a strong enough word."

Emmaline reached to take Doan's hand in hers, her bracelets clanging as she did. She held his hand tight as she said, "We now understand, don't we? Thank heavens KT came to town, and thank heavens Georgia Albright saved William Walker Brown's manuscript! History lives at this spot. I am grateful, too!"

Others added words of gratitude, and after several moments of conversation and hugs, they dispersed. Graham and Al, holding Gabi's arms as they navigated the gravel path, approached KT with an invitation to dinner.

"It's a quiet spot with marvelous Italian food," proclaimed Al. "Gabi and I will meet you and Graham there. Graham can ride with you and direct you to the spot. Please join us!"

KT responded to the invitation with an enthusiastic, "I'd love it! I have questions for you and Gabi! Thank you."

Al chuckled, "Uh, oh," with a smile as he and Gabi drove away.

Graham climbed into KT's car, and he directed her to the restaurant on the eastern outskirts of Hillview. Annie's story moved him. For the entire seven miles, Graham expounded on Annie's bravery, her resolve, and her devotion to Miss Mittie, Blink, her family, and every other person who became her friend.

****

Al and Gabi were preparing to sit at a table when KT and Graham arrived. Gabi gave KT a massive hug and peck on the cheek.

"Congratulations on your triumph at the courthouse and fulfilling your goal at the cemetery!" called Gabi as Al helped her into her seat. "I'm pleased you found the lovely graveyard and got permission to bury your beloved grandmother's ashes there. It's marvelous and relieves you of worry. Your words were simple and loving, KT."

"I am relieved, thank you. An incredible range of emotions has washed over me since I arrived in Hillview a few short weeks ago."

Al ordered a bottle of wine. The four chatted and gave their selections to the server.

"Excuse me, but I must ask a question," announced KT. "I am reading letters from Blink Hill to Nonnie, and several letters discuss a man named Mr. Berger who owned a shoe store here in Hillview. He had a sister in Holland during World War II. It's likely a curious coincidence, but his sister's daughter was named Gabi. Could . . ."

Graham recoiled and turned to his mother. Al took Gabi's hand as if to protect her. Gabi Wessler appeared to shrink into her chair, but her pleasant countenance never wavered as she straightened her back and spoke in a muted voice, "I am Gabi Schorr."

KT's mouth flew open as she cried, "Oh, my goodness! Blink's letters speak of your family and how your circumstances worried Mr. Berger. Last night, I read what happened to your father. I'm beyond sorry; I'm heartbroken. How horrible for you. I can't express my thoughts appropriately. Oh, Gabi!"

Gabi patted KT's left hand and winked at Al as she pushed her hair from her face.

"I was young, a baby, really. I cannot recall much before we went to the country home of my father's cousin near Amsterdam. My memories begin there."

"Mr. Philips?"

"Yes. We endured a most unusual existence. The adults did not allow my older brother David and me to play outdoors where a passerby on the road might see us. We spent our outdoor time behind the house or barn near the woods. The four adults always required silence and whispers from us children. My parents didn't venture far from the house either, although Mr. Philips went to work in town each weekday. He must have been older than forty-five, because Nazis made men eighteen to forty-five work in their factories. I remember every morning arranging our bedroom to make it appear unused. Our clothes became too small as David and I grew, and Mother could no longer let out seams, so Mrs. Philips, we called her Tante, gave Mother an old dress and an old shirt and pants belonging to Mr. Philips, whom we called Oom. Mother altered them for us as best as she could. We practiced running to a shelter inside the barn to prove who was the fastest and quietest. I can't imagine where Mother got chocolate, but when we performed those drills, she gave the winner a teeny piece. The cramped hiding space in the barn held six chairs and a dinky table with a water jug and cups. A covered bucket for human waste sat in one corner."

"Mom, you don't need . . ."

"No, Graham! KT spoke today of her grandmother's history. I don't mind sharing mine."

KT reached out to Graham's mother and said, "No, Gabi. It's painful for you; I sense it, and I merely wanted to learn if you were the little girl in Blink's letters. Please don't divulge painful memories. I shouldn't have mentioned it."

Gabi shook her head. "I am over eighty years old. I relate the story to make sure others accept what happened there."

"Mom has spoken to school kids and described her experiences during the war. She spoke to civic clubs, too."

Gabi said, "I have. Young people must learn and absorb these truths so history will never repeat itself. Despite such an existence, David and I found happiness and did not consider ourselves unfortunate. Mother and Tante tried to teach us since we couldn't attend school, but such an endeavor proved difficult without schoolbooks. This meant when we came to the States, David especially, since he was older, and I found ourselves behind in our education, plus we knew no English."

Al inserted, "David and Gabi's teachers in Hillview spent hours after school helping the children learn English after Elise, David, and Gabi arrived. Within a few months, both children became fluent, and Elise did, too."

Gabi's voice grew quiet. "Father and Oom stood near the road late one Saturday afternoon, which was unusual. Quite unusual. My brother and I were behind the barn drawing pictures in the dirt while Mother and Tante hung clothes on the clothesline. We overheard a commotion by the road and German voices, so the four of us ran to our hiding space in the barn and huddled together. A man speaking Dutch asked Oom where his wife was, and Oom repeated over and over she was visiting relatives in a neighboring town. Loud crashes came from inside the house. Tante and Oom's dog barked and barked. He was a big, gray, fuzzy dog. We heard a shot. No more barking. The soldiers, or whoever they were, entered the barn, shooed chickens outside, and hauled off the cow, but they didn't come near our hiding space. By luck or providence, they didn't have dogs with them, or they would have discovered us."

Al poured a glass of water and handed it to Gabi, who sipped it in silence for a moment.

"We listened to vehicles drive away, but we stayed hidden in the barn for what suggested forever to us. We kept silent until darkness fell. Then, we left the barn, but we found no one except for the dog lying on the ground near the road. Mother and Tante began crying because they realized Nazis had taken the men. David and I held onto each other and cried. The Nazis wrecked the house, overturning and smashing furniture, breaking lamps, searching, I suppose, for jewelry or money, but we had buried valuables, as well as Jewish items, in the woods earlier. Mother and Tante dragged the dog's body behind the house and buried him in the woods."

"Gabi, I don't know what to say! This distresses you." KT's voice cracked.

"No, no, I want to tell. In the following months, life became more challenging. We never lit lamps at night, and we did not light any fire lest we alert someone of the home's occupation. A few times, someone entered the house and looted more, but nobody checked for us. The forest became our safest refuge because its density prohibited discovery. Mother and Tante constructed a makeshift tent of heavy canvas they found in the barn, which worked remarkably well to shield us from the elements. We moved mattresses into it. Oom's elderly employer and his angelic wife became our saviors. They brought food, blankets, heavy coats, hats, gloves, clothing. In the latter part of the war, the Dutch Famine caused by the German blockade of food meant hunger emerged as our constant companion. Thank the heavens we were not in Amsterdam where starvation killed thousands. We lived in an ever-present state of fear,

232

alternating our existence between the house, the barn's hiding space, and the forest until Canadian troops liberated our country in 1945. By then, we were malnourished and, frankly, alarming to see. Oom's employer and his wife were members of the Dutch Resistance, and they informed us what happened to Father and Oom."

KT noted a similarity between Gabi Wessler's World War II experience and the Poole family's Civil War story. Both families buried monetary and sentimental items, and both experienced extreme hardships without adequate food. The North Carolina Home Guard was vicious and cruel but not as organized and deliberate as the Nazis who grabbed Gabi's father and Mr. Philips, sending them to their deaths at Buchenwald.

"War brings out the worst in humanity, doesn't it?" KT asked. "If Noah had not escaped, he may have suffered a horrible death in a Civil War prison camp. Sheer luck and the kind bravery of others saved you, Gabi, as well as your mother, your brother, and Mrs. Philips. I cannot comprehend how those who inflict such cruelty upon others can live with themselves."

Graham agreed. "Meanness and hate continue and will until the end of time, I guess. It's tragic Noah didn't make it home, but if he had, your grandmother might not have unraveled the secrets or unearthed the truth which helped set Hillview free. Mom's father would be gratified that his loved ones survived and lived a noble life here. His sacrifice saved their lives."

Gabi continued with her story. "Our life in Hillview turned out better than we imagined. We lived with Uncle Max Berger. What a kind and generous man! Mother found employment as a clerk in a ladies' store on Main Street, where she worked until age rendered her too frail. Mother, David, and I became citizens of the United States as soon as possible. Uncle Max left Mother his house upon his passing, and she lived there until her passing. She corresponded with Tante for years. Tante moved to Amsterdam, where her sister lived. Mother also corresponded with our benefactor businessman and his wife. They undertook dangerous risks to help us stay alive and hidden. Others in the Dutch Resistance lost their lives."

Al took Gabi's hand, gave it a swift kiss, and told KT he thought Gabi was the prettiest girl in Hillview, asking her to marry him not long before leaving for Army boot camp.

"She agreed, can you believe it, and we tied the knot the day after I returned home. I'm a lucky old geezer! I took over a successful business, and Graham and I grew it more. Gabi and I are blessed with two talented kids and a couple of delightful grandkids. Much of our success results from Gabi's support and work behind the scenes. Thank you for advising us of Uncle Max's concerns for his loved ones during the war. It means a lot."

KT beamed. "You're a wonderful family, and I'm thrilled and honored to consider you my friends. Blink's letters to Nonnie yield such insight into this area and its people. We are all connected, are we not? Nonnie knew of you, Gabi, through Blink's letters. It's beyond extraordinary. Did your brother David stay in Hillview?"

"No. After he completed his education, he joined the Air Force. David adored flying. He never married. In the early 1960s, my brother sensed escalation toward war in Vietnam, and when his re-enlistment date approached, he retired. After experiencing the effects of war firsthand, he could not bring himself to take part in another war. He found employment with a commercial airline and remained with them until furloughed by a failed physical exam. His heart. David suffered a fatal heart attack not long afterwards, and we lost him in 1991. I blame our stress and near starvation during the war for his heart trouble."

Graham said, "Uncle David had a marvelous sense of humor. He brought trinkets from exotic locations to my sister and me whenever he visited. I adored my grandmother Elise, too. Her outlook on life served as an inspiration to me. When my wife and son died, I remembered what my grandmother experienced during the war when she lost her husband in a horrific way and kept her family together under threat of the same outcome. Food scarcity and fear of discovery persisted every minute of every day, yet she maintained her optimism. No sadness or pessimism ever overcame her!" Graham's wide grin acknowledged to KT his deep reverence for his grandmother Elise.

Al scooted his chair from the table and announced departure time had arrived. "This afternoon has been delightful, but Gabi and I must get home. My dang foot is tingling and giving me fits because I've been on my feet most of the day. I hate to be a party-pooper, but we'll excuse ourselves. I need to get home and rest this foot on the ottoman. Graham, I'll bet KT will be happy to drop you off at your house. Stay awhile."

"Of course!" proclaimed KT. "Thank you both for coming to the cemetery and for the delicious dinner. I appreciate your kindness and your friendship. Thank you!"

After hugs, Al and Gabi left, and KT and Graham enjoyed a last pour of wine from the bottle Al selected. KT returned Graham to his house, waving as she drove away, filled with satisfaction and gratitude for the day's events. Appreciation of Gabi's extraordinary survival during World War II and her family's subsequent life in the United States overwhelmed her.

"What a terrific day! Everything is turning out better than I ever imagined. I'll sleep well tonight!" she declared to the file box on the floor and to Stub's envelope on the desk.

DEAD AS A DODO

K T awoke in total darkness to the jingling and vibration of her cell phone. She fumbled to grab it from her nightstand but knocked it to the floor. Turning on the bedside light, she squinted at the clock. Two forty-five. The phone went silent. She leaned over the side of the bed to retrieve it when the clamor resumed.

"Hello," KT's groggy voice mumbled.

"KT, it's Graham." The urgency in Graham's voice alarmed her.

"What is it? What's wrong?"

"I'm headed to McCormick House. Sheriff Cortez called. There's been a shooting."

****

When KT arrived at the property, flashing blue, white, and red lights consumed the entire area. Three police cars, one fire truck, and two ambulances jammed the driveway and front yard, and another police cruiser arrived as KT parked on the street and bounded from her car.

Confused, she stumbled through the blinding lights, trying to figure out what had happened. As she made her way between the vehicles, she spotted Graham talking with Sheriff Cortez.

"What on earth has happened?" KT screamed.

Sheriff Cortez turned and reached out to her. Taking her hand, he spoke in a slow and measured tone.

"From what we can assess, Dr. Winslow, it appears Blane Martin tried to set the house on fire when Larry Finler and his cousin confronted him."

"Is Larry okay? Is Clete okay? Are they hurt?" KT's heart pounded, and her body trembled as she scanned her surroundings.

Graham said, "Both of them are fine. It's, uh, it's Martin."

"Martin?"

"He's dead," Sheriff Cortez said in a matter-of-fact tone.

KT scrutinized the chaotic scene again and spotted Larry sitting in the back seat of a police car, his head in his hands. Clete's back leaned against the car, his hands flinging in the air as he talked to two deputies, who took notes as he spoke. Another deputy unraveled yellow police tape, strung it around a tree, and extended it to the front porch, wrapping it around one of the stone porch pillars. In a moment, she spotted the covered form on the ground.

"Dead? Martin's dead?"

"Yeah, as a dodo," Sheriff Cortez said, as he left to speak with Larry.

KT's entire body shook, and she felt faint. She willed herself to stay upright but accepted Graham's steadying arm. He led her to the cruiser where Larry sat, and they listened as Larry relayed events to Sheriff Cortez and the deputies while Graham's arm encircled KT's waist to steady her. Another deputy came from inside the house and handed Larry a glass of water, which he held in his shaking hands and gulped in mere seconds.

"As I was sayin' to these fellas, Sheriff, Clete and me was sleepin' upstairs. Clete woke up first 'cause the dog barkin' like crazy woke him."

"What dog?" Cortez asked.

"Dunno. It's a dog what hangs around sometimes. We'll see it, and before you bat an eye, it's gone. Weirdest thing I ever seen. Anyhoo, it raised such a ruckus we come downstairs to see what was wrong. I grabbed my shotgun because we've had trouble out here before tonight. You know bout the trouble. I called, and a deputy come out."

"I remember," said Cortez.

"Well, Clete flipped on the porch light and opened the door. Right away we smelled gasoline. I come out on the porch to see the dog yappin' and pullin' at a dude's leg. Couldn't see who the dude was 'cause it was dark. He had somethin' over his head, but he was swingin' his leg around, and the dog didn't let go, and the dog was flyin' around while he hung onto the dude's pants. I seen a torch kinda thing on fire in the dude's hand. He started swingin' the torch at the dog, but I swear the torch went right through the dog! Didn't hurt it one bit. Honest, Sheriff, I ain't been drinkin, neither!"

"I believe you," Cortez said as he addressed a deputy. "Get Larry more water. Clete, do you need something to drink?"

Clete shook his head, slid to the ground, and crossed his legs.

Larry said, "Anyhow, I started hootin' at the dude, and Clete started yellin', too, and the dog kept barkin', and the dude threw the torch-thing toward the side of the house. It missed the house, but it landed where them spent daffodils is over there. Next, the dude pulled a revolver out of his pocket and fired at the dog before he turned the gun on me. He missed me, but he hit the post over yonder. He aimed at me again! Sheriff, it was plumb crazy! The dog kept yankin' on the feller's pants leg and barkin', and Clete kept yellin', and I aimed and shot. I thought he was gonna kill me! Honest, I did. Honest, I did! I swear, Sheriff! I done thought he was gonna kill me!"

Sheriff Cortez nodded and patted Larry on his shoulder. He instructed Larry to stay seated and not to worry before turning to Graham and KT. He ushered them to a spot away from Larry and Clete and surveyed the surroundings before speaking to them in hushed tones.

"Dr. Winslow, my deputies found an empty gasoline can over yonder. Gasoline odor is powerful at the side of the house. The evidence is overwhelming. Martin was trying to burn down this house. If he had hit your house with the torch, he would have set it on fire. My deputies searched for the dog Larry keeps referencing, but they haven't found it. Did Martin miss hitting the house with his torch because the dog pulled him off balance? Probably. We found Martin's car parked at the dead-end. He pulled it into the weeds where it's not visible from here, and another can of gasoline is inside his car."

This information rendered KT speechless. She stared at the Sheriff and stared at the ground before her bewildered stare returned to Graham, then to Sheriff Cortez again.

"What happens now?" she asked.

"Well, I won't arrest Larry, if it's what you mean. Martin's gun is on the ground next to his body, a bullet is lodged in the stone pillar, and Larry has a corroborating witness in his cousin. Forensics will determine whether the bullet in the pillar is from Martin's gun. To me, we've got a clear-cut case of self-defense. Plus, you fortunately have No Trespassing signs posted. Martin had no reason for being here. In the

240

middle of the night? Torch? Gasoline? Come on, folks. He was up to no good!"

The forensics team arrived, followed by the county coroner. Deputies and others scurried hither and yon. One ambulance, the fire truck, and two police cruisers left the confusion, and as daybreak arrived, an ambulance departed the scene, carrying the body of one Blane Martin. Sheriff Cortez stayed behind, only leaving after the forensics team completed their work. He advised Larry and Clete not to leave town.

"Boys, I doubt if the prosecutor will bring any charges, but stay close because he will question you more. I'll return to my office and make out my report. We need to find Martin's next of kin and notify them, but where does he live, and who's his kin? It's baffling how elusive he is. He didn't want to be found. It's plain as day."

Graham's watch read eight o'clock. He left KT at McCormick House with Larry and Clete and drove into town to bring breakfast for everyone. KT, Larry, and Clete returned inside, where Larry continued recounting the events. Clete inserted, "That's right, that's right," each time Larry made a comment. When Graham returned, KT had calmed the two men and made coffee for everyone.

"Thanks for this chow, Graham Cracker," Larry gasped. "I didn't reckon to be hungry, but it sure tastes yummy."

Clete's bobbing head signaled his approval of the egg, bacon, and pancake platter.

KT said, "Larry and Clete, I want you to go upstairs and rest. Try to get some sleep, please. You've been through a lot, and you need rest. Doctor's orders, guys. You hear me?"

Graham reiterated KT's admonition. He insisted the likelihood of prosecution did not exist, and Larry and Clete should relax.

"No more work today, boys."

"Okay, Graham Cracker. We're plumb wore out. Right, Clete?"

Speechless, Clete's head reminded KT of a bobble-head doll as he nodded in agreement.

After these exchanges, Graham drove home to shave, shower, and go to work, and KT arrived back to her hotel room. She intended to relax, but nerves intervened. She kept reliving the early morning horror, alternating between pacing the room, plopping into the desk chair, and flipping through Blink's letters. Slamming the letters on the desk, she sank into the chair, collapsed forward onto the desk's top, and broke into massive body-wracking sobs.

"I should have sold to Martin the first time he sent me a contract!" she wailed. "Oh, Nonnie, why didn't you want the damn house demolished? Your time here in Hillview left you scarred. Why did you care? Susie Rutledge hung this albatross around your neck where it stayed until you died, and now the godawful piece of real estate is mine. How stupid, how arrogant of me to assume I could turn it into a home somebody might want because nobody will want to live where a killing occurred. I've created a monster, an expensive, worthless monster! What folly on my part!"

No answer came to her questions nor rebuttal to her comments. Silence. KT raised her head and searched the room as if she expected to see Anna Ruth sitting on the bed, but her grandmother did not appear.

KT placed her flushed face upon her folded arms. She regretted her return to Hillview. A simple phone call to Graham, instructing him to sell the property, would have prevented this mess, and she wished she had never heard the name Blane Martin. KT lamented she did not bury Anna Ruth's ashes next to her own mother Joellen instead of answering an imagined subpoena from within her heart.

"What was I thinking? Nonnie was right. McCormick House is an albatross, a ball and chain. I hate it, and I hate Hillview!" she hissed before falling asleep at the desk.

****

KT's cell phone revived her from a groggy haze.

"Hello, Dr. Winslow, Sheriff Cortez here."

KT flipped on the desk lamp.

"Sheriff Cortez, how are you?"

"I'm fine. How are you?"

"Okay, I guess. Drained and shaken, but I'm okay."

"I'm trying to find any next of kin for Martin, Dr. Winslow. We believe we've discovered where he lived. The clerk at the mail drop store gave us an address they have on file for him. It's a rental house in Grover. I left a message for the landlord and am waiting to learn if Martin lived there. If he did, I hope the landlord can help us find the guy's next of kin. I swear, Martin was a piece of work. He used the name Thomas B. Martin at the mail store, but it appears the name he used for the rental house was Tommy Martin. I've seen nothing akin to this for someone who acted like a big shot. I can learn on social media what someone ate for dinner, but nothing on this character is there other than his address at the dang mail drop store!"

"It's weird, isn't it?"

"You can say that again. I turned my report over to the county prosecutor, and he wasn't convinced as to the truthfulness of the Finler boys' story. Of course, he never accepts things without a thorough investigation. He and I held an extensive discussion, and it's plain to me the shooting was self-defense. The matter requires no further investigation, in my view. I'd say Hillview is lucky to be rid of Martin. It's not my call, though. It's the prosecutor's."

For Sheriff Cortez to opine in such a manner did not seem to KT fitting for a person in his capacity, but KT replied with a simple, "Oh."

Their conversation concluded, and KT squinted at the clock by the bed. Seven o'clock. Still in a daze, she washed her face and trudged to the hotel restaurant, finding the dining room crowded. The hostess seated her at a table in a corner. By this time, KT's head pounded, and hunger pangs stabbed. She selected an entrée and placed her head in her hands, elbows on the table, as she observed the other diners. Most appeared to be attendees of a business conference, and their loud chatter and laughter intensified her headache. Four men at the table next to her rose, and one turned to her.

"Want the newspaper?" he asked as he handed her a copy of the *Hillview Gazette*.

There on the front page, a picture of McCormick House beneath a bold headline, "Prominent Developer Shot Dead," sent a chill through her body. The article detailed the shooting, naming the address where the incident occurred and names of those involved. It referred to Larry and Clete by their full names, Lawrence Finler and Clethern Finler, and it mentioned Dr. Kathryn Winslow several times. The coverage ended with the county prosecutor's statement, "The shooting is under investigation."

KT set the newspaper on the table and poked at her lemon chicken dinner, one of her favorites, but it held little appeal despite her stomach's growls for nourishment. After twenty minutes of food dabbling, she pushed the plate aside. Folding the newspaper under her arm, she left the restaurant's clamor and returned to the quiet of her room.

Nervous, she ran her fingers through her hair and phoned Larry to check on him and Clete. He said they drove into town for dinner, and when they returned, the elusive terrier waited on the front porch but scampered off as they got out of the truck. KT sighed at this evidence of Bitsy's existence and proceeded to the bathroom to draw a hot bath. She lingered in the tub until the water cooled, bringing a sense of calm and closure to the trauma-filled day.

She cared not to turn on the television and risk seeing more on the shooting; instead, she checked phone and email messages, replied to those needing a response, and drifted into a fitful sleep.

****

KT awoke early. She dressed and threw open the curtains to determine whether a sunny or cloudy day awaited, but darkness greeted her. Her stomach growled, and she dressed and hurried to the restaurant, hoping for a scrumptious omelet. The restaurant opened at six o'clock, but her watch read five-thirty, so off she went to the twenty-four-hour eatery one block away.

"Hi, honey," called the hostess when KT entered the diner. "Come this way."

The hostess seated KT at a table toward the rear. Even at such an early pre-dawn hour, customers filled part of the room. Her head no longer ached, and KT found the diner's clatter and chatter uplifting.

A minibus filled with senior citizens stopped for breakfast and took every remaining seat. The hostess approached KT and asked if an elderly gentleman might join her at her table. Without hesitation, KT accepted his company.

"Where are you headed?" asked KT.

"We're a group of Civil War enthusiasts, and we're touring a few sites in the valley. Springtime presents a delightful time for exploration. We visited Gettysburg, Antietam, and Schoolhouse Ridge, and now we're on our way to obscure spots not mentioned in lots of history books."

"Marvelous! My grandmother was a professor of the Civil War period. What a coincidence. Where are you going today?"

"Civil War battles and skirmishes fill this Shenandoah Valley. Today's itinerary is Fisher's Ridge, Cedar Creek, Tom's Brook, and New Market. We'll continue south before we head home Wednesday."

"How interesting! I'm not familiar with those places, but I'm sure my grandmother was. She died last fall, and I have inherited her filing cabinets filled with lectures and other papers. I haven't examined them yet."

The two engaged in animated conversation. KT informed him of Anna Ruth's name and where she taught, and the man filled her in on the significance of the day's tour stops. In what seemed to KT a flash, the bus driver announced the bus's departure. Her elderly companion bade her goodbye with a final comment.

"Before we head south this morning, we're going to drive past a house we believe was on the Underground Railroad. It's three miles west of Hillview, and we want to take a gander at it. A doctor lived in the house, and legend has it he helped slaves reach freedom. Have you heard of the man?"

Aghast, KT practically choked on her coffee. "Mueller?"

"Yes. Is the legend true?"

KT stopped. She thought for one solemn moment before her eyes twinkled, and she answered, "I believe it's true. I'm positive."

"Hot dog! We're on our way!"

The diner emptied as rapidly as it filled, and the gray-haired tour members boarded the bus for their first stop of the day, Doc Mueller's former home on Apple Ridge Road.

KT tarried at her table and requested a second cup of coffee. She marveled at the group's stamina and interest in historical sites. The fact they were aware of Doc Mueller left her astonished and gratified.

"What a tribute to a remarkable man," she whispered to her coffee cup.

As she paid her tab at the front counter, her cell phone emitted a muffled sound from within her jacket pocket.

"Hello, Sheriff," KT said.

"Good morning, Dr. Winslow. I hope I haven't called too early."

"No, you haven't. I'm leaving the diner near the hotel."

"The prosecutor wishes to speak with you. Can you be at his office at ten this morning?"

Startled, she answered she planned to be there at the designated time.

"Thank you. This is a formality, I believe. He will speak to the Finler boys today, too."

"Have you more information on where Martin lived?"

"Not yet. I'm hoping the landlord will call me this morning."

"Okay. Thank you," KT said as she drove toward the scene of the shooting, cursing Blane Martin and growling, "Annie's Albatross" as she drove.

As she turned off Apple Ridge Road, she spotted the tour bus, hazard lights flashing, stopped in front of Doc Mueller's. The driver stood outside taking photographs of the house, and KT saw tour members snapping photos from inside the bus. The scene quelled her anger while a satisfied smile crept over her face as she reached McCormick House. Larry's truck sat in the gravel driveway, and she called to him when she entered the parlor.

KT found Larry in the dining room, where they conversed for several minutes. Larry expressed his nervousness over speaking with the prosecutor later in the afternoon, but KT reinforced the optimism Graham and Sheriff Cortez put forth.

"Don't borrow trouble," she advised before complimenting Larry and Clete on their excellent craftsmanship. After leaving the house, she stood alone in the yard for several minutes, absorbing the silence and peacefulness of her surroundings. The horror unfolding there in the wee hours of the previous day marred their serenity, and KT's brow furrowed.

A car loaded with teenagers drove past at a snail's pace, honking the horn and breaking the spell. Following the teenagers' car came another, this one bearing a well-dressed man and woman gawking at KT. When KT stared back, they averted their gaze. Both cars drove to the dead end, turned around, and passed once more for a second view of the now infamous McCormick House.

"Oh, brother," snorted KT as she climbed into her car and headed to the prosecutor's office.

NOWHERE MAN

G ood morning, Dr. Winslow," the prosecutor intoned. In his mid to late forties, his stern demeanor personified total devotion to the business of law. He wore a well-tailored dark gray suit and a black and crimson bow tie. Standing a smidgen over six feet, his bulky bone structure presented an imposing figure. "Please take a seat. I need to question you on the shooting at your property."

KT sat and read the nameplate on the man's desk. Daryl Rich, Prosecuting Attorney, took his position behind the desk and eased into its high-backed wood and leather chair.

"Dr. Winslow, you had a recent court issue with the deceased. Please relate the circumstances."

KT discussed every interaction with Blane Martin, even the bulldozer incident on her second day in Hillview. She answered each of Prosecutor Rich's questions, but it appeared to her the man was painting a laser-focused accusatory picture aimed at her.

"Did you instruct Lawrence Finler to keep his shotgun at the house?"

"No."

"Did you threaten the deceased in any manner?"

"I instructed him not to set foot on my property or I'd call the Sheriff."

"Did your attorney threaten the deceased?"

"After Martin threatened me in the courtroom, Lyntha Bishop threatened to get a restraining order against him."

"How did he threaten you in the courtroom?"

"His exact words were, 'You won't sell the place to anybody else. I'll see to it,' which Lyntha and I took as a threat."

Daryl Rich pursued his never-ending barrage of questions. KT answered each one in as calm a manner as she could muster, but despite Sheriff Cortez's assurances, KT grew more uneasy with each question. Martin tried to set her house on fire, and it appeared Daryl Rich cared not one whit. Was the prosecutor attempting to frame KT? Or Larry?

As one hour of interrogation approached, KT addressed the county official.

"Blane Martin tried to burn down my house. He fired a gun at Larry Finler! I confess I am confused. I don't understand your line of questioning."

Daryl Rich's face expressed no emotion or reaction to KT's comments. He explained to KT the necessity of his questions to "get to the bottom of this shooting" and continued his line of questioning for fifteen more minutes before rising and thanking KT for coming.

"Please stay available in case I have more questions, Dr. Winslow," he instructed, while showing her to the door.

****

KT received a call as she pulled into the hotel parking lot. Sheriff Cortez had news.

"The house in Grover *is for sure* Martin's residence, Dr. Winslow. His landlord phoned and confirmed Martin lived there. My deputy and I are headed to the place now. The landlord will let us inside so we can search for information on his next-of-kin. We're empty-handed as of now. How was your meeting with the prosecutor?"

KT hesitated before responding. "I didn't comprehend it, to be honest. I felt his questions were accusatory. His approach bothered me."

Cortez hooted and said, "It's his job, Dr. Winslow. Listen, we're at Martin's house. I'll get back to you. Now, don't you worry, you hear?"

"If you say so."

KT entered the hotel and went straight to the restaurant, where she ordered a cup of soup and a salad. Lost in thought, she did not notice Graham's arrival.

"Pleasant lunch?" he asked.

Startled, she laughed as she motioned for him to sit. "Yes. What are you doing here? Don't you have houses to sell?"

"You're funny. Not today. I got a call from Sheriff Cortez a while ago. He's at the house Martin rented in Grover. I thought I'd keep you company until we hear more, and I wanted to learn how your meeting with Daryl Rich went this morning."

Graham ordered while she detailed her meeting with the prosecutor. She cited every question asked of her and reiterated her unease with several of the questions. Graham nodded his head at each recitation but expressed no concern. When KT finished, he reassured her with a "don't worry" admonition and ate his lunch.

"Larry's appointment with Mr. Rich is at one," KT said. "Clete sees him at three. If I became worried after my meeting, I worry for Larry and Clete. I suspect Rich will grill them hard. After all, Clete's an eyewitness, and Larry shot the jerk. Oh, I suppose I shouldn't speak ill of the dead."

"He was a jerk," Graham said.

"Yeah, and that may be the only truth belonging to the late Mr. Martin." KT rolled her eyes.

"Listen, I don't have appointments this afternoon. You're nervous about the Finler cousins and what Cortez finds at the Grover house. Let's drive to your place and discuss something else. Pricing and timelines for putting McCormick House on the market need to be decided. Besides, it may be wise for someone to stay there while Larry and Clete are in town."

The possibility of more trouble slammed her. She hastened from the table, signed the check, and grabbed his arm.

"Let's get out of here!"

****

Larry and Clete had left McCormick House by the time KT and Graham arrived. When Graham unlocked the front door, the scent of fresh paint greeted them. As they strolled from room to room, KT's pleasure concerning the home's rehabilitation was unmistakable. Concerns over Blane Martin's shooting retreated to her brain's back recesses, and she expressed amazement at the home's interior.

The cream and sage tones of the living room wall, complemented by original walnut woodwork, created the perfect spot for someone to snuggle into an oversized chair and read by the fireplace. A mason by trade, Clete's meticulous cleaning and pointing of the stone fireplace and mantle provided a majestic focal point to the room. In the dining room, the original chandelier, cleared of years of dust, glimmered in the sunlight. The kitchen, however, took KT's breath. Original cabinets painted to match cream-colored walls, a shiny, refinished porcelain sink, and modern appliances reprised a classic 1930s country kitchen, but with twenty-first century touches. The farm table, sitting on a tarp to protect the floor, sported navy-blue paint. Its four chairs, strutting their matching color, rested in the corner by the washer and dryer. Navy and white checked curtains, draped over the kitchen counter, waited to be hung at the kitchen window where Ellen Young's African violets' profuse blooms brought her joy during the Great Depression.

"Graham, you were right; the quality of Larry's handiwork is amazing. He and Clete are creating a desirable, welcoming home. I'm amazed at how fast this has gone and at their craftsmanship."

"Yeah, the interior will get finished soon. Painting the exterior, landscaping, and rebuilding your stone wall come next. Larry did a skillful job of replacing rotted wood on the outside of the house. He's a whiz. I took photos of its decrepit condition before you started this job, and the renovation will amaze potential buyers!"

They sat on the porch steps as Graham presented KT with a folder containing pricing possibilities. Following a productive discussion, they reached a decision. Graham's confidence in a fast sale boosted her spirits, too, but when an older, dented and rusty car stopped in front, and its occupants gaped at Graham and KT, her mood soured.

"Hello, there!" Graham called to the men in the car. "Can I help you?"

No response. The car sped to the end of the street, turned around, and blasted back toward Apple Ridge Road.

KT studied the ground and murmured, "I'm afraid suspicion and rumors are raising their ugly heads again. Blane Martin may have been correct; nobody else will get McCormick House."

"No, these are gawkers, curiosity seekers, nothing more. Don't worry. Study your surroundings! Similar properties are hard to find. Seclusion and magnificent trees create a private sanctuary here."

"I guess," she sighed as her cell phone disrupted the conversation.

"Dr. Winslow, Cortez here. Our boy Martin was something else."

KT put her phone on speaker so Graham could hear.

"We still have found nothing confirming who his next of kin is, but we've found a bunch of other stuff validating our suspicions Martin was a crook. He must have a dozen addresses he uses for different, uh, enterprises, shall we say?"

"Sheriff, Graham Wessler here. What else are you finding? He's a lawyer, and we've learned he's facing disbarment."

"I can't go into detail, Graham, but I've got a search warrant now, and we're going through everything. Shoot, we just wanted to find his damn relatives and tell them he's dead, but it appears we've uncovered criminal evidence. I've called the prosecutor to let him in on this. I can't say more."

"Thank you, Sheriff!" KT called as the connection ended.

Graham and KT sat in silence for several moments before Graham rose from the step and faced KT.

"Intuition always told me Martin wasn't on the up and up with his home building business, but Cortez's comments suggest there's more to this story. I guess we'll know soon enough when they dig through his house, won't we?"

The crunch of gravel on the driveway interrupted Graham and KT. The turquoise pickup slammed to a stop, creating a swirl of gravel dust as Larry hopped from the driver's seat. With a slight grin on his face, he approached them with a slow stride before stopping in front of Graham and KT.

"Well, folks, they ain't throwin' me in the slammer! The ole prosecutor dude sure can put a body in a worried state, though. He ain't givin' me my gun back yet, but he directed me to hang around town and not leave the county. Kinda tough, he is! I got to admit, I ain't been this nervous in a month o' Sundays. It almost made me take a drink or spring a leak! I didn't, Graham Cracker. I'm sober as a judge and dry as a bone!"

KT rose and rushed to Larry, taking his arm. "I'm sorry you had to experience this whole awful affair. Shooting Martin is devastating enough, but questioning by the prosecutor is harrowing. I'm sorry! I'm so sorry."

Larry patted her arm, his nervousness apparent. He related his answers to the prosecutor and confessed Daryl Rich's questions intimidated him. KT nodded in agreement when Larry expressed concern for his own well-being. Was the prosecutor intending to charge Larry with murder? Larry's countenance turned darker as he spoke. He moved to the front porch steps and plopped his skinny behind on one.

"Graham Cracker, you know I been in a bunch of trouble before. My drinkin' and fightin' days put me in the clink a bunch of times. I ain't never tried to shoot nobody or knife em or nothin', though. Ole Larry here ran with a rough bunch of boys, and lots of em got themselves into bad trouble. Not me. I gave the dude everything he asked and more, even bout the spooky light at the stone wall. He asked why I brought my shotgun. Now, I'll be honest with you,

Katie Doc, I was kinda scared. It's the reason I brought the gun out here."

"I know. Graham, isn't there anything we can do to make the prosecutor realize Larry wasn't trying to hurt Martin?"

"I believe he'll come to that realization."

Larry said, "Clete, he's with Rich now. I offered to wait for him in town, but he wants to walk the three miles here to clear his mind. Clete's a quiet sorta fella. He don't say much. I asked him not to let the dude spook him because we didn't do nothin' wrong."

"No, you did not!" Graham insisted. "Larry, can KT and I bring you and Clete dinner from town?"

"Nah, I stopped by the chicken and catfish joint and got me two of their combo meals. It's tasty, and cousin Clete loves it! You go on and don't fret on me and ole Clete. We'll be okay. You eased my mind a tad. I don't reckon the prosecutor will make Sheriff Cortez arrest me."

"We must not borrow trouble," KT admonished. "Nonnie often repeated those words, and she was right."

Graham patted Larry on the shoulder and signaled to KT they should leave. As KT and Graham climbed into the red Jeep, they left Larry with reassuring proclamations. As they headed to town, Gabi Wessler phoned to invite them to dinner, so Graham and KT drove straight to the Wessler home.

"This has been a trying day for you, honey!" Gabi blurted as she hugged KT and kissed her cheek. "Come in, you two. Let's have a relaxing meal on the patio. Each of us is shocked and befuddled by this dreadful development, aren't we? How is Larry handling the situation? I hate he found himself in such a spot. What was wrong with Martin, anyhow? Was he mentally ill or plain evil?"

"It's buffet time!" announced Al. "Food's on the kitchen island. Grab a plate and help yourself."

After everyone sat around the patio table, Graham and KT familiarized Al and Gabi on the day's developments.

"Martin was a strange bird," Al said. "I don't remember him around these parts until around fifteen years ago, maybe less, when he arrived in town and began building like a house-a-fire. The subdivision behind your property is his, and the other three houses on your lane are part of it. He built a subdivision on the land next to your cemetery off Creek Road, too. He built houses in other locations, but no more subdivisions, only individual homes. When somebody experienced a problem with one of his builds, they had a heck of a time getting any resolution. He didn't hire the best workers and used substandard materials. Lots of surplus and junk scrounged from other jobs."

Graham agreed and added, "Yeah, people have sued him several times. Nobody can get hold of him, and his employees are as mysterious as he is. I've never met a person who comes close to his baffling behavior. Operates under the radar. Appears and disappears. Goes by variations on his name. Sheesh, I can't wait to hear what Cortez has to say!"

****

Graham returned KT to her hotel after the enjoyable meal and welcome diversion at the Wessler home. Settling into the desk chair in front of her computer, she checked her phone and email messages. KT needed a distraction from the Blane Martin mess, but she could not bring herself to engage in deliberations involving the Maine job opportunity at that moment. As a result, she started clicking away on her "Find Noah's Relatives" project.

The Poole family contact, Euladora Monroe, lived in Virginia Beach, Virginia. KT's watch read eight-fifteen, which she deemed not too late to phone Euladora, so KT drew a deep breath and punched the numbers into her cell phone.

"Hello, is this Euladora Monroe?" Upon confirmation, KT introduced herself and launched into an explanation of the call. She avoided any mention of the murders Noah witnessed so long ago.

"My grandmother tried to find Noah's kin, but she never learned his last name, which rendered her attempts futile," KT said. "But modern technology enabled me to find you. I read the document you posted online written in 1924 by Ibby Poole, Noah's older sister. I can't imagine how awful it was for Noah's family not to know what happened to him, but now I have found you, and it's important for me to finish what my grandmother started."

Euladora Monroe expressed joy and amazement, and she did not question how a teenaged Annie Young learned Noah's story in 1934. This relieved KT, because she did not wish to elaborate on the mystical narrative unless she deemed it necessary. Euladora launched into the account of Noah Poole's legend in her family's lore and stated whenever the subject of the Civil War arose, someone always recounted the family mystery of the sixteen-year-old boy who vanished during the war.

KT and Euladora spoke for two hours, and KT promised to send Euladora copies of her grandmother's notes regarding Noah's journey. Euladora countered by inviting KT to Virginia Beach to deliver the documents in person. She wished to meet the woman who undertook the challenge to fulfill a grandmother's fervent dream. KT agreed and ended the call, satisfied with the outcome of her research. Noah Poole would no longer remain a mystery to those who came after him. KT and Euladora settled on an upcoming date for the visit before KT returned to her home in Bluff County.

"Ah, Nonnie," KT murmured. "I found them for you, and I sense you're here and are pleased. Noah's family is found, and McCormick House is reborn."

KT readied for bed and soon drifted to sleep after contemplating the following day's likely turn of events. What might she and her friends learn involving the mysterious man whose body lay unclaimed at Jones and Little Funeral Home? Blane Martin caused plenty of trouble, no matter what moniker he used, but did any family exist to mourn his demise? Innumerable riddles surrounded the man, and for a moment, one fleeting moment, KT felt sorry for him.

"Oh, well, we'll learn more tomorrow," she addressed her pillow as she gave it a punch. "I'm betting tomorrow will shed light on Mr. Martin."

CURSES AND BLESSINGS

K T received Sheriff Cortez's telephone call as she emerged from the shower. Could she come to his office at ten-thirty? He had already spoken with prosecutor Daryl Rich. KT agreed.

Following a hurried breakfast, she spoke on the phone with Dr. Rightmore, who insisted the clinic needed her to return posthaste. The man's incompetence and his lack of concern with her plight frustrated KT. She seldom took time allotted for vacations and often worked into the wee hours of the morning and on weekends. Rightmore needed KT because he struggled, not because he appreciated the difference she made with patients, and his phony flattery annoyed her. She promised to return as soon as possible but reiterated she did not plan to return until she settled matters in Hillview. She also pointed out a premature return to work could cause additional trips to Hillview, but Rightmore's curt dismissal of the call projected his dissatisfaction with her responses.

After scolding herself for her indecision regarding the Maine opportunity, KT opened the envelope from Stub O'Connor and analyzed its contents. Stub's contract guaranteed better monetary compensation, better working conditions, better facilities, plus a teaching professorship in the medical school. The prospect of providing excellent medical care to those in need without the corruption and widespread anti-public health sentiments of Bluff County enthused her the most. The sooner she resigned her Bluff County position, she reasoned, the sooner Rightmore might get forced out and replaced by a more competent director. Maybe.

KT exited her hotel room after running a brush through her hair one more time. Upon arrival at Sheriff Cortez's office, she straightened her shoulders and proceeded to his private office, where Graham waited.

"Hello, Dr. Winslow," Cortez bellowed. "Thank you for coming. Boy, do we have interesting developments with Martin! I've filled in the prosecutor."

"Did you find his family?"

"It's possible. We discovered a birthday card signed 'Mom,' and its envelope was in the trash can. We researched the return address and found a phone number, and I left a phone message asking the woman to call me. Boy, howdy, Martin had a lot going on! A lot."

Graham leaned forward and asked, "Like what?"

Sheriff Cortez leaned back and chortled, "Well, it appears he swindled folks and used fake names or maybe actual clients' names to open credit card accounts. We found fourteen envelopes addressed to fourteen different names at the house Martin rented. Every letter inside threatened legal action if the person didn't pay overdue statements. Amounts owed ranged from insignificant sums to eleven thousand dollars. The landlord advised us Martin lived alone in the house, which is a dump, a real dump. His landlord also received a recent telephone call from a lawyer in Florida who was hunting for Martin. The Florida lawyer had mailed certified letters to the Grover house, but Martin never claimed them. This lawyer wanted confirmation Martin lived there, and he revealed to the landlord Martin was part of a hefty swindle in Florida. I don't have details, though."

"Florida?" Graham asked.

"Yep, but we did find items of interest to you, Dr. Winslow. He had an enormous map of this county tacked to a wall, and Martin's subdivisions were outlined in blue, as were individual houses he built. Your property was outlined in red with a target drawn on it. A folder containing those trashed contracts he sent you sat on a chair next to the desk, and a heap of contracts he sent to your grandmother lay under those. Her notes to him refusing to sell were there, too."

"Everything he blabbered to the judge was a lie, and there's the proof!" KT exclaimed as she gripped Graham's arm.

"Hold on," said Cortez. "He cut out your grandmother's signature from one of her letters, glued it to one contract, and photocopied the document to make it appear as if she signed it. That's evidence to me he planned to forge a signed contract. It's a snazzy piece of work, you'd better believe. It might pass for real because it's so well done."

"He's facing disbarment for forging a client's signature and stealing her money, Sheriff," Graham said.

Cortez chuckled and placed his chin in his left hand, elbow on the desk. "What a piece of work Martin was. We found a book of Bible quotations filled with bookmarks and underlined quotes. What a blarney-filled piece of work!"

The phone on his desk buzzed, and Cortez asked Graham and KT to wait in the outer office. Martin's mother was returning the sheriff's call.

"Boy, what a sleaze!" exclaimed KT as they took a seat on a vinyl couch in the waiting room. "What a sleazy scumbag!"

"I figured there was more to him than the shady dealings we knew," Graham responded as he stroked his mustache. "I don't get it. The guy rents a dumpy one-bedroom house in a town away from Hillview but drives a luxury car. He cheats folks and never pays, the entire time pontificating Bible verses in his insufferable manner."

"Blane Martin did those things. Past tense. He's dead." KT nodded toward the door of Sheriff Cortez's office. "I don't envy him the job of telling a mother her son is dead."

"Even Blane Martin's mother, KT?"

"Even Blane Martin's mother."

****

After twenty minutes, the door to Sheriff Cortez's office opened, and Cortez signaled Graham and KT to enter. His drawn face validated a tough conversation with Martin's mother.

"She's heading here as soon as she gets a flight. Lives near Miami. Doesn't believe he was trying to set fire to your house, Dr. Winslow. Claims the shooting was intentional because he was such a successful businessman. Jealousy. The woman kept repeating what a devout Christian boy he was. Her last name isn't Martin; it's Noland. God, I don't enjoy this part of my job."

KT agreed in a low voice, "I can imagine. I suppose she'll learn the truth about her son after she arrives, huh?"

"No way to hide it. Grover is in this county, which means I'll oversee an investigation. I have a deputy sorting out the credit card business, and I left two deputies at Martin's house to go through everything. They may find more incriminating material. We roped off the house as a crime scene."

Graham asked, "Will the Noland woman's accusations hurt Larry? Do you have any idea whether the prosecutor might bring charges against him?"

"The self-defense evidence is straightforward to me, but Daryl Rich has fooled me before. He's one tough customer and a real lone ranger. Unpredictable."

Sheriff Cortez's words did not bring KT comfort. On any given day, saving McCormick House brought joy, yet other days brought doubt and despair. On this day, doubt and despair gained ground. Graham took her arm and suggested they leave.

"Sheriff Cortez will alert us to any developments. Let's leave him to his work. Come on," he urged.

They headed to Birdie's Bistro for a quiet lunch. Upon arrival, they found it empty except for one other couple seated at a table by the window. Graham and KT selected a private table-for-two in an isolated corner. When a server greeted them, they gave their order and sat without speaking.

KT broke the silence. "I wish I never started this renovation. I'm responsible for Larry's troubles and Martin's death. It's my..."

"No! It's not your fault! Quit!" He reached across the table and gripped both of her hands in his. "You stop! Listen, Martin wasn't a decent person. If you sold to him, you'd have stepped into a quagmire. Nothing he did turned out simple or straightforward. I have no clue why he was desperate for McCormick House, but from what we've learned today, it's obvious the guy had no scruples. You can't blame yourself. Please. Stop!"

She peered at him as tears welled in her eyes. Graham withdrew a handkerchief from his pocket, reached across the table, and dabbed the tears away, still holding her hands in his free hand.

She spoke in a borderline inaudible murmur. "I'm sorry. I'm not an emotional person, but it's like I'm always on the verge of tears since I got here. I tried to do what Nonnie wanted. Oh, I believed it was the right thing to do."

"It's the right thing. It *is*. You aren't responsible for Martin. He brought it on himself, and as for Larry, thank God Larry was there! Larry saved the house. He and Clete may have died in the fire if Martin succeeded. Think of it in that respect. Please be grateful for what happened. Please. You're doing the right thing, and I'm not saying this because I'm your realtor."

"Oh, it's everything, not only this. My clinic director is giving me grief for not returning sooner. I have another month's vacation time due, and I sent in a request for it, which put him into a rage this morning. It's overwhelming and makes my stomach turn. At the same time, I have this job opportunity in Maine I already mentioned; it's intriguing and exciting. I'm considering it more each day, and my mind constantly flits from one problem to the next."

"Graham and KT! Welcome! How are you on this fine day?" Birdie's voice boomed from behind the counter.

Startled, KT saw Birdie hurrying toward them, carrying an envelope. Graham waved at her and squeezed KT's hand.

Birdie placed the envelope on the table in front of KT and planted her hands on her hips before whispering, "I've been waiting for you to get in here! See what I found upstairs in the odds and ends Olivia Watson left in a closet! I went through the photos one by one after you said your family patronized her diner when they lived here."

Puzzled, KT withdrew her hand from Graham's grasp and opened the envelope. Inside lay three old, creased black and white photographs. One featured a group of five men dressed in 1930s business suits. The second showed a man with one arm around a woman and his other hand resting on the shoulder of a teenaged girl, but the third, a closeup of the teenaged girl, drew a gasp from KT.

"Lay your baby brown eyes on the back of those pictures, KT!" Birdie exclaimed. "It's your family, girl! Olivia Watson wrote their names on the back!"

KT read the names written on the back of each photo. Penciled notations identified the family of three as Dr. Carter Young, Mrs. Ellen Young, and Annie Young. KT had never seen a close-up photo of her grandmother as a teen, and she locked onto the two photos of Annie, absorbing every detail of the girl's earnest face, her freckles, her dress, and her stance. Of the five men in the first photo, KT recognized only two names—that of her great-grandfather Carter Young and his physician friend Jack Morrison.

KT handed the photos across the table to Graham and addressed Birdie. "Birdie, you can't imagine how much these mean to me. I can't ever thank you enough. I'm speechless." She held the pictures to her breast when Graham handed them back to her.

Birdie stooped and embraced KT. She winked at Graham as she kissed KT's hair.

"I almost fell out of my chair when I found those!" Birdie hooted. "Olivia Watson must have photographed gobs of her customers because a box is full of pictures of people at the diner. I need to make my wall display bigger, don't I? I love the history here. Graham, aren't you glad KT came to town?"

Graham glanced at KT and back at Birdie before proclaiming in a firm voice, "You bet I am! It's a marvelous thing KT is doing with McCormick House." His gaze of admiration lingered upon KT.

"Oops, here's your food!" Birdie exclaimed as the server approached the table. Birdie squeezed KT's shoulders again and announced, "I better get back to the kitchen. I'm glad you two came in today. Enjoy, now, you hear!" She bustled through the kitchen door.

For several minutes, KT and Graham ate in silence, Graham alternating between glancing at his dining companion and taking bites of his salad. His voice interrupted the silence.

"I see kindness in your great-grandparents' faces and sweetness in your grandmother's." He raised the photo and said, "See how these men are laughing? They were having one heck of a time, weren't they?"

KT inspected the photo. Carter Young and the man beside him, Jack Morrison, appeared to enjoy a shared joke while the other three men looked on. One man's index finger pointed at the camera, but his eyes aimed at KT's great-grandfather and Morrison. KT spied a clock reading twelve-thirty through the diner's window, so she assumed the group had enjoyed or were preparing to enjoy lunch at Olivia Watson's Diner.

"These are wonderful, Graham. I *needed* to see these today. Dr. Jack Morrison was Carter Young's best friend. He urged the family to move to Hillview. They were friends in college, and Dr. and Mrs. Morrison were with Carter and Ellen Young when they married. The two couples remained friends here and after my great-grandparents returned to Oklahoma. I learned of their friendship on the afternoon Nonnie and I sat next to the stone wall."

"You will treasure these always," Graham said.

KT twisted in her chair before directing her gaze at Graham. She pushed her plate to the side and rested both hands on the table.

"I will. This Martin mess tore me apart and made me question my decision. My brain jumps from one conclusion to another every few seconds, and I find myself in unfamiliar and uncomfortable positions. I've always been a decisive and impatient person, and this chaos makes me feel wishy-washy. You're correct about Martin. It's not my fault Blane Martin is dead; it's his own fault. We're innocents affected by his no-good self, but I can't let this turmoil dissuade me from moving forward. What will happen will happen but seeing my family's faces in these pics and appreciating what they faced, I believe Carter, Ellen, and Annie are with me here, and they command me to go forward. I *must* do it to honor them, to honor Miss Mittie McCormick, to honor Blink Hill and his parents Ned and Cora, and to honor the people who lie in the cemetery with my grandmother. To honor myself, I must do this. I can't turn my back on you, your parents, Emmaline, Birdie, or Lacy Albright, or Larry and Clete. After everything that's happened, I *must* press forward."

Graham's grin stretched across his face, and he pointed an index finger at her in the same gesture as the unknown man in the photo pointed at the camera. She returned the gesture with a smile.

"Way to go! Let's finish lunch, and I'll get you to your car. I have a showing at four o'clock. Will you be okay? As for your job opportunity, you must fill me in on specifics. A gleam came across your face when you mentioned it. It's got to be great!"

"I'm much better now," KT said. "I'll reveal more soon."

"You'd better! Maine is gorgeous country! I bet you'd love it there."

"I'm driving out to Creek Road Cemetery and the house to see how Larry and Clete are doing. If time permits, I'll gather materials to take to a print shop. Nonnie wrote Noah's story on notebook pages, and I want to give copies to a lady in Virginia Beach who keeps his family history. I'm okay. We'll take whatever developments unfold and handle them."

KT's old determination returned.

****

Creek Road Cemetery gleamed in the bright sunlight. KT stood in silence before Anna Ruth's stone for several minutes, her lips moving as if in a quiet, two-way conversation. After closing the gate and dawdling on the path to her car, she drove to McCormick House. Inside, Larry stood at the bottom of the stairs, arms loaded with tools and a folded drop cloth. He greeted her with his usual chirpy, "Hi, Katie Doc!" and placed his load on the floor.

"How is it going today, Larry Locks?"

"Fine and dandy! Clete's clearin' more brush from the stone wall with a brush hog so he can get it in shape. I ordered a load of rocks from the quarry, and they deliver tomorrow. Clete also cleared a wider path to the wall so the truck can get there with the rock. He'll take the brush hog back to the rental store in the mornin'. Quick and easy. We're gettin' near the end of this project, and I ain't been arrested yet, neither!"

KT had almost forgotten the possibility of arrest hanging over Larry. She assured him no arrest was forthcoming, and no one blamed him for defending himself and Clete from certain death.

Larry's tattooed arm brushed his wavy hair from his face as he thanked KT for her trust. He spoke of remaining chores to be completed and hurried upstairs to retrieve more supplies after bidding KT goodbye. She strolled through the rooms on the main level, appreciating the results of Larry and Clete's labor. Each room's fresh paint, each piece of cleaned and polished woodwork, the refinished hardwood floors, and the gleaming kitchen brought a satisfied smile to her freckled face. She peeked into the half bath under the stairs, winked at herself in the mirror, and skipped through the front door to her car.

At the hotel, she gathered her grandmother's notes detailing Noah Poole's journey and the murderous tale. She arrived at the print shop thirty minutes before it closed, and the shop promised to copy the pages and bind them into two spiral books, one for Euladora Monroe and one for Emmaline Conrad. KT retired to her hotel and spent a fair amount of time answering emails and returning phone calls from her brothers and her father. Her family's calls comprised simple check-ins on the progress of her project. She did not disclose Blane Martin's death and reassured her father and brothers everything was fine. None of the four understood her desire to spend Anna Ruth's inheritance on a dilapidated and abandoned house in a place unknown to them.

"I don't get it," her father scolded. "Who cares if the house gets demolished? You're wasting money, honey. Money you can put to good use." Each of her three brothers replayed the same tune. She laughed at each one and ended each call with, "Love you lots!"

Another review of Stub O'Connor's proposal solidified her decision. As much as she yearned for better times in Bluff County, the Maine opportunity meant a beginning, an appropriate time to embark on the next chapter in her travels along her life's road. Success in taking Anna Ruth to her ultimate resting site, bringing closure to Noah's family, and saving McCormick House from demolition marked the perfect end to her current chapter.

FAMILY TIES

A groggy KT awoke late the following morning. Upon her arrival at McCormick House, KT found a frantic woman standing near the porch, screeching and cursing at Larry in a high-pitched voice.

"You killed my boy; you killed my boy!" the woman bawled as KT rushed between the woman and Larry, who stood on a porch step.

"Excuse me, please stop yelling," KT pleaded in a quiet and measured voice.

She assumed the woman, smelling of cigarettes, dressed in skintight flowered pants, a flowing sheath around her shoulders, and a low-cut blouse unable to contain her ample breasts, to be Blane Martin's mother. Four or five bracelets clanked away as the woman flailed her arms near KT's face. Her bleached hair, the color of vanilla ice cream, moved nary an inch thanks to heavy application of hair spray, and eyelashes laden with black mascara flashed as she screamed and stomped her sandaled feet on the grass.

"Ma'am, please. I understand you're grieving, but please! Are you Mrs. Martin?" KT asked.

"My name's Violet Noland, and you bet your life I'm grieving! This, this piece of trash killed my boy! My precious Christian boy! Dear Jesus, help me!" She clasped her hands as if to pray and gaped at the sky before resuming her verbal attack.

Larry's head hung, his hair falling in his face in reaction to the woman's insult, but KT stood firm, her body blocking Larry from Violet Noland. When KT noticed a knife protruding from Violet's handbag, she turned to Larry and instructed him to go inside the house and lock the door.

"Call Sheriff Cortez," KT whispered in a calm voice before she turned to face the enraged visitor.

The two women glared at each other for several moments. KT assumed a rigid stance and planted her feet to optimize her height and confidence. Although her insides fluttered and churned, her outward demeanor presented a picture of controlled calmness. Violet Noland shifted her weight from one leg to the other, her eyes shooting daggers through KT.

"I'm gonna get him!" Violet Noland screeched as she went for the knife. In an instant, KT slapped the woman's hand, causing the knife to hurl through the air, landing in the grass.

"No! Calm down and step back! You're trespassing. Did you not read the sign at the entrance? I am sorry about your son, but his own actions caused his death. Your grief is understandable, but . . ."

The sound of Sheriff Cortez's cruiser spitting gravel as it sped up the driveway aborted KT's plea. She breathed a sigh of relief when he leaped from the vehicle and approached.

"I was on my way here when Larry called," Sheriff Cortez said to KT before he addressed the ranting female. "Now, Mrs. Noland."

"I *told* you it's *Miss* Noland, you stupid pig! You're in cahoots with this broad and the trash inside the house. They killed my boy because they're jealous, and I don't believe a single thing you people say! Tommy was a genius. He did wonders for your sorry town, with his magnificent homes. I kept nagging him not to bother with this pathetic junk-hole because it's not worth spit, but he insisted on putting every bit of our land back in the family. Now I've got to bury my boy! He's the only thing I have left, and he's gone! I'm getting out of here, but you wait. I'll get even with every one of you!" She jabbed an orange fingernail toward Cortez, KT, and the front door of McCormick House.

Miss Violet Noland shoved past Sheriff Cortez, climbed into her rental car, and almost hit a tree as she wheeled through the front yard to the driveway. Gravel flew behind the vehicle, pieces smacking the Sheriff's vehicle.

Larry and a sheepish Clete emerged from the house. They stood on the porch and gaped at the Sheriff, their faces revealing worried minds. KT stayed put on the step, but her hands trembled, and she took deep breaths in a futile attempt to calm herself.

Sheriff Cortez said, "Well, now, she was something, wasn't she? I'll take the knife to the office, Dr. Winslow. I'm glad she didn't use it."

"You and me both!" shouted Larry in a defiant tone. "She dang near started to beat me up before you got here, Katie Doc, and I done never hit a girl before, but I was ready, yes I was! I was awful glad to see you, Katie Doc, and you, too, Sheriff!"

Sheriff Cortez chuckled. "Can we go inside, folks? I need to speak with you."

The four headed to the kitchen where the kitchen table chairs rested, tucked under the table. Each took a seat, and Cortez cleared his throat. Larry swept his hair behind his ears. A pale and frightened Clete stared at the window, and KT rested her sweaty hands in her lap.

"I have good news. Larry and Clete, Daryl Rich has declined to prosecute you. He says it's an open and shut case of self-defense. You boys can rest easy. As for Martin, Thomas or Blane, or whatever-the-hell he called himself, that boy was in for it. He's been swindling folks here, there, and everywhere! The shyster borrowed money using each of the variations of his name, too, and he skips from one town to another to make it hard for anybody to find him. With Martin as a common surname, it's easier to hide under the radar. We got lucky when we found the birthday card. Otherwise, we might still be searching for his kin."

KT said, "What marvelous news! Larry and Clete are relieved, and I am, too. I'm sorry for Martin's victims, though."

Cortez agreed but added, "Dr. Winslow, we are his victims, too. My deputies and I will crack the puzzle and notify the proper authorities. I doubt anyone owed money will see a penny."

Larry asked, "What did Violet Noland mean about Martin wanting to get land back in the family, Sheriff? It don't make no sense."

"The whole thing is mystifying. Listen, folks, is everyone okay? Larry? Clete? Dr. Winslow? I need to get to my office. Glad you called me, Larry. I want to make sure Miss Noland gets her son's body and herself out of town pronto. Until she's gone, I'll send a deputy to drive by day and night."

The three assured Sheriff Cortez of their well-being and bade him farewell. Cortez drove off with a wave, and Larry slapped Clete on the back.

"Whoa, Nellie, Clete! Everything's gonna be fine, cousin! Let's get this joint ready so Katie Doc here can sell it and go home. You and me gonna go fishin', ain't we?"

Clete nodded, and a slight smile crossed his face. "Yup," he said. "I'm headed to work on the stone wall. Bye, Dr. Winslow." He grabbed a water bottle from the kitchen counter and slipped out the back door.

"Clete, he's kinda shy, Katie Doc," laughed Larry. "He's a decent dude, and he's been powerful worried bout me goin' to jail. We're both glad this mess is done! You okay?"

"Yes, Larry. Thank you for everything. I'm sorry I put you two in such a terrible plight. Thank heavens Daryl Rich came to the correct conclusion."

Larry leaped up the stairs two at a time as KT exited the house and hopped in her car. Her cell phone, sitting on the passenger seat, alerted her to several missed calls from Graham. When she returned the call, she related the morning's events to him. In addition, she mentioned Violet Noland's comment dealing with family land.

"Isn't it odd? What did she mean?"

"I can't fathom it, but I'm glad you're okay. It worried me you didn't answer your phone. The news Rich isn't filing charges against Larry is fantastic. Makes sense, though, because he was protecting the property and himself from Martin. That's all. What a sorry excuse for a human being Martin was. Listen, I have a closing to attend soon, but I got a call from Doan Hill earlier inviting you and me to dinner tonight at his house. Since I couldn't reach you, I said we'd be happy to join Amy and him for dinner. Is it okay with you? I hope I wasn't presumptuous."

"Oh, how kind of them! I'd love it. What time?"

"I'll get you at six."

****

From the print shop, KT retrieved the two spiral booklets filled with Annie's notes containing Noah Poole's story. One she reserved for Euladora Monroe, and the other she delivered to an appreciative Emmaline. Emmaline and KT enjoyed a lengthy conversation, and Emmaline showed KT the drawing for the commemorative plaque to be placed at the front of McCormick House.

"I've wanted your property to have the historical designation for a while, KT, always hoping we might receive permission to include it. If this design is fine with you, I'll take it to the sign maker in the morning."

"It's grand! A historical marker might help the property sell faster, too, don't you think?"

Emmaline shrugged. "You'd better ask Graham. This entire region holds a tremendous volume of history, and various folks find historic homes desirable. The sign maker should have the sign ready in a couple of weeks and will install it as soon as it's finished. What's left before Graham puts the place on the market?"

"Exterior stuff for the most part, but the interior will soon be ready. I hope Blane Martin's shooting doesn't put a damper on the sale. The last time I hope to see McCormick House is the day the For Sale sign gets pounded into the ground. My clinic director isn't happy because I requested more time off, and I need to get home sooner than later. I'm planning a brief trip to Virginia Beach to visit a descendant of Noah Poole's sister, who has invited me to deliver Nonnie's notes in person. I must finish this one last task for Nonnie. My work here in Hillview is almost done!"

A slight frown crossed Emmaline's face. "It's satisfying, I'm sure, but I'll miss you. I hope you'll visit us after you return to your home. You've made friends here, and I'm one, you'd better believe!"

KT grabbed Emmaline's hand and held it tight. "I know," she whispered.

As KT opened the door to leave, Emmaline admonished her in a stern voice, "Don't you leave here without coming to bid me goodbye, you hear?"

"I won't. I promise!"

****

Doan and Amy Hill's home, built by Blink years before, sat tucked in a clearing of the dense woods directly across the street from McCormick House. KT noticed at least two additions to the original construction of stone and wood. With its wood stained a deep brown, the home blended into its serene, forested surroundings.

Doan greeted the visitors with warm handshakes, but Amy grabbed KT and enveloped her with a tight hug before giving Graham a quick peck on the cheek.

"Come in, come in!" Amy exclaimed, ushering them into the living room. As they chatted on recent events and sipped iced tea, dappled sunlight streamed through trees surrounding the home. Doan expressed relief Larry and Clete faced no prosecution. He thanked KT again for sharing his family's history, and Amy echoed his gratitude.

"I want to kick myself for not asking Grandpap Blink more questions and not paying attention to his stories," Doan lamented. "I held enormous love for him, but I didn't find family history interesting. What wasted opportunities!"

"I get it," KT replied. "I didn't truly appreciate Nonnie until the day we sat beside the stone wall, and she shared her story. At least you spent consequential time with your grandfather over the years. I didn't with my grandmother, and the reality pains me. Once I gather the letters your Grandpap Blink wrote to Nonnie, I'll copy and bind them into a book. If I can't get the job done before leaving Hillview, I promise to send it to you."

Amy announced dinner. Graham knew Doan and Amy as acquaintances, but by evening's end, the four appeared to have been close friends for years. KT observed the two men retreat to the screened-in porch to discuss landscaping and Hillview politics before she entered the kitchen to aid Amy with clean-up duties after dinner. Amy was a pediatric nurse at the hospital, and an instant bonding over their shared professions developed. Each of the Hills' twins, away at college, left Doan and Amy empty nesters, and Amy expressed eagerness at her children's upcoming return for summer vacation. Graham and KT did not leave the Hill residence until after ten-thirty.

"Well, I haven't enjoyed an evening this much in ages," Graham confessed to KT as they approached the hotel.

"It was delightful, wasn't it? Thanks for taking me. I'm glad I got better acquainted with Doan and Amy. They're fantastic. See you soon!"

Despite the late hour, Blink's remaining letters beckoned. After climbing into her pajamas, she propped herself in bed and grabbed the last stack of letters.

May 3, 1948

Dear Annie,

I'm sorry I did not send you a letter with the news Zell and I were getting married. I was busier than you can imagine and only found time to send a telegram. Please forgive me. Yesterday, we received the tray you sent. Zell says it is the most beautiful tray she has ever seen. We will use it many times. Doctor and Miss Ellen sent an elegant china bowl. We have gotten generous gifts from our friends. Berta brought an enormous cast iron griddle. We will make lots of pancakes with it. Mr. Berger and his sister Elise gave us a set of flatware. Mr. Edwards and the band boys gave us a console radio and record player. My college roommate Abe mailed embroidered napkins and towels his wife sewed.

Pap and I are planning to build Zell and me a house here on the property. We start next week. Harvey Woodard's crew will do most of the work. Harvey has a construction business now. He is a talented carpenter and has plans for a three-bedroom house. Right now, we live in my room in the cabin with Mam and Pap, and it's crowded.

I have enclosed a photograph of Zell, me, Mam, and Pap at the wedding. We got married in Longtown since that is where Zell's people live. Mr. Berger came, and Berta and her brother-in-law Frank Simmons came, too. Mr. Edwards and the band boys played after the ceremony. What a surprise! A picture of Mr. Berger, Berta, Frank Simmons, and the band boys with Zell and me is also enclosed.

Thank you for the photograph of you and Joellen. You both have cheerful faces. Does she enjoy school? I appreciate the article you sent describing your lecture at the history conference. You learned truths from Noah that give you bountiful knowledge of those old times. It is grand you get paid for your lectures. I hope you get more lecture jobs.

Will you ever come for a visit? I hope you will because Zell wants to meet my best friend. We want to meet Joellen, too. Consider it, will you? Mam and Pap would love to see you again.

Your friend,

Blink

KT cradled the black and white photographs in her hands and studied each face. She scrutinized every feature and stance, clothing, smiles, trees in the background—everything. Her hands caressed visages of those of whom Anna Ruth spoke with reverence. And Mr. Berger, Gabi Wessler's Uncle Max! Blink and his bride beamed with joy as they stood with their arms around Cora and Ned Hill, Blink's beloved Mam and Pap. The photo of Blink and Zell with Cora and Ned radiated joy. In the other photo, Berta Simmons and her brother-in-law Frank, without whose legal assistance James Hinshaw's inheritance would have been lost, stood beside each other. Berta folded her hands in front of her dress, and Frank's hands rested in each of his pants' pockets. Blink and Zell stood in the middle of the group, and the band boys crowded behind everyone. Blink identified each person on the back of the photo, which KT appreciated.

"I wish I had a magnifying glass," KT complained to the photos. "Oh, what a marvelous surprise! I must show these pictures and Blink's letter to Graham and his parents, as well as Doan and Amy. We *are* all connected to each other, aren't we, Blink? Like branches growing from a sturdy trunk or a tapestry whose threads weave a random portrait."

KT placed the two photographs on the bedside table with loving care and checked the clock. Despite the late hour, she lifted the next unread letter. It described the construction of Blink and Zell's home and acknowledged the couple planned to inhabit the house within a week. Blink spent multiple Saturday nights performing with the band in nearby towns, but he expressed dissatisfaction with time away from Zell. He and Ned built on to the greenhouse behind their barn, and Ned ordered a supply of tree seedlings and flower seeds. Blink's dream of a nursery came to fruition.

Pap and I are converting the cornfield for the trees he ordered. He says harvesting corn is hard for him these days. The war is over, and food is not scarce anymore. I cannot wait to plant the trees and watch them grow! I still go into our woods, dig saplings, and plant them in pots, but I will plant them in the field when they grow more. We may convert the pumpkin patch into a tract for blueberries and Christmas trees. Blueberries are a gamble, but Pap likes them because they don't require much care, and they fetch a pretty penny. My idea with the Christmas trees is when they get at least five feet tall, we let people cut their own. It might be fun for families, and it might be helpful advertising for the nursery and our crops. Less work for us, too. Pap is thinking on it. His back hurts awful bad sometimes.

Another letter mentioned Blink's decision to play less with the band. Two musicians joined the band, so Blink's absence did not cripple it. Ned's health deteriorated after a fall from the truck, which threw increased work on Blink, Cora, and Zell.

Sometimes Pap's arthritis flares, which means the three of us must do more. I hired a young man from church to help us two days a week. Zell and I will miss the money the band brings in, but we will do fine. Berta is friends with an older lady in town who is ailing, and the lady needs someone to help clean her house and cook. Zell started working for her three days a week. I bought a car and taught Zell how to drive it, and she takes the car to town those three days. The money she earns helps pay for the fellow who works for us.

This information concerning Ned distressed KT. She was unaware of Ned's age at the time of Blink's letters, but she assumed years of farm work took a toll on his body.

"I have an uneasy feeling about where this may be headed," she addressed the letter in her hand as she laid it aside and read Blink's next correspondence.

January 28, 1949

Dear Annie,

I am sorry I haven't written in a while. Please forgive me. We received your Christmas card and photograph of you and Joellen. Zell and I enjoyed your note describing your trip to visit Doctor and Miss Ellen for Christmas. It is grand you can spend time with them. Joellen enjoyed the train ride, I bet.

Pap's health improves. He must be careful, but he can do various tasks. We cut back on our vegetable crops and are growing close to the same number as we grew when you lived here. I planted blueberry bushes and tiny Christmas trees in the old pumpkin patch. We bought them from a nursery in Pennsylvania. It was going out of business. I transplanted little pines from the woods in Zell's family's land near Longtown, too. They will not be ready to cut for a few years. I heat the greenhouse so seedlings won't freeze, and I want to make the greenhouse bigger come spring. Mam still sells eggs to several people from town and members of our church. I convinced Pap to put an advertisement for Mam's eggs in the newspaper, and she got new customers from the ad.

Guess what? Zell and I are expecting a baby! It will arrive at the end of May. We are elated, and Mam is making baby clothes. Zell plans to continue working for the lady in town as long as she can. The lady uses a wheelchair now, and Zell is of considerable help. She gave Zell a raise in her wages recently, and the extra money helps us. She asked Zell to bring the baby with her after the baby arrives. An old crib is in the lady's attic, and she wants to put it in her second bedroom for our baby. I plan to get it from her attic and put it together.

Let me hear from you.

Your friend,

Blink

The hour was late, and a weary KT slipped into a deep slumber with Blink's letters surrounding her on the bed, bedside lights blazing. As she slept, faces of Blink and others cherished by a youthful Annie Young danced through her brain. She engaged in imagined and nonsensical conversations with each one until jolted into reality by the jingle of her phone.

CHICKENS COME TO ROOST

Larry's voice boomed through KT's cell phone. "Mornin' to you, Katie Doc! You gotta have a look-see at what me and Clete done. We're almost ready, I tell ya. I got the inside cleaned, and the stone wall is lookin' fine. The outside is a waitin' for Doan to work his magic with landscaping and me to finish painting. Dead trees got hauled off yesterday."

KT chuckled, "I'll be out soon, Larry. This is marvelous news. I saw Doan last night, and I gave him free rein to plant whatever he thinks will make a splash and flourish. Thank you! I'll see you soon."

KT gathered the letters strewn on her bed and placed them in a neat pile on the desk. Larry's report pleased her, and she enjoyed a casual breakfast reading the local newspaper. A four-sentence blurb confirmed the county prosecutor planned no charges against Lawrence and Clethern Finler for the death of Blane Martin. Such relief! Now, the prosecutor's decision was public, and gossip might dissipate. Her thoughts turned to the upcoming trip to Virginia Beach to meet Euladora Monroe and present Annie's notes divulging Noah's ordeal. The prosecutor's decision and Larry and Clete's progress at McCormick House left KT free to leave the next day for Virginia Beach.

She took a deep breath and jotted a text message to Stub O'Connor expressing the honor she felt to accept the position. Satisfied with her decision, she viewed her upcoming move to Maine with eager anticipation. As she hit 'send,' the phone jingled, causing her to drop it and miss the call. The call came from Graham, so she signed the check, walked outside, and returned Graham's call.

"KT, I got to ruminating on what Martin's mother said about family land. I'm at the courthouse checking on something for a client, and I asked Mrs. Jennings to research past ownership for Martin's subdivision behind McCormick House and the one next to your cemetery. I've put in a call to Sheriff Cortez, too. Remember, he noted Martin circled properties he owned on a map posted in the house where he lived? I want those addresses. Something is strange."

"Violet Noland's comment came out of the blue, didn't it?" KT agreed. "The old orchard behind McCormick House was owned during the Civil War by Morse Blanton. Land on the cemetery side of the creek was, too, but Blanton sold the cemetery parcel to a Mr. Taylor after the Civil War. Letters I'm reading from Blink Hill to Nonnie say Blanton properties got auctioned off for non-payment of taxes in the 1940s."

Graham replied, "Interesting. I'll let you know what Cortez says and what I learn from Mrs. Jennings. Hey, I really enjoyed last night. Doan and Amy are delightful."

"I did, too! They're fantastic, and I'm thrilled to know them better. I promised to keep in touch with them. Thanks for accepting their invitation! Oh, I promised *you* a description of the Maine opportunity. I accepted it right before you called." KT elaborated on the healthy professional environment, her new responsibilities, and her anticipation of living near mountains and the ocean.

"I'm thrilled for you, Dr. Winslow! Listen, the job sounds perfect, and Maine is spectacular. I understand how much you care for the clinic in Bluff County, but you've made an excellent decision, the perfect one for you right now."

"Thanks. I'm eager to go—haven't been this energized about my profession in months because of poor decisions I can't control. Now, I can't wait to get home and tell Rightmore I'm leaving, and I'm confident everything will work out for the best. Call me if you discover interesting tidbits about Martin."

Graham's laughter rang through the phone. "You bet I will!"

KT took the elevator upstairs and settled into the corner chair in her room, where she phoned Euladora Monroe to confirm the next day's visit. Euladora reiterated her hunger to learn details of her mysterious ancestor's 1863 journey. The two chatted for several minutes, and KT began preparations for the trip. Before long, she realized she had not visited McCormick House as promised to view Larry and Clete's progress, so she hustled to her car and drove to the property as a light drizzle began.

The revived exterior gleamed through the drizzle, catching KT's breath. With dead trees and overgrowth eliminated and flower beds readied for new plantings, the place awaited Doan's magical touch with landscaping and fresh gravel strewn on the driveway. A grand dwelling it was not, but McCormick House radiated an immaculate transformation. She ventured its vintage charm would overwhelm potential buyers.

KT tooted the horn as she pulled in behind Larry's truck. Drizzle turned to steady rain, so she darted from the car to the flagstone sidewalk and up the porch steps. Inside, Larry greeted her with an enormous grin.

"Howdy do, Katie Doc. Are you pleased?"

"It's miraculous! I'm thrilled! We'll soon be ready, Larry Locks!"

Larry nodded as he leaped onto a stair as if to deliver a speech. "I'm dabbin' paint boo boos, and guess what?"

"What?"

"A dude knocked on the door about thirty minutes ago. He and his wife been watchin' us get this place to somethin' a body can be proud of. He asked if it's for sale, and I said it will be soon. I gave him Graham Cracker's phone number. Didn't show him through the house, though. Don't think Cracker might approve, since he's an expert at showin' houses. It ain't ready anyhoo. The dude said they have a daughter and a pup. They live in town but want to live on acreage, and four acres with lots of trees is right up their alley. Ain't it great?"

"It is!" KT clapped her hands. "It won't be long! I'm leaving tomorrow for Virginia Beach, but I'll be back in two or three days. If you need me, call."

"Will do. Going to the beach, are ya? Clete's at the wall out back puttin' it together. It don't bother him to work in rain. He wants to get done so we can go fishin'."

"Marvelous! I won't go back there, though, because I didn't bring my rain jacket today. Oh, my trip isn't for pleasure. It's, uh, it's unfinished business."

Larry and KT bid each other goodbye, and KT dashed to her car. Progress at the house pleased her, and she held faith the man who inquired about the property might be the buyer she desired.

"A husband, a wife, a daughter, and a dog. Just like Nonnie's family." she exclaimed to the steering wheel as she fidgeted with her key. "Oh, my, how perfect!"

Rain kept falling as KT stopped for a haircut and drove to Birdie's Bistro. As she entered the restaurant, her cell phone vibrated. The tone of Graham's voice on the other end of her telephone alarmed her.

"Where are you?" he asked.

"I'm walking in the door at Birdie's. Why? Is something wrong?"

"Not wrong. Peculiar. Listen, I'll be there soon. Will you get a table? A secluded one? Please order whatever you're having for me, will you?"

"Um, okay. What's going on, Graham?"

"I'll explain when I get there."

****

When Graham burst through the door, KT straightened in her chair, watching as he approached the table. Within one hurried second, he shoved his umbrella under the table, plopped into the chair, and leaned forward to speak. He did not see Birdie waving from behind the counter.

"Mrs. Jennings got back to me on the records for Martin-owned properties. She researched back into the early 1800s."

"Uh, huh," said KT as she accepted her salad from the server and observed Graham's irritation with the intrusion.

"The orchard which once lay beyond the rock wall at McCormick House and the farm where the graveyard sits belonged to Morse Blanton before and during the Civil War. Isn't he the man who?"

KT broke in with an impatient sigh. "Yeah. I'm aware he owned those properties. Morse Blanton sold the plot where the cemetery is to a man named Taylor after the Civil War.

Taylor owned the farm across the creek. Mr. Taylor's son Charlie deeded the cemetery to James Hinshaw of Philadelphia. James, you may remember, was the son . . . "

"Right," Graham chimed in. "Morse Blanton or his grandson Clay owned most of the other plots of land scattered around Hillview, the ones Martin built houses on in recent times."

"It makes sense. Morse Blanton was a banker. From what I gather, he foreclosed on people's homes and kept them for himself as rental properties. His grandson, Clay Blanton, inherited everything and continued the despicable practice."

"You're right. Clay Blanton got hold of even more homes in Hillview and around the county. He was a banker, too, right?"

"Yes, and not an honest one, either. From reading Blink Hill's letters to Nonnie, I've learned Clay Blanton stole customers' money and absconded from Hillview, never to be found by authorities. He died in Florida. According to Blink, the county sold Blanton properties for non-payment of taxes at public auction not long after World War II ended."

Birdie's peppy voice disrupted the conversation. "How's your meal, folks? You come off dang serious. Everything okay?"

KT turned to Birdie and took her hand, patting it as she spoke. "Everything is wonderful as usual, Birdie. We're talking real estate, and real estate is serious business!"

KT's forced laughter did not dissuade Birdie. "All right. I'll get you more tea and send one of my special brownies to split for dessert. They're humongous." Birdie left the table but turned and studied the two diners. She appeared unconvinced nothing troubling pervaded their conversation.

Graham spoke in low, muted tones. "You're correct; a public auction disposed of Clay Blanton's properties. At the auction, an orchardist by the name of named Ellis bought the orchard behind McCormick House. The farm where the cemetery sits sold to a local farmer at the auction. Other houses Blanton owned around the county got auctioned off to various people. The old farm next to the cemetery and most of the Blanton houses around the county have had several owners since the auction."

KT's demeanor expressed impatience. She thanked the server for replenishing tea and cut the enormous brownie in half, handing Graham one of two forks. She sighed and took a bite of the brownie as she searched Graham's face in anticipation.

"Here's where it gets interesting, KT."

KT's left eyebrow cocked. "Interesting?"

"Seventeen years ago, the Ellis family sold the orchard behind McCormick House to Martin. The land where the other houses on your lane are located sold to Martin two weeks later. Three years later, the original farm that included the cemetery sold to Martin. One by one, those rent houses, several of which had been demolished, leaving vacant lots, turned up in Martin's hands."

KT's impatience grew as she gulped her tea. She waved her hand and said, "Yeah, well, it's how he developed the two subdivisions, right? And built houses on the lots around town? A developer on the prowl for deals found deals, I suppose. It's an odd coincidence."

Graham leaned in closer. His eyes darted around the restaurant before locking with KT's, and he blurted, "What is Martin's full name?"

KT sneered, "Thomas Blane Martin. He used variations of the name. We've discussed this before." Her hand gesture and eye-roll implied annoyance.

"A year before he began buying properties in and around Hillview, he legally changed his name to Thomas Blane Martin."

"Okay, that's weird. What was his name before he changed it?"

"His full name prior to changing it was Thomas *Blanton* Martin, KT."

KT gasped and almost dropped her glass of tea. Tea sloshed out of the glass on to Graham's left hand as she set the glass on the table with a wobble before steadying it with her other hand. She stared at Graham while he dried his wet hand with his napkin. He stroked his mustache in his now familiar gesture before speaking again.

"Thomas Blanton Martin. Blanton. This explains his mother's comment about family land. Martin must have been Morse and Clay Blanton's descendant. We can guess why he wanted McCormick House. He wanted to tear it down and erase its history. You're shocked, aren't you? I never expected this, either."

KT did not speak. Her brain swirled with details Anna Ruth exposed on the afternoon at the stone wall. Details about Morse Blanton, the murderer and crooked banker. The Morse Blanton who ruined his son Albert's future with Molly and James. Then Clay Blanton, Morse's grandson, following in his grandfather's vile footsteps, reprised the family *tradition* of dishonor and indecency. Graham and KT stared at each other and did not speak for several minutes.

Graham broke the silence. "Are you okay?"

"I'm stunned. Bumfuzzled! How did you get this information? Are you sure?"

Graham lowered his voice to a near whisper. "What I say next may stun you even more."

"Oh, Lord, what?" Her eyes widened as she gulped more tea.

"You remember I retired from government employment?"

"Yes, I do. You and your wife both were federal employees. It's how you met."

"Yes. I didn't say what branch of government, though."

KT shrugged.

"I worked for the CIA, KT, as an operations officer."

"You mean you were a spy?"

He burst out laughing.

"Well?"

"We don't use the term. Let's say I kept a low profile and worked overseas a fair amount, but it's why I planned to leave the job. It meant too much time away, and danger was a consideration. My wife had left the agency and adored being a mom."

"My God! No wonder you could throw Martin's henchman over the stone wall! Crazy!"

Again, Graham responded with laughter before speaking. "I have a friend who works for the FBI. He owes me a favor, and I called it in. My buddy is going to investigate Martin further. Off the record."

"This is nuts! I'm flabbergasted. I mean, this Blane Martin news and now your history. It's bizarre, to be honest with you. Do your parents know what you did for a living?"

"They do. I divulged my secret after the accident when I came home to join Dad in the business. Of course, I didn't furnish them details, but it amazed them, shook them. Once in a blue moon, I receive a call. I guess I'm still on the job, in a way. When I left town the other day, I traveled overseas on a brief follow-up. Ummm, this is confidential, KT."

"My lips are sealed," she said as her finger ran across her lips. "Zipped shut!"

"How was the brownie, folks?" Birdie yelled from behind the counter.

Both KT and Graham gave her a thumbs-up.

KT asked, "I'm scheduled to go to Virginia Beach tomorrow. Should I wait?"

"No, go ahead. You want to go, and McCormick House is almost ready. Go! Nothing I learn will affect the sale of your place."

KT hesitated and mumbled, "I guess you're right," as she fumbled with her napkin.

"I am."

Her face softened with a smile as Larry's news about a potential buyer for McCormick House popped into her brain.

"Oh, we have a potential buyer! Someone stopped by the house and is interested. Larry gave him your phone number. Has he called yet?"

"Hmm," Graham said as he peered at his cell phone resting on the table. "I have six messages. Maybe one is his. I won't show it until it's ready, though, but the day will come real soon. I'll install the For Sale sign when it's ready and get busy promoting."

They both waved to Birdie as they departed the bistro. By this time, rain had ceased, so they lingered in front, chatting, before Graham climbed into his red Jeep and left. KT stood a moment, spun around, and scrutinized the front of Birdie's. Once a thriving diner for whites only, it withstood multiple owners and abandonment before a persistent and talented black woman from New York City revitalized it into a flourishing business once again.

"Thomas Blanton Martin, huh," she mumbled to no one.

Birdie waved from inside, and KT returned the gesture and headed to her hotel. She settled into her familiar corner chair and resumed studying Blink's letters, absorbing each detail of lives well lived and of Hillview's evolution from Jim

Crow into a diverse and vibrant town nestled in the Shenandoah Valley.

August 18, 1949

Dear Annie,

Thank you and Joellen for the rattle and bibs! Baby James is growing the same as weeds in my fields. I am glad you approve of us naming him after James Hinshaw. I hope he will grow to be as fine a man as James Hinshaw. A baby is tons of work, but Zell and I are doing fine. Mam and Pap help, and Zell's folks come over from Longtown, too. Zell works for the lady in town three days a week and takes James with her. The lady is caring. She thinks of Zell as a daughter, she says. The lady is white, so it is kind of funny, isn't it? She is a friend of Berta's.

Doctor and Miss Ellen sent James a handsome blanket Miss Ellen sewed. It is almost too pretty to use.

Our vegetable crops did well because we had enough rain and sunny days. Our young blueberry bushes were so bountiful we let folks pick their own for fifty cents a gallon. Most of the plants are still small, so next summer should be even better. Flowers in the greenhouse were dandy, and customers bought most every one of them. I sold a few trees, too. Pap's health improves, and he helps more with crops and the nursery. Pumpkins are coming in now. I kept a scant section of the pumpkin field since they are popular in the fall. Christmas trees are growing.

Blanton's orchard behind Mrs. McCormick's house belongs to the Ellis family now. They bought it at the auction. They own the orchard south of Blanton's, but you may not remember them. It took hard work to get Blanton's orchard in shape again, and apples should come in okay this season.

Pap and I took crops, mostly green beans and squash, to the Farmers Market. Mrs. Rutledge bought several things, and she was friendly again! She congratulated me on the baby and asked about you and Joellen. She is glad we write to each other and has listed Miss Mittie's house for sale again. This time, she is using a different real estate man, Harry Wessler. The last family who lived there stayed for six months, but they bought a house near Grover. I spoke to the gentleman two or three times. He was kind of rude, and he complained about weird happenings. Ha! Ha!

Mr. Foster, the owner of the Mueller property, comes from Washington most weekends. He and his wife keep the home and grounds in excellent shape. Pap and I no longer care for the place because the chap who worked for Mr. Foster before the war cares for it. Mrs. Foster buys eggs and vegetables from us. She stayed and had coffee with Mam last weekend, and it reminded me of how Miss Ellen used to have coffee with Mam. The Fosters are decent folk.

Hug Joellen from us. I wish for a visit in person again. Thanks for the picture of you and Joellen. I will send pictures of us and James.

Your friend,

Blink

"Thank goodness for Blink's letters! Without them, so much would be lost to time," KT said to herself.

Following James's birth, Blink and Zell had two more youngsters, a boy, and a girl. The land flourished under Blink's prowess, and bit by bit the farm took a back seat to the nursery. Blink and Ned built a larger greenhouse to grow annuals and perennials. A variety of shrubs and trees planted in straight rows replaced vegetable fields. Blueberries flourished while spruce and pine seedlings grew into Christmas trees. By the mid-1950s, Hillview and county residents flocked to the nursery to purchase flowers, shrubs, and trees and to pick blueberries and cut their own Christmas trees. Other food crops fed only the Hill family and friends. Blink completed a correspondence course in horticulture, using the remainder of James Hinshaw's money. Blink and Ned placed a wooden sign at the entrance proclaiming the business Tobias Hill Nursery, and Ned and Cora continued to live in the cabin. A letter written in 1958 brought three pieces of delightful information.

The radio station called. They want me to do a radio show on Fridays! Local news is from noon until 12:15, and my show will run from 12:20 until 12:30. The station will call it The Friday Farm and Horticulture Report. What do you think? It scares me somewhat, but Zell says if I write everything out first, I can read it slowly. I'm confident I can do it! This should help business.

I am playing with the band again. After Mr. Edwards died, two fellows joined, but they don't have a mandolin player. I enjoy it. Zell supports me, and the jobs bring extra money. Yancy Barnes is retiring, but a chap who moved here will step into his spot. We practice on Wednesdays, still in Mayfield's back room.

Mam found out the library started a new policy. Your librarian friend Mrs. Albright got the town council to agree the rule saying Negroes cannot use the library was not right. Mrs. Albright said the rule was "downright immoral." Now I can check out books on flowers and such, and Zell can read mystery stories. Zell enrolled James in a summer library program for children. Three other Negro kids attend, too.

"Ah, progress. Finally!" KT proclaimed. "The nursery thrived, Blink and Zell had two more babies, the band played on, and lo-and-behold! The library opened to non-whites. In 1958, for Pete's sake. Thank you, Georgia Albright!"

She read more letters until encountering one with a dreaded opening line. KT knew its contents would come eventually, but such anticipation did not lessen the pain. She took sharp, quivering breaths and trudged to the bathroom where the tile acoustics further amplified her heart wrenching sobs.

September 4, 1962

Dear Annie,

This is a hard letter to write. I started to send a telegram but thought better of it. Mam died last Thursday. Doc Morrison said it was a stroke. Pap found her lying on the kitchen floor when he came home from town. It was too late to save her.

We held services for her this morning and buried her with her people in the church cemetery off Rock Howard Road. It is peaceful and well kept. Pap is lost without her, as are we.

Annie, I can't write to Miss Ellen and Doctor to pass on this sadness. Can you do it? I hurt too much. Please don't forget Cora Hill. Always remember how she adored you and your family.

Your friend,

Blink

I RECKON IT WAS MEANT TO BE

T hunder and lightning aroused KT early the next morning as gully-washer rains drenched the region, and a check of the weather showed widespread storms threatened to produce flooding in low-lying areas across the mid-Atlantic and east coast region.

A phone call from Euladora urged her to postpone travel until the following morning. A one-day delay promised clear weather and an easy drive from Hillview to Virginia Beach, so KT agreed without hesitation and alerted Graham and Larry of her change in plans. Resolving to finish Blink's remaining letters, KT made a cup of coffee, settled into the comfy corner chair, and began reading as pounding rain and thunder reverberated outside her window.

May 11, 1963

Dear Annie,

This promises to be a busy summer for us. Customers are buying my flowers, and I may sell out. They are asking

300

when the blueberry crop will come in, too! I hired three fellows to help Pap and me. We provide landscaping services now. I completed another correspondence course on proper planting and landscaping to educate myself better in those subjects. Pap helps me when he can, but his arthritis keeps him in his chair much of the time. Zell and I worry about him, too, because he misses Mam something terrible. The children try to cheer him up, but he often sits on the cabin porch and stares into space. Zell prepares enough lunch and dinner to include him with our meals. He cooks his own eggs and toast for breakfast.

I bought six acres from Mr. Conroy due north of me, and I plan to move the pumpkin patch and expand the Christmas tree lot back there to free acreage closer to the front. I removed the sign by the road advertising Mam's eggs, and I sold the chickens because they created problems for nursery customers. Pap raised a fuss, but he refused to build a large enough coop behind the cabin to keep customers from having to shoo away chickens. Zell convinced him the eggs she buys from the store are as tasty. They are not expensive, either. Pap tends our family garden. It saddens him we don't have the quantity of crops we once had, but he realizes the nursery is easier to manage and I love it. Our garden feeds us well. Zell cans what we cannot eat.

Berta says Mrs. Rutledge thought she sold Mrs. McCormick's house, but the transaction fell through. The mill closed, and they transferred Mr. Rutledge to another mill in Pennsylvania. He comes home on occasional weekends. I am surprised he is still working because he is old. Last week Mr. Rutledge fell sick and is in a hospital in Pennsylvania. Berta doesn't work for Mrs. Rutledge anymore because she has a hard time bending over, so Mrs.

Rutledge hired a younger lady. Berta says Mr. Rutledge keeps working to pay for Mrs. Rutledge's spending habits.

My radio show is going strong. I enjoy it, and it brings us customers. The radio station let me advertise our band's performance at Spring Fling last Saturday. The town did not have a Spring Fling when you lived here. It's a festival with a market, artists, music, and prizes for funny costumes. I took James, and he sold flowers from a table while the band performed during the afternoon. I printed a flyer advertising the nursery, and he gave out every one I printed. Since Negroes don't have to be out of town after sundown anymore, James and I stayed after dark. We ate hot dogs, and I saw four colored guys I know and their wives from Longtown in the crowd. A band played rock and roll music until nine o'clock. Lots of young people danced. My band's bluegrass music isn't too suitable for dancing.

I can't believe Joellen is graduating from high school. You will miss her when she goes off to college, won't you? Will you visit us? Our children are doing fine. James is eager to attend high school next year. He is an excellent student. Jilly and Joseph are growing, too. Jilly is a solid student, but Joseph is more interested in what Zell and I consider silliness. None show interest in my occupation! There is talk of opening Hillview schools to Negroes, but our children will still attend the same school I attended on Rock Howard Road.

This is a long letter. The lecture you gave at your old college in Chapel Hill sounded interesting. I'm sorry your trip to where Noah came from didn't produce any information on his family, but your decision to stop searching for them is the right one, Annie. Do not regret it. Pap and I take excellent care of the cemetery, and Noah is *at peace. The lilac bushes are blooming, and they smell wonderful.*

Your friend,

Blink

As KT digested the contents of the 1963 letter, she put her head against the chair's headrest and sighed. Besides learning about Blink's family and Hillview's evolution on matters of race, the revelation Anna Ruth stopped her prolonged search for Noah's family brought a chuckle.

"Well, Nonnie, don't you worry one bit because I am finishing your unfinished business tomorrow!"

She paged through more correspondence, eager for details. KT learned Susie Rutledge's husband did not recover from his illness, leaving Susie a well-to-do widow in a too-big house who entertained society friends with bridge and gossip parties. KT found it sad to learn Susie apparently did not mourn her husband's passing. Blink's business grew more prosperous, and his son James left for college in Illinois. The radio show persevered, and the band played on, but two letters written within weeks of each other in 1967 brought heart wrenching disclosures.

December 8, 1967

Dear Annie,

Pap died Saturday. His heart gave out. He was helping a man cut a Christmas tree when he collapsed. An ambulance came quick, but it was too late. We had a fine service for him and buried him in the church cemetery next to Mam. Please pass the word to Doctor and Miss Ellen. Ned Hill was an honorable man, wasn't he? I can't write anymore.

Your friend,

Blink

December 29, 1967

Dear Annie,

I have more sad news. Berta Simmons died last week. She fell sick not long after she attended Pap's funeral and came to our house afterwards. We learned of her death in the newspaper. The obituary said she had pneumonia. Zell and I went to her funeral service. Mrs. Rutledge was there, too. Mrs. Rutledge does not seem healthy to me. Berta was a wonderful friend to us, wasn't she? She held the key to what happened at the stone wall and did not even know it! Please relay this sadness to Miss Ellen and Doctor. Berta and your mother wrote to each other often, and this will upset Miss Ellen.

It is hard to adjust to life without Pap. We miss him. We miss Mam, too.

Your friend,

Blink

KT realized in her heart Blink's correspondence could contain sorrowful accounts as years rolled by, but losing Ned Hill and Berta Simmons created a numbing pain in her chest. Ned, Cora, and Berta, whose friendships meant the world to Annie Young and her parents, no longer walked the earth. KT tasted the heartache Anna Ruth, Carter, and Ellen must have experienced when they learned of these deaths.

She turned to the window, scouring beyond the outside dimness. The storm had calmed, but rain persisted. Blink's revelations left her too drained for lunch downstairs, and she reached for the hotel telephone and called room service. She leaned back in the chair and closed her eyes.

"Room service."

KT rose and admitted the young man who held her lunch tray. After he left, she munched her sandwich and sipped hot tea as she digested Blink's correspondence. KT learned from Mrs. Jennings at the courthouse Blink passed away in 2001, and she knew Susie Rutledge died in 1970, so she steeled herself to study the remaining letters without emotion. She bit her lip and vowed to remain stoic. Letters from the next two years reported nothing extraordinary until 1969.

March 11, 1969

Dear Annie,

Thank you for the picture of Joellen and you. I'm glad you enjoyed your visit with her. It's wonderful she likes her job and you approve of her young man. I'm not familiar with the game of basketball. Will we get a wedding announcement soon?

Everything is fine here. I hired two more fellows to help me. James graduates from college next year but will not come home to help in the business. He is not keen on my kind of work. We are thankful he kept his grades up and didn't get drafted to Vietnam. Jilly graduates high school in May and has her heart set on a college in Georgia, but money is an issue. I am not sure we can swing it. Joseph is still a scamp! Zell is fine. She keeps books for our growing business, and she helps me in the greenhouse.

Miss Mittie McCormick's property is in terrible shape. I see the real estate sign still posted, but weeds and grass and saplings overrun the yard. The house appears in disrepair. Zell heard Mrs. Rutledge is not well. I guess she is not paying anybody to care for it.

The mill burned. It's stood empty a long time, and the fire department says arson caused the fire. The city cleared the remains last week, and the high school across the street plans to expand on the property.

Hillview is in a tizzy because a Negro family from Longtown wants to buy a house in town. No real estate agent agreed to help them until they contacted Harry Wessler. By the way, he still holds the listing for Mrs. Rutledge's house. He found a house whose owners will sell to the family. Mr. Wessler got death threats in the mail and on the telephone, and the newspaper wrote an article on it. Zell and I hope no trouble comes from this. They integrated Hillview schools, but only a handful of Negro kids go there instead of the Negro school where I went and where our kids go. Things are changing, aren't they? The theater owners allow Negroes to sit on the main level, too. Zell and I rarely go to movies, but Jilly and Joseph say most of our people still sit in the balcony to avoid trouble.

The Mueller place sold last month. Mr. Foster died, and it sold once before this. I don't know who owns it now, but I must introduce myself.

Mr. Berger sold the shoe store several months ago to the man and woman he hired a few years ago to help him. They are fine folks. I bought a pair of shoes last week, and Mr. Berger sat in a wheelchair greeting customers. He is frail, but I was glad to see him. His sister Elise still works at Lindale's Ladies Fashions. She is several years younger than Mr. Berger. Elise's daughter Gabi is engaged to Harry Wessler's son Al, who will enter the real estate business with his father when he gets out of the Army in June. Elise's son David is in the Air Force. I owe Mr. Berger an enormous debt of gratitude for helping me long ago. Not many white folks would have helped a colored kid like he did. He and I spoke for over an hour at the shoe store. I sat on a stool next to his wheelchair while we talked.

The radio station is keeping the current Friday format. That means for now my show stays the same. It presents time predicaments for me, and I may quit. During winter, it's not much of a problem, but during spring and summer, I am too busy! The band boys and I are disbanding. Our music is not popular now, and we get few requests for performances. It takes me away from the business and Zell and the children.

Your lectures sound interesting, and the extra money is grand, too. Please give Doctor and Miss Ellen my regards.

Your friend,

Blink

Sorrow is the frequent response when one reflects on lost loved ones. Instead, elation washed over KT. Although she mourned the loss of beloved characters from her grandmother's life story, she treasured the window into the past, which affirmed Hillview's transformation from a small-minded town to its current state of openness. Optimism concerning Blink's future letters, coupled with trepidation, brought a richness to her mood. As she rested her head at the back of her chair, an incoming call on her cell phone pierced the silence.

"Hi, KT!" Graham's voice boomed before the phone reached her ear. "Listen, I plan to put the sign out front of McCormick House first thing day after tomorrow. Doan called and said he will be out tomorrow to landscape, and a load of gravel for the driveway comes the next day. The inside is well-done and appealing, thanks to Larry and Clete. Clete should finish the stone wall tomorrow, and we'll enter the property into the listing services after Doan completes his work. The family Larry mentioned has an appointment to see it on Thursday. Okay?"

"Fabulous! Emmaline says the historical marker should be installed soon, too. I'll keep my fingers crossed for a speedy sale. This family sounds perfect with a dad, a mom, a daughter, and a dog. I wonder how old the girl is?"

"The gentleman told me she's twelve. Her name is Ann."

Astonished by the coincidence, KT caught her breath and replied, "Nonnie was twelve when they moved into the house. Oh, I hope they fall in love with it!"

"Have a safe drive to Virginia Beach. Why don't you stay an extra day or two to enjoy the beach? Things are fine here."

"I may do it. Thanks loads for your support and friendship through this ordeal. I doubt any other realtor has gone through what you have with a listing, and I'll never forget it. You've earned my undying gratitude!"

Graham guffawed, "It's been a pleasure! A unique and unforgettable pleasure, Dr. Winslow! I hope you consider me a genuine friend instead of simply your realtor. My folks adore you, as does everyone else you've met around here. You must keep in touch with the Hillview crowd. You will, won't you? Don't forget us when you're in Maine!"

"You bet I will! I consider each of you as, well, family, and I'll never forget. I'll be seeing you, each one of you!"

"Isn't that a song title? Wasn't 'I'll Be Seeing You' popular during World War II," asked Graham.

KT paused. "Why, you're right. Nonnie said it was a favorite of hers. I found a record of the song, an old seventy-eight, among her belongings." She paused again. "I believe I now understand why she loved it as much as she did."

Graham chuckled, and KT visualized him stroking his mustache. He wished her a safe trip once again before concluding the call.

KT resumed her study of Blink's remaining letters. She learned his son James found employment in Illinois, married, and had three children, the oldest of whom was Doan Hill. Blink and Zell's daughter Jilly attended Spelman College in Atlanta, married, and moved to Wisconsin with her husband where they had two children. Son Joseph, the scamp, became a Naval officer and sent his parents photos and memorabilia of every locale he visited or was stationed. Whereas Blink could not join the armed services during World War II, his son joined the Navy and thrived. Mr. Berger passed away not long after Blink's wistful reunion with him at the shoe store.

A letter from Blink to Anna Ruth not long after Susie Rutledge's death hinted at the care Blink bestowed upon the location where Annie and Blink's friendship took root. Their friendship lasted until death separated the two. Anna Ruth recounted to KT that she sent Blink money as payment for maintaining McCormick House, but he cashed no checks. Ever.

I'm not sure why Mrs. Rutledge left you Mrs. McCormick's house, but I am glad she did. With your permission, I intend to reclaim the yard. It's a scene from a horror movie, Annie, overgrown so much one can hardly get through the mess. Teenagers throw pumpkins at it on Halloween. They explode and make a terrible mess. Harry Wessler keeps a sign there, but nobody can read it because somebody splattered paint on it. Please let me care for it. Its condition pains my heart.

Heartfelt and emotional letters of condolence Blink sent to Anna Ruth when each of her parents died compelled KT to stop reading and clear her head with a long stroll in the waning rain. Blink's replies to his friend reflected her unmistakable pain of losing Ellen and Carter Young. Ellen, Carter, and Anna Ruth were an incredibly bonded trio, and KT assumed that without her parents' support and love, Anna Ruth experienced an acute sense of aloneness. KT's father and her mother Joellen, busy with their growing family, lived miles away, providing little solace to Anna Ruth. This truth pained KT.

The thought of tackling Blink's remaining letters brought more dread, but the letters compelled her to complete the task.

Ensconced in her room, KT read the entire day. When her legs begged to be stretched, she jogged down the stairs to the front desk and advised the clerk she planned to be gone for two or three days but would settle her bill when she returned. Because of her lengthy stay, the hotel extended a reasonable rate, which KT found generous. She ate dinner in silence as she replied to emails on her phone. Dr. Rightmore expressed relief regarding her upcoming return to work, but KT gave him no clue of her plans to resign. Plenty of time waited for the chore once she returned. In one message, KT's father suggested accompanying him and her oldest brother's family on a Caribbean cruise in the fall, but she declined. She mentioned no upcoming change in her employment.

When KT returned to her room and her faithful chair, the dread of reading more letters disappeared. She learned of the cancellation of Blink's radio show because of a change in station format. As bluegrass music staged a comeback, Blink occasionally filled in with one of the local bands. Tobias Hill Nursery prospered each year as younger generations arrived to cut their Christmas trees, pick blueberries, and purchase flowers, trees, and shrubs cultivated with tender care by Blink and his employees. Several times, Blink mentioned his grandson Doan, enlightening Anna Ruth to the boy's interest in the nursery and of his help at McCormick House. One letter provided a glimpse into a typical summer.

Grandson Doan is with us for six weeks. Doan is a tremendous help to me and Zell. He learns fast and is a joy to have here. He and I mowed your McCormick property yesterday. I always have Doan mow a path to the stone wall and alongside to keep it clear. We trimmed shrubbery, too. It is not obvious to me why nobody buys the property, but real estate is not selling now. My business this summer has also been slower than usual. Please stop sending me money because I will not accept it.

I put more rocks around Bitsy's grave and installed another cross because the old one had rotted away. I mowed and trimmed at the cemetery and whitewashed the surrounding fence. Doan does not go with me there. I don't want to explain to him. He would not understand or believe everything. Maybe I will explain it when he is older. I have told him pieces of my family history, but it does not hold his attention.

A 1993 letter contained heartbreaking details of Zell's cancer diagnosis. The fast-moving disease attacked her body with vicious brutality, and within six months, she was gone. Blink's grief poured forth in subsequent letters, revealing his devastating sense of loss, yet his former optimistic self gradually emerged. Jack Morrison, Carter Young's physician friend, once described the child Blink as "happy-go-lucky," and within a few years, it appeared to KT this description once more proved appropriate.

Age took its toll on Blink's health as it had on his father Ned years prior. Arthritis interfered with his ability to perform strenuous tasks at the nursery. His letters spoke of Doan's help and of his employees' loyalty as Tobias Hill Nursery flourished. Hillview changed even more. Younger generations did not remember the days of Jim Crow, and its hateful remnants no longer haunted the town. An influx of visionary residents brought an energy Blink found refreshing. The last letter in the pile, written in a more scrawling, uneven penmanship than others, ended thus:

Your friendship has been a constant in my life, and I cherish it. Whoever might have thought in 1933 the black boy and the white girl would stay friends forever? I reckon it was meant to be. Take care of yourself, dearest Annie, and I will write when I can.

Your oldest friend,

Blink

KT trudged to the desk and pulled the letters together into a neat stack, returning them to the file folder from which they came. She placed the folder into the cardboard file box on the floor and secured the lid with string. As she closed the window drapes and turned on the lights, she smiled.

"Well, Nonnie, tomorrow I'm off to meet Noah's family and complete your mission. I hope you are pleased."

THE TAPESTRY

Brilliant skies and no wind provided the perfect start for KT's excursion to Virginia Beach. KT tossed a few items into her overnight bag, bounded out of the hotel to her Honda, and programmed the GPS to Euladora Monroe's home in Virginia Beach. The spiral booklet detailing Noah Poole's journey, supplemented by recent photographs of Creek Road Cemetery, rested in the passenger seat next to KT.

She quizzed herself aloud about Euladora's lineage as she drove.

"Let's see, is Euladora Monroe Noah's great-great-grandniece? I should have verified who is who. Euladora's great-great-grandmother was Noah's sister, Ibby. Do I have the relationship correct? Oh, I can't wait, Nonnie!" KT's comment addressed her deceased grandmother as if Nonnie herself sat beside her in the car.

KT whizzed past the entrance to Skyline Drive, making a mental note to check out this byway through Shenandoah National Park on her return trip. Reflecting on Blink and his band, she tuned in a bluegrass music station.

When she stopped for gas and a restroom break, she spotted a diner next door, went in, and seated herself by a window. While waiting for lunch, KT scrolled through phone messages. She ignored a plea to return the next day from Dr. Rightmore. Another from Doan advised he and his crew were at McCormick House and should complete the landscaping job by late afternoon. The third from Graham requested a response. KT gobbled her grilled cheese sandwich, returned to her car, and called him from the parking lot.

"Hello, KT. Are you interested in what my FBI friend learned about our boy Martin?"

"I am! What did he find out?"

"As I told you, his name was Thomas Blanton Martin, but he changed it to Thomas Blane Martin not long before buying most of the tracts once owned by Clay Blanton."

"Clay was old Morse Blanton's grandson, remember. Who'd have thought?"

Graham replied, "It's extraordinary, isn't it? The only thing I figure is the clan passed on the false tale Clay Blanton got rooked out of his properties or whatever nonsense. Fact is, Clay Blanton stole his bank customers' money and fled to Florida. Bank fraud is a federal crime, and he should have done time in prison. I wonder if family lore mentioned this little detail?"

Incredulous, KT remarked, "Blane Martin tried to recover those Blanton properties out of a sense of what? Loyalty? Revenge? It's absurd. Ludicrous."

"Regardless, he was a snake, as your grandmother aptly put it, a crook the same as Clay and his granddaddy Morse. Martin's business dealings weren't on the up and up. The swindle in Florida involved racehorses, performance-enhancing drugs, and organized crime. Wonder if old Clay got in with those criminal types in Florida way back when?

If so, it might explain where Blane Martin got money for the houses. Can you believe a crime boss tried to sue him? Hilarious! My buddy found no criminal proceedings against Martin, but he discovered a long list of civil lawsuits, close to twenty. It's hard to comprehend."

"Have you given this information to Sheriff Cortez?"

"Yeah. With Martin dead, I doubt if the individuals he cheated will recover a dime, but his trail of deceit is now an open book. Perhaps it will help put other bad actors away. He robbed Peter to pay Paul, as the saying goes, and his hatred for McCormick House and what it represented must have consumed him. It's got to be the reason he tried to steal McCormick House from you, and when he didn't succeed, he decided to burn it to the ground."

KT stared out the car window. "You're right. His family, doubtless, blamed my grandmother for their problems. If she hadn't brought Morse Blanton's evil to light, maybe they. . ."

"Listen, KT, none of the Blantons can blame their crooked ways on your grandmother. It's providence you came to Hillview and saved McCormick House. If Blane Martin had gotten hold of it, he would have erased an important part of our history and desecrated an idyllic part of the county with more of his shoddy houses. Doan is working his magic on the outside landscaping right now. It will sell, and when it does, you'll move on with your life with the knowledge you accomplished an honorable thing."

"Thanks. You're right. The Blanton tribe put a blight on Hillview, didn't they? Listen, I must get on my way. I'll see you when I get back to Hillview."

"Safe trip, Katie Doc!"

They both laughed and ended the call.

"My word, Nonnie! What a journey!" she chuckled as green, rolling hills gave way to larger towns, and she pressed on to Virginia Beach.

****

"Hello, hello, hello!" sang Euladora Monroe as she threw open the front door to her cottage. "I haven't been this excited in years and years!"

KT returned the tight hug Euladora lavished upon her and entered the charming home nestled in a historic neighborhood known as Alanton. Euladora had explained earlier that she and her deceased husband purchased the cottage as a weekend getaway over forty years prior. After her husband's death, Euladora moved there on a permanent basis. The cottage's pale blue exterior, complemented by shutters and a front door painted a salmon color, blended with the coastal setting in a perfect marriage. White trim around the windows provided a striking accent, and window boxes overflowed with brilliant flowers. An enormous long-leaf pine stood in the heart of the front yard, peppering the house with shade. Inside, the casual décor provided a relaxing environment for visiting.

Euladora's auburn hair, streaked with silver, framed her dimpled face in a most pleasing fashion. She offered KT coffee and directed her to the dining room table, which was strewn with photos and memorabilia. Side by side, the two sat as Euladora showed KT photographs, beginning with ones from the late 1800s. Her pink, manicured-to-perfection fingernails shuffled through a stack of fragile photographs as she spoke.

"No photos exist before Noah's disappearance, so I have nothing to show us what he looked like," said Euladora. "I say disappearance, KT, but family legend refers to his departure as a kidnapping."

"Kidnapping, abduction, conscription, whatever one calls it," replied KT, "Confederates took a sixteen-year-old boy from his family when the family needed him most. After reading my grandmother's notes and Ibby's recollections on the genealogy website, I can only imagine how difficult it was for Noah's mother and sisters after he vanished."

"Oh, yes. Of course, you read Ibby's notes, but her younger sister Mamie left us tidbits of the family's plight in a letter written to Ibby's first-born son when he was a boy. Ibby named him Noah after her younger brother. You'll be interested in what Mamie wrote to the boy." Euladora handed KT a yellowed birthday card.

I send you the happiest of birthday wishes, my darling nephew Noah. You, in your sixteenth year, are at the cusp of adulthood. Your precious mother, my sister Ibby, conveyed to you the name of our brother, Noah Poole, when you came into this world. It is a noble name to carry. Your namesake was sixteen when he left us.

We have passed our recollections of our beloved brother to you, and my fervent hope is you will grow to be the man I am positive he would have been. Carry your name with pride. Strive to be noble, honest, and true.

Aunt Mamie

Euladora presented a letter Mamie wrote to her sister Ibby not long before Ibby's death. Mamie's memories revealed a loving, hardworking family who endured grueling times after three brothers left to fight in the Civil War, a reduced family with no resources tasked with keeping the farm going. The patriarch's sudden death plunged the three women and young Noah into a maelstrom of backbreaking work and worry, which intensified after Rebel soldiers absconded with Noah. Mamie's letter provided more insight into the misery following Noah's departure.

Oh, sister, you must believe what an inspiration you were to me after Noah's kidnapping rendered you, Ma, and me vulnerable and alone. Because I no longer attended school, you and Ma did your best to guarantee I did not grow to adulthood illiterate. I despised your efforts then, but I am grateful now. When I feared starving and the horror the Home Guard might thrust upon us, you remained calm and steadfast. You did not express anger when I took the bonnet bestowed upon you by your beau and sold it to Old Man Gimble's wife. She admired it many times, so when I suggested it to her, she paid a paltry sum, one I, in my childish ignorance, did not realize constituted an insult. You embraced me rather than scold. When my finger snapped as I dug for sweet potatoes, you set it as gently as possible while I cried in pain. The splint with which you wrapped the broken appendage accomplished its goal, and my finger is straight today. You comforted me as I wept because I found no sweet potatoes. Wild pigs had eaten the remaining morsels. We ate nothing the rest of the day, do you remember? After we sold the farm and relocated to Raleigh, you remained my guiding star. Brothers George and Jacob protected us upon their return from the ravages of battle, but you, my much loved Ibby, inspired me to the highest rung of womanhood. Be forever aware of what you mean to me.

"KT, here is a photo of Mamie and Ibby taken in 1928. Mamie is on the left; Ibby is on the right. The notation on the back says they were visiting Ibby's daughter."

KT examined the photo and remarked the similarities between the two were striking.

"Did they have auburn hair as you do, Euladora?"

Euladora scrunched her face and responded, "Nobody ever mentioned it. Maybe."

KT recalled her grandmother's description of Noah as having auburn hair, but she did not relay this to Euladora. KT strove to keep the exact details of Anna Ruth's involvement with Noah Poole known only to herself. While her Hillview friends appeared to accept the story, she did not perceive Euladora well enough to expose the entire truth.

As Euladora shuffled through photographs and letters, KT gained a distinctive understanding of the Poole family of North Carolina and their descendants. They were hardworking, decent people who scattered across the United States and entered a variety of professions. KT learned of teachers, soldiers, nurses, sailors, aviators, physicians, farmers, a federal judge, a nurseryman like Tobias Hill, a congressman, an autoworker, and more. A microcosm of America.

"I wonder what Noah might have become if the Confederates hadn't taken him," KT conjectured.

Euladora said, "We have discussed the possibilities. We have ingrained the mystery of Noah in our family history for generations. Since you have brought me the record of what happened to him, I will make certain my relations receive the information. I'd love to see Anna Ruth's notes now."

KT gave Euladora the spiral booklet.

"I hope you can read my grandmother's handwriting. If I had more time, I would have typed her notes."

"Oh, I was a teacher, KT. I learned how to decipher every sort of handwriting. Besides, the handwriting makes it more authentic. It allows us to see it as Annie wrote it. Let's sit on my screened-in porch while I devour this fascinating tale."

They moved toward a wicker couch with thick cushions, KT carrying a scrapbook containing photos and clippings, and Euladora clutching the booklet.

While Euladora read, KT alternated between examining the scrapbook and observing her companion. She found it difficult to discern Euladora's thoughts. The afternoon waned, a breeze fluttered through the porch, and soon evening descended upon the two women.

"Oh, gracious!" Euladora shook her head and moaned, "How tragic. Noah wanted only to return to his family. His travails show what a determined and perseverant young man he was, don't they? Such bravery. What awful things he experienced! The horror of war, being taken from his people, witnessing cold-blooded murders. It's tragic, isn't it? I'm sorry he failed in his quest to get home. You say this picture shows his burial plot?" Euladora scrutinized the photograph of Creek Road Cemetery and the tombstone marked with Noah's name.

"Yes. I had the last name of Poole added to the refurbished stone a few weeks ago. I buried Nonnie's ashes next to him."

"Who are these other men? Israel Hill and Ben Hill?"

KT indicated Israel and Ben's history was lengthy. Euladora retreated to the kitchen and brought a tray filled with cheese, fruits, crackers, and shrimp cocktail. "I assumed we might need nourishment! There's plenty more if we consume every bit of this."

Euladora's somber mood lightened. Noah's journey pained her, but her sunny disposition returned as the women enjoyed their snacks. KT relayed the narratives of Israel, Ben, Albert Blanton, and his beloved Molly. She introduced Euladora to James Hinshaw and his gift of the cemetery to Ned Hill. KT detailed Annie Young's friendships with Blink and Mittie McCormick and the town's ugly reaction when Annie exposed the murders. Euladora listened, captivated by the story.

"Your grandmother created a furor, didn't she?" Euladora asked.

"She sure did!"

The women visited until midnight before embracing and promising to keep in touch. KT bade Euladora goodbye and departed for the beachfront hotel where she had secured a reservation, relieved that Euladora never questioned how a teenaged Annie Young spoke with Noah in the 1930s.

"I wonder if Euladora might have believed the story, Nonnie," she ruminated as she strolled to the hotel entrance, breathing in the night ocean air. "I wonder."

****

When KT awoke the next morning, she delighted in the ocean view and the sun beaming upon the shore's pale blonde sand. She had not visited a beach in years and in an instant realized its calming effect upon her soul. Professional focus dictated her life, leaving limited opportunities for simple pleasures. Vacations or even brief getaways never found their way into her world. The doctor was fine with this because she loved her career, but not the current scene at her clinic back home. Deep in her consciousness, KT acknowledged there should be more on her life's road, and the opportunity waiting in Maine opened the door.

KT donned a wide-brimmed hat and took a lengthy stroll on the beach. The cool sand massaged her feet, and an ocean breeze dampened her hair and face as she reflected upon her time with Euladora Monroe. They examined countless photographs, letters, and newspaper clippings concerning the Poole family and its descendants. One photo stood out in her mind.

The picture of Noah's older brother George as an old man showed him lounging in a chair with a cane resting against his knee. KT recalled Ibby's essay describing an exquisite hand carved cane given George by the physician who cared for him after a Civil War skirmish. Russell Hill carved the cane, and Doc Mueller had to have been the physician.

"You and I concede it's the truth, don't we, Nonnie?" KT shouted into the pounding surf.

The surf responded with a continuous roar, which KT answered with a lingering smile as she trod the length of the beach far beyond the boardwalk. The rest of the day she spent wandering through stores, people watching from an Adirondack chair shielded by an enormous umbrella, wading in the surf, and ignoring phone calls from Dr. Ron Rightmore. No calls came from Hillview. When night fell, she enjoyed tacos and beer in the taqueria next to her hotel and took one last hike on the beach before returning to her hotel room. From a chaise lounge on the balcony, she gazed at stars until midnight before retreating inside to her fluffy king-sized bed. Crashing ocean waves lulled her into a deep slumber from which she did not awaken until eight o'clock the following morning.

****

Buoyed by a hearty breakfast and a sound sleep, KT loaded her car and bade farewell to Virginia Beach. The return trip to Hillview began with a full tank of gas, a full cup of coffee, and a full heart. Only one item on KT's agenda remained: sell McCormick House. She did not need to be present to complete the sale because Graham often handled those details for clients, so she planned to bid her Hillview friends a warm farewell and "Get out of Dodge" as soon as she returned to Hillview. Joyous in her accomplishments, she began to sing, and KT Winslow sang loud, and she sang long, and it felt invigorating and wondrous.

Near Rockfish Gap, she exited the interstate and proceeded toward Skyline Drive. The thirty-five mile per hour speed limit assured a leisurely drive through Shenandoah National Park with its multitude of breathtaking vistas. The side trip lasted around three hours, and when she bid adieu to the park near Luray, she embraced a refreshing new love for nature's artistry. KT stopped for fuel and left a phone message for Graham, giving an approximate arrival time at McCormick House.

The drive resumed, and her thoughts swung to people she encountered throughout her journey. As late afternoon sun streamed through the trees, her car crunched up the gravel driveway to her "albatross" where Graham's sign officially proclaimed the property to be for sale.

Doan's landscaping provided an inviting setting for the once dismal structure, and the home's white paint glistened in the late afternoon sunlight. KT climbed from her vehicle, but instead of entering the house, she raced to the rear boundary to be greeted by the old stone wall. Restored with Clete's tender touch using techniques he and Larry described as from "olden days," the wall stood between three and four feet tall and ran the entire length of the rear property boundary. A cleared pathway ten feet wide lay in front of the wall, allowing one to stroll alongside with ease. The elegance and sheer beauty of it overwhelmed her. Annie Young spent hours upon hours trying to rebuild the dilapidated wall with Carter Young and Blink's help, an impossible task for amateurs in 1934, but now it appeared as it must have in 1863 when Phoebe Mueller rode her horse named Blaze along the pathway. Trees on the far side of the wall, at the bottom of the rock ledge, mostly hid the homes Blane Martin erected on the former Blanton apple orchard.

"Nonnie, see the wall! It's gloriously different from how it was when you and I were here last fall. Are you here? Are you pleased?" KT rotated her body in every direction, taking in the sky, the trees, the opening in the woods. "Bitsy? Are you here?" No answer.

She jogged the path Clete cleared through the woods to the house. KT unlocked the front door and entered the dwelling where the living room's stone fireplace begged for a wintertime blaze. She trotted straight upstairs to inspect Larry's handiwork on the second floor. The new shower added a sleek, modern touch to the bath, but the clawfoot bathtub evoked images of times past. Annie's bedroom, complete with a lovely quilt and pillows covering the iron bed frame, allowed KT to imagine her young grandmother reclining on the bed as she pondered her circumstances and wrote her notes.

After a fleeting glance into the two other bedrooms, she hurried downstairs. She peered into the half bath, dwelt a few minutes admiring the room lined with bookshelves which once served as Ellen Young's sewing room, and moved through the dining room into the kitchen. Modern appliances, paint, and a shiny floor presented a picture of immaculate efficiency, while the kitchen's still-vintage charm created an appealing heart for the home. When KT saw three flowerpots filled with blooming African violets on the kitchen windowsill above the sink, she whispered, "Ellen Young's violets. Graham thinks of everything. Mission accomplished!"

Her eyes turned to the kitchen table, its navy paint coordinated with the navy and white checkered curtains on the window. Several papers and a bouquet of flowers in a vase rested on the table's surface. She recognized Larry's handwriting on one paper, lifted it, and read:

Katie Doc, I hope you are pleased with what Clete and me done. Tell me if something is not right, and I'll fix it. We gone fishing. I enjoyed working for you. You are a real nice lady. Have a safe trip home. Don't forget old Larry!

She removed the note attached to the flower vase and saw it came from Stub O'Connor. The message read:

Looking forward to completing paperwork on your position after you return to Bluff County. We'll have Maine "lobsta" when you get here. Can't wait!

KT put her hand over her heart in response and examined the next set of papers. They included a contract to buy McCormick House. KT assumed the buyer was the husband with his wife and their twelve-year-old daughter. With a solid, full price contract, this was the buyer for whom she hoped. She eased into a chair. Her mind mulled over everything that had happened since she and her Nonnie trudged through the property's overgrown woods to the broken-down stone wall.

KT reflected upon her observation that although Hillview was not a perfect town, it appeared isolated from the divisiveness of the day and handled the problem better than many locales. No longer dominated by a greedy few, it had traveled far from an ugly past and today embraced diversity, neighborliness, and civility. Hillview had excellent schools, libraries, health facilities, and a range of recreational and cultural assets. She believed her soon-to-be home in Maine was made of similar cloth.

The stories of Hillview, Miss Mittie, Blink, Phoebe, the Blantons, Ned, Cora, Carter, Ellen, Berta, Doc Mueller, James Hinshaw, and finally, Noah Poole, etched themselves in her brain and heart for life. Thanks to her new Hillview compatriots, she more fully understood the precious value of connection—connection with each other, with a common purpose, and with those who went before. Maybe it is pure luck, but places exist where those connective threads truly thrive, touching and feeding everything that is noble. Such threads form a magical tapestry of trust and friendship. Hillview was such a place, she sensed. Graham and his parents, Doan and Amy, Emmaline, Lacy, Lyntha, Birdie, even Larry and Clete were connected to KT, wherever she may go.

A deafening, "Yoo Hoo!" from the front door jostled her from her musings. A beaming Graham entered the kitchen, where KT remained seated at the table fingering the sales contract.

"Pleasant trip, KT? I knew we'd sell soon, but in one day? Full asking price, too! The buyer is the family with the twelve-year-old daughter, and they adore the house and grounds, especially the stone wall. You said you wanted to keep the bed upstairs and this table, but they wrote those into the contract. Will you part with them?" His grin stretched from one ear to the next. "Hope you approve of the violets in the window. You said Ellen Young kept violets there, and I thought they might add a homey touch. Mom loaned me the pillows and quilt for the bed upstairs. Oh, those flowers came to the office, and I brought them here." With a satisfied grin, he stroked his mustache and leaned against the kitchen counter as he surveyed the room with a satisfied sigh.

KT did not speak for several moments before her hushed voice broke the silence. "The violets are lovely, and the quilt is exquisite. Thank you."

More silence, a lengthy silence. KT stared at the violets and turned her gaze toward Graham before re-examining the contract by flipping through its pages. Her eyes returned to the violets before they rested on Graham.

In a near whisper, she said, "My time here has helped me understand what is most important in life. I've learned what makes a community exceptional and what makes a friend a genuine friend. I've accepted the professorship at the medical school in Maine, you know, and it's in a pleasant town, much the same as Hillview, I'm told. No matter where I may go, you, your loving family, and each of my friends here will live in my heart for the rest of my life. This is gratifying but *remembering* those you love isn't the same as *being* with them."

Graham smiled and shifted his feet.

After another prolonged pause, KT's voice grew stronger. "I believed I had just two choices, two roads out of my current situation, but that's not true. What I'm trying to say is, I can't sign this contract. I can't sell McCormick House, Graham. Can you please pull up the sign out front? This is where I belong. I'm home."

"Indeed, you are, Katie Doc, indeed, you are!"

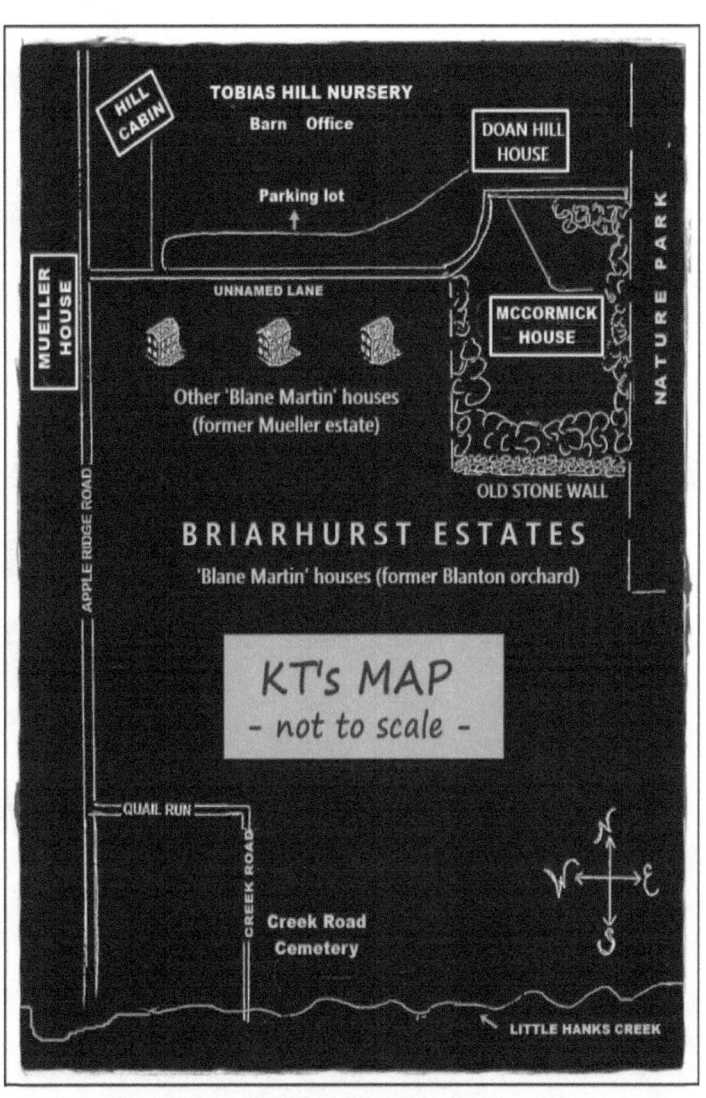

- HILL CABIN
- TOBIAS HILL NURSERY
- Barn   Office
- DOAN HILL HOUSE
- Parking lot
- NATURE PARK
- MUELLER HOUSE
- UNNAMED LANE
- McCORMICK HOUSE
- Other 'Blane Martin' houses (former Mueller estate)
- OLD STONE WALL
- APPLE RIDGE ROAD
- BRIARHURST ESTATES
- 'Blane Martin' houses (former Blanton orchard)

KT's MAP
- not to scale -

- QUAIL RUN
- CREEK ROAD
- Creek Road Cemetery
- N W E S
- LITTLE HANKS CREEK

HILL FAMILY

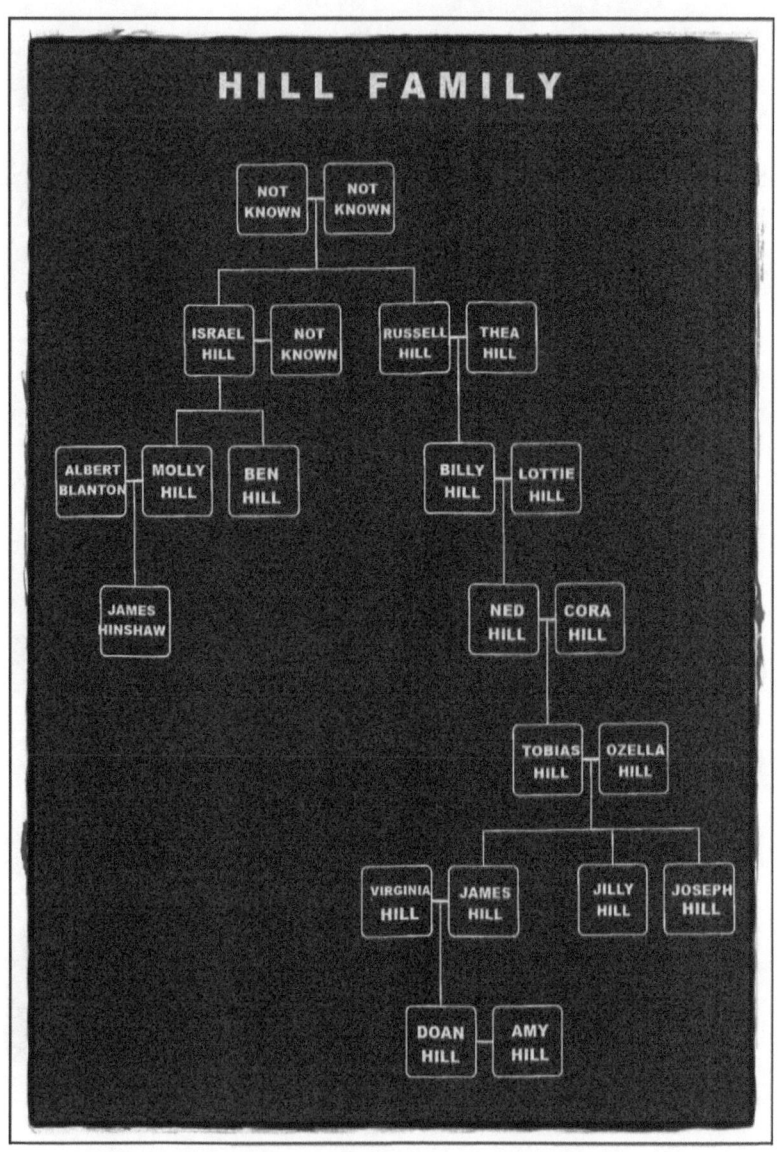

BLANTON FAMILY

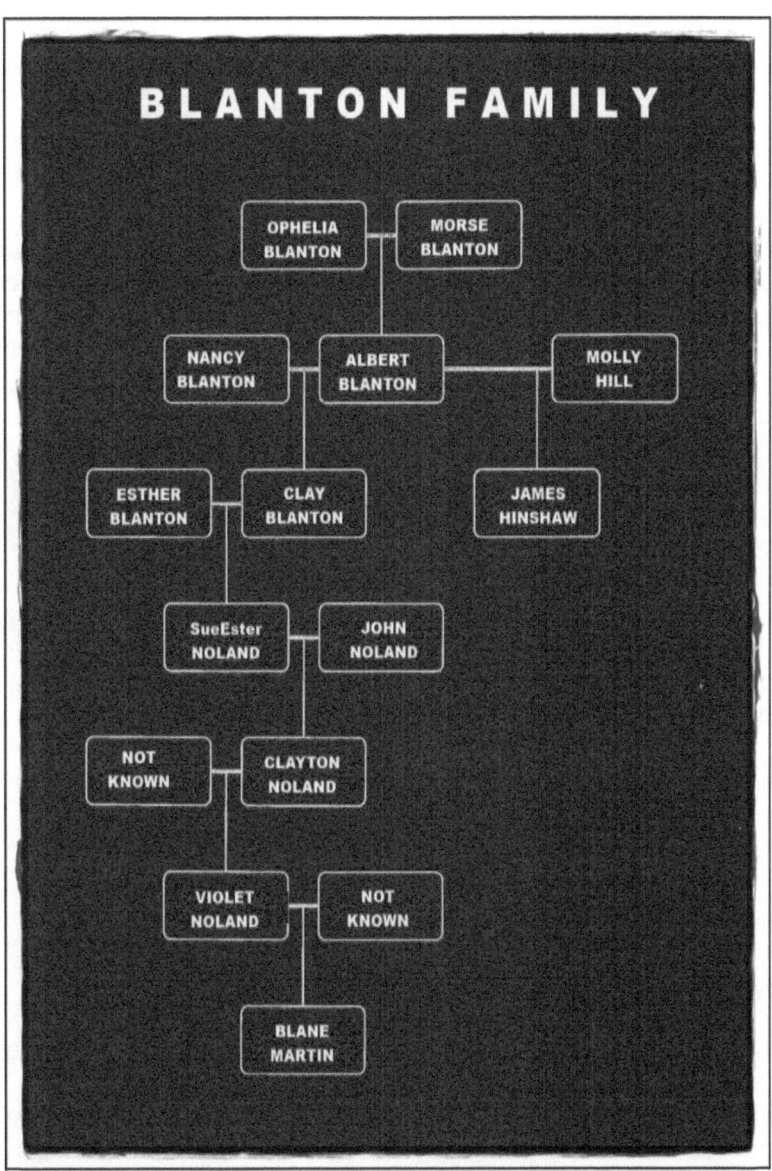

About the Author

I was born in Kansas City, Missouri and grew up in Norman, Oklahoma. Good public schools and access to the University of Oklahoma drew my grandparents to Norman in 1920. They viewed education as the key to better opportunity. By the time of my birth, those hard times that defined Oklahoma during Great Depression had been replaced by considerable optimism and prosperity, at least in Norman. I grew up within a few blocks of the main campus. Like most of my friends and family, I was a diligent student and predestined to attend college at OU.

Upon graduation, with a major in English and a minor in Journalism, I struck out on my own to accept a teaching position in Houston. Despite the miserable heat and humidity, Houston expanded my horizons. Here, I met my husband, gave birth to our child, and spent several rewarding years teaching 8th grade English before co-founding a group of travel agencies with my husband. Those travel agency years were always interesting, and thanks to our dedicated employees, the business grew and was respected for its attention to customer service. After seventeen years in Houston, we were exhausted. We were hungry for a four-season climate, fewer seven-day work weeks, and a more family-friendly lifestyle. We sold the business, and in 1987 it's off to Kansas City.

If Houston was hard, Kansas City was delightful. Over the course of thirteen years, I enjoyed a career in the field of educational publishing, we raised our son, became involved in civic activities, and forged some lasting friendships. My career ended abruptly, due to a series of mergers and acquisitions. We were empty nesters now, and my husband was offered a nice promotion that required us to relocate to the D.C. area.

Our new home was in the historic Eastern Panhandle of West Virginia, about an hour west of Washington. This spot of heaven in the upper Shenandoah Valley was to be our home for the remainder of our years. It offered natural beauty, cultural opportunities, good friendships, civic involvement, retirement, and easy access to our grandchildren in Washington. What could go wrong?

Our son's family did exactly what my grandparents did so long ago. They sought a community with better schools for our grandkids and better opportunities for themselves. The place—Overland Park, Kansas. After a couple of years, we followed and are happy to be back in the Midwest. Once again, we are close to our dearest ones and their pets, projects, and shenanigans.

My home office looks out on what was an old farm with a primitive grass runway. Occasionally, a small plane will taxi to the end of the runway and go up for a spin around the countryside. I am inspired by my new setting and am more than ready to share a few tales.

Special Resources

RATINGS (AND REVIEWS) ~

I hope you enjoyed this story as much as I enjoyed telling it. If so, a nice RATING on the site where purchased and on GOODREADS is deeply appreciated. Should you have comments to share with other readers, a written *review* may be added to the rating. I don't hire companies or people to post ratings or reviews because I think they should only come from actual readers. Thank you.

WHERE TO BUY MY BOOKS ~

Print and eBook versions are sold worldwide. For a list of all sellers with direct links to my books (signed/unsigned), please visit my website, ASHFOARD.COM.

BOOK CLUB RESOURCES ~

Signed books for reading and screening. Live Zooms (single or multi-location.) In-person meet-ups/Kansas City area. I absolutely love doing these free sessions. For details, please visit my website ASHFOARD.COM.

ASHFOARD.COM. (MY WEBSITE) ~

Where to buy. Signed copies. Book Club resources. About the author. Reviews. Backstories.

ON FACEBOOK & YOUTUBE ~

Jane Yearout, Author (my Facebook page) is where I post material of general interest to my readers. This is also where readers may chat with me and others about the stories, characters, societal themes, things they like or don't—and pose their own burning questions. It's a friendly place. Please stop by.

My YouTube channel is where readers may enjoy music and videos that relate to my writing. Some of the artists are special to me and may not be widely known. Also archived here are a few of my own videos, some with commercial content.

www.ingramcontent.com/pod-product-compliance
Lightning Source LLC
Chambersburg PA
CBHW031435240626
47154CB00001B/279